7-20

2.90

CURSE THE DARKNESS

Lesley Grant-Adamson divided her childhood between Wales and London and now lives in London and Somerset. She was a feature writer on the *Guardian* before going freelance, writing television documentaries and fiction. With five previous novels published, *Patterns in the Dust*, *The Face of Death*, *Guilty Knowledge*, *Wild Justice* and *Threatening Eye* – Lesley Grant-Adamson has a secure place in the brilliant new wave of British women crime writers.

LESLEY GRANT-ADAMSON

Curse the Darkness

faber and faber

LONDON · BOSTON

First published in 1990
by Faber and Faber Limited
3 Queen Square London WC1N 3AU

This paperback edition first published in 1991

Photoset by Wilmaset Birkenhead Wirral
Printed in Great Britain
by Cox and Wyman Ltd, Reading, Berkshire

CIP data for this book is available
from the British Library

ISBN 0-571-14197-8

For Betty and Jim Knights who let me use Butlers

CONTENTS

BOOK ONE

Sudden Death

First she saw the shadow, the thin line of the rope, the shape of the hanging body. Her mind cut out the sounds of the people on the stairs behind her. Her hand thrust the door and she confirmed what the shadow foretold.

Then she tugged the door shut, killing the sight in the room, denying his neighbours the sunlit corpse with its livid face and its elongated, elegant shadow.

A tweedy old man with a military air, the one who had said his name was Ratcliffe, pushed up against her. 'He's done it, hasn't he? Done himself in?' His voice was high, excited.

Rain Morgan nodded, unable to prevent him throwing back the door, striding in, leading the way for the rest. She marked their eager rush, their anticipation of shock, their acute silence once the thrilling notion became reality.

Only Mrs Dobson – or Dawson? – a rotund pensioner from the basement flat hovered outside the door. 'Poor bastard,' she said, fiddling with the buttons of her amorphous cardigan. 'It wasn't much of a life was it? Not in the last years.'

'I'll call the police,' said Rain.

She borrowed Ratcliffe's telephone on the ground floor. He and the others stood in the hall outside his flat, murmuring a background to her call. The hall was dark and cold. Like the rest of the house, it appeared uncared for.

Behind her a woman's voice said: 'His phone was cut off, you know. He used to borrow mine, claimed his was out of order but I soon saw through that.'

Ratcliffe drew a handkerchief from his jacket pocket and blew his nose noisily before commenting. 'He did it in style, I'll say that for him. Hanging himself from a chandelier!'

The police came. 'Which one of you found him?' the sergeant asked. He scanned the group expectantly. Apart from Rain Morgan they were all old. Apart from the woman from the basement they wore the stigmata of the upper middle classes: poverty with a good address.

'We all did,' said Ratcliffe.

Nods of confirmation. Mrs Dobson, or Dawson, did up an extra button on her cardigan. She said, her flat London accent in contrast to Ratcliffe's public-school precision: 'It's what he wanted, you see. He got us all up here.'

Ratcliffe refused to let her be spokesman. He interrupted her observations, his mood pompous now that the questions they had already asked themselves were being posed officially. 'During the night Wilson pushed notes beneath our doors asking us to call on him at 9 a.m. today. Apparently he intended that we should all participate in the macabre discovery.'

'I see, sir. You were all friends of the dead man, I take it.'

There was sufficient hesitation before the reply for the sergeant to gather that Mr Alfred Gervase Wilson, deceased of Flat 4, 18 Hunt Road, London sw3, had been on rather bad terms with his six neighbours. But Ratcliffe said no more than: 'He kept himself to himself.'

Mrs Dobson amended that. 'In recent years, that is. You could say he withdrew into his shell.' She paused, hoping the sergeant would write down the phrase in his notebook. Then she said: 'Before that he used to be friendly with everyone. Used to cut the grass in the garden for us. Always whistling, he was.'

The sergeant was concerned about more recent events. 'How did you get into his flat this morning?'

Rain Morgan supplied the answer. 'He gave me his keys. I live a few streets away and last night he dropped through my letter box an envelope containing his door keys and a request to call at nine.'

'And that's a funny thing,' said Ratcliffe, pre-empting the young sergeant's next question. 'He could have given any of us in the house his keys yet he preferred to walk over to Kington Square to involve Miss Morgan. Can any of you

4

imagine why that should be?' He cast around but the faces were unhelpfully blank.

Rain kept her guesses to herself. The questioning was taking place in Ratcliffe's flat, the big Victorian room accommodating them all with ease. It was a dated and drab setting but comfortable enough, with solid old furniture and oriental rugs, and ephemera, things he had lived with for a long time. He had told the sergeant he lived there alone, and Rain made deductions about the woman whose face was prominent among a collection of framed photographs on the mantelpiece.

From overhead as they talked came the sounds of the sergeant's colleagues carrying out other, more unpleasant duties. Men tramped through the hall and up the stairs, and came down again with the heavy tread of the burdened. Outside, the doors of a van slammed. Unidentifiable noises continued overhead.

Freed, after another half-hour, Rain escaped to Kington Square. Plane trees in the gardens were spring-budded, anemones bowed from window boxes on balconies along the Georgian terraces, and blackbirds were amorous on tender grass. Refreshing, after Ratcliffe's flat.

Her long airy sitting room opened on to a roof garden. She unlocked the french windows and went out. Alf Wilson had admired her home, she remembered. He had remarked that his own living room was bigger, but hers was brighter, prettier.

And that was how long ago? Three years? No, four or five at least. It was shortly after she had brought back from Antibes her white vase, a sinuous form that played wavy shadows along her white walls. Alf Wilson had admired that vase too. Five years? Six?

Instinctively her eye went to the shelf where she displayed the vase, although she knew it was not there. Nothing was there. The room was stripped, ready for the decorators who were due to arrive that day. Variations of white against white were all that proved her room was normally a gallery of paintings, *objets* and woven fabrics, the random accumulation of her travels.

Alf Wilson had been her guest at a party here. She had met him in a pub near by, an acquaintance of an acquaintance, and recognized his name from the days when it went rolling by with television credits. She had trawled from her memory the names of his plays, his serials, and he had been flattered and had warmed to her.

He had offered to buy her a drink but she had insisted on buying one for him. 'My pleasure,' she had said, 'to reward the genius who wrote *Dead and Alive* and kept a nation transfixed for six weeks.' Embarrassing, the quips one remembered.

They had spoken about *Dead and Alive*, which had written his name into entertainment history. It had been a significant development in television drama, a breakthrough in an era before breakthrough was a word.

'What are you doing now?' she had asked. And he had confessed to a fallow patch but said there was 'a new thing' under discussion and he would be back on the screen before long. She had known better than to expect him to risk his new idea by divulging it to her, or anyone else, and she had not pushed for details. Instead, they had reverted to *Dead and Alive*, and when it was time to say good night and go home she had impulsively added an invitation to her party.

And now he was dead and he had summoned her to discover his body. She was very much afraid she could guess why.

Shivering, she turned back to her garden. Without her possessions around her she felt vulnerable, exposed. And the shadow slashing across her floorboards was too insistent a reminder of her first sight of Alf Wilson's room.

His had been empty too. No, not that exactly. His possessions had been sparse. A table with an old typewriter on it, three ill-matched wooden chairs (one overturned in the centre of the room), a sofa and bookshelves, and that was all. In a different room the pieces would have been ample but his was spacious, the width of the house, and it was intended to be a grand room. Swagged curtains at the massive full-length windows lived up to that grandeur. So did the chandelier from whose hook Alf Wilson had hung his rope.

Her telephone rang, jarring. Rain knelt on the boards beside it.

Holly Chase, her deputy on the *Daily Post* gossip column, was characteristically breezy, 'Hi! How are the decorators?'

'They haven't shown up yet.'

Holly laughed. 'Oh-oh. Could be bad news.'

'They said mid-morning. I refuse to panic yet. I'll be with you once I've settled them in.'

'Fine,' said Holly. 'We've had a string of calls for you, but nothing that can't wait. I'll leave you to your lonely vigil then.'

Rain prevented her ringing off. She asked her to send their secretary to scour the library for the file on Alfred Gervase Wilson.

Rain squeezed into the editor's office for the morning conference. She was late as usual. Holly Chase smiled at her, a flash of white teeth in a dark face. The office lawyer, whose duty it was to steer the newspaper around the libel laws, nodded glumly. Rain pretended not to understand he was perturbed because her story about an errant judge had overstepped the mark, and because she and the editor had conspired to overrule his objection. 'Nice morning,' she said to him with an innocent smile.

He grunted a reply and looked away.

The news editor, a willowy young Irishman with an unexpected talent for holding down a job nobody thought he could do, tapped her shoulder. Was it true, he wanted to know, that Alf Wilson was dead?

'Yes. I'll write you an obit, if you like, unless the television critic is keen.'

Riley accepted. 'He says not. He says you knew Wilson.'

'Slightly.' The word was a rejection, a snub to Wilson who, she feared, would have claimed something more positive than their vague acquaintanceship, the occasional drink together when they happened to be in the pub at the same time, the one visit to her flat, or the hand raised in greeting on occasions they spotted each other across the King's Road.

'Suicide, wasn't it?' Riley persisted.

One of the leader writers hushed him. The editor, a colourless man who favoured vivid ties, was talking, asking the defence correspondent whether a strong follow-up to that day's front-page lead was in the offing.

'Woe betide him if it isn't,' Riley whispered to Rain. And the leader writer hushed him again.

Rain read the list typed on the sheet of paper Riley held, a rundown of the main stories he intended the home news pages to carry next day. Beside Alf Wilson's name he had sketched a question mark in red biro. She teased herself, trying to make out what the other words meant. What story was signified by 'Ultimatum', for instance? Or by 'Sanctuary', for that matter? Her mind roved over his list until it was time to attend to her own brief jottings and declare what she meant to run in the diary.

The ritual of the morning conference, first step on the long road to next day's paper, seemed faintly comical to her. Ordered by clocks, heads of departments and specialists converged, clutching scraps of paper with their lists of ideas. They ticked or crossed out, depending on the mood of the meeting and whether, as frequently happened, someone else had been inspired with the same thought.

Then they returned to their niches and set their staff to work to turn the ideas into researched and written stories. And always, all the while, actual news was happening and making the lists obsolete. Better stories replaced weak ones, good ones were hustled out in favour of up-to-date items and reporters jockeyed to get their copy in, preferably played up on the front page.

The morning conference settled nothing. No edition of the *Daily Post* had ever reflected its decisions faithfully, and none ever would. Rain was inclined to use this as an excuse for her customary lateness.

As they trailed out of the editor's office again, one of the reporters said provocatively: 'A pretty dull crop you've got there.'

Holly obligingly took issue with him. Rain sauntered back to her desk, not deigning to argue, and reflecting that she required no further excitement that day. Just this once she would be content if nothing more interesting happened and the dull crop appeared in print unscathed.

Holly came running up behind her. 'Honestly, I don't know where he gets his cheek. When did *he* last have a decent story?'

'Yesterday,' said Rain. 'The one about . . .'

Holly's indignation wilted. 'Oh, yes. Well, even so, he shouldn't . . .'

Her telephone rang and she became engrossed in scandalous tittle-tattle about a pop star.

Rain put out a reluctant hand and opened a cardboard file of yellowed newspaper clippings. From several, twenty years old, the jaundiced face of Alf Wilson regarded her.

'Another Winner for Wilson', said a headline. 'TV's Alf Takes Top Award', said another. 'Wilson Serial Wins Ratings War'. And so forth. Rain sighed.

Rosie, her fashion-conscious young secretary, glanced up. She misinterpreted the sigh as criticism of the impecunious *Post*'s failure to fully computerize its library.

Computers were a prickly matter at the *Post* because there were hardly any of them. Journalists' attitudes had changed. In the beginning they had believed it an advantage to be employed by a company too impoverished to modernize its news-gathering and production methods, because, had they been threatened with it, the *Daily Post* staff would have resisted the 'new technology' as ferociously as any group in Fleet Street.

Instead they had seen the paper sold by its likeable proprietor, who had declined to sacrifice his inherited country estate

9

to pay for necessary changes at the *Post*. They had seen his successor, an American businessman, murdered at his desk before he could carry out those changes. And they were still enduring the limbo while a fresh buyer was sought.

Theirs was the only daily national newspaper labouring in the traditional way and they were weary of being the butt of Stone Age jokes. Only at the *Post* did compositors continue to stand at the stone and make up pages, dropping metal type by hand into formes. The wit of those Stone Age jokes eluded people outside the printing industry, but everyone understood why *Private Eye* had dubbed the paper the *Daily Past*.

And worse by far than the mockery, the staff found their ignorance of modern methods a hindrance when they wanted to change jobs. It was months since anybody had been poached by Wapping or Docklands. Resistance had crumbled. *Daily Post* journalists craved computers.

Rosie explained to Rain about the Wilson file. 'They said it was too old to be put on their computer. They don't bother with the ancient ones that nobody uses any more. This was in the Not Currently Active section.'

Rain dredged up a wry smile. 'It would be,' she said. The most recent of the cuttings in the file was eleven years old.

She wrote Alf Wilson's obituary. It was distasteful to set down that she had herself found the body, that Wilson had arranged for her and his six neighbours to call at his flat together and that he had delivered a key to her. She could not shirk the details. Other newspapers would interview Ratcliffe and the rest of the tenants, and everything would eventually be made public at the inquest.

Holly came and read over her shoulder. 'Do you know why he killed himself?'

'He was a hasbeen. Perhaps that was it.'

Holly tutted. 'Most people don't even achieve that. At least a hasbeen has been someone.'

'Sorry, it's the only explanation I have. His flat was bleak. His telephone had been cut off. He led a withdrawn, depressing life.'

'Was there a suicide note?'

Rain said: 'The police told me they searched but there was nothing.'

Holly said: 'Perhaps he was ill. People with terminal illnesses sometimes . . .'

She left the sentence incomplete and went back to her desk, where she concentrated on the scurrilous news about the pop star, a big name whose has been years were still a long way off. Holly said that the way it was shaping the story was definitely worth a place in tomorrow's column.

Rain flipped the file shut and pushed it towards Rosie's desk for it to be returned to the library. But she could not finish so easily with the Alf Wilson story. It haunted her for the rest of the day. As news of her involvement spread, colleagues came to commiserate or probe, and journalists on other publications optimistically begged her help.

Rosie filtered out calls from rivals but one from a television company slipped through. Frances Keene was a former reporter with the *Post*. She was on the line before Rosie or Rain realized why.

'Look, Rain, it won't take any time at all,' she pleaded. 'A swift interview about how long you'd known him, what he'd been doing since he dropped out of the public eye . . .'

'And why he wanted me to find his corpse?'

'Er . . . yes. That was extraordinary, rounding up a posse.'

Rain refused the interview, adamant that she had no answers to Frances's questions and was as baffled as everyone else. 'Try the rest of the posse, Frances,' she suggested and rang off.

But when she left the office that evening, Frances Keene and her crew were waiting for her on the Fleet Street doorstep. Left with no choice, Rain Morgan walked towards the camera.

David Gerrard swirled his whisky around his glass and eyed Rain Morgan speculatively. 'You don't believe my little story?'

She dismissed it with a smile. 'David, I don't even believe *you* believe it.'

He pursed his lips. 'But it's such a good line. Now admit that much, at least.'

She burst out laughing. 'Yes, it's brilliant. But it's no part of my job to run stories you've faked to promote your authors. *You* admit *that*!'

He swooped a fleshy hand at the tray borne by a passing waiter and plucked a glass of wine for her. She objected half-heartedly. 'David, I should have gone by now.' Gone from him, gone from the party. But the glass was in her hand, he had detained her a mite longer with his unwanted gift.

'Rain, you must see that in these tough times one has to employ every device.' He was claiming poverty, a hard life, a reluctance to buckle the rules. None of it was true. If anyone was helping himself in a greedy self-help society, it was David Gerrard.

She said: 'All I see is that you'll stop at nothing to publicize your authors in my column. *Anybody's* column.' She wagged an admonishing finger. 'You're getting yourself a bad name, you know, as one of the Fleet Street hustlers. Literary agents used not to be so raffish.'

But her schoolmarmish tone amused him, the censure was lost. He vowed to call her immediately he had a story that would interest her. He was incorrigible.

Rescue came, a very young man whom Rain did not know but who felt free to talk to her because he recognized her face. She encouraged him to introduce himself to David Gerrard and she slipped away. Before she was out of earshot she heard him telling the literary agent about the unpublished novel he had written.

Rain looked about, taking in who was there and who had failed to turn up for the opening of the nightclub. Silently she repeated her first editor's advice to her years ago: 'Never trust a promise, always see for yourself.'

A photographer was clicking at a giggle of soap-opera actors, a couple of David Gerrard's authors were getting lugubriously drunk in a corner, a few people were dancing, a lot of people were having a good time. The owner of the new club was exultant. But the young royals he had been promised had let him down.

When Rain left Gerrard followed her out, but by coincidence not design. 'We can't share a taxi,' he said, although there was not one in sight to argue about. 'Kington Square is quite the wrong direction for me.'

'I have a car,' said Rain, gesturing towards the street where she had parked it. 'And Chelsea is out of bounds to me for a week. I'm house-sitting in Islington for friends who are taking a holiday. I can drop you off on my way.'

'Tell me,' said Gerrard, as he folded himself into her tiny red car. 'Who's flat-sitting for you while you're house-sitting?' Settled, he had to hunch down but still his fair hair brushed the roof.

'The decorators.'

'Ah, I see. Having the decorators in is an unchallengeable reason to decamp.' He wriggled, trying to get comfortable but he was so overweight that he overlapped the seat.

Rain had driven several hundred yards before he mentioned the other advantage in leaving Chelsea for a few days. 'And you won't be bothered by the locals greedy for details about poor old Alf Wilson.'

Slowing at red traffic lights she asked: 'Did you know him, David?' Her tone was casual but her interest had quickened. David Gerrard might have answers she did not.

He disappointed her. 'Not professionally. I was a youngster when he was in his heyday, but one hears things.'

Avoiding his thigh she pulled on the handbrake. 'What things?'

'That he'd left one agent, gone to another. That his work wasn't being sold. That he was on and off the teams . . .'

'Teams?'

'Yes, they write television series like that. They hire a team of writers, hand them a set of characters and a story line and tell them to get on with it. If one's good and one's compatible, one stays on the team. If not . . .'

A tabby cat slunk across the road, taking advantage of a

green matchstick man pedestrian-crossing light. Rain said: 'But Alf Wilson originated some of the most successful drama we've ever seen on British television. Why should he be handed characters and a plot?'

'Because he needed to be on the teams. He had his success early and it died early. Then he turned to run-of-the-mill television writing. That ought to have worked for him, but apparently it didn't. He had ceased to travel hopefully, had ceased to labour.'

'You suggested he might not have been compatible.'

'No, I meant that was one of the reasons people are dropped. I don't know why Wilson faded out but many of them do. Remember that, an awful lot of them do.'

He spoke the last words with an air of finality, but she had not finished with the subject. 'I simply don't understand how a talent like his could have been wasted.'

Replying, Gerrard reminded her how the producers who had worked with Wilson had also been swept away; how the system that had allowed writers to progress from single plays to full series had been changed so that writers beavered away on the teams hoping to be allowed the chance one day to write a single play; how there were far too many writers competing for television work; and how the importance of influential contacts led the hasbeens to hang around pubs frequented by the currently successful, desperate to be remembered when writers were sought for new projects.

Gerrard concluded: 'If you want to know whatever happened to Alf Wilson, the answer is probably some of that.'

Amber. Green. The car moved forward. Rain said: 'Would you do something for me, David? I don't mean for the paper, I mean for me.'

'Well, on the basis that you're a nice girl who'll return a favour, why should I refuse?'

She ignored his inference that he could wangle his authors' way into her column in return. She said: 'I wish you could find out precisely what Alf Wilson did for the last eleven years.

Purely for my own curiosity.' And, she might have added, to test how far she ought to feel guilty.

David Gerrard said it would be no trouble at all, that everyone was certain to be talking about Wilson and he would merely have to keep his ears open. 'Will you give me your Islington telephone number or will the office do?'

She said the office would do.

She dropped him off outside his flat and drove on to Islington. Endeavouring to obey a night-time traffic ban she became lost and drifted into territory she did not know. Eventually she cheated, skimmed past a No Entry sign and headed confidently towards the Dudleys' house. There was exactly enough space between vehicles parked at the pavement's edge for her to drive up to their garage.

As she opened the car door she heard the dog barking. Her chief duty as house-sitter was to feed and walk the dog. Rain yawned, decided it was too late to do other than let him race about the back garden for five minutes. She braced herself for his energetic welcome. She could already hear his claws clattering on the tiles of the hall, and the thuds as he bounced against the front door.

'It's all right, Fred, it's only me,' she called in a reassuring voice that did nothing to quieten him as she slotted her key in the lock.

He barked louder. Rain called louder but he was too deafened by his own noise to hear her. He continued to bark. The door opened a crack and she glimpsed him, dancing about, wagging his tail, joyful at being saved from his loneliness. His owners kept more respectable hours than their house-sitter did.

And all she had was a glimpse because suddenly Fred was in the street with a speed that defeated her reactions. He circled once, reared sideways at her command to 'Come!', and then he was gone.

Futilely, she ran into the road after him. 'Fred! Come here, Fred!' With a flick of his black tail he was round the corner. Rain dithered between the unlocked house and the escaping pet. She locked the house then ran to the street corner. But Thornhill Road had bends and angles and thick black shadows. Fred was invisible. She went indoors.

He'll come back, she thought as she switched on the hall light and straightened the doormat the dog had sent skidding. *He'll stretch his legs and then he'll come home. They've got fantastic sense of direction, they return from anywhere.*

She hesitated, the doormat dangling from her hand. *Or is that pigeons?* She had never owned a dog, she was about to find out.

Fred's escapade prevented her going to bed. She grudgingly accepted that and prepared to wait up for him, taking up position in the sitting room at the front of the house and leaving the curtains open.

'Fred, you've got an hour,' she told the absent animal. 'After that you're on your own.'

She filled the first few minutes of the hour by writing her piece about the new nightclub and she spent the rest thinking over what David Gerrard had told her about Alf Wilson's slide from fame to obscurity. Unfortunately she had missed seeing how the television news programmes had handled the story. They might have stopped some of the gaps in her knowledge. His family, for example. Was there an ex-wife somewhere, children? The file had not said. There were bound to be relatives of some degree, but when the police had asked her, and had asked Ratcliffe and Mrs Dobson and the other tenants of that sad house, no one could suggest where to start seeking his next of kin.

That morning she had lied to the police. She had told a small and insignificant lie and she was puzzled as to why she had done it. Yet when the sergeant had asked her to hand over the note Alf Wilson had put through her letter box, she had denied having it with her.

An unconscious decision to withhold it forced her to say: 'I left it at home. I'll drop it into the police station later, if you like.'

The sergeant had thanked her and asked her to do so. And

while Ratcliffe and the bald man from the husband and wife team in the flat across the hall had handed over theirs, and the wife of the man with the tremor had produced the note slipped beneath their top-floor door, and Mrs Dobson had bustled down to the basement for hers, Rain had realized that she wanted to photocopy her own before letting the police see the original. Yet why she should want to do so, she could not say.

They were in her shoulder bag now, copy and original. She took them out and stared at the one Wilson had delivered, although she knew the words by heart.

Supposing, she thought, he had delivered the note a day later, when she had left Chelsea for Islington? Unwittingly, she would have failed him. But what difference would it have made after all? He had invited people from the other flats at 18 Hunt Road to call on him too, and when their knocks went unanswered they would have grown alarmed and had the door opened, either by force or perhaps with the landlord's key.

Alf Wilson had not truly required her attendance to ensure that his body was discovered within hours of his death rather than days later or however long it took for neighbours a man normally avoided to become concerned about his absence. Her presence had been irrelevant – and yet Wilson had described it as essential. Rain wished she knew why.

The Dudleys' sofa was deeply comfortable. Rain dropped off to sleep. Three-quarters of an hour later the chimes of a clock on a shelf in the dining room woke her. Her mouth was dry, she felt dishevelled. It had not been a restful sleep.

Dutifully, she looked out into the street in case Fred had scrabbled at the front door while she dozed. He was not there. She bolted the door and went to bed. Despite her tiredness, falling asleep again was difficult. She never like to be on her own in a house at night, never liked the dark. Fred was not merely the reason for the Dudleys asking her to look after the house while they went to France, he was also the chief reason she had said yes. With Fred in the house, she had carelessly

17

assumed, it would be as good as having another person around.

Each unfamiliar creak of the house's timbers, each switching on of the fridge, each clamour of the dining-room clock brought her nervously alert. After a time she got out of bed, tramped downstairs and examined the clock, seeking a means to prevent it chiming. Unsuccessful, she muffled it beneath tablecloths in a drawer and headed back to bed.

Before mounting the stairs, she detoured to the sitting room to check on Fred. Directly she entered the room and approached the window, she saw something that made her falter. A man was outside the house.

Her instinct was to draw back, tuck herself out of sight and watch. The silk of a curtain stroked her cheek. She moved further into the room, keeping the figure in sight.

He was standing beneath one of the twin willow trees that flanked the Dudleys' front path. Street lamps were lit all night through and the man was concealing himself in the black shadow of a tree. He was perfectly still.

For minutes he did not move. Then he shuffled his feet. Then he stayed stock-still. Rain heard her anxious breathing, absurdly loud. She believed he had his back to her but the top half of his body was obscured by the fronds of willow and he was wearing something dark above his jeans.

Weighing up what to do, she let further minutes pass then ran upstairs to test whether a different window would let her see down the street, whether she could make out what or whom the man was watching. But the luxurious growth of trees cut off her view. She opted to scare him away and turned on the front-bedroom and hall lights. When she returned to the sitting room he had gone.

The remainder of her night was passed in restless sleep interspersed with nervous sorties in search of Fred and the lurking man. By five-thirty she gave up and showered and dressed. Obliged to search the streets for Fred, she regretted having invited Holly Chase to drop in for breakfast because Holly might well arrive before Fred was found.

The morning was crisp and bright, with a sharply cold breeze shivering the willows. Rain looked closely at the one beneath which the man had stood, but there was nothing to confirm his presence. No dropped cigarette end or sweet wrapper, no footprints, nothing. No Fred, either. She turned towards Thornhill Road and, for want of any other clues, she set out in the direction Fred had taken.

From time to time she called his name, particularly when she came upon public gardens and shrubby corners where a dog could forage unseen. Once she heard furtive movements among rhododendrons and grew hopeful, but she found a drunk sleeping rough. If he had seen a great black dog in the night, he did not tell her.

She wished she knew the district better. At this time of day it was quietly suburban, with scant traffic and hardly anyone walking about. She was too early for the youngsters doing newspaper rounds, although at one newsagent's shop an Indian man was bent double marking papers with street numbers ready for delivery. There was no one else she could appeal to for news of Fred.

When the streets had become a degree meaner and the cars parked in the gutters were older and tattier, she doubled back. N1 had long given way on the street signs to N7, she had walked a considerable distance.

Returning, she missed Thornhill Road, her main landmark, and zig-zagged uncertainly, reassured that she was in the correct territory but relying on luck to guide her to the Dudleys' house. At a junction she hesitated, made her choice and stepped into the road. A car horn hooted, frightening her until she realized she was not at risk because the car was on the other side of the road she had just left. The driver was Holly Chase.

'Where are you off to?' called Holly, and saved Rain from a long tramp in the wrong direction.

Rain was still recounting the night's adventures and the morning's follow-up as Holly drove up to the Dudleys' house.

Holly interrupted: 'Is Fred a large black dog with shaggy hair and a great fan of a tail?'

'Yes.'

'Just like the one sitting on the doorstep?'

'Oh.'

Holly pealed with laughter. 'They always come back, didn't you know that?'

'After the first hour I decided that was pigeons, not dogs.'

Rain went to Fred, doubtful whether he deserved to be patted and greeted affectionately for displaying his fine homing instinct or treated with contempt for the trouble he had caused. He provided his own solution, leaping up to lick her face, a treat she fended off in the nick of time.

'I bet he gets that from his owners,' said Holly, locking her car. 'I bet the Dudleys are the sort of people who greet their friends with exuberant kisses.'

Rain was sceptical that dogs imitated human behaviour, although Holly's guess was correct about the demonstrative welcome Marion Dudley gave visitors. Holly looked admiringly at the solid double-fronted house with the fancy fanlighting above the Georgian door. Fred grabbed her attention. She patted him, saying: 'He's spent many an hour in the hall watching the Dudleys bounding up at their guests, haven't you, Fred? It's that kind of neighbourhood, isn't it, Fred?'

'Snob,' said Rain as she let them into the house.

'Oh I don't fool anyone, not even me,' sighed Holly. 'What wouldn't I give for a house like this?'

Holly was house-hunting but in Hackney, not among these streets. She and Daniel, who had shared each other's lives longer than Rain had known either of them, had their modern semi-detached outer-suburb house on the market and were trying to move nearer the centre.

'I can tell you precisely what you'd have to give,' said Rain, lifting a paper from a stack on the hall table. They were all from local estate agents advertising properties on their books and touting for new business.

Rain tossed the paper back on the table. 'Coffee?' She

marshalled cups and saucers, milk and sugar, while the coffee-making machine offered a sibilant contribution to the conversation.

Holly was comparing the wonders of the Dudleys' kitchen with the inadequacies concealed behind the Hackney estate agents' cunning prose. The Dudleys had employed an architect and an interior designer who had put them to enormous expense. Their home was a world away from Holly's brick box in Spinney Green and the below-par flats she was being offered.

'Drink that to steady your nerves,' said Rain sliding a cup of coffee along the marble table, 'then I'll show you round the house.'

She began the tour upstairs and when they descended to the sitting room Holly spotted the note and the photocopy where Rain had left them during the night. Rain asked her to read Wilson's lines.

Holly's great dark eyes grew serious. 'You said there wasn't a suicide note, but what do you think this is?'

Rain shook her head. 'It didn't read like that. Not the first time, not later. Now I simply don't know.'

Holly read it out: ' "I need to ask you a favour. Please come to my flat at 9 a.m. tomorrow (Monday). It's desperately important, I wouldn't be writing this otherwise. Don't fail me, Rain. It's imperative you come." That's an emphatic way of wording it, if he meant he hoped you'd be free to call round.'

'Not necessarily. If you'd known him . . .'

'Rain, I *didn't* know him. Tell me.'

Rain sank on to the sofa where she had spent too much of the night. 'Did you see the television news?'

Holly nodded.

Rain said: 'I was out, I missed it. The television will have told you more than I know about him.'

Holly ticked off points on her perfectly manicured black fingers. 'One, it told me where he'd lived, how his body had been found and how the police did not suspect any other person of being involved in his death. Two, it told me he'd written *Dead and Alive* and various other plays in the sixties and early seventies, and that he'd won a selection of awards. Three, it said he'd been born in Yorkshire and brought up at various places in the South of England. Four, it said that the BBC was planning to screen *Dead and Alive* and some other work as a tribute to him.'

She spread her hands. 'That's all, Rain. It told me nothing about Alfred Gervase Wilson as a personality. The nearest it got to that was in your interview with Frances Keene when you said he was a quiet man who always had a friendly word when you met him in the street.'

Rain winced. Could she have been so banal?

Holly continued. 'I interpreted that to mean he was lonely and you caught him hanging around in a pub.'

Laughing, Rain shooed Holly into the kitchen, promising to tell as much as she could about Alf Wilson but only if they could eat while she did so. Holly refreshed Fred's bowl of water and made a fuss of him while Rain cooked. Fred was going to be on his own again most of the day, except for the couple of hours the Dudleys' Portuguese cleaner would spend at the house.

Telling all to Holly did not take long, and Holly accused Rain of holding back.

'I promise you,' Rain protested. 'That is it. The total.'

Holly pulled a face. 'It's very difficult to know as little as that about somebody you've known for years and regularly seen around the place.'

'You've pinpointed the problem,' Rain's words came in an eager rush. 'I saw him around. I had very few conversations of any length with him and they were spread over several years. Most of the time it was a smile and a wave as we passed on opposite sides of the King's Road.'

She paused, then confessed. 'Holly, I can't help wondering whether if I'd bothered to cross the road and spared him a few minutes of my time he'd have avoided reaching such depths. Our meagre relationship was far more valuable to him than I realized. Why else would he have come to me with his key?'

Holly said gently: 'You hadn't seen him for months. You don't know how he'd changed or what peculiar ideas he'd fostered. His neighbours said his behaviour had altered, remember. Perhaps dragging you into it was an aberration, something he'd never have done if he'd been rational.'

Rain finished her breakfast and said that yes, she imagined Holly to be right. She did not confide the suspicion she was struggling to quash, the suspicion that she understood why Wilson had sent for her, that far from it being an irrational act it was an entirely reasonable one.

During the morning, after the editorial conference and before lunch, she received two telephone calls about Wilson. One was from David Gerrard to tell her he had stumbled across someone who would talk to her about Wilson. The other was from a BBC producer asking her to appear on a programme about the dead man.

Gerrard said: 'Nicholson's leaving town this afternoon but perhaps you could trap him at lunchtime. Sorry I won't be available to introduce you but I have a lunch today.'

'I'll manage,' said Rain, writing down Nicholson's telephone number.

'I'd be interested myself to hear what he has to say, but alas there's this frightful lunch.'

'Don't fret, David, I'll report back.'

'Well, not too early.'

Rain laughed. 'One of *those* lunches, the long, long type?'

'I fear it could turn out that way. One has to look after one's authors, you know. Occasionally one has to go so far as to buy them lunch. Especially when they come up to town to discuss why their books aren't selling. Soften the blow and whatnot.'

Rain made a noncommittal mmm. She discounted the theory that an author's pursuit of financial reward would be deflected by the sight of a West End restaurant full of richer people stuffing down expensive lunches. But she kept the thought to herself.

It took several attempts by Rosie before Rain's telephone

call to Nicholson succeeded. 'Sure,' he said. 'Let's talk about one-thirty. Is the Groucho OK?'

A Fleet Street pub would have suited her better but she said yes. And this was what the Groucho was for: a meeting point for media people, a club for those who would not ordinarily join a club.

Nicholson was already in Soho; Dean Street was handy for him. He was a television writer who had worked with Wilson. He had not stated he was a friend, which is what Rain most hoped for, but she was willing to go to the Groucho or anywhere else to meet him. He was not simply leaving London that afternoon, he was leaving for Hollywood. She needed to catch him while she could.

Her taxi dropped her outside 45 Dean Street. A drunken gossip columnist from one of the disreputable tabloids was wedged in the revolving doors, arguing with someone. Rain hurried in through the adjacent door, thankful he neither noticed nor accosted her.

She entered the bar, to the left of the foyer, and immediately Nicholson moved forward to meet her. He was a hefty man with hair unfashionably long, particularly on a man of forty plus. His first words, after the drink buying and the pleasantries, alarmed her.

'He talked about a new project,' he said, 'but it wasn't true. It never is with people like that. They fool themselves and they think they fool everybody else too, but it doesn't do them any good. It's not surprising he got so depressed he killed himself, it's only surprising that anyone's surprised.'

2

'You'd be better off dead,' said David Gerrard. He was leaning back from the table, twitching ash from a small cigar.

The diffident man opposite gave him a wry smile. 'Thanks.'

Gerrard gestured with the cigar. 'Well, to be perfectly frank, John, one sees it all the time. Publishers have to be coerced to look at their back lists. They are adept at allowing books to go out of print, forgetting the enthusiasm that made them buy the titles in the first place. Unless the author finds a niche in the news, his books are unlikely to be dusted off and reissued.'

John Gower inclined his head to avoid cigar smoke. 'But if I were to walk under a bus, all my troubles would be over?'

Gerrard looked askance. 'One would have to secure a classier niche than *that*. Blundering beneath buses smacks of incompetence and short-sightedness, not at all the attributes one would wish to promote. You deserve better.'

'Such as?' Gower shifted in his chair. The restaurant was emptying, they had been there a long time and he felt cheated. Gerrard was famed as the pushiest agent in London but he had done nothing to popularize Gower's books. The publisher, Pegwoods, had been miserly about increasing the advances for successive novels; had failed to sell paperback rights; and had pitched the print runs of the newer books at a lowly level that effectively curbed sales. The outlook was not propitious, but Gerrard had cautioned against moving to a different publisher, saying that they were all the same and a switch might make it less attractive for Pegwoods to reissue books, should they ever be so inclined.

Gower sipped the brandy Gerrard had bullied him into accepting. He had asked for the meeting to thrash out the difficulties that hindered his career, but the agent had turned it into lunch at a fashionable restaurant in Charlotte Street; he had wanted encouraging news of Pegwoods' plans to promote the next book, *The Secret*, due out in a couple of months, but Gerrard had none; and now, when Gower was dispirited and angry, he could not leave, he had to sit it out until Gerrard had finished his cigar and paid the bill. Gerrard was taking his time about it, talking nonsense as the meal drew to its desultory close.

'Such as?' imitated Gerrard, drawing on the cigar and exhaling smoke with luxurious slowness before going on: 'It would be awfully effective if you were murdered. Murder is a headline maker, you know, never fails. I can see it now, John. "Top Writer in Death Probe".'

'*Top* writer?' challenged Gower.

'Oh, it's always top this and top that in the tabloids. Doesn't mean anything, it's a non-word but they like it because it's short.'

'Ditto death, ditto probe?' suggested Gower.

'Ye-es,' said Gerrard absently. He picked up the bill from the silver tray, then reached into a pocket and tossed a gold credit card on to the tray. With the cigar he summoned a waiter.

Gower said, with more asperity than he intended: 'Well I'm sorry to spoil your fun with the headline writers, David, but I'm not prepared to get myself murdered or squashed by a country bus.'

Gerrard flinched. 'Not *country*,' he corrected. 'A *London* bus. The accident would have to happen here. It's the journalists' prejudice that if news hasn't happened in London, it probably hasn't happened at all. Please, if you project yourself beneath the wheels, John, make absolutely sure you do it in central London.'

Gower was saved from a reply by the arrival of the waiter, the business of the credit card, the waiter's demand that they say they had enjoyed their meal, and Gerrard's compliance with the demand. Then, simultaneously, Gower and Gerrard looked at their wrist-watches, Gerrard's sleeve scooting back to reveal a heavy gold watch and a cuff link set with a ruby.

Gerrard surveyed the clutter of empty glasses, cigar ash, coffee cups, crumpled napkins, the disorder of a good meal. He said: 'Wine maketh merry, but money answereth all things. I must away and make some money, John. I'll speak to Pegwoods about *The Secret* but I hold out no hope. I know how they're spending their budget this year, and the next, and it isn't on your kind of fiction.'

A great deal of it was not going on fiction at all. As Gerrard had already mentioned, Pegwoods were ecstatic about having outbid other publishers for the autobiography of a dead parrot, the world's most loquacious pet who had, from beyond the grave, communicated his story to a medium. Pegwoods were reportedly the envy of the publishing world: animals *and* the unknown – what more could they ask?

Gerrard had not pretended Gower's book would command the respect accorded the ramblings of a dead parrot, and his resumé after the meal was a reiteration of the gloom he had dispensed throughout. Then he said: 'I'm taking a taxi to Queen Square, can I drop you anywhere?'

'No, thanks. I'd like to walk.'

'Well, then . . .' Gerrard slid his credit card into his pocket and rose. The meal was over, they were free of each other.

They parted a few yards from the front door, Gerrard diving for a taxi. He waved through the window as it departed. Gower crossed the road and hurried away, needing to put the street, the lunch, the conversation behind him.

He would have invented a destination had he been asked for one, but Gerrard had not asked. Gower did not have a plan, he wanted only to walk. He had never held out extravagant hope of a satisfactory outcome to the meeting and was surprised at his chagrin.

What's 'satisfactory' in this context, anyway? he reasoned. *If Pegwoods were planning an energetic promotion for* The Secret *I'd have been told before today.*

Gerrard had diverted him with anecdote and steered him

into talking about the book he was currently writing. Gerrard abhorred the perfidy of publishers, but had unveiled no scheme to lift him from the ranks of the average, and that was all Gower had wanted to hear.

John Gower considered himself a realist. Any writer who set out to make his living from fiction needed to be that. He had been realistic about letting his reputation build novel by novel instead of praying for a soaraway success with one of the first. He had taken practical steps, like moving out of London to live more cheaply and with fewer distractions. Coolly, he had weighed the limitations of the writing life and he had taken the risk.

There were six books, each of them two years of toil and mental tussle. The reviewers liked them. He had stepped up from 'promising' to 'reliable'. Yet, for all that, his certainty grew that the promise was to remain unfulfilled.

Hard work and talent had proved inadequate. They could not tip the scales against luck and he was repeatedly reminded how much luckier other writers were. Every bookshop window told him, every station bookstall rubbed it in and the books pages of newspapers and magazines emphasized what he knew to be true. The novels of John Gower were being overlooked, the attention they deserved was being paid to other people's work.

But attention was hardly a finite thing, even if there could be only so many column inches on a books page or only so many yards of shelving in a bookshop. Gower was neither jealous of other writers nor dismissive of the output of those money-spinners who produced for the mass market, 'Fat books for thick readers,' as Gerrard had once acidly described them to him. Yet Gower's life was becoming a torment of frustration.

Linda had left him six weeks ago. She had discussed and argued and packed and gone. Six weeks ago he had been getting down to the new book – not the next one to be published, the one Gerrard and Pegwoods meant when they talked about the new book, but the truly new one, the one that was in the process of forming itself inside his head.

Starting off was invariably a delicate phase for Gower. The story was building and being shaped. Very little was on paper. All he had was a tentative story, a central character who needed clarifying, an idea of the manner in which he would like to tell the story and the notion that he might use a particular setting. Six weeks ago, the new book was as nebulous and fragile as that. And that is when Linda walked out.

Their arguments over the years and on the day she went were ritual and uninteresting. She had never liked the country, had given way to persuasion when he needed to leave London, her own work had reached a plateau with no prospect of promotion away from the city, and she was fed up with being short of money.

'You do realize I'm subsidizing you, don't you?' she had said. 'Subsidizing you and Pegwoods. Why should I? Don't tell me they are too poor to make you a decent advance, look what they paid for that trashy novel by . . .'

But he had walked out into the garden rather than hear it all again. Anyway, he had not expected her to go, not even when she had packed and put her suitcase by the front door. Linda could say a great deal without ever actually doing anything. Then she had called him over.

'Look,' she had said, keeping her voice low to prevent anyone who might be in the lane hearing, 'I'll need the car to get to the station. Do you want to drive me there or – '

'Linda, for heaven's sake!'

'No, I mean it. I've told you. Now, about the car . . .'

'I'm driving you nowhere,' he had said.

She had taken a deep breath, said nothing, waited. But he had not asked her to stay. Then she had said: 'All right, John, I'll leave the car in the car park and give the keys to whoever's in the booking office.' They had resorted to this arrangement in the past when one or other of them needed to go up to London.

'Please yourself.' He had moved away. The house had instantly acquired an abandoned air, although she was audibly opening the garage doors, dragging into place the heavy stone that held one of them open while the vehicle was manoeuvred in or out.

Gower's sense of the house became acute: its narrow passage with the faded wallpaper they had hung when they had moved in ten years earlier, the scuff marks on the newel post at the foot of the too-dark staircase, the crazy slope of a window disturbed during settlement a century and a half ago.

He had gone into the room with the slanting window, his study. There were bookshelves, neat papers on one side of a very big desk, a computer and its ancillary items stowed on the other side, and a pile of typing paper in the centre in front of a captain's chair. Gower had felt more comfortable. His study.

He had pulled out the chair but changed his mind and had not sat down. Instead, he had leaned over the back of the chair and read what he had written on the topmost sheet of paper. The pile was stapled, roughly a dozen sheets at a time. 'Richard Crane,' he had read, his lips moving the words. Beneath the name was a list: 'streetwise, tough, uncompromising'.

On the back was a full page of text, printed out from his computer. His working method was to write his notes and eventually his first draft of a new book on the back of the printouts of the previous book. It reassured him in his slower patches, reassured him more than the published novels on the shelves near by had the power to do, that he was equal to the massive creative effort with which he had burdened himself.

He had heard the car engine, muffled at first inside the garage, then louder as Linda had reversed into the open. He had jerked away from the desk, run along the passage and out of the front door. The words had been there, he had meant to say he loved her and that he wanted her to stay. But he had not spoken them. He had stood on the threshold and Linda had driven away.

She had not stopped to close the gate to the lane. Gower had done that for her, walking to the gate on weakened legs, pulling it shut and anchoring it by dropping the vertical bar into the socket. With detachment he had watched his body go through these routine actions, each movement automatic yet seen afresh. Then he had rested a moment, hands on the gate's cold iron. There had been a hardening of his throat, a fear he was going to cry. Faintly, very faintly, he had heard the car zig-zagging through the lanes.

In the wake of her desertion he had set aside Richard Crane and the new book, and he had written to David Gerrard requesting a meeting to discuss what was left of his promising career.

The lunch he had eaten with Gerrard was weighing heavily. It had been rich and elaborate, the menu offering nothing simple and light. No doubt Gerrard's choice of wines had been impeccable, the brandy admirable, but at the time Gower had found it all unnecessary and by mid-afternoon he regretted it.

He wished home was within easy reach so that he could sleep off the meal. As it was, he had to stay in London a while longer. The rules about using cheap return tickets prevented him travelling on a train during rush hour. Peak period began, according to these rules, peculiarly early. Gower was resigned to delaying his return until after it.

He headed for bookshops – Hatchards, Waterstones, a wealth of them, all treats after the privations of country life. He browsed and bought, revived himself with espresso coffee when he faltered, and scoured the non-fiction shelves for anything that impinged on the subject of his new novel and might prove useful. By the end of the afternoon he was laden with books.

Coming out of one of the shops, brooding how to pass the rest of the time before going to the railway station, he thought he saw Linda. The woman was racing along with home-going office workers, and for a second Gower thought she was his wife. The mistake was enough to convince him that what he should do with the rest of his time was to meet Linda.

He used a pay phone in a hotel near by. Linda's sister's telephone number was engaged. He sat in the foyer and waited, ringing the number again a few minutes later. Engaged still. He read for a while, his concentration on the book interrupted by picturing Linda on her way from her office – wherever that was – to her sister's house where she had taken temporary refuge.

Gower did not know exactly where the sister lived either. He had the telephone number that Linda had left him when she had called in at the cottage one day while he was out, to collect some of her personal things.

'If there's anything urgent,' she had written, 'you can reach me at this number.' And then, in a slightly different hand, as though it were an afterthought, she had squeezed on to the bottom of the slip of paper: 'Sorry I missed you today.'

He had pondered those words for a disproportionate amount of time, warming at first to the belief that Linda was genuinely sorry he had happened to be out when she arrived and then reflecting that Linda was the only person who could have calculated he would be out at that time on a Tuesday because he generally was. Then he had brightened at the thought that maybe she had intended to avoid him but had, when it came to the point, been sorry.

He tried her sister's number again. At the second ring a breathless woman answered him. 'Hello?'

'Er . . . Mary?'

'Yes. Who's that?'

'It's John, Mary. John Gower.'

Cagily: 'Oh?'

'Is Linda with you?'

'We-ell.'

'I thought she might be there.'

'She told you, John. I mean I understood her to say she'd told you she was staying here.'

They were at cross purposes. He and Linda's sister usually were. He said: 'Yes, she did. I'm asking whether she's there now, at this very minute.'

'Oh, I see.' Mary sounded relieved.

'Well?'

'No, she won't be back for a while. She's gone to . . . She said she'd be late this evening.'

Gower asked how late but Mary said she did not know. Then she hazarded that Linda would be no later than eight. She said: 'I'll tell her you rang, shall I?'

'Yes. No. I'll ring her after eight.' But then another thought crowded in. 'Yes, tell her I called. Tell her I'm in London.'

'And you want to see her.' Mary made it a statement, not a question. 'Where shall I say you are?'

He did not pause to consider the irrelevance of that, he gave her the name of the hotel he was in. Setting down the receiver he took stock. Linda ought to be at her sister's within the next couple of hours, and he would arrange to meet her. He would have to buy her a meal, it would be too late to offer anything less although he was so full of Gerrard's lunch he would not be hungry himself. What *he* needed was a shower and some rest, not more food.

He fell headlong into a fresh plan. He booked himself into the hotel, bought a shirt, underwear and socks at a shop a few doors away and took a shower. When he met Linda he would be looking good. It would not suit his purpose to be grubby, dishevelled and tired.

Not until he was running a comb through his hair did it occur to him to question what his purpose was exactly. To *talk* to Linda? He could do that on the telephone, it did not require all this preparation and expense. To take her to dinner with a view to persuading her to go back to Dorset with him? He winced, accepting that Linda had made her feelings about country life extremely plain and she was unassailable once her mind was made up.

Had he seriously intended to invite her to spend the night with him at a hotel? And if he had not, what was all this about? If he had wanted sleep, he could have dozed on the train home, as he had done on other occasions.

The trouble with you, he told the combing reflection, *is that you're treating your wife like a character from one of your fictions. But Linda, as she's proved, is not a woman to be confined by the scenes you imagine for her*. And certainly he could not imagine a favourable reaction if he were to suggest she slept at the hotel with him.

He did not mention the hotel when they spoke on the telephone. The time was a little after seven-thirty but he had been impatient to know whether she was going to be as late as Mary had believed. Linda did not sound displeased to hear him, but neither was she keen to meet.

A pity, he thought too late, *about getting involved in explanations to Mary. If I'd spoken to Linda initially her reaction would have been different, but Mary's allowed her time to decide how to respond.*

Linda softened her refusal by changing tack. 'What brings you to London?'

'Lunch with David Gerrard. He's pressuring Pegwoods to do something special for the next book.'

'Does he think they might?'

'Oh there are one or two ideas.' Like walking under a London bus or becoming a murder victim. But the lie slid effortlessly over the tongue.

Linda said: 'It would be terrific if Pegwoods did do something. You do deserve it, John.'

'Thanks. But don't I also deserve dinner with my wife tonight?'

Linda laughed the throaty chuckle he used to find sexy when he first knew her. He might not have remembered that if it had not sounded sexy now. She said: 'I don't see the point. Nothing's going to get me away from London again. I wish you'd face that. Whatever we had is finished.'

He cut in. 'We can't talk about this on the phone.'

'We didn't, John. We talked about it at the cottage, over and over.'

'*You* talked . . .'

'All right, it was a monologue. I couldn't force you to say what you wanted.' A pause neither of them would fill. Then she said: 'Anyway, we both know what you want and you've got it. A quiet corner to write your books. Now I'm going to have the things *I* want.'

Although he wheedled and cajoled, he could not win her. He concealed his annoyance, preferring to end the conversation on friendly terms. Linda had not said she did not want to see him ever again, she had not mentioned divorce or any of the ending-it-all things. She had left everything casually open-ended. It was merely that she was not living with him at present and that she was too weary after her day's work to spend an evening going over old ground.

He ended with a joke: 'You'll be sorry when I'm rich and famous.'

That was one of their long-standing jokes, what would happen when he was rich and famous. Linda countered with a joke of her own.

'I might change my mind under those circumstances.'

They rang off. As her voice died in his memory he took in the impersonal room, noted the creases in the impulsively bought shirt and sensed a creeping depression. He had been rash to delay, not to have caught the train. He sighed and lay down on the bed. A book was to hand but after a page or two, he dropped it on the floor beside him and stared, unseeing, at the ceiling.

Some other guest had a television set on, its sound throbbing softly through the wall behind his head. His head was aching, not severely but enough to reinforce his dislike of drinking alcohol at lunchtime. He closed his eyes, thinking that he should try to buy painkillers from the chemist's where he had earlier shopped for a toothbrush and razor, and trying to recall whether the chemist stayed open late into the evening.

He slept until roused by shrieks of laughter on the landing and the crash of a noisily closed door. Disorientated, Gower lurched to his feet, headed for the bathroom for a drink of water and switched on the television set in passing. *News at Ten* had reached the end of the preliminary headlines.

He fetched his water and perched on the end of the bed to watch the spate of recorded catastrophe, thinking that at least breakfast television provided some let-up and some laughs, essential ingredients for those who live alone with no one to chat to when they get up in the morning. Gower had watched a lot of breakfast television since Linda's departure.

The newsreader he liked was on duty, a woman with the same frank blue eyes and shoulder-length fair hair as Linda's. But their voices were dissimilar, Linda's lighter and the newsreader's a shade nasal. Gower compared his wife and the newsreader, oblivious of what was being read from the autocue.

Then there was some film, then the male newsreader with a different item, then the woman again. To and fro they went, not capping each other's stories but rather producing a diminuendo effect until the final, trivial joke that brought the programme to an end.

Gower reached for the button and switched the set off. He had the glimmer of an idea for a scene with Richard Crane, his fictitious hero, in a hotel room. Crane would be experiencing the hollowness Gower himself was feeling, he would be at a turning point and the hotel scene would be the mechanism for forcing the change in his life.

Perhaps, he thought, *Crane will be influenced by something viewed on television? No, too corny. Something else, something subtler. Think about it, work it out. But why should Crane be in a hotel room? He isn't a tourist, he's a Londoner.*

Gower unconsciously nibbled the nail of the little finger of his left hand, a tic that accompanied his deepest concentration. *Well, obviously a hotel room is a no man's land, a place that exists outside a man's normal life and that concept applies to what goes on there. Walking into a hotel room is walking out of real life with real responsibilities into another, artificial existence. And Richard Crane would . . .*

Gower released the bitten nail and rubbed his hand over his face. He had not succeeded in grasping the idea. Crane was not making himself clear. Gower could not bring him into focus and until he could he would be thrashing around the subject without pinpointing what Crane needed from that hotel room, that step out of his real life.

Gower put on his jacket and checked his wallet in the pocket. He lingered with his hand on the doorknob and looked around the room. Of course he could not have brought Linda here. This was the sort of room where men took other men's wives or prostitutes.

In the hotel bar Gower watched people. He especially watched the men, that is to say the kind of men he believed Richard Crane to be. Crane would be in his late twenties, more youthful than Gower himself. He had noticed he usually wrote about characters slightly younger than himself as if this were a quirk devised to ward off his own ageing.

There was one man he suspected came close to the elusive Crane. He was solid muscle with a direct way of looking at the person talking to him and an easy grace. Although his clothes were casual they were not worn carelessly. Gower visualized the man shopping, the recognition of the staff in the expensive boutique he frequented, the swift decision about the trousers and shirt and the long time selecting precisely the right leather belt.

Across the bar, the man felt Gower's gaze and glanced over. Gower deliberately let his vision grow hazy, claiming he had been staring into space and not studying the man. He dropped his head slowly, looked into his glass and drank off the last of his lager. His characters, he mused, were generally richer, more stylish than he was himself. He supposed that was a compensation too.

A couple of American tourists entered, seeking somewhere to sit. He made way for them, leaving the bar and crossing the foyer to the street. The brightness left him foolishly surprised. In the country April evenings were dark, the nights black. But in the London street traffic swished by, pedestrians scurried, groups of friends jostled to read menus outside cheap restaurants and a few shops were open.

He stepped on to the pavement and strolled past the restaurants. He was excited by the confusion of accents and languages, by the way people from everywhere in the world had been lured to holiday or live in London, and by the smaller purposes that had drawn such disparate characters together on one street at the same time.

Pushing by, a knot of youngsters bumped against him and he realized the folly of wandering in the centre of the pavement while everyone else was hurrying to get somewhere or do something. He moved aside, walking closer to the shop windows and letting the eager tide roll past unimpeded.

Towards the end of the street, where traffic lights rhythmically passed away the time, there was a bookshop. Gower loitered by its window enjoying its glut of titles, wishing he could get inside and browse. He noted the display, the kind of books that were chosen for it.

His own had never been arranged around a showcard or touted with publishers' breathtaking claims as several of the books in this window were. Three of them were what Gerrard called 'Fat books for thick readers', books that in Gower's experience were invariably badly constructed, overwritten, padded and inflated as desperately as their publishers' praise. They sold in millions (if the publicity was to be believed) and he cursed his bad luck at not writing them. Why should it be a disadvantage to care about syntax, cadence, shape and style, let alone originality? But in the marketplace it was.

His thoughts were slipping into a familiar groove but he tugged them away. Instead, he considered the covers in the window. There were stills from television or films if the book was linked to either production. There were startling abstracts, details of famous paintings, silver words proud on glowing coloured backgrounds, there were bucolic covers on books for women, there were leaping, dashing figures on thrillers and static dead ones on crime novels. In the centre of the window was a . . .

Gower stiffened. He sensed someone close by. People were passing along the pavement behind him, and the daring handful risked crossing the road diagonally at traffic lights to join them, but apart from all that activity he was aware of someone else. Someone who was scarcely moving. Someone to the side of him.

He balled his fists and turned his head fractionally in the direction of the furtive movement. He saw nobody. Next to the bookshop with its festive lighting were three unlit windows, protected with steel grilles. His eyes adjusting to the darkness, he peered along the row but spotted no one. Just as he was telling himself his imagination had misled him, he heard a sound, soft but distinct and from within a few feet of where he stood.

His curiosity would not permit him to walk away, as his caution urged. Resolutely, Gower went towards the sound. And then he saw something he had been too distracted to notice earlier. Between the bookshop window and the first of the unlit shops ran a meagre alley, perhaps a yard wide and in utter darkness.

He took a couple of paces inside the alley and his foot struck something soft. He gasped, his mind unravelling with frustrating slowness the detail of what he had discovered. A black plastic dustbin bag lay at his feet. Its top was ripped open and papers spewed out. Beyond it were two more bags, each torn apart. A man stooped over the third, his arm deep in its contents. He took no notice of his watcher, he sifted the rubbish, silently except for the occasional papery sounds of wrappers that someone had secured for cleanliness and that he was undoing in his search.

A breeze along the alley made Gower aware of the man's stench, filthy clothes on a filthy body. Gower backed off. The man heard, looked up. Through the dimness, his eyes gleamed. He shuffled forward. Gower could see him better. He was very old, or maybe he merely appeared very old. His hair was uncut and straggled in dirt-encrusted strands around a grimy face. Shoes, trousers and overcoat, with its ripped collar and pockets, were ancient and blackened. The smell intensified as he drew nearer.

Gower, sickened, was unable to move. Disgust rooted him until the creature was within reach. A curled hand snaked towards him, palm uppermost. The supplication was a mumbling incoherence. Gower backed into the street. A passer-by clipped him with an elbow, called: 'Sorry, mate' and was away without breaking step. Three youths scampered across the road between traffic, whooping at their own courage. A few people came cheerily out of a restaurant. A young couple were kissing in the bookshop doorway. Gower had rejoined the real, acceptable world.

The clean comfort of the hotel room flashed through his brain. His feet started to carry him there. Then compassion overcame revulsion. Pressed against the bookshop window to conceal his actions, he took notes out of his wallet. The couple in the doorway broke off their embrace long enough to confirm he was not spying on them. He ran back into the alley. The down-and-out was back at his business with the rubbish bags.

'Here,' Gower called roughly. 'Have this.'

He advanced, holding his breath to avoid the smell. Near the third bag the man's stink mingled with that of decomposing food scraps. 'Here, take it.'

Stupid and alarmed, the old man was disconcertingly reluctant. It seemed an age before he was willing to draw his hand out of the rubbish bag and extend it to accept the money. Then Gower moved sharply away, to dodge the embarrassment of the man's gratitude.

But the man did not speak, appeared not to understand or care. Gower felt himself to be rudely abrupt, and turning at the end of the alley called back: 'Goodnight.'

Goodnight! How ridiculous that sounded, how inappropriate. What could possibly be good about a night passed in an alley with the detritus of someone else's good living? What possible hope could the old man have of a good night, this night or any other? Gower squirmed as he made for the hotel.

His pace was equivalent to everyone else's now, he need not hug the walls to prevent obstruction. He wound through the other pedestrians, kept his eyes on his route and ignored everything extraneous. Spurred on by the distant hotel sign, he speeded up. He was moving as fast as the fastest fast-moving Londoner. He was running away. They were all running away.

That night he slept in his skin, unaccustomed to doing so and missing the comforting warmth of pyjamas. Now and then he awoke, when a random movement allowed draughts to creep in beside him. The room was actually hot and the windows were locked against intruders, or perhaps drunken guests falling out. Airless and uncomfortable, he anticipated a restless night, but was unduly pessimistic. Most of it went by in peaceful sleep.

At the back of the hotel, undisturbed by street noises, he was awakened early by the commotion of garbage collectors. They forced on him the memory of the old man in the alley, a distasteful incident he pushed aside as he remembered the previous day's failures: his lack of success with Linda and with David Gerrard.

Gower showered and dressed in the new shirt. The refuse collectors had him up well before his usual time but he meant to hurry through breakfast and catch an early train home. The London trip had achieved none of the things he had wanted, he acknowledged he would have been better off staying at home and working on the next book. The change of scene had not helped it, as a change of scene occasionally did. Richard Crane continued to be imprecise, an impression rather than a personality he knew.

In the dining room Gower was overwhelmed by the energetic enthusiasm of the foreign tourists mapping out their day's sightseeing. There was much flapping of Underground plans and guidebooks, much chatter. He helped himself at the buffet and sought out a secluded corner, unfolding his newspaper for company while he ate.

The *Daily Post* was not what he read every day but once in a while he enjoyed its verve. More substantial than the brasher tabloids, it offered the fun the solemn upmarket papers scorned. Gower turned to the gossip column, to a page topped with a photograph of a smiling blonde woman beside her handwritten name: Rain Morgan.

Is it, he wondered, *actually her signature or has it been designed? Mine would look pretty mysterious blown up to that size and stretched across four columns. I'll have to ask David Gerrard one day, he's always tossing her name into conversation claiming she's a great friend. Somebody he uses, anyway.*

Then he began to read. Halfway down the page was another photograph, not the main illustration but what police and journalists called a mug shot. This was of a middle-aged man, and Gower knew him at once.

Alfred Gervase Wilson, he read, was to be favoured with repeats on television of his spectacular successes of the sixties and seventies, or he would be if the BBC could put its hands on the recordings. Apparently they were not all present and correct, someone had removed them without permission. Rain Morgan hinted who that might be.

'Poor old Wilson,' muttered Gower as he poured himself a second cup of coffee. Surely Wilson was not to be cheated out of his tribute as well as everything else? Gower had not truly known Wilson, which is to say he would have recognized Wilson anywhere but Wilson would have had no recollection of him.

When Gower was a student, Wilson had given a talk on writing drama for television. Aspiring writers had crammed themselves into the room. Wilson was the best of television dramatists, and television was going to be the most important medium for drama in the future. Or so they had all thought at the time.

Gower knew what had happened to theatre. It had given up moaning that people did not travel to cities to watch new productions of old things; it had gone out into the pubs and small halls to meet the people, it had embraced new ideas and new writers and it had flourished. He understood that cinema had trimmed and tacked and entered into a financial alliance with television film-makers. But he could not say what had happened to Alf Wilson.

On his way to the railway station Gower stopped at a bank cash machine and checked the sum in his current account. It was adequate but not good. Foreign sales of his last three books had been disappointing, the trickle of cheques he had come to expect had all but dried up.

He took out some cash, regretting his emotional response to the down-and-out. The fellow had either been robbed of the money or drunk it by now. He had parted with £20 and for no very good reason. Walking smartly to the Underground station, he did what everybody else was doing and averted his eyes from the huddled figures in shop doorways, their bedding of newspapers or, if they were lucky, sleeping bags, not yet stirring to meet the day.

When he arrived at Waterloo the train was ready to leave. He raced through the barrier and sprang aboard, encumbered by his heavy bag of books into which he had stuffed yesterday's dirty clothes, placing the garments at the bottom so that no one need know they were there. The train was almost empty, he had space to stretch his legs and flop.

When the backs of inner-city houses were left behind and the suburban gardens and allotments were gliding past, he got out one of his books and skimmed it. But his attention was not gripped. He set the book down and concentrated on Richard Crane, giving him the firm jaw and muscles of the man in the hotel bar.

Finding a suitable face for a fictional character helped hugely, although with two of his novels he had never managed it and that had not harmed the books in any way. It was simply that the right face made it easier for him to develop the story.

A woman got into the carriage when the train stopped at Basingstoke, saw Gower and shied away to the other end of the carriage. He sat up, smoothed his brown hair, tidied his bag which had spilled books on to the seat opposite him. She had not trusted the look of him. Crane would have been a different matter. She would have admired his appearance, his confidence and gracefulness. However empty the carriage, Crane would not have sprawled across the seat.

Gower pulled a thin notebook from his pocket and wrote

43

down a phrase depicting Crane. He paused, then in brackets after it he jotted a qualification. He did not want to stress Crane's physical attractions, the sexual aspect that would be apparent to the reader but which must remain understated if Gower was to avoid creating an uninteresting copycat figure, a slick, tough young man ripe for sexual adventures. Fictional characters like that abounded and readers would be puzzled when Richard Crane subsequently veered from the stereotype.

Gower put the notebook away. He was feeling pleased, recognizing in himself the welling up of the urge to create. He could pass months between one book and another when it felt impossible that he would ever know that joy again. Only experience convinced him that the day would dawn when he needed to begin the long, tiring, tortuous journey from inkling to final draft. He smiled faintly at the villages and fields winging by the window. When he got home he would write.

He had always wanted to do that as long as he could remember, to write. This was not an ambition that had commended itself to his family – school teachers and minor civil servants to a man and a woman – but he had stuck to it because he had never been able to see a more preferable way of spending his time.

After university he had seemed to bow to the pressures and had taught for a while, precocious little boys in a snobby school in London. Then came the first book, fitfully pieced together in evenings when he ought to have been doing other things and in school holidays when he ought to have been travelling as his colleagues did.

The book prevented him going on with the teaching, for two reasons. For one, he had been handed an escape plan to get out of a profession he disliked, and for the other he knew how much better the book could have been if he had been able to give it all his mind.

A good while passed before the escape plan came into operation, because Linda arrived in his life. She was the

44

daughter of one of his colleagues, and she blundered upon him one end-of-term day while she was seeking her father. He had not heard the words of her apology, all he knew was that a young woman with the deepest blue eyes was standing in the doorway with brilliant July sun filtering through her lint-fair hair.

By the time he had wrenched his attention free of the scene he was writing, the door had closed, Linda had gone. Gower had flung himself at the door, inspected an empty corridor, wondered whether it was possible he had invented her. That was how Linda had entered his life: suddenly, startlingly. That, too, was how she had left him.

Anticipation about writing the Richard Crane book buoyed his spirits for the remainder of the two-and-a-quarter-hour journey west. He did not mind that it was raining heavily at Sherborne where he had left the car, or that the seal around the windscreen was damaged and water pooled beneath the pedals, or that the car hated starting in the wet. He read the time off the Abbey clock, viewed across the Pageant Gardens opposite the railway station, and congratulated himself on getting out of London early.

Even a delay at the level crossing and the evidence that he would be trundling along part of the journey behind heavy farm machinery could not crush his optimism about the day ahead. Things that were not favourable were at least bearable.

The shower was thinning as he climbed to the brow of the long hill south of Sherborne and a view of small fields, high hedges and wooded hilltops. He wound down a window to dispel condensation inside the car. Farmyard smells came and went as he drove through ragstone villages, past the long profiles of barns, and turned east on to a narrower road that led him, ultimately, home.

Stream Cottage. First the willow tree, then the slate roof of the cottage, greening with lichen, then red-brick walls, then the bad grey slab of rendering on the flank that bore the brunt of the weather. Home. John Gower was whistling as he whisked open the gate and drove up to the garage, stopping short to allow space to swing the doors back.

First he closed the gate, waving and calling hello to his nearest neighbour, a woman from a cottage some way off, who happened to be walking up the lane. Then he garaged the car, removing his bag of books from it beforehand as the garage, in truth an old wooden shed, was too narrow to give adequate room for manoeuvre. He chanced putting the car away without anchoring the garage door with a stone, but he was lucky. The wind held off and the door did not slam and scratch the car.

Then he was letting himself into the house, leaving the front door wide open as he stooped to gather letters and that morning's *Independent* from the passage before carrying them through to the kitchen. The house was cold. He filled a kettle to make a hot drink. Then he tipped his bag upside down on the table and when all the books had slithered to a halt he extricated his dirty washing and tossed it into the washing machine to join other garments lying there ready for him to run a programme when he had a full load.

Gower shivered and inspected a damp stain on the rear wall, daring it to have grown in his absence. He was certain the house was colder than the fields outside. When the kettle finished hissing, the silence was palpable. He was relieved when a tractor started up and a farm worker began to sing raucously above it. Jed Mullen was notoriously noisy. How often had Gower cursed him when the lumpen Jed was working in the field beyond his study window and Gower was attempting to write through his witless hollering? Now he was grateful to Jed for the affirmation that he was not alone.

The instant coffee was low in the jar. He scraped together enough for one mugful. The fridge contained sufficient milk but it was clear he had been too hasty in rushing home without shopping. He would have to go out again, a few miles across country to a real village that had a shop and not a mere scattering of farms and cottages.

Gower sat at the kitchen table with his hands around the hot mug. He ran an eye over the letters. An electricity bill, by the look of one. A circular, judging by the franking on another. And a letter from London. He opened that.

The letter was from his wife. Its contents hurt him to the core. Linda had said none of the ending-it-all things to his face, she had sent him a letter instead. He fought to take in every phrase, every nuance, but his eye retreated repeatedly to the single word in the third line. Divorce.

Then he was on his feet, making for the passage exactly as though she were in the sitting room and he could barge in and have it out with her. But there was no Linda. There never would be. Linda had left him for good. She had been to see a solicitor and was planning a divorce. He could not bear this. Yet he had to bear it and alone. There was no Linda, there was only Jed Mullen riding by the gate on his tractor and yelling a ribald greeting as he doffed his woolly hat in pretended deference to 'our hinterlectual', a tag he had attached soon after Gower had moved into the cottage and been unwise enough to ask Jed to keep his noise down because he was writing.

Gower did not remember getting from the kitchen to the doorstep. He slammed the front door on Jed and turned into the sitting room. There he re-read Linda's letter. He took it sentence by painful sentence, forcing himself to weigh it and miss nothing. Finally he screwed it up and threw it at the fireplace. He had been able to find no loophole in it, no 'if' he could latch on to. She was not offering conditions for her return, she was absolutely adamant that their marriage was over.

He had never seen it like that. He had known she was tired of the country and of her job and of being short of money, but he had not known she was tired of him. Thinking back, he could say with total honesty that she had never suggested that. And because she had not, he had assumed that when she had taken time to reflect she would be back. After all, she had gone to stay with her sister, she had not run off with another man. Linda had given him none of the pointers he would have

47

expected if things were so utterly hopeless that she wanted a divorce.

He picked up the telephone, half dialled Mary Green's number, put the receiver back on its rest. Linda would be at work, not at her sister's home. He did not know what to do but needed to be doing something. There was no point in calling Mary, she was unlikely to be there either but if she answered there was nothing he could say to her. Their conversation the previous evening troubled him. He suspected Mary's defensiveness had concealed knowledge.

Gower searched the room for the envelope his wife's letter had come in, realized he had opened it in the kitchen and found it beneath the table, lying on the black splodgy pattern of the worn linoleum floor-covering that had been there since before they had owned the cottage. The stamp on the envelope was a first-class one but he refused to accept that as incontrovertible proof that Linda had sent it the previous day.

The postmark was more interesting to him. He took the envelope to the window because the mark was faint. He still could not see plainly. For better light he opened the back door and stepped into the garden, holding the envelope inches from his nose and angling it. But the mark was smudged as well as indistinct and he was uncertain what it said.

Jed Mullen's tractor turned in at the field gate and plodded in the direction of Stream Cottage. Birds flurried away at its approach. Jed was bawling, a song or insults, it was all the same in the cacophony. Gower was oblivious until the vehicle lumbered nearer. Then he went inside, banging the door behind him.

Through the window he spotted Mullen staring at the cottage. Under his breath, Gower damned Mullen for an inquisitive oaf. He returned to the sitting room, anxious not to be seen. It seemed typical of Mullen's insensitivity for him to be clowning during somebody's anguish.

From the floor by the grate Gower recovered the letter, smoothed it and gently slipped it into the envelope. At the back of his mind was an idea that he ought to preserve it, like crucial evidence. But he did not want to read it again. He knew it by heart. He took it upstairs and hovered in the bedroom, his and Linda's room, deciding where to put it. The room was cold and shady. The weeping willow, planted much too near the house, blocked the view from the one small window. At sunnier times of day the room was washed in willow-green light.

He opened a drawer that had been Linda's, one that she had emptied that Tuesday when she had returned, and he laid the envelope face down in the centre of it. Then he walked softly away.

Later, it was hard to remember what he did next. He must have been shopping, because a supermarket carrier bag full of groceries was in his car, but he had not the haziest recollection of the drive to Sherborne and back. He did, though, remember walking into a village pub that evening, being greeted by people he had not seen in a long time. And he remembered leaving, very late, long after the legal closing time and walking up interminable lanes to Stream Cottage with a torch borrowed from the landlord.

He ought to have been drunk. He had certainly downed enough, but a dogged lack of co-operation by his body prevented it. Through the conversations, the card games and the buying of rounds of drinks, he remained relentlessly sober, the pain underlying his cheerfulness unabated.

As the torch picked out his cottage gate, he cut the light and held his breath, standing stone-still in the lane and enjoying the illusion, the *peace*, of his own invisibility. Until he moved, clicked the beam back on and freed his breath in a sigh, he felt that he had suspended his very being. Dark-clothed in the darkness, he had been nothing. And the impression had brought both relief and excitement. In that prophetic moment of oblivion, he and his cares had ceased to exist.

Sleep evaded him that night. Much of it was passed in the study where, with commendable detachment, he pored over the reviews of his earlier books, on the lookout for misguided praise rather than unfair criticism. Gerrard had been unable to help, now he wanted to work out for himself why the 'promise' of the early books had atrophied.

Eventually he came to the conclusion that the reviews were no help either. The same reviewers whose acclaim had seemed excessive to him when the first book appeared were equally enthused by its successors. Because he was no longer a newcomer, they were obliged to stop mentioning promise in favour of (and how he disliked this) 'reliable'. The word made his efforts sound like repetition whereas each sharp, crystal-line novel was painstakingly groped for. If only *he* had also believed in his reliability, how much more carefree life would have been!

A line in a *Punch* review niggled at him. 'John Gower's novels have become a minor cult.' He ground his teeth. Nobody was saying the books were trash or unappealing, and *Punch* had intended a compliment by claiming a cult. But Gower, dismayed that he had been flattered when the review was fresh, saw the exclusivity of a cult as the antithesis of what he must achieve if he were to break through to the mass market.

The books were good – critics found fewer flaws than he did himself – but Pegwoods had failed to exploit them. David Gerrard, active on behalf of a handful of his other writers, had nothing constructive to say. For half an hour Gower calmly considered whether he ought not to give up writing. He could pick up a job, not necessarily teaching, he had various useful qualifications, and there was no disgrace in retiring after a well-received half-dozen novels. In fact, he thought that more commendable than muddling along, as many authors did, from bad book to worse while talent and imagination failed them.

But it was *not* half a dozen books; the nub was that within weeks there was to be a seventh published. There was still much to play for. Thinking about number seven, *The Secret*, fanned all the hope and all the passion Gower had been assiduously setting aside.

Why shouldn't it be 'lucky seven'? This time the book might take

off, Pegwoods might reprint. Someone might pay a fortune to publish
an American paperback. Hollywood might be on the phone begging for
the film rights.

He pictured David Gerrard scratching his immaculate blond head and pondering whether it was more fruitful to risk a big-name producer the other side of the Atlantic or to squeeze as much as could be got from the BBC who would be simultaneously pleading to be allowed to make a six-part television serial. Once Gower had let his thoughts wander down this trail of fantasy, it was natural for Linda to appear in each imagined scene. Five of the books had also been her sacrifice, she was entitled to share in the good fortune of a lucky seven.

Long before the first brassy blade of sunshine was slicing across the corner of his desk, Gower was plotting to ensure that *The Secret* could not be ignored in the way its predecessors had been. He refused to sit back this time and count the reviews, he was going to ensure the novel escaped the confines of the books pages and became news in a broader sense.

Gower drew up a sheet of paper from the pile in front of him, the heap he had intended to devote to writing about Richard Crane, elusive hero of his embryo book. He uncapped his fountain pen and wrote a neat and slowly considered list. The adventures of Richard Crane would have to wait because John Gower was embarking on an adventure of his own.

3

'If I didn't know myself better,' said Rain Morgan primly, 'I'd wonder what I'd been up to.'

'A diamond cuff link?' gaped Holly Chase. 'On the back seat of your car?'

'Well, quite.' Rain twiddled the cuff link between her fingers. 'I didn't find it until this morning, but it must have been there since Monday night. A pity I feel obliged to give it back, it would probably go some way to paying my decorators' bill.'

Holly giggled. 'Don't even be tempted. David Gerrard must realize where he lost it.' Her telephone interrupted them. 'That's probably him now, demanding its return forthwith.'

She lifted the receiver. It was not Gerrard, it was an estate agent badgering her for a decision about a flat she had viewed in Hackney. Holly parried. Not quite what she had in mind, one or two other places to see, and so on.

Rosie came along with a handful of mail. Rain said to her: 'Come on, let's have the important stuff first.'

Rosie shot her an indignant look. 'I haven't opened it yet, it's only just arrived.'

'No, no, I mean the gossip among the secretaries. What were they whispering in the ladies' cloakroom this morning, what nuggets did you overhear in the huddle around the coffee machine?'

Rosie's eyes narrowed and, sitting at her desk which abutted Rain's, she drew her chair a scrap closer and leaned forward. 'Well, Rain, the only gem, if I may put it that way, is that Lucy on the switchboard took a call first thing this morning from a frantic man who claimed he left his cuff link in your car on Monday night. He's been trying to reach you ever since he realized where he'd lost it. Apparently it's terribly valuable and you're to . . .'

Rain winced. She held up the cuff link. 'I suppose it's no use explaining he's an enormous man and he was snarled up with the seat belt when he got out and this must have flown off as he battled to free himself?'

Rosie had sucked in her cheeks like a schoolteacher listening to an unlikely excuse. 'No, none at all,' she said. 'Nobody is going to settle for your version when there's more fun to be had from innuendo.'

'Do you know,' said Rain, 'I think you might well have the makings of a journalist. Gossip-column branch, preferably.'

Rosie said she was not going to listen to insults, she was going to open the mail. And did.

Rain rang David Gerrard to say she had found his cuff link and to object that the way he had bubbled the story out to the telephonist meant that she, Rain, had lost her reputation.

'The biter bit?' suggested Gerrard without pity.

'How would you like this returned? In a taxi? On the back of a motorbike? Through the post?'

'My dear,' gasped Gerrard. 'We are talking real diamonds, you know.'

Rain reassured him. 'It's only your stories I accuse of being fakes; your diamonds I trust emphatically.'

'Very well then. No more talk of motorcycle messengers and other risky ventures, please. We shall have a personal handing over. I will buy you lunch as a reward for finding it and returning it safely.'

This was not what she would have chosen. For months she had been ducking out of lunch invitations but his gratitude gave him an advantage over her. She tried saying: 'You ought to be blaming me for a seat belt that savages passengers.'

'Ye-es, getting out of your car is distinctly reminiscent of waltzing with an octopus. However, I don't think we should let that stand between us and a good lunch.'

She capitulated and agreed to lunch the following Tuesday.

'You'll get fat,' scowled Holly, lamenting that no smooth-talking, diamond-clad, money-soaked gourmet ever wanted to take *her* to lunch.

When Rosie left her desk, on one of the mysterious journeys with which secretaries fill their days, Holly became conspiratorial. 'Has she said anything to you?'

'About what?'

'She's looking for a new job.'

Rain looked pained. 'Three years teaching a youngster how to do the job and once you've settled into a nice comfortable groove she's up and off!' She hesitated. 'It *is* a nice, comfortable groove, isn't it?'

Holly nodded, beaded plaits jangling. 'She really likes working for you.'

'But?'

'But any secretary who isn't mistress of a computer these days feels she's missing an essential in her life. Her career, anyway.'

Rain rested an elbow on her desk, cupped her chin in her palm. 'Any other newspaper would have shifted her into the late twentieth century. Poor Rosie hitched herself to the only one that denied her.'

'Afraid so. From her point of view, it makes sense to abandon us.'

'Why has she told you and not me?'

'She's going to tell you. She's waiting for a good time.'

'Good heavens, am I that scary?'

Holly said it was a question of Rosie feeling disloyal. 'That's flattering, in a way.'

Rain was finding it hard to feel flattered. 'Did she also explain to you how she defines a good time?'

'After the decorators, perhaps. Once the gruesome scene at Alf Wilson's flat has faded a bit. When things are more settled, less tense.'

Rain snapped that things were not tense at all, that she did not know why Holly should say so.

Holly raised hands in surrender. 'OK, OK, forget I said that.'

Rain's fingers had tightened on the edge of the desk. She held the grip a moment, then relaxed, saying mildly: 'Sorry. Of course you're right. I'm not a creature who likes to be unsettled and for the present everything is very unsettled.' She meant the decorators and living at the Dudleys' house in Islington, of course. But she also meant more private matters, like Paul Wickham who was hovering on the edges of her life.

Holly knew that. 'Have you heard from Paul since . . . ?'

Rain thrust blonde curls back from her face. 'No, but I don't expect to. It was left that *I* would . . .' She felt Holly watching her keenly and she let her sentence hang. She said brightly: 'And I haven't. Not yet. Maybe never.'

Holly adopted her most understanding expression: 'Pride,' she said, 'is a great waste of life.'

Rain let it pass. She could not expect Holly to truly understand. Holly had Dan and a steady domestic kind of life. Holly had a lot of family not far in the background. Holly lived in a different sphere.

And then Rain swept sombre thoughts aside with a laugh that caused a passing reporter to remark: 'Nice to hear someone happy around here.'

Rain said to Holly: 'It's almost possible for me to envy you that little semi-detached in Spinney Green, and that choice of mediocre flats in not-so-very smart Hackney! There's a lot to be said for knowing what the boundaries are, how far you can go.'

'I didn't,' said Holly quietly. 'And I don't. You're forgetting we didn't start from the same place.'

And by place she did not mean which part of London, she meant the huge social divide that could have curbed her talents if she had been a shade less lucky at any crucial stage of her twenty-five years.

Rain mimicked a well-known television interviewer. 'Tell me, Miss Chase, to what do you attribute your success?'

Holly simpered, in the style of the man's typical interviewee. 'Absolute stupidity. I didn't know what I was doing was impossible.'

They smiled at one another. Then Holly pointed out that it was time for the morning conference and there was a scramble to cobble together a list of diary items that would sound interesting when Rain explained them to her assembled colleagues. As usual, she was among the last to enter the editor's office.

The meeting jogged along as it did every day. The features list seemed a drab one (yet another politician writing a piece explaining something or other, one more actor chattering about a film, and a broadside in the latest campaign by a woman who was an immoderate campaigner).

The news list was better. The news editor's Irish accent intensified as his enthusiasm was shared by his audience. He ended with a quip, turning to Rain as he finished outlining his stories and saying: 'That's all, unless Rain plans to bring us any more dead celebrities.' He was rewarded with kindly amusement. He was not a man who attempted many jokes.

He cornered her as the meeting broke up. 'They haven't said when the inquest on Alf Wilson is to be held, have they?'

'I've heard nothing.' A suspicion flickered through her mind. 'You're not going to ask me to cover it as well as be a witness, are you?'

He grinned. 'I think my budget will stretch to an agency report.'

She thought: *Poor Alf. He doesn't merit a staff reporter. Twenty years ago journalists would have been queueing for a seat.*

Rosie came up to tell her there was a woman in the foyer who wanted to speak to her about Alf Wilson. Rain went down immediately. The woman rose from a chair as Rain stepped out of the lift.

Rain saw a short, neat figure, top-to-toe Marks and Spencer clothes, middle-aged, a couple of stone overweight and with a permed hairstyle that was unflattering to her broad face. The gold of her hooped earrings glinted as she came forward. 'Rain Morgan?'

Rain held out a hand. 'So I am.'

The woman's touch was cold, fleeting. She said: 'I'm sorry to bother you at work. I know you're a busy woman.'

Rain thought: *North country accent. It said on the television that Alf Wilson had been born in Yorkshire.*

The woman got the Rain Morgan smile, the welcoming but guarded variety. 'How can I help you?'

'You could tell me what happened, whatever you know of Alf Wilson's death, that is.'

Rain raised an eyebrow.

The woman said: 'Oh, dear, I haven't explained myself. I'm Pat Jarvis. Alf Wilson is – *was* – my cousin.'

Rain took Pat Jarvis into the canteen to talk. This was an uninviting subterranean place avoided by those who were free to leave the building for their refreshments. Therefore it was a good place to take Pat Jarvis. No one would overhear.

The guest wrinkled her powdered nose at an atmosphere redolent of elderly rissoles and cabbage. Mrs Jarvis looked like a fastidious housewife, the sort who would insist on an efficient extractor fan going full pelt while she cooked and on blue, scented disinfectant fresh in her lavatory bowl at every flush. She eyed the two cups of coffee Rain set down on the table between them.

Rain said: 'The coffee's good, it's only the ambiance that's off-putting.'

Mrs Jarvis delayed her acceptance of this reassurance until she had spooned in sugar, stirred, taken a sip. 'Oh yes,' she said. 'Very nice.'

'Look,' said Rain, deciding to own up. 'There's not much I can tell you about your cousin's death that you won't already know. I found him, but so did a handful of other people, his neighbours. I used to meet him by chance and chat to him on and off over a few years.'

Pat Jarvis studied her coffee, swirling where she had stirred it again. 'I see.' Rain waited. Pat Jarvis said: 'Yes, well, Alf wasn't one to say much, ever.'

Rain resisted agreeing. She did not want Pat Jarvis to conclude her visit was a waste of time and then abruptly leave.

She wanted the woman to tell her about the dead man. She said: 'What was it you wanted to know in particular?'

The woman laid her hands on the table, cradling but not touching her cup and saucer. The question was never answered directly. She seemed to have half her mind elsewhere, had done so ever since she had met Rain.

She said: 'He was a mite mysterious, was Alf. At one time he used to be up to Yorkshire for the odd weekend and he never missed the family things – you know, weddings, funerals and whatnot. But then he went very quiet. To tell you the truth, he didn't respond to Christmas cards for the last couple of years and I formed the impression he'd moved away.'

Rain asked when she had discovered this was untrue.

Pat Jarvis said: 'When the local police came round to my house and said he'd died and they thought I was the next of kin. It was only then I knew he'd shut us out on purpose. To think of him getting my Christmas greetings and deciding not to send cards to me! I don't mind saying, it gives me a peculiar feeling to think of him doing that.'

Rain murmured sympathetically and asked whether Pat Jarvis herself had moved house, whether he might have mislaid her address.

'No, I've stayed put for years. Besides, if you want to find somebody you always can. The post office would probably know if they'd moved, or you could write to a neighbour. Of course, I'm talking about the sort of place I live in where, generally speaking, you know who's who around you. I don't mean London. This must be the easiest place to lose a person.'

She shuddered slightly and Rain regretted leading her into the canteen. There were nicer alternatives, not too many since the newspapers had moved out and the area had begun to die, but some. She opened her mouth to speak, but Pat Jarvis got in first. 'I didn't say about the letter, did I?'

Rain confirmed she had not.

'Well it was about a month or five weeks back,' the woman said. 'Suddenly, out of the blue, there it was on the mat. Alf, writing from London to say could he come up for a couple of days. A weekend he said it would be. To do with something he was working on. Would I have a spare bed for him?'

Catching the bewildered look on Rain's face, she rushed on. 'Oh, he hadn't set his address down, only the date at the top of the page. It was the postmark that said London. And so how he expected me to reply to him, I couldn't say.'

'Did you bring the letter with you?'

'Bring it to London? Whatever for?'

'Er . . . to show the police.' She meant she would like to see it herself.

'Well, the police wouldn't be interested in that. No, it's at home. If they ask they can be shown it, I'd have no objection. But it was written weeks ago, it was about coming up for a couple of days, nothing to do with killing himself.'

'I see.' Rain drank her coffee. Pat Jarvis was speaking about the time and the cost of travelling to London and back. Then Rain asked her: 'When did you last see Alf?'

'To talk to at our Tracey's wedding. And that's going back a while, I can tell you. Tracey's had three children and a divorce since then.' She toyed with her spoon before adding, her voice low: 'But I suppose you could say I last saw him this morning.'

Rain imagined the scene: this middle-aged woman being led into a cold room, going through what had to be gone through, accepting the meaningless sympathy of professionals.

She said: 'That must have been very unpleasant for you.'

Pat Jarvis stroked the edge of her saucer. 'I won't pretend I'd like to spend every Wednesday visiting a mortuary. But it's a duty, isn't it? If the occasion arises in your family, then it's a duty you have to carry out.'

Despite the resignation, she shuddered once more. Then, briskly: 'I'll have to come back for the inquest. Not for the opening, which won't be much, but for the full one. The policeman they called the coroner's officer explained that. They'll open the inquest shortly and adjourn it until a time when everybody they need can be there to give their evidence. I'll have to come then. Well, I'd want to really, wouldn't I? To hear what happened. To take an interest. It's a responsibility, being the next of kin.'

Rain murmured appropriate comments. Concerned, she saw the woman's features sag as though she were about to cry. But Pat Jarvis pressed a hand to her mouth and when she took it away she had recovered sufficiently to force a weak laugh. 'He was supposed to be a clever lad, was Alf. But he did some daft things. I mean, what can you make of a man who writes asking to stay with you and doesn't give you an address to write back to? And then hangs himself from a bloody chandelier?'

Over the next few minutes Rain outlined what she knew about Alf Wilson and she promised to tell his cousin anything else she learned. Having mentioned the television programme to which she was contributing, it seemed only fair to offer to pass on any snippets the research might produce about the 'missing' years.

After that Pat Jarvis became anxious about the time, saying she planned to visit the flat in Hunt Road before she caught the train north. 'The police said it would be all right. They've finished there now so I shan't do any harm looking around. Not that I can say what I'll be looking for. It's only a feeling I have that I'd like to see the place.'

'Have you got keys? I handed the police the ones Alf sent me.'

'There were two to the flat and one to the street door. The police gave me a set.' She checked in her handbag to see they were safe. 'Presumably there'll be stuff I'll have to clear out before the landlord can relet. Although how I'm to tell what might have been Alf's and what might have been the landlord's, I haven't a clue. Anyway, I'll take a look today, then when I come down next I'll know how much I have to tackle.'

She gathered her coat around her and stood up to go. 'They all say it, I know. All families do. But he was the last person you'd have expected to do a thing like that.' She bit her lip before going on, in a weakening voice. 'If he'd known how distressing it would be . . . I wonder, you see, whether there was anything I ought to have done for him. There's always somebody left behind wondering that, isn't there?'

When she parted from Rain in the foyer, Pat Jarvis repeated the cold brief handshake but her words were friendly. 'You can go there, if you like. To the flat, I mean. You seem the nearest thing Alf had to a friend lately. If it'll help you at all to go there, then I won't mind.'

Rain thanked her. Pat Jarvis patted her handbag, saying: 'I'll send you the keys. Once I've finished there today I'll put them in a taxi for you. But I don't want them getting lost, mind. You've to promise to look after them and let me have them back when I come up next.'

The woman said a final goodbye and walked away down the street, past poignant boarded-up buildings abandoned by the newspaper industry in its chase after the new. Fleet Street, like Alf Wilson, had had its day.

There was a tremor in the fingers that gripped the key, her palm was moist as Rain let herself into the dead man's flat, although reason decreed there could be no repetition of the sickening discovery. The speed with which the keys had arrived by taxi at her office surprised her until she remembered how eager Pat Jarvis had been to get away from London and home to Yorkshire.

Yorkshire in April, she thought. *Pale blue sky whipped with cloud, flowers breaking colour against stone walls, moors where only wind stirs. No wonder she preferred to hurry home.*

She rejected her tourist's postcard opinions of Yorkshire and returned to reality as the door eased open. Hastily, silently, she closed it behind her. She intended to speak to the neighbours later but until she was ready for them she wanted to keep her presence secret. Her reasons were as ill-defined as her reasons for wanting to poke around in the flat, or for lying to the police and initially concealing from them the note Alf Wilson had sent her.

She stood, shoulders against the closed door. Sun barred the room with the pattern of window panes. There was no overturned chair, anything that had been disordered had been tidied. Three wooden chairs were grouped around a dining table, the elderly typewriter was standing on the table exactly as she had seen it before. The sofa appeared unmoved near the fireplace. Books leaned drunkenly on their shelves.

Her eyes were drawn to the chandelier. It dominated her mind, dominated the room too but perhaps it had always done that. Probably it was one of the original fittings in the house, certainly it was of the correct period. She wondered whether the landlord would be sufficiently sensitive to remove it and spare the succeeding tenant the discomfort of knowing a man had hanged himself from its hook.

Rain took a step forward, then stopped and caught her breath. Outside on the staircase she heard barely perceptible footsteps. Then silence. She waited, hoping she had not after all disturbed any of the neighbours, that no one had come to investigate.

After a minute she decided she had been wrong, that the footsteps had not halted on the landing by Wilson's door, that someone had gone about their normal business ignorant of her presence. She advanced across the room, towards the full-length windows with their swagged curtains in faded velvet. For the second time she heard the footsteps outside.

She tried to quell her nervousness, thinking: *What's there to be so jumpy about? I have a right to be here. Pat Jarvis invited me and gave me the keys. It's no one else's business if I come in here.*

But she wished she could be certain no one considered it his business.

The windows deserved window boxes, but Wilson had not provided them. They would have obstructed his view of the pavement below and maybe he had liked to look down on the people trailing to and fro. 'Maybe.' If she had been his friend, or even what his cousin described as the nearest thing he had to a friend, then there would have been fewer maybes.

Not for the first time she felt fraudulent. Guilty about it too. When he was alive she had not behaved as a friend, now that he was dead she was taking the advantages of one.

She urged herself to look and absorb and attempt to learn about the man. Rooms were said to report on their owners but this one was keeping mum, after stating straight off that the occupant had lived without money.

The books were a jumble of fact and fiction, trash and literature. None of the titles was new, except two paperbacks published within the past year. Both were stories based on television drama series, one about a glamorous but neurotic woman who grows rich through business acumen and rises up the social scale, the other about a gritty but sensitive man who grows rich through wheeler-dealing and throws off the shackles of a humble background.

Fables for our time: when in doubt, make a fortune. Rain pushed the books back on to the shelves.

She went to the typewriter, her facial expression lapsing into a sentimental smile. *Thirty years old, sure to be, but they've lasted, these Olympia Monicas. There'll be a case somewhere, a rigid grey box. A semi-portable, meaning it could be carried, but not very far.*

Next she went to the bedroom, visible through a lobby off the main room. The bedroom had awkward proportions because at some stage in the history of the house a spacious rear room had been hacked up to create bedroom, lobby, and diminutive kitchen and bathroom. Whatever period features or charm the original room had possessed had been sacrificed during the alterations.

A cupboard had been built across an alcove in the bedroom. There was an old kneehole desk with a stained leather top scattered with personal things, and there was an unmade bed. Blankets and sheets slumped messily to the carpet.

Rain opened the cupboard. Alf Wilson had been as mean about clothes as about furniture. A couple of suits hung there, beside a haphazard collection of casual garments. The cupboard was far from big but could have held more. Alf Wilson had not owned more.

She lifted out one of the suits, picturing him in it. But it was no use, she had never seen him in a suit. *Hardly surprising*, she thought, *this style is years old*.

She lifted out the other one. This was newer but in a different colour. They had one thing in common: the dust on the shoulders. He had not had occasion to wear either of them for a long time.

With a finger, Rain drew open the drawers down each side of the desk. She touched nothing within. Papers were piled neatly to the brim of each drawer. Pat Jarvis might have flicked through them, perhaps the police too. Rain closed the drawers.

In the kitchen a used cup and saucer stood on the draining board by the sink. A tap dripped, complaining of a worn-out washer. Rain twisted the tap hard and the drip ceased.

This scotched her assumption that the tap had dripped since Wilson's death. She came up with another guess, that Pat Jarvis had made herself a drink while at the flat. Rain examined the cup for confirmation in the guise of lipstick traces. There were none. She set it back on the saucer and peeped in the fridge. He had not stocked up on food either.

The bathroom, plain and utilitarian, took even less of her time. She returned to the sunny sitting room, gave it one more assessing glance and let herself out on to the landing.

Ratcliffe was at home, on the ground floor, but was tardy opening the door, and Rain had almost given him up. She explained she would like to speak to him about Alf Wilson, because she was to appear in a television programme about him.

Ratcliffe rubbed the side of his face with an age-blotched hand. 'I thought you'd done it. I saw you, the day he died. On the news.'

'There's to be a feature programme about him as well.'

Ratcliffe appeared reluctant. 'I don't know what you think I can tell you, but I suppose I do know a bit more about the chap than the others here. Keep my eyes open, you see. Not everybody does that.'

Rain hinted that this was why she had come to him first.

Flattery opened the door to her. Ratcliffe ushered her into his room with the solid old furniture and its family photographs. He scooped a *Daily Telegraph* out of an easy chair in the sunlight and apologized.

'Bit of a mess, I'm afraid. Don't have many visitors, matter of fact. Visitors keep you on your toes, you know.'

Ratcliffe had been an army man. Rain had always assumed it, but he said so in the next sentence. She allowed him a digression into the value of army discipline in a fellow's life, before tugging him back to his dead neighbour.

He sat opposite her, in a twin of her chunky chair. He plonked his elbows on his chair arms and steepled his fingers. 'Wilson, then. Well he was living here when I moved in, so I can only talk about the last twelve years. Mrs Dobson in the basement has been here the longest but I doubt she'll be able to help you. She has her own outside entrance, you know, and doesn't have much call to be in the main house. The others meet going in and out or popping into the hall to collect the post, but she has her own letter box too.'

Rain nodded encouragingly. 'How often did you see Alf Wilson?'

'Often didn't come into it. We like to keep ourselves to ourselves in this place. One doesn't want people darting in borrowing sugar and what have you. It's best not to get overfamiliar, I find.'

Rain put her question another way.

Ratcliffe said: 'We have a bit of a garden at the back. Wilson used to cut the grass for us at one time. We told the police, if you remember.'

Rain remembered fat Mrs Dobson had said so.

He said: 'There's meant to be a gardener, but the agents didn't keep him up to the mark and therefore Wilson got into the way of doing it for us. Now the reason I'm harking back to that time is that those were the days when I saw him frequently. We all did. Literally, I mean. We could look out of our windows and see him, cutting the grass. And if we bumped into him later we'd thank him for doing it and he'd say it was growing fast at that time of year or it had been a bit damp and he wished he'd waited, whatever was appropriate. We talked, you see, about the job in hand. No call to stray into other areas, was there?'

She wished they had strayed. She asked: 'Did he ever mention what he was writing?'

But he had not and Ratcliffe assured her he would never have asked. 'I knew who he was. He was a big name, wasn't he, twenty years ago? Of course, I was abroad and missed a lot of it, but from what I heard he was a very big name in his field.'

Out of her memory came David Gerrard's words about Alf Wilson: 'He had his success early and it died on him early.'

Ratcliffe was saying: 'Not always a good idea, you know, to press a chap about what he's up to. If he's still at the top of his tree, you'll find out soon enough. And if he isn't, he'll probably lie to you.'

His words provoked another memory, Nicholson's words before he flew off to Los Angeles and television scripts: 'He talked about a new project, but there wasn't one.'

Rain looked up at the ceiling. No chandelier, only an ordinary light fitting. Through that ceiling was Wilson's flat, a few feet away but contact between the two men had been minimal. They kept themselves to themselves in that house, the old people endeavouring to keep up appearances on slender fixed incomes, and Alf Wilson, younger, disappointed, bitter perhaps, fighting to remake his career. A truth? A lie? Nothing but Wilson's own words – to her in the street, to his cousin in a letter – suggested it was true.

Rain became aware of the silence, needed to fill it. 'I expect you heard him typing.'

'On summer days when the windows were open. That kind of thing. We're fairly well insulated against sound, on the whole.'

'You were telling me about the garden, Mr Ratcliffe. Why did he stop mowing it?'

The steepled fingers dropped to rest on kneecaps, bony

through gingery tweed. 'Couldn't say. He stopped, just like that. The woman from the top floor asked him about it but we couldn't make head nor tail of the answer. After that we pushed the agents and a youth started coming round. Was he temperamental, Wilson?'

'I haven't heard that.'

'No, nobody's heard much at all, have they? That television stuff, on the news, that didn't give anything away. What about his family?'

Rain explained that the police had traced a cousin in Yorkshire.

Ratcliffe said: 'He'll be coming here, then, this cousin.'

She did not correct his assumption that the cousin was a man, she wanted to get Ratcliffe to the point. But her attempts to discover what Alf Wilson had done with himself day in and day out – whether he had received visitors and, if so, who – were frustrated. Ratcliffe could remember no particular visitors, although from what he said any visitor would have been remarkable.

In a while she said her goodbyes and left him to go back to the doze she guessed she had interrupted. He had told her useful things about the other tenants, though. The man and woman on the top floor had set off that morning on holiday. The couple across the hall were at work and it was Mrs Dobson's afternoon for going to the library. Ratcliffe knew that because she was good enough to change his books for him.

Rain made for Mrs Dobson's flat regardless. This was reached down stone steps from the front garden. There was no answer to her ring on the bell, but when she climbed back up she spotted roly-poly Mrs Dobson coming along the pavement. Rain sat on the garden wall and waited for her.

The cardigan Rain recognized from Monday flapped out of the front of an unbuttoned jacket, emphasizing the shambling roll of the woman's gait. Mrs Dobson was burdened with two shopping bags. She took Rain into her flat. It was deep, it was dark. Mrs Dobson was a troglodyte. She had hung net curtains at her low windows to avoid being spied upon, and had grown used to life with scant natural light.

The woman rested one shopping bag on her kitchen table and began to take groceries out of the other and store them in a cupboard and an old yellow fridge. 'My day for the library, you're lucky you caught me,' she said over her shoulder as a lamb chop went into the fridge.

'Mr Ratcliffe told me.'

'Oh, you've been talking to the Colonel, have you?'

'Is he?' She had mistered him, he had given no clue.

Mrs Dobson chuckled. 'No, he's plain mister, but that's what I call him. Likes to act the military gentleman. Likes to claim he knows everything that goes on. Bet he didn't tell you anything, though.'

'We-ell.' No, he had not, but Mrs Dobson looked as though she might.

Mrs Dobson filled a kettle, not pausing to inquire whether her guest wanted tea. 'Measuring out life in teacups, that's what my late husband used to call it. One in the morning when I wake, another when I get dressed . . . Rituals. This is my day for the library, that's another ritual. Only the Colonel's books and mine from now on. Heavy enough, mind. I promise myself a cup of tea as soon as I get in. Sticks and carrots, my late husband used to say, penalties and rewards to prod and coax me through life.'

Rain asked her what the penalty might have been.

Mrs Dobson hung an empty bag on a hook behind the door. She cackled. 'The penalty for not going to the library is not having a book to read in the evening.'

Rain picked up a point that had been left behind. Had Mrs Dobson meant that she used to fetch books for Alf Wilson?

Mrs Dobson nodded. 'That's right. Four, he had. That's what's going to make the difference, you see. Four for me, two for the Colonel (that one nods off in his chair most of the day, if you want to know what I think) and four for Mr Wilson. Books can be quite heavy.'

'Yes, I wonder Mr Wilson didn't fetch them for you instead.'

'He couldn't have done the choosing, could he? With his books, he'd write on a piece of paper what he wanted and I'd bring them. Now I couldn't send him off with a piece of paper like that, though he did offer, to be fair to him. I enjoy the browsing, you see.'

She dipped into the bag of books and hauled out a fat romance. 'They said in my magazine this was a good read.'

She opened the book at the lending record. 'Look, you can see how many times it's been taken out. I always check on that myself, unless a book's very new or I've heard of it before. Well, I don't want to trudge all the way home with a heavy great book that I won't be able to get into. If the page at the front shows lots of other readers have borrowed it, then I reckon I can be sure it'll do for me.' She dropped it back into the bag.

'What do you bring for Mr Ratcliffe?'

'He's easy. I find him a couple of stories about the army. There's adventures – you know, things with men in uniform on the covers – and then there's books by old soldiers who used to be in Burma or wherever. Oh I can keep him supplied for years. You'd be surprised how many old soldiers write their memoirs.'

Rain was not. Neither was she surprised that Ratcliffe dropped off in his chair with such frequency. She accepted a cup of tea.

'Today,' Mrs Dobson told her, 'I got poor Mr Wilson's books from last week out of his flat. A woman came to see in there, said she was a cousin come to give the place a look over. I found her on the doorstep when I popped outside to sweep my steps. She said she couldn't get the street door to work. There's a knack to that lock. She'd rung a couple of times but, if you ask me, the Colonel's hearing isn't what it might be.'

Rain sipped bitter, strong tea.

Mrs Dobson heaped a mound of sugar into her own tea and then held the cup up with both hands and drank noisily before describing how she had accompanied the woman into Wilson's flat. Together they had discovered the library books in the bedroom and once she had them safely in hand, Mrs Dobson had gone away leaving the woman in the flat. She was determined Rain should hear the minutiae of it.

But then Mrs Dobson threw in a remark that roused her interest. 'She called down here before she left, asked me whether I could give her a plastic carrier bag because she wanted to take some papers away. I gave her a Boots bag, that was the strongest I had. Some of those supermarket things are that flimsy, the handles go on you. "Thank you very much, Mrs Dobson," she said, and then she asked me where she could find the landlord. She'd decided she wanted nothing out of the flat and the best thing was to tell the landlord to relet.'

'And where,' asked Rain, 'is the landlord?'

'Jersey,' said Mrs Dobson. 'But it's managed by Catchmans in Fulham Road. That's where I sent her.'

She raised the teapot to offer more tea, saying she supposed there would be no problem reletting, plenty of people would be happy to move in exactly as it was, that's why the house never got done up properly but, speaking for herself, she would be none too keen on a flat where she might find a ghost hanging from her chandelier.

Rain declined the refill and left.

'But you've got a wonderful flat of your own!' Holly Chase was so taken aback it had been thirty seconds before she could find any words at all.

Rain shook her head, blonde curls bouncing. 'No, I've got a wonderful flat that the builders are going to be tearing apart for several weeks.'

'I thought it was decorators, not builders.'

A messenger passing Rain's desk delivered a memo. She set it aside unread. 'Yes, it was, until I called in this afternoon and found they'd come upon rotting woodwork. I sent for my friendly local builder who said he'd have to take off the plaster, and then it occurred to me that as I was going to have to endure all that disruption and mess I might just as well go ahead with some alterations I've had in mind a long time.'

Holly knew about them. There was a door that Rain wished was further along a wall and she hankered for a bigger kitchen which could be achieved only by slicing off part of the entrance lobby.

'Even so,' said Holly doubtfully. The Kington Square flat was a magazine dream home compared to her options in Hackney. 'Even so, fancy renting Alf Wilson's flat.'

'It's only for a few weeks, and I've got to go somewhere. It's too long to camp on friends.'

'Hmm,' said Holly. She could not help feeling there was more to it than she was being told.

'I shan't move in until the Dudleys are back from France and I can stop riding shotgun in Islington,' Rain added, as though that made the enterprise any less peculiar.

'Hmm' repeated Holly.

Rain read the memo, an announcement of staff changes. She passed it to Holly, saying wearily: 'What this paper needs is a new owner, not new staff.' After months on the market, serious bidders had been few.

'And computers,' said Holly, handing it back. She glanced at Rosie but the secretary was on the telephone and had not heard.

That evening Rain drove to Islington early. She appreciated the welcome she got from Fred, yet he contrived to make her feel guilty. The Dudleys' plush home was wasted on a dog, and for most of the day Fred had it to himself.

'Never mind, Fred,' she said, patting him and trying to restrain his bounding. 'We can have a nice long walk to the shops together.'

Not being a dog owner, she had not considered what she was to do with Fred once she reached the shops. Although it was essential for her to buy food, it was illegal to take the animal into a food shop. The predicament did not strike her until she and Fred neared the local supermarket, an obliging store that stayed opened until nine in the evening. Outside was another dog.

She was alerted by Fred's rumbling growl and he pulled forward on his lead. Her response was to tell him not to be silly and to tug him back, but the dog provoking Fred was a moth-eaten Alsatian standing in front of the shop doors. It was not alone. Beside it slouched a filthy, long-haired man who was begging.

He had positioned himself and his pet – although pet was too benign a word for the beast – where no one could enter or leave the shop without tangling with them. Fred rumbled again. Rain did not want to tangle, especially as Fred appeared likely to be the aggressor.

On the wall to one side of the entrance were metal hooks, hitching posts for dog leads. She advanced, but the Alsatian quivered and Fred barked and the man sidestepped to block her, demanding money to buy food. Embarrassed and unsure how to react, Rain backed off. She heaved Fred away from the fight he was looking forward to, and she walked up the street until she found a small corner shop open. She had to shop there instead.

Shopping, she decided, was a one-woman business. Dog walking and food shopping did not mix. She took a different route home, through residential streets. Then she let Fred into the back garden, where he raced around and failed to outpace a fleet cat while she cooked her supper.

During the evening she wrote letters, made telephone calls, read and watched television. Quite late, she decided to take her letters to the local postbox and give Fred another airing. He padded meekly beside her, neither pulling ahead nor dragging back to sniff at gateposts, and she fooled herself into thinking she had imposed her authority.

The flaw became apparent on the return journey when a cat dived over a low garden wall in front of him and fled across the road. Before Rain could tighten her grip in response, Fred had the lead from her grasp and was away. Cat and dog went down the slot between two houses and vanished. Rain dashed after them.

If Fred had not barked, she would not have guessed where he had got to. But his noise revealed he was on the other side of a high wall to her right. The wall was topped with broken glass and wire. Fred had found another way in.

'Fred! Fred, come here!' At her voice he stopped barking. That made it worse, she no longer knew exactly where he was. Running alongside the wall, she reached a dilapidated wooden gate. Its lock held, but it was shoved off its hinges, and she had room to squeeze through the gap.

The garden she entered was overgrown. Beyond a sea of weeds, was the roof of a shed. From an apple tree near it, the cat seethed. A swishing and a swaying of what had once been someone's lawn gave away Fred's location reasonably accurately.

'Fred! Here, Fred!' in her most commanding tone.

But Fred resisted and she had to wade in after him, following the serpentine trail made first by the cat and then its pursuer. Seeing Rain's arrival, Fred put on a display of penitence, wagging his tail at her while dropping low and wriggling about. He interrupted this with occasional thoughts of his prey, thoughts that made him squirm away and raise nose, ears and an ineffectual paw in the direction of the top of the apple tree. While he was thus engaged, Rain clutched the end of his lead.

When she had him secure, she looked around. No lights had come on in the house at the end of the garden. The performance and intrusion had disturbed no one. Going back into the alleyway, Rain tried to close the gate behind her, but it was heavy and she had only one hand as Fred was frisking on the end of the lead. She left the gap a little worse than when she had found it and took Fred home, scolding him with threats of a ban on future outings until he showed more obedience. Fred was unimpressed.

With him safely dozing in a favourite corner of the kitchen, she telephoned her flat to listen to messages on her answering machine. She always felt absurd hearing herself answer, and her invitation to callers to leave messages seemed interminable. Then, pen poised, she jotted down the gist of each message.

There was one from the builder, the rest from friends or colleagues. One was about Alf Wilson. It was from Frances Keene, the television reporter who had filmed her for the news item and who was also working on the planned feature programme about Wilson.

'Afraid there might be a hitch, Rain,' said Frances. She was rapid, like someone bursting to pass on scandal. 'There's a rumour that he didn't hang himself after all.'

Not hang himself? Rain felt her face pucker in a frown. *How could anyone believe Alf Wilson didn't hang himself?*

Frances's voice purred on. Something about an anonymous telephone call to the television studio. Something about Frances not being able to confirm any of this. Something about her hoping Rain, deeply involved as she was in the Alf Wilson story, might be able to throw light on it.

But all Rain could see was the blinding sight of a man's body hanging against the sunlight.

Frances's recorded voice continued to come at her out of the Dudleys' telephone. Frances was worried that a prolonged investigation into the death would hinder the scheduling of the television film, that background material that she would be free to use in the normal way might be prejudicial, that the kind of film they had planned might become impossible, she knew Rain would understand.

And all Rain could see was the shadow, the thin line of the rope and the shape of the hanging body.

Frances kept on talking, but there was one word she was not using. The word was murder.

4

John Gower began his adventure in the public library at Sherborne on Thursday morning. The young librarian was dimpled, with bra straps sketched darkly beneath a fine white cotton blouse. She was apparently used to being chatted to by her customers. Gower did so, deliberately letting her know that the information she was seeking for him was research for his next book.

'I'll be going down there in a day or two,' he said, while her eyes were on her microfiche screen waiting for enlightenment, 'but it would be helpful if I could find out a few details in advance.'

'I'm sure we've got something.' Her eyes left the screen long enough to flash an encouraging smile. 'You're writing a book about coastal wrecks, are you, Mr . . . er . . .'

'Gower. John Gower.' He ought not to have been disappointed that the name meant nothing to her, but he was. 'No, it's a novel.'

'Ah, background,' said the librarian, who had heard tell of such things. Then the machine threw up the name she wanted. 'We have one called *The Wreck of the Charity* by J. B. Mullen.'

He registered the coincidence of names. Impossible not to grin at the notion of Jed Mullen taking time off from bawling songs on his tractor in the fields around Stream Cottage to pen a serious work on a mysterious shipwreck.

The librarian noticed the smile, failed entirely to appreciate that it was nothing to do with her and, blushing, lowered her eyelids. She took a piece of paper and scribbled down the details in a girlish hand.

Schoolteacher, thought Gower. *She trained as an infant-school-*

teacher. Where else did women ever acquire that childish way of writing with flat, undeveloped forms?

He took a chance and asked whether she had ever been a teacher. Her mouth widened in an 'Oh!'

'Yes,' she admitted. 'I was. I didn't know you, did I?' Perplexed, she was thinking he was too old to have been a contemporary, asking herself whether he had ever been a tutor of hers.

'No.'

'Then how did you know?' She had her hand on the scrap of paper, not prepared to pass it over until he had explained himself.

He smiled at her confusion. Tell the truth? Invent an entertaining lie? He told the truth. He pointed at the paper, teasing. 'All is revealed in the handwriting.'

'Gosh,' she said, looking down at her handwriting. 'You could tell *that*? Upside down!'

'Oh yes,' he said airily. 'Upside down, sideways, any way you like.'

'Gosh. It's not even as though I did any teaching. They ran out of jobs. I went into library work instead.'

A woman with a creaky basket on wheels rattled up beside him and Gower accepted the piece of paper the librarian pushed forward. 'You should find the book on the non-fiction shelves over there, Mr Gower, second stand along.'

He thanked her and moved away. Behind him the woman with the basket said: 'Hello, Margaret. How are you today? Mother any better?'

Later, Margaret would remember him. Perhaps the older woman too.

Gower found *The Wreck of the Charity* where he remembered it from earlier visits. He did not meet Margaret again when he queued at the black-topped counter to borrow the book. She was talking to the creaking-basket woman, and the counter was the other side of the door from her desk. A brisk older woman served him.

Gower sat in his car close by in the Old Market car park and took from the dashboard shelf the sheets of paper on which he had drawn up a list of things to do. He made a neat cross beside 'library'. Then he put the sheets back on the shelf.

They were the key to his future, those listed words. He had a plan and it was dangerous and he could only attempt it once, but it was the only means he knew of avoiding the penury that had destroyed Alf Wilson, and it was the surest means of bringing Linda home.

The library visit had been more successful than he had hoped. Luck had given him the friendly youngster on the way in and the terse woman on the way out. It could so easily have happened the other way round. Gower pictured Margaret on television before long, her bra straps tantalizing beneath her pretty blouse, as she told the whole country how Gower had asked her to find anything about a wreck off a Cornish headland because he was going to use it for background to his next novel.

She would never know that this copy of J. B. Mullen's book would stay unread, or that Gower had already read it long ago, had once owned a copy that he had discarded along with other possessions when he and Linda had moved from their London flat to Stream Cottage. He picked up the library copy from the passenger seat of the car.

'J. B. Mullen,' said the blurb on the dust jacket, 'has recreated the intriguing story of the *Charity* and the men who failed to find her. Although a score of witnesses reported the millionaire's yacht sinking off the Lizard in 1908, the wreck has never been pinpointed. Rumours about the wealth on board her have sent three men to their deaths in the search. Now J. B. Mullen has written a gripping story about the mysterious *Charity* and the curse that claims the lives of those who will not let her rest.'

Gower snorted. J. B. Mullen, in his opinion, had tacked together unsubstantiated newspaper stories and local rumour. Mullen had not written very well, either. However, this hack writer and the elusive *Charity* were going to be of inestimable value to Gower. He chucked the book on to the dashboard shelf and got out of the car to walk down Hound Street and find a stationer's.

Anonymous among the stationer's lunchtime shoppers in busy Cheap Street, he bought a rent book and a slim ruled notebook with a smart green and gold cover. Notebooks were a weakness. He liked a fresh one for a fresh project, but not any old notebook. He preferred to have one with a pleasing colour or design. Having paid, he put the paper bag in which he was handed the purchases into the inside pocket of his raincoat. Back at the car he marked another cross on his list, beside 'rent book'.

Gower drove out of Sherborne, to the south. Sheep and Friesian cows dotted the fields, and the buffed paintwork of vehicles on a second-hand car lot, where he ought to have traded in his limping car long ago, winked in splashes of sunshine. The way ahead was unclear, part shaded, part bright, as the day had not settled into one kind of weather or another.

He kept to the main road until a little short of Cerne Abbas when he pulled off, cut the engine and slid across to the passenger seat. Using as a rest the copy of *Yachting World* he had bought that morning, he opened the rent book on his knees and with a black ballpoint pen filled in one column with a series of figures, the same figures each time. Then, referring to his pocket diary, he wrote weekly dates beside those figures and in another column he initialled each line of entries. The dates ran back two months. The initials were chosen at random: YW for *Yachting World* or, if he were challenged, for Mrs Yvonne Williams.

He had given the fictitious Mrs Williams neat, round handwriting. Without flourish or individuality, it would pass an amateur's scrutiny as totally different from his own slanting hand with the affectation of embellishments on certain letters. Gower was pleased with the result. He shut the diary, returned it to his pocket and, taking out his fountain pen, he prepared to personalize the record with a tenant's signature.

His hand wavered above the rent book. And into his mind

came that difficult, cunning character who was never there when he wanted him: Richard Crane. On impulse, Gower signed Richard Crane in the appropriate space, using his normal handwriting and happily bringing off a fluid line that made it appear a practised signature and not merely two words written down. Gower was ready to drive on.

In Dorchester, a town he rarely visited, he followed car park signs until he was safely in one in the town centre, a brief walk through a shopping arcade to the main street. But first he studied the discoloured map displayed near the Tourist Information Office, chose an address, and went to see it.

Orchard Street seemed entirely suitable, Victorian brick terraces curving round the hill below the dark prison wall. Gower used the biro to complete the record in the rent book. Richard Crane was now the tenant of 39 Orchard Street. In reality, Orchard Street ended at the river and allotments after number thirty-seven.

Gower walked back up the hill, mildly nervous about what he was going to do next. It might not have been crucial, he did not know, but it was a valuable means of putting Richard Crane to the test. If the rent book failed him, he would have to retreat and think of another way. If it succeeded, he would feel confident about the bigger thing to be done afterwards.

Dorchester Library was also modern, not unlike the one where he had acquired *The Wreck of the Charity*, but there was no one with the soft-centred appeal of Margaret with the white blouse. Gower advanced on a man sitting at an inquiry desk. The man gave him an interrogative look. Gower said he would like to join the library.

'Have you been a member before?'

'Yes,' said Gower, realizing stupidly late that the man would not be interested in his membership elsewhere but only in this particular library. He chose not to correct the mistake until he was forced to.

'Name, please?'

'Richard Crane.' Gower cleared his throat. This was absurd, he was scarcely able to speak the lie. How could he bring the rest of his plan to fruition if he was going to make a fool of himself over this simple, harmless, deception? The hand inside his jacket pocket clenched, nails biting into skin. He told himself: *Pull yourself together. Relax.*

The man was tapping his computer keyboard. 'Hmm. Some time ago, was it?'

'Yes.' Gower lied confidently. The man had invited a yes.

'I expect it was too long ago, we'd better start again.'

He produced a card from beneath the desk and began to fill it in. Questions: Name, address, name of library branch that had previously been used. Answers: Richard Crane, 39 Orchard Road, Dorchester, this one.

'Good,' said the man. 'Got some form of identity, have you?' His pen struck through another section on the card. 'We needn't trouble with references as you've been a member before. I expect you're in a hurry to use the library.'

Feeling for the rent book, Gower said that yes, he was in rather a hurry. He held out the book. 'I've got this. Is it good enough for you?'

The man skimmed it. 'Yes, anything with an address gets past me.' He gave the book back. 'Sign this, would you, please?'

Gower signed for Richard Crane.

And then there was a snag. The man said: 'If you'd like to choose your books, you can give this to the librarian on your way out. Your card will be ready for you next time you come.'

Gower's thought was a protest. *Next time!* He fixed a grateful smile on his face and fought down an urge to argue about it. He wanted the card now, immediately. He had depended on it.

Keeping the smile in place he strolled to the fiction shelves. He had to decide whether to delay the rest or to press on, assuming the rent book would be sufficient, although to his mind one piece of identification was less than half the value of two. He bit his little fingernail as he mulled it over. Anyone watching would have thought he was scowling his way along the fiction shelves in pursuit of a book he could not put his hand on.

And then he was by the Gs, looking straight ahead at three John Gower novels. He took an impish delight in borrowing them, hoping this library was one of those whose annual record was used as the basis for calculating Public Lending Right payments to authors. By taking the books out he might earn himself a few pennies.

The librarian who checked out the books repeated the information about the card being available next time he came in. Gower wished someone would say whether that meant as soon as next day, perhaps he could bear to delay the rest of his plan until then. But he preferred not to ask and appear anxious, and he decided anyway to go ahead without the card.

There was a choice of banks in South Street, one very busy and the others not so. He picked the busy one and said he would like to open an account. A clerk led him to a table in a corner and whisked through a series of questions about the kind of banking facilities he required. He kept it simple, asking only for a current account.

Forms were produced, answers filled in on his behalf. The rent book was proffered and approved. He was asked about his date of birth and gave Richard Crane's, lopping five years off his own age but keeping the same day and month. That way it would not be too difficult to remember. Asked whether he had accounts with other banks he said not, adding that he had been working in Australia for a number of years and only recently returned.

He was asked for references. The clerk said: 'Your employer, your doctor – the usual thing.'

Gower said he had not registered with a doctor but he would ask his employer. When she inquired about his occupation he said he was a barman.

He had already transferred cash from his deposit account to the current account, and had drawn a sum to pay into the new Crane account. The notes were in his pocket now but they

81

would have to stay there. Opening a bank account was tougher than getting access to a library.

Leaving the bank, he was worrying about the need for two references. Mrs Yvonne Williams, landlady of 39 Orchard Street, would be useless for this purpose because the bank would want to contact her. As neither she nor the house existed, the ruse would collapse. But finding a genuine resident to help him out should not be hard. Gower was hopeful he could fix that.

And Richard Crane need not fret about a second reference: John Gower, author, of Stream Cottage, Lydden, had already typed him one.

Before lunch, Gower was drinking in a pub on the fringe of Dorchester with an elderly jovial landlord who enjoyed his work, was on good terms with his brewery and loved meeting new customers. Stan Hawes, this wholly exceptional character, was a godsend after the setbacks Gower had experienced during the morning. Settling in to listen to Stan's tales, he weaseled pieces of information about Richard Crane into the conversation.

Stan had a story about a New Zealander who had taken a local pub and enlivened gossip at the Licensed Victuallers' Association branch by his forthright way of dealing with troublesome customers. Eventually two of his customers went to hospital and the New Zealander went back to New Zealand, hastily. Gower vaguely remembered a newspaper story about the assault.

Gower asked: 'Done much travelling yourself?'

'Aussie,' said Stan. 'Spent three years down under.'

While the landlord reminisced aloud, Gower revised Richard Crane's history. Crane would still be a barman, because it was a job Gower knew slightly having worked in pubs in his student days, but he had been to Canada and not Australia.

Gower confided, when the moment seemed ripe. 'Shall I tell you what I miss most, coming back?'

'Bears? Maple syrup?' laughed Stan Hawes.

'No, a bank account.'

Stan paused, in the midst of pouring the fresh pint Gower had ordered. 'Eh? So how come you can't have a bank account?'

Before the froth had settled on the beer, Richard Crane had hooked his second reference.

Gower played it well. He stayed on a little longer, joining in a three-cornered conversation when one of the regulars came to the bar to talk to the landlord and then ordering a snack. He left with the promise to drop in again soon.

Returning to the bank he met the same clerk. She took the two written testimonials, did not read them in front of him but disappeared from view for several minutes. He managed to look puzzled when she returned saying: 'I'm sorry, Mr Crane, I can't reach Mr Gower. His telephone isn't answering. But I've checked with Mr Hawes and that one's all right.'

He said ironically: 'Funny about John Gower, I thought writers spent all their time alone with a typewriter.'

The clerk smiled. Perfect teeth, perfect lipstick. She said: 'I expect they also have to go shopping sometimes.'

'Or to the bank?'

She thought that was witty, but not nearly as witty as Gower did.

'I'll keep trying him. I know you must be keen to get the account opened.'

He fingered the wodge of £10 notes. 'Yes. I want to put some cash somewhere safe.'

The clerk hurried off again, came back with a senior's approval to open the account on the basis of the letter from Mr Hawes, the pub landlord. She said: 'I'll contact you and let you know once I've spoken to Mr Gower.'

'Thank you.' He was ready to go to the counter where there was a cashier free to take in his money. The clerk was giving him a paying-in book, a temporary cheque book without his name printed on it, some other things. But then she spoke again.

'Can I telephone you somewhere?'

They had established that morning that he had no telephone at 39 Orchard Street. He thought fast. 'Not at home,' he said, playing for time.

'Work, perhaps?'

He remembered he was a barman. 'Yes, you could do that. Mr Hawes's number. It's on his letterhead.'

'We'll let you know when you can come in and collect your cheque card.' Her professional smile flashed. The bad moment had passed and he was free to pay over his money.

The notion of further involving Stan Hawes forced him to return to the pub to warn him to expect another telephone call. Gower marvelled at his own cheek: on the briefest acquaintance he had persuaded the man to write a testimonial to his honesty and now he was going to use him to take telephone messages. He wandered nonchalantly into the pub.

Instead of the jolly Stan, there was a thin-lipped woman behind the bar, tidying up. Two customers whispered over their pints at a table in the centre of the room. There was a definite *froideur*. His heart sinking, Gower ordered a half-pint of lager and asked after Stan.

The woman dusted an optic before saying, over the shoulder of her pink synthetic blouse: 'He won't be here again today.'

'Oh?'

She ignored the questioning tone and rang up the money. Gower gulped down the first two mouthfuls and pushed her for more information. She had started the next optic along. He said: 'Taking a well-earned rest, is he?'

'Some might put it like that, I don't know that I would myself.'

He gave a nervous laugh, although it was unlikely she had meant to be funny.

She said: 'Bournemouth, he's gone to. Caught the train half an hour ago.' She finished with the optic and looked round. 'A message, was there?'

At last the opening he needed. Gower said yes, there was.

'Someone might be leaving a message here for me. I talked to Stan earlier on.'

'What sort of message?'

'Oh, it's about . . .'

'Telephone or letter, or just a message?'

'Telephone.'

'I see.' Gimlet eyes stated what she thought about the way people exploited pub folk. A friendly landlord was forever being used by people: for cashing cheques, as a noticeboard, for taking messages. Hawes enjoyed it, Mrs Hawes did not.

'Probably tomorrow,' Gower hazarded. 'Will Stan be here then?' He did not trust Mrs Hawes; the sooner Stan got back the better.

'He'll be here.' The third optic got her attention.

'Good. Well.' He drank up the lager. 'I'll be off then.'

She looked over the synthetic pink a second time. 'Who's the message for then? You never said your name.'

'Crane. Richard Crane. Stan knows me.'

She watched him leave.

He drove to Stream Cottage, the stream an uninspiring trickle but its bank rich with primroses. Later on there would be campion, violets and bluebells although he could not be there to see them.

In his garden the grass was ready for the first cut of the year. He took pleasure in ignoring it. Before he reached the kitchen the telephone rang. The bank clerk politely checked that Mr Gower had indeed provided a written reference for Mr Richard Crane.

Gower confirmed it, disguising his voice with a tinge of American lest she recognize it as the voice of the man she knew as Crane. All he had said before she identified herself was 'Gower', not enough to make a switch discernible.

As he came away from the telephone he felt moderately confident. The Crane bank account was open for business, he had been invited to collect his cheque card and personal cheque book next week. He congratulated himself that rather than blunder forward he had thought the venture through step by intricate step. He had prepared better than he need have done, because the library ticket had been unnecessary at the bank, but better that than be ill-prepared. Overall, the plan was sound. Mishaps were beyond his control.

And yet Gower was shunning one aspect, perhaps the trickiest. He faced up to the problem. *I'm going to have to confide in someone. I can't do everything. It's impossible to do it alone.* He delayed a decision about that and made a telephone call.

Rob Watson was astonished to hear from John Gower. It had been a long time.

'It's been a long time,' Rob said, and said it again as surprise denied him anything more intelligent to say.

'Afraid I've been busy,' Gower apologized, hinting at a frenetic life style that allowed scant space for old friends. 'I should have been in touch way back . . .'

'No, my fault,' Rob butted in. 'I was going to ring you after I moved down here, wasn't I? We were going to have a day's sailing now and then.'

'Perhaps we still might,' Gower was getting to the point as quickly as he decently could. 'You've still got the *Jumble*, I take it?'

'The *Jumble*! My God, you're way behind the times. Just goes to show how long it's been.'

'What happened to her?'

Rob's laughter blared down the line. 'I sold her, that's what happened to her. *Sold* her.'

Gower heard himself echoing. 'Sold the *Jumble*?'

Damn, he thought, *Rob hasn't got a boat any more. I've depended on using the* Jumble, *and he hasn't got her. And I don't know anybody else who might let me . . .*

Rob's laugh was reduced to a hiccoughing sound. Then he said, between splutters: 'Yes, you wouldn't believe it, would you? I remember thinking at the time: if old John Gower knew what I was getting for her, he wouldn't believe it.'

'I'm not sure I do,' said Gower in disbelief. 'You mean someone paid you a decent price for her?'

'Oh, very decent. And she went to a good home. A fellow up the coast liked the line of her . . .'

'But she didn't have a line, she was ugly, she was . . .'

'Yes, you and I noticed that but you've got to take my word for it, this fellow didn't. He set his heart on her and before I understood what was happening he was writing a cheque.' Rob laughed loudly again, named a figure, laughed some more.

Gower made an effort to enjoy the good news about the *Jumble*, but was thankful Rob could not see his face. The news was remarkable indeed. The boat had begun life as a kit that a man had failed to complete. Gower and Watson had finished her while they were students in Exeter, supplementing the kit with odds and ends they picked up cheaply or scrounged, and adapting her to a highly individual design – and, yes, an ugly one.

The man who had bought the kit mentioned he had intended calling her *Sea Dog*. Gower and Watson had the happier idea of *Jumble*, the dog in the *Just William* stories. It suited her pedigree perfectly. They had kept her at Fowey, Rob's home before he had moved further west.

'I bet,' Gower guessed, 'her name's been changed.'

'Oh sure, he didn't care for that. But at least he didn't twig why she was called *Jumble*. I wasn't going to risk that ridiculous cheque by telling the truth and drawing attention to her certain defects.'

Gower listened to more laughter, joining in despite his anxiety. He put a key question: 'Do you sail at all now, Rob?'

'Of course I bloody sail! What do you think? I'm not going to chuck it up on the say-so of a pushy wife who'd rather have a fitted carpet, am I?'

Rob had never liked Linda, seldom hid it and was equally seldom fair to her. Gower had always let the gibes slide by. Who were they aimed at really, him or Linda? He asked what boat Rob sailed these days.

Hearing Rob bubbling about the finer points of his racy new craft, Gower felt his own long-suppressed enthusiasm resurface. He wanted to stand again on the deck of a sailing boat, to dip and bend with the tide, be spattered with spray and feel the tug of the sail in the wind. Never mind that he was pinning his future on an afternoon's sailing, he was burning to sail again for the sheer joy of it.

Rob was saying: 'What do you say? Come down and see her. We'll take a trip around the bay. Just like the old days.'

'I'd love to,' said Gower. But he meant he would love to go alone. While he had been assuming Rob still owned the *Jumble* he had thought it would be easy to ask to be allowed, for old times' sake, to take her out alone. A pacy modern boat was a different matter. It would be like asking whether he could borrow his wife for a night if Rob had ever had one, which he naturally had not because wives wanted three-piece suites more fervently than they wanted boats.

Gower swallowed hard. He had no choice but to ask Rob, but he must make it seem as though it was Rob's offer rather than his request. Timing would be the key, because Rob worked in an insurance office all day. If he could make it appear that he was only available at a time when Rob was not, then Rob might accept that.

When Rob realized that Gower could not meet him at the pub near the harbour after work, he tried desperately to think of a way round it. Gower, with faked reluctance, blocked each attempt. Then Rob started talking about taking next day off work, holiday he was prepared to sacrifice to spend a day sailing with the man who had once been his best friend.

Gower was ashamed of what he was doing. His deceit was glaring set beside Rob Watson's open-hearted eagerness to renew their lapsed friendship and share the pleasure of his new boat. Yet Gower could not capitulate too swiftly. Having invented obstacles, they must be made to appear substantial even if, eventually, negotiable.

He thought: *You're going too fast. Let him take you out the first time, then press for an afternoon on your own.*

He backtracked, took Rob up on his offer. 'I've got a lot on tomorrow but I'll make it. Won't be until the afternoon, though.'

'Great,' said Rob. 'Meet me at the harbour, say any time after two.'

'And in the pub if I'm early?'

They laughed together, as they had used to do.

After the call, Gower gathered up items he needed to take to the boat. Deck shoes, waterproofs, things he had never had the heart to part with but had not touched for years. In the morning, tossing them on to the back seat of the car, he reversed into the lane and spun away in the direction of the Cornish coast.

He was tremendously excited. The years fell away. He felt a student again, skiving off tiresome lectures to escape aboard the *Jumble* with his closest pal. They had built the boat together, had learned to sail on her together, had almost sunk her together. Rob and he shared a treasure of memories, the best ones to do with sailing. He could not prevent himself smiling in anticipation of the reminiscing they would do before the silhouette of Rob's new boat disappeared against a darkening sky.

Gower was halfway there before he let any of the less palatable memories revive. They did not trouble him because they were less to do with himself and Rob than with Rob and Linda, and their antipathy to each other. If Rob was obliquely scathing about Linda, then she had not a good word to say for him either.

Gower laughed, remembering how he had sold his share in the *Jumble* to Rob, and Linda had been adamant the price was pitifully low. Now it seemed she might have been correct. But Linda had objected because she objected to Rob as a matter of principle. No one could have dreamed that a future buyer would be bewitched by the *Jumble* and pay the figure Rob had named.

A few years ago, thought Gower, *I'd have been telling Rob my plans. It would be a damned sight easier if I could do that today.* He chewed over the possibility, then decided against it.

Rob might have changed. He knew he had himself. People did.

And so, driving to meet Rob, he faced up to the fact that he had to confide in someone and that he had a choice of only two people: Linda or David Gerrard, his literary agent.

If she had not left him, the option would automatically have been Linda because it would have been heartless not to have let her in on it and because she wanted – *had* wanted – his success as much as he did himself.

'When you're rich and famous,' she used to say in the days, not many years back, when she had believed it was bound to happen, that the people at Pegwoods who decided which books to promote would no longer resist the critics' opinion and would print and sell huge quantities. 'When you're rich and famous we can have one of those.' She might have been referring to a London flat, a big country house, an ocean-going yacht or simply a handyman to call once a week and cut the grass. 'When you're rich and famous . . .' It had become a refrain.

Looking back, grimly, Gower understood what that refrain had actually meant. Behind the lighthearted remarks about expensive holidays and servants, there was the wretched truth that their lives were in limbo until his luck turned. The inability to pay for wild extravagances did not grieve them (most of the population was deprived of those and none the worse for it) but what hurt was the scrimping, waiting for the worst to be over and finding that it never was and, increasingly likely, it never would be.

They could live contentedly without world cruises and mansions, but they had been forced to trim away at the small pleasures and the basic needs. He had sold his share in the *Jumble* and cut back on non-essential books. Leaving London had destroyed their social life and done away with the expense of theatres and entertainment.

Those friends they had in the country were more accurately her friends, largely her colleagues. The London days, when the Gowers' flat had been an open house, where friends arrived willy-nilly, sure of food and drink and good company, and any Saturday evening could turn into an impromptu party, seemed like another life. Their country life had been meanly different. When they were rich and famous, they would be generous once more.

Children had been on the waiting list too. Linda had grown up in threadbare, schoolmasterly penury and would not inflict that on any child she brought into the world. She had been the youngest of four, which was several more than her parents could afford to support in comfort.

'Darling, we aren't poor,' Gower had said, accusing her of exaggeration. 'Not exactly. It's just that we haven't much spare cash.'

'Then how would we manage if I had to give up work?'

And it was true that they could not have coped. Her income was essential. She had said: 'It's not as though I could go back to work and leave you to mind the baby, is it?'

It was not, because his books were fragile creations that took all his time and concentration. Without dissent, children became one of the things the Gowers were saving up for.

'Well, what do you think of her?' Rob Watson oozed pride. He could not take his eyes off the boat. After the initial back-slapping greeting, he had not given Gower another glance. If ever a man was in love, Rob Watson was in love with his boat.

Gower teased him. 'She lacks the grittiness of the *Jumble*.'

Rob aimed a playful punch that stung Gower's arm. He had forgotten this aspect of Rob, the puppyish aspect. Rob said: 'John, I promise you, this lady lacks nothing.'

Behind the smiles, the attempt to share Rob's enthusiasm and the expressions of genuine admiration, Gower was heavy-hearted. *Never*, he thought, *never, never will Rob let this thing out of his sight. I'm wasting my time coming here. He isn't going to lend a beauty like this to anyone, not even me.*

Rob was saying they should stop ogling and go on board. He led the way. The *Fleur* was a streamlined racer, a sleek shape built for slicing through water. Her styling and her finish were impeccable. She was everything Rob had ever craved, everything John Gower had once craved.

Gower asked: 'Is she all yours, Rob?'

'Yes. No, the marine mortgage can't be overlooked, I suppose. But there isn't a partner in this enterprise. Come on.'

They went into the cabin. Not a scratch, not a blemish, not a bit like the scarred *Jumble*. The *Fleur* was what could happen to a man who lived alone, lived for sailing. Rob was confirming it, describing how she had handled when he had raced her. Then he was anxious to make the most of what was left of the day. There was a light offshore breeze, there was sunshine and there was nothing better than to be sailing away.

With grace and agility they entered the open sea, leaving Mount's Bay behind them, riding the swell as they passed St Clement's Isle and hugging the coastline as far as the headland of Carn Du. Gower glimpsed the stubby granite pier of Lamorna Cove, its boulder-strewn beach and quarry cottages, then the *Fleur* was on to Boscawen Point and Rob made her do this and that, putting her through her paces like an owner with a dog in a show ring. Gower understood, and thrilled to the feel of the boat. His sentimental affection for the *Jumble* dissipated on the sea breeze. Anyone could be forgiven for preferring the *Fleur*.

'Who do you sail with mostly?' Gower asked.

But Rob Watson mentioned a handful of names, people who went out with him from time to time, no one who had replaced Gower as his regular partner. Gower supposed that being sole owner made all the difference. Also, Rob said he enjoyed sailing alone.

'These boats make it easy,' he said. 'It's something I've got into the way of. Sometimes I go right over to . . .'

But his words were lost to the wind. Gower tried to be crew, not passenger, but Rob was adept at handling the *Fleur* alone and Gower suspected his friend would be happier still if left to demonstrate.

In the old days, thought Gower, *we used to take turns to be skipper. All those names who go out with him, they must all be crew, he must always be skipper.*

Rob was shouting across to him: 'Remember that time off Muddle Head?'

Muddle Head was the name they had given the point where confusion had almost scuppered the *Jumble*. Gower roared with laughter. 'We're not going to do that to the *Fleur*, I hope!'

Rob shouted. 'I always remember it, every time I go that way. I swear I saw my past flashing before my eyes.'

'I should think you saw mine too.'

Rob ducked beneath a sail, adjusted ropes. He was taking the *Fleur* far out and fast. A long way off there was a big ship, a tanker, further still a small island, no more than a rock. Gower's fingers fastened on the guardrail.

Well before the tanker, Rob sheered away, arcing the *Fleur* towards the coastline. He was pleased with the performance. Gower teased again. 'Shame, I thought you were going to loop around the island.'

Rob said something about a deep shipping lane, about yachts keeping clear when possible. 'Besides, look at that.' That was the view of land, the hump of green hills topped with moorland, the foaming sea around cliffs. Gower was taking it in when Rob sent the *Fleur* skittering away and the shore view was hidden by spray. Gower guessed Rob could keep this up for hours.

They did the reminiscing as they sailed home across the bay, the *Fleur* dawdling along with the tides and Rob relaxed and expansive. 'I see her sometimes, the *Jumble*,' he said.

'Where does she lie now?'

Rob tipped his head eastwards. 'Down that way, can't remember exactly where she's moored. I think it might be one of those swanky new marinas.'

'Surely not. They wouldn't find space for a creaky old bath tub like that.'

Rob raised an eyebrow at the change of allegiance. 'Never thought I'd hear you be so rude about the old girl.'

Ruefully, Gower admitted he had been won over by her successor. *Get on with it*, he thought. *Soon we'll be mooring, then there'll be the pub, and he's sure to be surrounded by other boating types swapping yarns. If you don't get around to it pretty quickly, it'll be too late.*

And into his mind came a cleanly focused picture of the fictional Richard Crane, steady-eyed and firm-jawed, a steely character who was never one to dilly-dally when he wanted something, who made things happen.

Gower cleared his throat, but Rob spoke first. 'Look, John,' he began awkwardly. 'Before we get ashore, there's something I want to say.'

'Oh?' Gower was at a loss, his own resolve vanishing as he watched Rob's embarrassment.

Rob said: 'I'm going to make a mess of this, I know I am. But, well, the thing is I feel I owe you some money.' He hurried on through Gower's puzzled denial, saying: 'No, let me explain. What I mean is I feel you were rather done down over the *Jumble*. I've told you what I got for her.' He shrugged. 'Well, that's it. When I bought your share, I paid far less than I ought to have done. Now we know what her true value was, I want to pay some more.'

'We agreed a price, there wasn't even any argument about it. We both felt it was a reasonable price and you paid it. End of deal.'

Rob persisted. 'We were wrong. Until that fellow rolled up three years later, it was all guesswork.'

Gower argued but Rob shut him up, saying: 'I'm going to do it, I'm the skipper around here and you can't stop me.'

He said how much he proposed to pay, said he had felt guilty about it ever since the *Jumble* sale, and they both caved in laughing at the sound of that. Then Gower seized his opportunity.

'I'll tell you what, Rob. Why don't we commute your offer? Instead of the cash, why don't you give me what I'd really like most of all?'

Understanding glimmered in Rob's eyes. Gower spelled it

out for him: 'Let me take the *Fleur* out once in a while. What do you say?'

Rob said yes. To Gower's immense relief, Rob said yes. Rob mumbled once or twice that Gower ought at least to think over the cash offer and Gower assured him he already had and that the high price of the *Jumble* was Rob's good luck and he was entitled to every last penny of it. By the time they entered the harbour, the matter was closed.

In the bar of the Ship Inn where, true to form, Rob was greeted by boating friends, Gower managed to ask whether he might be allowed to sail the *Fleur* on Monday. The tiniest frown touched Rob's face before he said that yes, of course, that was fine. Before long Gower left him there, using the excuse of the long drive home to get away.

Walking to the car, he cast a longing glance at the *Fleur*. 'Monday, if that's all right,' he had said casually over the beer glasses. 'Monday afternoon, weather permitting.'

This had been unfair of him, Rob could not discuss it while he was in the midst of the hubbub. That's why Gower had done it then. He ran the last few steps to the car, imagining Rob chasing after him having marshalled objections or having invented an excuse to take Monday afternoon off work too and sail with him. Gower looked in the rear-view mirror as he started the engine but the pub door stayed shut, no one came out. Whatever Rob's discomfort, he had agreed to lend the boat on Monday and so he would.

Rob Watson was a decent, straightforward man, so good-hearted that he had actually tried to pay money he was not obliged to. And yet Gower knew that the money was relatively unimportant to Rob, although he did not have excess to splash around. Gower had refused his money and was going to take the thing Rob valued most.

He would have felt shabby acknowledging this, but the resolute face of Richard Crane came to his aid. John Gower changed up a gear and sped away.

Home, he dropped into a chair, exhausted, and switched on the television set for company. He found himself watching an independent channel, a late-night offering billed as a tribute to Alf Wilson. Actors and directors were trundled forward to say what a great fellow Wilson had been, how his triumphs had founded their careers. There were clips of his plays that had been recorded and fond verbal recollections of those that had not or whose tapes had been mislaid.

Critics compared his achievements for television drama with the advances in theatre or film. They skirted around the tragedy of the silent years. Little was said about his private life until a Mrs Pat Jarvis filmed at her home in Addingham, Yorkshire, explained that she was Wilson's cousin and provided a few seconds of background to his professional life.

Most remarkably, Rain Morgan, the gossip columnist, was filmed walking through a Chelsea square and talking about her acquaintance with the dead dramatist and her impression of a quiet man who had his success early and suffered when it died early.

She said: 'If ever I asked him whether he was busy, he would always say he was working on something new. The last time I met him he said he expected to be back on the screen soon.'

Then viewers were shown a twenty-year-old publicity photograph of a smiling Wilson sitting at a typewriter. Over it, Rain Morgan said: 'But there's no evidence that he *was* writing anything. I'm afraid it was all a face-saving pretence.'

A close-up of her pretty face replaced his, as she wistfully concluded: 'He was right about being back on the screen though. All those repeats that are being planned, programmes like this one, everyone clamouring to say they worked with him or how much they wish they had . . . He's had more attention this week than he did in the last ten years.'

Gower went to make himself a sandwich, switched channels and settled to watch the BBC repeat of Wilson's *Dead and Alive*. Cutting bread, opening the can of tuna, he was thinking about Rain Morgan.

David Gerrard's always dropping her name into conversation, showing what great pals they are. He ought to be able to use her to

*publicize me, when I'm ready. Whether I take him into my confidence
or not, he ought to be prepared to do that.*

Any misgivings Gower had ever admitted about what he
was undertaking were dispelled by that evening's television.
What was happening to Alf Wilson vindicated him completely.

A shade after eight the next morning the telephone at
Stream Cottage began to ring. Gower was more than half
expecting the call. Slowly he set his coffee cup down and
walked across to the telephone.

This is it, he thought, and braced himself before lifting the
receiver.

Rob's voice conveyed all his *angst* in the time it took him to
say hello and that he hoped he had not got Gower out of bed.
Then: 'John, about Monday, I've been thinking . . .'

'Oh no, there isn't a problem is there?' Gower sounded
plausibly disappointed.

'Not really, but the thing is . . .'

'I see. You're having second thoughts about lending me the
boat.' A statement of plain and predictable truth but Gower
made it seem like a criticism of Rob's unreliability.

Rob floundered. 'Nobody's ever taken her . . . I mean, I just
don't . . . John, she isn't the *Jumble*, I used to let people use the
Jumble, but . . .'

Gower listened coldly, letting Rob stagger from one unfinished sentence to another, revealing through his inarticulacy
how desperate he was for Gower to free him from his promise.
Gower did not. Gower laughed.

'Listen, Rob. I'm not going to do anything I wouldn't do
with you aboard. It's not as though I'm a novice, is it?'

He threw in that he thought he might make use of the *Fleur*
in a book he was writing. Gower had often noticed how
willing people were to help if they believed that to be the case.
Flattery, he supposed, and a vicarious way of taking part in
the great mystery of creating a book.

And gradually, by keeping the tenses right, so that they
were always discussing what Gower 'was going to do' on

Monday and not what he 'would have liked to do' if Rob had not changed his mind, he wore down his friend's objections. By the time the call ended, Rob was reconciled to Gower using the *Fleur* on Monday. For Gower there was only one faint worry.

Rob had said: 'As a matter of fact, I'm not very busy at work right now, I might scrape some time off that afternoon. Don't be too surprised if you find me waiting on board for you.'

After the call, Gower spent some time with charts retrieved from a trunk in the stair cupboard. He spread them over the frayed sitting-room carpet, taking a special interest in the stretch of coast from where the *Fleur* was moored to the site where the *Charity* sank in 1908. Then he flipped through the J. B. Mullen book about the wreck.

Around nine o'clock he poured himself another cup of coffee and steeled himself to make a telephone call, a call so important that his whole future hung on it. The thought made him queasy. His inclination was to ring Linda instead and right up to the moment his finger was poised over the dial he could not trust himself not to do that. But the number he dialled was David Gerrard's. Practical common sense had defeated sentiment. His agent could deal with the future in a way his wife could not.

The connection was poor and Gerrard seemed a world away. Gower had to raise his voice. He apologized for bothering him during a weekend but said it was imperative for Gerrard to be free to help with something on Monday.

Gerrard, not troubling to conceal his annoyance at being disturbed, shouted back that he had a full diary on Monday and whatever it was would have to wait. He did not ask what it was, he wanted to get off the line.

Gower said: 'I've taken your advice, David. I'm going to die. On Monday.'

At the other end he heard nothing but a stupefied silence.

5

When Alfred Gervase Wilson had been dead for five days, the inquest was opened in a dingy room that did nothing to raise morale. A police officer said he had been aged forty-eight, was found dead at his home, had been identified by Mrs Pat Jarvis, and that a post-mortem examination had been carried out by Dr Steven Elwood. The coroner adjourned the hearing for two weeks.

Rain Morgan had sat through the five-minute formality along with reporters from freelance agencies and a local paper. Once it was over she left, the others staying for the lengthier business of the day. She had not fulfilled any purpose by her presence, except to satisfy a muddled feeling of duty, a feeling brought on by Pat Jarvis's speech about the responsibilities of the next of kin. Friends, however loosely the term was applied, had responsibilities too.

Lying in bed on Saturday morning at the Dudleys' house, she thought about this. Then she stretched luxuriously and listened to birdsong. All those small gardens, all those trees, all those birds – could it really be only two miles from Charing Cross? She had taken to the place, to Fred also now that he had an inkling that he ought to obey her. After the business of chasing the cat into the derelict garden further down the street, Rain had kept him bossily under control.

Tomorrow the Dudleys were due to return from their French holiday and she would be packing her car and moving out. She would be sorry to go. Their house was what people called a luxury home, not merely estate agents but real people. Rain felt she could quite happily settle for that kind of luxury.

She threw back the duvet and walked to the *en suite* bathroom, loving the curl of deep carpet around her toes. In her sleep-warmed state she could envy Marion Dudley's life.

Marion had a vague and part-time job at an art gallery, but was able to set it aside at every whim and Marion was a woman with plenty of whims.

She had married a man making City money and they had both inherited houses. She had no financial constraints, responsibilities or cares. Her days were filled with walking Fred, having her neighbourhood friends for lunch, fitting in that undemanding gallery job on the occasions it pleased her to do so, visiting the beauty parlour in Thornhill Road, calling taxis to take her to a Knightsbridge hairdresser, and deciding which costly outfit to wear to the theatre or opera in the evening. She could hardly avoid noticing the beggars outside her local food shops but the spectacle did not shame her.

Rain squeezed toothpaste on to her brush, smiling at the memory of Marion telling her that Fridays were hell because of the packing and the drive to the Dudleys' cottage in Gloucestershire. It had transpired that often the packing was actually done by the daily help who looked after all the other chores at the Dudley house. Marion was wilfully underemployed. With a contrastingly frenetic and independent life, Rain Morgan was fascinated by such indolence.

'Fascinated,' she murmured beneath the sounds of running water, 'but prepared to give it a try. Any time a rich suitor comes along.'

She was dressing when the doorbell rang. Fred made a hullaballoo as she ran downstairs, wrapping her dressing-gown around her. She peered through the security glass in the centre panel of the front door. This minute window gave her a round picture of a red-haired man standing on the doorstep. He was from the house next door. She clattered with bolts and chains and locks.

'Hello, Rain,' he said, 'I've come to see whether you're all right.' His face explained that something, somewhere, was not all right.

'What's happened?'

'We were done last night. Didn't hear a thing, slept through the lot though we'd been half expecting trouble because a couple of lads have been seen hanging around the street recently. Police on their way now, of course, but that'll be a waste of time.'

'A break-in? Did they take much?'

'Yes, plenty. But thank God they didn't make much mess. I suppose they had to be careful because we were upstairs. You didn't hear anything, did you? Or see anybody?'

Rain shook her head. 'Not a thing.'

The man retreated. 'Well, expect the police to call. They should be up from King's Cross any time now.'

Not until she was upstairs again and finishing dressing did she remember the night she spotted the legs of a man beneath the tree outside her front door. When a policewoman arrived, during Rain's breakfast, Rain mentioned the man.

'Did you get a description? Young or old?' the policewoman asked.

'Young I think. The shoes had some white on them, that's what caught my eye.'

'Trainers, perhaps?'

'They could have been. And he appeared to be wearing jeans, with a dark garment on his top half. But the branches obscured my view of everything except the legs.'

The policewoman politely noted this apparently useless information. She said: 'Could you tell which way he was looking? Towards your neighbour's house or at this one?'

Rain explained she was almost sure he had his back to her and was looking across the road, not directly, but obliquely down the street. That was also written down.

When she left the house that morning, she locked up with extra care, double-checking each window lock and security grille before saying goodbye to Fred. *Absurd*, she thought. *This is the one day I can guarantee nobody will break in, not with a police car outside the next house.*

Although Saturday was theoretically the day the paper closed down, she had to look in at the office. There she encountered an especially bright Holly Chase. 'Guess what?' said Holly. 'I have found *the* flat.'

'Wonderful. Where?'

'Hackney. But wonderful for Hackney. You know, there are some very good bits of Hackney.'

'Does Dan like the flat?'

Holly shrugged. 'Dan's away on location, but he'll love it. I'll tell him to.' Dan was a television cameraman.

'Let's see.' Rain held out her hand for the estate agent's details.

Holly hesitated before passing them over. 'Rain, it's better than it sounds. And don't take any notice of that photograph. It doesn't look like that at all. I don't know how they do it, unless there are special courses for estate agents' photographers to ensure that every property looks like a heap of rubble.'

Rain peered at the smudgy photograph, photocopied on cheap paper. 'Looks like a heap of rubble. What's this?'

Holly and Rain bent over the page together, Rain's index finger on an enormous lump projecting in front of the first-floor window. Holly said: 'That's a clematis.'

'Up there?'

'From the basement. There's a big tub in the area and a net that the clematis climbs up. But you can't see that in the picture because it's obscured by the sale board.'

'Must keep out the light,' suggested Rain.

'And lets in the scent,' said Holly more positively. 'They told me, a fabulous scent wafts right through the first floor. That would be our floor, that and the one above.'

'You'd have to hack it back,' said Rain. 'You need light as well as fabulous scent and as this room faces north . . .'

'OK. Fine. I'll hack it back. But never mind the clematis, read on, Rain.'

Rain read, breaking off to discuss room sizes and views from windows and the facilities of the kitchen. Holly filled in the details, projecting how things would be when she lived there. She wanted a minor change to the kitchen but nothing complicated or expensive, and she wanted better wardrobes in the main bedroom.

The flat would always fall short of Rain's and further short of the Dudleys' house, but it had one outstanding advantage: it was what Holly could afford and she liked it sufficiently to buy it. She told Rain she was longing to make an offer, once she had Dan's approval.

A messenger delivering mail interrupted them. Among Rain's was a letter from Pat Jarvis.

> 12 Cragg View,
> Addingham,
> Ilkley,
> N. Yorks.

Dear Rain Morgan,
Thank you for sparing time to talk to me about my cousin. I trust the taxi driver delivered you the keys to his flat. Having looked over Alf's letter, the one he wrote me a while before he died, I decided to send you a copy. I was wrong about the date of it. I think I told you he wrote five weeks ago but really it was six. When you read it you will notice that he asked about coming here to stay last week.

Poor Alf. There's been such a lot in the papers and on the radio and television about him, saying what an important man he was. I feel very sad that he will never know how much people in his line thought of him.

Yours sincerely,
Pat Jarvis

Alf Wilson's letter was shorter and sharper. It was dated early March and told her he needed to be in the Dales on the weekend of 9 April and asked whether she could provide him with a bed for a night or two, possibly three. 'It's research for a new project, so I can't be precise,' he wrote. 'Sorry I haven't been in touch for a while. All the news when I see you.'

Instead of going to do his research in the Dales, Alf Wilson had died. Rain showed Holly the letters. Holly's skinny plaits quivered but what she said was: 'None of this substantiates the rumour that he didn't kill himself. His mind could have gone through any number of contortions since he typed this.'

The rumour, based on an anonymous telephone call to the police after Wilson's death became public, had not developed. There had been no more calls and nothing to back up the claim. Journalists who knew of the incident were as well used to frivolous allegations as the police and equally inclined to ignore it.

Rain refolded the letters and replaced them in the envelope, conceding that Wilson's behaviour had been bizarre. 'He wrote to her, didn't give an address, and didn't contact her again when there was no reply. It's as though having sent this, he forgot about it.'

She put the envelope in her bag, saying she was going to go to Kington Square to pick up post and check on the builder's progress, although the prospect was appalling.

But Holly asked: 'Did you find anything in Wilson's flat to indicate that he was going to research in Yorkshire?'

'I haven't searched for it.' And, as an afterthought, 'Pat Jarvis probably did. She cadged a plastic bag from Mrs Dobson because she needed to carry papers. A script, perhaps? Notes for a play?'

Too early to go from Kington Square to the television studios where she was to be filmed by Frances Keene, she was drawn to Wilson's flat. This time she concentrated on the kneehole desk in the bedroom, lifting out Wilson's papers a batch at a time, flicking through them, keeping the batches in order. She was halfway down the second drawer when she found it: a single sheet of paper covered in jottings, the word ILKLEY prominent and underlined.

Rain sat on the edge of Wilson's bed and gazed at the paper, striving to make sense of the scattered notes. There were other place names on the page, but most of the writing was speedy scrawl, disjointed words and doodles, the kind of thing that happened when one was on the telephone.

That set her wondering how old these notes were, because his telephone had been cut off. This was one of the first things she had learned about him since his death. While she had been ringing the police, and the other tenants of the house had been talking in shocked whispers in the passage outside Ratcliffe's flat, a woman had mentioned it: 'His phone was cut off, you know. He used to borrow mine, claimed his was out of order, but I soon saw through that.'

The telephone stood on the floor in the sitting room, near the window. She lifted the receiver and heard the dialling tone. Either the neighbour had been misled or Wilson had paid to have it reconnected. Rain stayed by the window, struggling to make out the scrawled words on the page. They were not written in smooth sentences that ran left to right across the paper, but were higgledy-piggledy, a phrase here, another there, but grouped in several areas. And there had been a change of pen. All but one of the groups were in black biro, the odd one out in red. Only Ilkley was perfectly clear, because that was in capital letters.

She read off the other place names, identifying London, Brighton and Sussex with comparative ease. There was a swirl that might have been Birmingham, but the red pen had slashed through this word. Bibey and Gomer and Slaborne, if that is what they were, were inexplicable.

She took the paper with her and caught a taxi to the studio. Frances Keene, who claimed a special relationship because she used to work for the *Daily Post* before being enticed into television, tempered her greeting with the accusation that Rain had allowed herself to be filmed for a rival channel's programme on the same subject. Frances had been very cross when she had seen the programme on Friday night. Her rather horsey face grew even less pretty as she grumbled about it.

Rain pleaded guilty and said in mitigation that her very first appearance had been in Frances Keene's item on the *Nine O'Clock News*. At that, Frances stopped looking sulky and said: 'If you're willing to give the time I think we ought to film elsewhere today.'

A sixth sense told Rain what was coming. With a display of obtuseness she asked 'Where?'

Frances did not own up immediately. She wanted to demonstrate her problems first. 'We've filmed the sister in her garden in Yorkshire.'

'Pat Jarvis is a cousin.'

'That's right. Well, we've done that and we've caught a couple of theatrical types in theatre foyers, but otherwise it's been telly people filmed in the studio. I want to break it up a bit.'

'Yes?'

'Your flat would be marvellous, Rain. All those beautiful things and white walls, its elegance would come over superbly. Perhaps we could involve the roof garden too and get your fabulous camellia with chimney pots in the background.'

'Sorry, Frances,' said Rain. 'You're too late for the fabulous camellia and I can't do you chimney pots. They are nicely screened by the massive trees in neighbouring gardens. All too bosky for what you have in mind.'

Frances recovered from her disappointment without pause. 'Forget the garden then, we'll concentrate on the flat.'

Rain pictured her flat. No plaster on the walls, part of a ceiling down, rubble everywhere. 'Forget the flat, too,' she said, and admitted that its elegance was currently below par.

This time Frances looked dejected. But with the ease of a woman switching on an electric light, Rain changed Frances's mood. 'Why don't we film in Alf Wilson's flat?' She held up the keys.

The crew trooped over to the flat. *En route*, Rain pressed Frances for anything fresh she had learned about Wilson during her research, or any twist to the rumour about the manner of his death. Frances let her down. 'I was going to ask you, Rain.'

Wilson's sitting room astonished the crew with its size, emphasized by its near emptiness. There were comments about its lack of homeliness, about the hopeless task of keeping it warm in winter, about the architect's intentions for it when he designed such a room. The cameraman became ghoulish. 'Can't we have Rain sitting on the chair beneath the chandelier?'

'No,' said Rain and Frances together.

The cameraman looked up at the chandelier. 'How did he do it?'

The faces swivelled to Rain, awaiting explanation. She said: 'A chair – that one, I think – was on its side. It appears he stood on it, put the noose around his neck and then kicked the chair away.'

The cameraman persisted. 'That was a lot of weight to put on the chandelier.'

'He didn't,' said Rain. 'The rope was through the hook.'

The faces tilted to the hook from which the chandelier swung. The cameraman said slowly: 'Well, how did he . . .'

'Oh come on,' said Frances impatiently. 'We haven't got all day. Let's get on with it, shall we?'

She was a reporter beginning to be a producer. The film about the death was more important to her than the details of the death. Besides, this line of talk was giving her the creeps.

Frances was efficient, it was soon over. When the others had gone, Rain sat on Wilson's sofa and sighed, wishing she had expressed herself better in the interview. The least and the most she could have done for the man who had placed disproportionate value on their slight friendship was to have talked well about him.

She pulled the table back into position. Like the sofa and the telephone, it had been moved to arrange matters for the camera. Abruptly she stopped, hands rigid on the edge of the table. An idea had touched her mind. She battled to bring it into focus.

Then with rapid movements she pushed the wooden chairs out of the way, dragged the table into the centre of the room and looked up. Her eye measured the space between the table top and the chandelier. Rain snatched a wooden chair, brought it up to the table, and used it as a step to mount the table. Then she lifted the chair up beside her and climbed on to that. Staring up at the chandelier, she stood on tiptoe and stretched her arms high above her head. The thought had clarified into a question: *How had Alf Wilson reached to put the rope through the hook?*

Admittedly she was shorter than Wilson, but the hook which held the chandelier was beyond her reach, and it would have been beyond his too. The hook could not have been reached in this way and yet the stacked furniture brought her closer to it than any other arrangement of pieces in the room. Having searched the flat previously, she knew there was no ladder.

Rain began to shake, at the horror of what she was doing. For her it was a game, an exercise, but when Alf Wilson had stood on this chair it had been utterly serious. There had been a rope around his neck. He had died.

Rain's hands went protectively to her throat. And as they did so she saw the door handle turn.

Then she was looking into the alarmed face of Mrs Dobson. The fat woman was red after the exertion of the climb from her basement lair. 'Oh my!' gasped Mrs Dobson, clapping a hand to her heart. 'What are you doing? For a second I thought . . .'

Carefully Rain stepped down to the table, then jumped to the floor. 'I was . . . er . . . inspecting the chandelier.'

'Inspecting the dust more like.' Mrs Dobson passed the hand from her heart over her face and came to lean heavily on the table with her other hand. 'She can't sell it, that next of kin. Fittings of that nature belong to the landlord.'

'Ah. Well, I'll tell her if I see her.' She wanted to know why Mrs Dobson had blundered in, badly frightening them both.

Mrs Dobson said: 'I thought you'd gone with those people with the camera. Television people, weren't they?'

Rain explained them, interested that Mrs Dobson had called once she assumed the flat to be empty. 'What did you want up here?' Rain hoped Mrs Dobson would miss the unfortunate directness of her question.

The woman said: 'Books.' She flapped a podgy hand at the bookshelves. 'I was going to borrow something to read, if the door was unlocked.'

'Feel free, I don't see why not.' She was not convinced 'borrow' did not mean 'steal' in Mrs Dobson's parlance, but it could scarcely matter. Pat Jarvis wanted nothing from the flat.

Mrs Dobson duly approached the bookshelves, edging her way along each one with a hand poised to snatch at likely titles. 'Stories,' she said. 'That's what I like, a good story.' The hand popped out and snared a book. She read the blurb thoughtfully. Then she laid the book on the table and returned to the shelves. Rain picked up the book. It was one she had never read, *A Candle Lit* by John Gower.

Mrs Dobson, without looking round, sensed what Rain was doing. She said: 'I had one of his from the library. Very good it was. Made you think. I like a book that gives you something to think about. Long words, though. I didn't care for the long words. It's not what ordinary people understand, is it? Mind you, I expect writers have got to use them, dust an unusual word off and put it in to stop it disappearing altogether. My late husband used to say that when an author sticks difficult words in he's not showing off as much as doing his duty by the English language.'

Her hand flashed out for another book. Rain riffled through the pages of the Gower novel. No especially obscure words caught her eye, but she noticed the book was annotated in pencil. It looked like Alf Wilson's handwriting. There was more of it on a page near the front that bore the dedication 'To Linda' and an epigraph: 'It is better to light one candle than curse the darkness.'

Mrs Dobson came to the table with a second book. Rain suspended belief. Mrs Dobson was never going to read a translation of a Czech academic's novel of ideas. Quite simply, Rain no longer believed the story about borrowing books. Equally, she was not going to reveal this. There was little enough to take and Mrs Dobson herself owned next to nothing.

When I've gone, she thought, *she'll be back and she'll help herself to whatever she fancies.*

Aloud she said: 'Is there a ladder anywhere in the house?'

'Under the stairs,' said Mrs Dobson picking up the two books. 'But I've told you, that chandelier wasn't his. And if you take my advice, you'll leave it alone. Nasty heavy thing it is, and it's seen one death already.'

Rain assured her she had no intention of removing the chandelier. Then: 'Did Alf Wilson bring that ladder up here recently?'

'I wouldn't know. Can't say I saw him with it.' She had taken a step towards the door, ready to return to the darkness of her home in the ground.

Rain said: 'When he was found, when we all saw him . . .'

'*I* never did. You opened the door, the others went inside.'

She was correct. Rain had looked in and shrunk back, the rest had rushed in led by old Mr Ratcliffe, but Mrs Dobson had stayed on the landing fidgeting with her cardigan buttons.

Rain said: 'Yes, I remember now.' And so it would be no use asking Mrs Dobson what had happened in the room during those initial moments of revulsion.

But Mrs Dobson said: 'They cut him down, didn't they? The Colonel, that's what I call Ratcliffe, well the Colonel kept on telling us afterwards how he'd sliced through the rope and what a good thing he'd had his knife with him. He says that's what you always do when somebody's hanged, you cut him down right off.'

'Yes,' Rain agreed, that's what you do.

'Just in case,' said Mrs Dobson.

'Just in case,' Rain echoed.

Mrs Dobson decided to confide. 'They didn't like him, you know.' She bobbed her head towards the living-room door, suggesting the other occupants of the house congregated outside, overhearing.

'I'd guessed that. But why not?'

'Colonel Ratcliffe, well he opened a letter that came for Mr Wilson. A few years back, it must have been all of four. Anyway, the Colonel said it was a mistake but Mr Wilson obviously didn't believe him. There was quite an argument. I was sweeping the front steps – well, I sometimes do them the same time as I'm doing my own, it doesn't take a minute and it's a minute well spent. I'm the only one to bother. You couldn't expect the Colonel to lift a broom, now could you? And the others aren't any keener. So . . . where was I?'

Rain said Mrs Dobson had been sweeping the steps, and Mrs Dobson went on: 'They were on the stairs, speaking very loudly, as you might say. I put my head inside to see what was going on and there they were, at the bend of the stairs. The Colonel was saying he'd made an honest mistake like anybody could have done, and Mr Wilson was saying nobody had ever done it before and the Colonel was to be more careful. I don't remember them swearing, but it was all said very nasty.'

Mrs Dobson then recalled the Colonel stumping away in high dudgeon and Alf Wilson pounding down to the hall and out into the street, slamming the door behind him. Rain asked about the other tenants' relations with Wilson. However, there had been no other dramatic incidents, or if there had Mrs Dobson had missed them, which appeared unlikely.

Mrs Dobson explained: 'Mr Wilson withdrew into his shell, that's what it was. He had nothing to do with any of them. I reckon I was the only one he bothered to talk to in the end, and that was because of the library books, you see.'

Mention of books reminded her of the two on the table and the need to carry them to her dungeon. She did, Rain watching her begin to waddle down the steps, convinced that if the woman tripped she would roll like a ball the rest of the way.

Alone again, Rain moved the furniture to its usual position, tore a sheet of paper from her notebook and inserted it in Alf Wilson's old Olympia.

'I need to ask you a favour,' she typed. 'Please come to my flat at 9 a.m. tomorrow (Monday). It's desperately important, I wouldn't be writing this otherwise. Don't fail me, Rain. It's imperative you come.'

She knew it by heart. She sat at his typewriter, where he

had typed that appeal, his fingertips striking the keys hers now struck. The pathos was making her miserable, she wished herself anywhere but this dreary flat with its wretched associations. And yet she was held to it by a gnawing guilt. She had mattered to him, and if she had known it she would have been kinder.

How many others, she thought, *might also be pretending to know me better than they do? My work gives me a wide acquaintance, I'm a familiar figure in the neighbourhood where I live . . . how many other lonely people are elaborating my everyday courtesies into friendship?*

At work she received letters from readers who addressed her by her first name, wrote to her about their intimate problems and sought her advice. Rosie wrote the letters back and Rain signed them. Such correspondence was part of her job, went with having her name and photograph in the paper each day. Alf Wilson was more troubling because their slender contact was not professional. They had been two locals introduced in a local pub. That was all.

Rain removed the paper from the typewriter, returned the carriage to the rest position and flicked up the shiny steel lever that locked the carriage in place. A small voice in her head corrected her. *That wasn't all. You invited him to a party. It was one summer, after you'd been to France. He liked the vase you bought in Antibes. He complimented you on your garden, the sweet peas especially. He admired your home and the way you decorated and furnished it. As a guest he was ideal. He said the right things but not to excess, he committed no gaffes and caused no embarrassment and he mixed with your other guests. So why was it you never invited him again?*

Accused by her conscience she had no defence, except that she could not remember. She gave a lot of parties, especially on summer weekends or evenings when a few phone calls were adequate to fill her home with people for informal drinks and snacks whenever she liked. All kinds of people came but Alf Wilson had only come once.

The truth, said the voice inside, *is that you forgot about him.*

You only ever thought of him when you bumped into him. And then you forgot about him again.

Unfortunately, he had never forgotten her.

The Dudleys' telephone was ringing as Rain entered the house. She hushed Fred, blocked his attempted escape as she closed the front door, and stumbled to grab the receiver. Marion Dudley was calling, from France.

'Is everything all right, Rain?'

Fred was making a dreadful row. Rain said: 'Yes, that's just Fred saying welcome home to me. How's France?'

'Didn't you get a postcard?'

'Not yet.'

'France is superb. And guess what?'

Fred had thrown a leg over the telephone wire and was rolling around trying to free it. Rain said: 'You'll have to tell me.' She stooped to help Fred.

'We're buying a house here!' Marion's triumph took Rain by surprise. She jerked up, cracking her skull on the hall table.

Marion said: 'Rain? What's going on?'

'Nothing, everything's fine.' Rain, rubbing her head, hoped this was true. She clapped a hand over the mouthpiece and told Fred to *sit!* He obeyed, dropping down on the wire that was now entwined around his body like convolvulus up a tree, and foreshortening it.

'Rain?'

'I'm listening. You're going to buy a house?'

'Yes. Well, what with the channel tunnel coming, *and* the terminal to be at King's Cross, it'll be absolutely marvellous. And we thought, why not? Prices are bound to shoot up once the tunnel's open. The children love it and it'll be a terrific investment. Of course, it'll mean spending less time in Gloucestershire, but I expect we'll soon get into the swing of it.'

Rain murmured what might have been encouragement to Marion or a warning to Fred who was wriggling.

Marion's voice crackled on about her new acquisition. 'You'd love it. It's about a hundred and fifty years old, pretty crumbling if you want the truth, but nothing that a few thousand and an imaginative architect can't mend. Oh yes, it's got several acres, mostly woodland, and a pond. The agents called it a lake, but that's overstating it. In fact, it was a millpond. We think we might do up the mill sometime but of course the priority will be the house. They said it was fit to move into but quite honestly if you'd seen . . . Rain?'

Rain indicated that she was still listening.

Marion said: 'Well, look, I mustn't go on about it. The point is, there are heaps of things we've got to do now we've decided to buy and we want to stay for another week and get stuck into it. Do you mind hanging on at our place, or are you frantic to get home to Chelsea?'

Rain said she wasn't frantic at all, quite content to avoid it until the builder had finished. Marion said how wonderfully convenient life was on occasions, and started on a series of goodbyes and see you soons and take cares that occupied another two minutes. Her last words were: 'Give my love to Fred.'

Rain gave him a look that could kill.

She tutted and set about unravelling him from the telephone wire. Once he was freed and shooed into the back garden to frolic, she had time to be grateful to the Dudleys and their extravagance. How much nicer to have the run of their beautiful house for a further week than to camp in Alf Wilson's depressing flat. And as for her own home, she did not want to see it again until there was at least some plaster on the walls and a coat or two of paint on top of that.

It was true, what she had said to Holly Chase. She did not care for disruption. When this whole episode was over and she could go home to a home that looked like one, then she would be happy. Until that day she would continue to feel adrift, putting a brave face on it, showing off the Dudleys' house to Holly and other friends and making light of her urgent dash to the builder (and of the extra funds she had been obliged to find to bribe him to get to work instantly) but hating, deep down, the rootlessness thrust upon her.

Whatever risk and challenge she faced in her professional life, however far she travelled in pursuit of her quarry, she liked to climb those familiar stairs to her own home each evening. She liked it best when there was someone there waiting for her, but was wary about allowing a new man to move in. Moving Oliver West out, bringing herself to make a firm decision and then forcing it on him, had been exhausting.

Their relationship had foundered long before he had gone, but she had delayed admitting it because it had been an undulating affair and it had taken her ages to notice that it had settled into a trough from which it was impossible to emerge. Besides, their failure was unavoidably public. That was the most painful part, not losing Oliver, because by the time he moved out she had nothing to lose.

Her caution about inviting a new man to move in was overdone. No temptation had arisen.

'I need space,' she had said to Holly, talking soon after Oliver's departure. 'I need time to discover what I want and how I like to do things. What I don't need is the pressure of another person.' In her life there were many people, graded from the tight band of friends down to the ever-expanding circle of social and professional acquaintances. It was part of her job to know everybody, but that made it no easier to choose wisely which relationships to foster.

'Oliver was a lot of pressure,' Holly had said. And so he had been, with his unwitting selfishness and his exploitation of Rain's generosity. As Holly spoke, Oliver, who owed his job to Rain, had been down the end of the office, laughing loudly with his cartoonist colleagues.

Rain opened a can of pet food and tipped it into Fred's bowl. She topped up the water in his other bowl. *Oliver*, she thought, as she threw the can into the rubbish bin, *was a mistake from which I'm entitled to take a long time to recover*.

She was equivocal about whether Paul Wickham had also been a mistake. In one way the timing had been bad, but

Paul's reappearance in her life had been the catalyst that crystallized her intention to rid herself of Oliver. If Detective Chief Superintendent Wickham had not been conducting the investigation into a murder in the *Daily Post* office, then they might never have met each other again and Oliver might have continued to live in Kington Square.

'I'm sorry,' she had said to Wickham, only weeks later, her cheeks burning with embarrassment. 'I seem selfish, I know, but I can't make any commitment. It's all my fault, I shouldn't have rushed into . . .'

When she faltered he provided an end to her sentence. 'Bed?'

'I was going to say a serious relationship, then I realized I meant any relationship at all. Paul, I really have to give myself space. Can you understand that?'

He said he could, obliging her but not convincing her.

And so, at her instigation, the thing between them cooled. The two urgently happy weekends they had scrounged from his overburdened working life would always be good memories. Since then the spur-of-the-moment restaurant dinners when he was suddenly free, and the phone calls that cheered her when he was not, became occasional rather than frequent.

'He's going to get fed up with you being too busy washing your hair,' said Holly Chase, watching from the sidelines one time.

'Paul understands,' Rain said.

'A man's understanding is so big.' Holly measured a gap with her finger and thumb. 'Besides, what's there to understand? You're playing the fickle female.'

Rain objected to that, and Holly said: 'If I were to come in one morning and say I saw Wickham in a nightclub the previous evening with . . .'

'He doesn't go to nightclubs.'

'All right,' said Holly extemporizing, 'let's say he was raiding it, accompanied by a glamorous WPC . . .'

Rain burst out laughing. Holly said: 'I mean what I say,

you'd be quite put out if he took you at your word and left you alone.'

'You mean I'd be jealous.'

'Believe it.'

Rain dismissed this with a shake of the head. 'Anyway, he can't take me at my word, I haven't said anything definite.'

Holly had said: 'Don't you think that makes it worse?'

Rain called Fred in from the garden and watched with pleasure as he skidded across the kitchen floor to the corner where his bowl of brown sludge awaited him. She preferred to think about Fred and what went into pet food rather than recall her last, faintly acrimonious telephone call from Paul Wickham. The acrimony bothered her less than the silence that followed it. It had been left that she would ring him, and she had not.

As time went by it became easier not to ring. Now and then she tried the Holly test, imagining him fondling a buxom WPC and calculating her degree of jealousy. It was nil.

While she watched Fred guzzling, she admitted that it was the tragedy of Alf Wilson that had set her worrying about her reluctance to make the phone call. If she could feel guilty about unintentional neglect of an acquaintance, how ought she to feel about deliberately hurting a man who loved her? She looked slyly at the kitchen clock, and was relieved to see it was an inappropriate time to telephone him.

6

They met on the windy ramparts of Figsbury Rings. David Gerrard, having chased down the motorway from London, was irritated at being there first. He was scowling when John Gower arrived.

'We'll walk this way,' said Gower, without apology, indicating they should climb up and walk along a ridge.

Gerrard fell in step beside him. 'John, this is absolutely the craziest thing . . .'

'You told me so on the phone yesterday. But you're going to help, aren't you? I can go ahead without you but it makes more sense for you to help.'

Gerrard was having trouble keeping up with him. He gave Gower a cautious look. He was discovering a side to the man that he did not know. He had always believed him to be a quiescent, dreamy character but this weekend Gower had whipped off a mask to reveal a pushy and determined nature. It was unsettling.

Gerrard said: 'Hold on, I'm not used to this sort of thing.' He came to a full stop and gasped to recover his breath. A vein was pulsating in his forehead. Now that he came to think of it, John Gower always looked terribly healthy, with his shining dark hair, a certain brightness of the eye, and a fresh-looking complexion. He had thickened slightly in the years Gerrard had known him, but was still worryingly athletic.

'Sorry,' said Gower. 'I forgot you never walk anywhere.'

'Walk? You call this walking? You were positively running. Anyway, I walk fairly often, as it happens. But only as far as the nearest taxi. I see no reason to overdo things.' He filled his lungs with grass-scented air and then nodded. 'All right, we can go on now – but carefully, please.'

Gower matched his pace to Gerrard's crawl. There was no

one else in sight, as he had anticipated. By afternoon there were sure to be one or two families on Sunday-afternoon outings, scrambling around on the chalky ditch and ramparts, come to marvel at the encompassing view and to argue about identification of distant landmarks. Early on a Sunday morning, it was a good place to talk unobserved.

Gerrard was whining about the dangers of the enterprise. Gower countered that the physical dangers were negligible, that the plot was as punctiliously researched as any novel he had ever written, and that, however it panned out, the scheme offered maximum potential for publicity.

Gerrard anchored his fair hair with both hands and spoke against the wind. 'If I'm involved and it goes wrong, it would be very damaging for me. I do see that *you* have nothing to lose.'

The remark amused Gower by its bluntness. He bit back a sardonic retort. 'That,' he said, 'is the point. I couldn't be in a worse position than I am. But I'm prepared to do something about it. I'm showing enterprise – isn't that what we've all been told to do these days? The books are good, everybody says so. All I've got to do is draw attention to them.'

Gerrard accused him of oversimplifying, but Gower spoke over him. 'You're supposed to be clever at that, David.' He named a couple of Gerrard's other authors who were seldom out of the public eye and whose sales were healthily high although reviewers shunned the books.

They wrangled, Gerrard torn between admitting on the one hand that he manufactured stories to promote his authors and confessing on the other hand that his reputation as a vigorous publicist outstripped his achievement. Gower kept him on the knife edge, then challenged him on another front: 'David, what bothers you about my idea is that you wish you'd thought of it yourself. Own up, you really do.'

Gerrard turned into the wind. He buried his hands in the pockets of his green padded jacket.

Where, thought Gower, *does he wear a jacket like that? Can he*

possibly keep an up-to-date wardrobe of country clothes in case he's
ever forced to leave town?

The thought ought to have prompted a sobering sequel about Gerrard's suitability for the adventure that lay ahead, but it did not. Instead, Gower gave his mind to what Gerrard was saying.

'John, I think I've decided to do it. But I want you to go through it again. One needs to be utterly convinced of its practicability.'

'It *can* work, I'm certain. And if you help me it can work perfectly.'

'From the beginning,' said Gerrard, sitting down on the grass, high above the empty road and the Sunday-quiet villages. 'And tell me every detail.'

Several times he interrupted Gower's flow to pose questions but not to offer comment. When Gower had finished, Gerrard laced his fingers and looked stonily across the landscape. But it was the look of a man who is not seeing anything except what is inside his mind. Eventually Gerrard said: 'You skirted around what you do after the *Fleur*. You haven't arranged anything?'

'Not yet.'

'Well don't. I know a place that will suffice. It's not romantically remote but it's secluded.' Then David Gerrard added a number of suggestions of his own, minor things that he believed would be useful lines to feed to journalists, when the day dawned.

The traffic below them increased. Church bells began to ring. They returned to their cars, the heavily overweight Gerrard puffing with the strain of unaccustomed air and exercise, and Gower chanting the key things to be done. Gerrard held up a hand: 'All right, John, I know.'

'Sorry,' said Gower, 'but we're short of time.' He made an effort to stop fussing but it was difficult when they had only the remainder of this Sunday in which to make arrangements for what could prove to be months ahead.

They paused by Gerrard's car. He had the door open before

he said: 'To be perfectly frank, the part I find repellent is the boat.'

'The *Charity*? You can't possibly believe that nonsense, that the wreck draws sailors to their doom?' He laughed nervously. It would be just his luck if Gerrard confessed he was a superstitious fellow who could not outface a legend.

'No,' said Gerrard, irritably, 'not that rubbish. I mean the boat you want me to take out.'

Gower's incredulity was beyond disguise. 'You can't steer a motor boat?' The tone said: Anyone can do *that*.

And the tone did not escape Gerrard. He pursed his lips, then said: 'You're no doubt correct, John, but I can't remember the last time I tried. In fact, leaving aside the occasional cross-channel ferry, I find it hard to recall the last time I was on a boat.'

'Oh.' Gower recognized his own folly. Why should he have assumed everyone was as familiar with boats as he was? The evidence was quite to the contrary. He said: 'Why didn't you say at once?'

Gerrard jiggled his car keys, abashed. 'Boating isn't such a jolly pastime in my view.'

'Oh. Seasickness.'

'No, or not that I remember although there was some nasty lurching outside Dieppe one time. Boating has always appeared a rather unnecessary and wet way of spending time.'

Gower said patiently: 'David, no one is going to get wet. You pick up the boat, you point it where I told you to go and you go there. That's it.'

Gerrard forced a smile. He said: 'All right,' but he said it in a way that showed he meant it was all wrong. With a stifled sigh, Gower accepted that the trickiest part of the enterprise depended on a very weak link, David Gerrard.

When Monday came, Gower gathered up the charts and other items he intended to take to Mousehole and then left Stream Cottage for Dorchester where he returned the John Gower library books and received a laminated plastic card that he was made to sign on the spot with Richard Crane's signature. He also called at the bank and was handed Crane's bank card and personal cheque book. Then he raced to Mousehole, terrified that Rob Watson would have wangled a whole day off work and be waiting aboard the *Fleur*.

Rob was not there. A man was working on a boat near by, painting and pottering, but he took no notice of Gower who boarded the *Fleur* and prepared to set sail. As Gower cast off, the man straightened, put a hand to an aching back and watched her glide away on an ebb tide. Recognizing him from the group Rob had drunk with at the Ship, Gower raised an arm in greeting. Gower scanned the harbourside, scared he would see Rob, but there were only gulls and a dog. Sun licked at the cowering granite cottages, slate roofs speckled orange with lichen and busy with gulls. Then the snapshot scene was a memory and Gower was through the harbour mouth.

The *Fleur* was a joy. Well-balanced, responsive, light to steer, there was as much pleasure to be had from her silky movement as from her crisp lines. A smile of sheer happiness transformed Gower's face as a keen wind took her past St Clement's Isle. With sheets pinned, she turned her back to Mount's Bay and set off to the west.

A cutter was coming up. Gower pushed the tiller hard over using the other boat as an excuse for lively manoeuvres. Then he was on course again. He stayed at the helm, alert for tankers in the deep water lane. Off Land's End he swung south-west.

The rock came into sight, the mainland had faded to an indeterminate blur. Gower looped around the rock, then made a straight run downwind. He looked at his watch. He had miles to go but when he arrived there would be hours to kill. Time-wasting was part of the plan.

For a moment he was tempted to detour. The *Fleur* was eager to go anywhere, it was a shame to disappoint her. But there was danger in improvisation. The simpler the plan, the easier to achieve.

He reefed the sail, reducing speed, and let the boat move gently on her way. He looked about, at the fine wake, at the gulls like flotsam on the waves, at a splash of oil and at a patchily blue sky creating shafts of sunlight over the water. That was all, there was nothing else to see.

A worrying thought destroyed the pleasure of the moment. *Supposing David Gerrard messes it up? What if he gets lost, or doesn't come?*

Common sense replied that it would not be the end of the world, that at worst he would have to return the *Fleur* to Rob Watson as though he had been for nothing more exciting than a joyride, that at best he could amend the plan and push on alone.

After a time he hove to, letting the boat drift while he opened a carton of orange juice and a packet of biscuits. The rations he had brought with him were scanty and he had to make them last until evening. Soon after, he moved her smartly downwind again, noticing how the clouds were coming up from the west and the shafts of sunlight were being obliterated.

The shipping forecast that morning had threatened him with nothing frightening, except the loss of a few hours' sunshine in an otherwise bright day. But the change in the mood of the sky persuaded him to make for the site of the *Charity* straight away and waste whatever time was necessary once he was there.

He moved north-east, identifying the headland that ended in Lizard Point and watching it take shape, the details of the land mass multiplying as he drew nearer. Specks became houses, windows winked out at him and dark patches turned into woods. The countryside was tricked out in spring colours.

Gower met shipping but none especially close, although he assumed that in a day or two its crews would recall the *Fleur* and report her position, allowing a record of her movements to be compiled.

The area where the *Charity* went down in 1908 was a

featureless stretch of water to the east of the reefs and rocks of Lizard Point. No peculiar currents, no treacherous shallows explained her sinking. Farmworkers in cliff-edge fields noticed her sailing by in a light squall and remarked how she began to circle, then to show every sign of distress. In minutes she unaccountably sank. The reason was never discovered. J. B. Mullen, in *The Wreck of the Charity*, latched on to her curious circling and described it 'as though she were being sucked down a giant plughole'.

He presented a similar theory about two boats, craft with powerful engines, that had been lost at the same spot while attempting to locate her wreck with sonar equipment. Neither of these had been witnessed sinking, one of them had not actually been seen at the site of the *Charity*, but the legend built up all the same. While it did not rank alongside the notorious Bermuda Triangle, and few people, apart from tabloid journalists, were willing to embrace a 'plughole' theory, the loss of the *Charity* had become one of the insoluble mysteries that human nature fervently encourages.

The *Fleur* sailed around the area. Then Gower rested, sitting on deck with the chart on his knee and his eye on the pencil cross he had drawn years ago to mark the *Charity*. Her true position had never been ascertained, but after reading Mullen's book and some magazine articles he had reached his own conclusions. If two groups of people on shore had given accurate accounts of what they had seen, and assuming those descriptions had been written down correctly by those who listened to them, then the *Charity* had probably gone down at the pencilled cross.

She was tantalizingly close to the shore, from the point of view of wreck hunters, and it was claimed she was stuffed with valuables including a chest of gold. Personally, Gower found the treasure hard to accept, especially the chest of gold. Although J. B. Mullen cited newspaper reports about the gold, going back decades, no reason had been offered for the *Charity*'s owner, albeit a millionaire, cruising the coast with a chest of gold on board. He was not a merchant adventurer returning from a business trip, nor was he a pirate. Gower had dismissed the gold along with the plughole.

He moved the *Fleur* on to the pencilled cross. *Go on, then*, he thought. *Let's see the giant plughole effect.*

Nothing happened, except that a gull perched momentarily on his guardrail. Gower went below and emerged with fishing tackle. This was also a hangover from his sailing days and had seldom been used since.

Within the hour he had caught three fish, nothing spectacular but good enough to support the cover of a fishing trip. He cast the line again and went down to the cabin.

The radio told him nothing that the sky had not already explained. The wind was to be heavier than the early forecasts had predicted and there were to be showers. *If I'm lucky, I'll only catch the edge of a squall. I don't want one, I want cloud. Plenty of cloud.*

On deck he saw how the wind was veering. A bank of grey, oblique streaks linking sea and sky showed him distant rainfall, and the new direction of the wind was bringing it closer. As the first drops spattered on the cabin roof, Gower went below to pull on waterproofs.

He had to choose between riding out the squall or sailing ahead of it and waiting for the wind to veer again. He let out the mainsail and the *Fleur* ran before the storm.

She showed him then what she could do in a race. Gleefully, he forced her on, demanding more and more. She never refused him. At length he swung her round to beat down the wind. He laughed off the raindrops stinging skin, making rivulets on waterproofs. A shower, that was what the forecasters had predicted. They had been wrong about the strength of the wind, but perhaps they would be accurate about the shower. If not, he was in trouble. If steady rainfall set in, Gerrard might chicken out. Gerrard was a weak link looking for an excuse to snap.

The shower blew away to the north-east. Sky lightened. *That's right. Nice and dry, but keep the cloud cover. Please keep the cloud cover.*

He reefed the mainsail and dawdled back towards the *Charity*. Sea air had given him an appetite that the rest of his rations could not satisfy. He ate slowly, picking up crumbs from the wrappers with a moistened fingertip. He had nothing to do but wait. There was plenty to think about but he preferred not to think about it. Unless Gerrard failed to keep the rendezvous, there was no going back on anything.

For April, the day was fading early. Gower stripped off clammy waterproofs and tidied his own possessions into his grey canvas bag. Whenever the moment came, he would be ready.

Reaching the *Charity*, he reefed again and let the boat drift leeward, curbed by the drag of the anchor. Seas had reduced to a comfortable swell. And that was that. He had to hang around like this for two hours more. He yawned and went below, bored by the compulsory inactivity, but it was a major part of the plan that he should be noticed at the site of the wreck. Tedious it might be, but the delay was indispensable.

He dozed off, waking in panic and guilt. Single-handed sailors were meant to keep a watch at all times, otherwise they might drift on to rocks or into shipping lanes. Single-handed sailors were acting illegally if they indulged in anything other than day sailing, but there was no legislating for fools who nodded off in the afternoon!

He banged his head against a locker in the scramble to get on deck and check whether he had drifted into trouble. But before he surfaced, he knew instinctively that something was wrong.

The sounds had changed. The familiar swish of the water and the creak of the boat were different. A dozen horrors came to mind in the seconds it took him to stumble from the bunk to the deck. Shallow water? A cliff beside him? Not a tanker, he would have heard the noise of its engines if it had been that. Whatever it was had not overlain the usual sounds with other noise, it had subtly altered them.

Gower staggered to the guardrail, with a wail of despair. *Fog!* It was not thick, it was not bad – *yet*. But he could not see the shore, could not be positive where that was or where he was. He listened hard but there was no approaching engine. Unlikely for him to have wandered as far as the shipping lanes, because the wind had dropped, but might not shipping be off course because of the fog? A light shroud of it here could mean impenetrable patches elsewhere.

According to his wrist-watch, he had slept for a little longer than half an hour. Comforted that it was no worse, he began calculating where he might be. As his head cleared and panic subsided, he worked rapidly with chart and compass until he was virtually confident that he knew where he was and where he ought to go. He took the *Fleur* back to what he hoped was the pencilled mark.

There was a snag. Unfamiliar with her compass, he had no way of knowing its margin of error. The compass had not been discussed when he was sailing with Rob three days earlier. Suddenly he pictured Rob, distraught on the pier at Mousehole, pacing about, never taking his eyes off the harbour mouth and praying for the *Fleur* to come into sight. Gower knew that whatever else the outcome, this afternoon's escapade had destroyed his friendship with Rob Watson.

I'll make it up to Rob, he thought, assuaging remorse. *I'll think of something*.

And then he heard an engine. He pulled the *Fleur* away from the noise and minutes later watched the silhouette of a fishing smack ride by. Alert for other dangers, he hovered around the *Charity* convincing himself the fog was lifting. Eventually it was true. The shore appeared to him as a blue-grey smudge, all colours stolen from the countryside as evening came on. He was close to the pencilled mark. The position of the Lizard lighthouse in relation to buildings above Bass Point promised him that.

Gower gasped his relief, admitting only at this stage how disturbing the uncertainty had been. With the shore in sight and the light too dim for anyone on land to see him in detail, he was happy. His eyes swung from Bass Point northwards, along the shoreline where the harbour lay. In that direction there was lingering mist, enough to scare the wits out of David Gerrard. Philosophically, he accepted that Gerrard would be late.

But not very late, please. There's a lot to do, a long way to go.

When the man was forty minutes late, Gower grew fractious. The coast up to Cadgwith was as clear as any other, yet Gerrard did not come. Gower had to start deciding what to do if darkness fell and the weak link had broken.

He gauged how far he could get, whether he could find a safe berth somewhere up the Helford River, among the wooded creeks and secret crannies, or whether he should chance anchoring in a cove near the Lizard. The maps offered countless possibilities, although picking one at random was hazardous. The boat might be damaged, he might have difficulty swimming ashore.

When he next glanced up, he spotted a small dark boat tossing about, to the north. Instantly he was on his feet, grabbing binoculars and focusing with trembling hands. He could not identify the man at the wheel but the motor launch was heading from Cadgwith towards him. 'Come on, David,' he shouted. 'Come on.'

And on it came, the dark boat expressing with every zig and every zag that it was in the hands of an incompetent. Gower began to laugh, and could not stop laughing. Gerrard's crassness suddenly seemed the funniest thing in the world.

He sobered as the motor launch drew nearer. The solid figure at the wheel was presumably Gerrard, but whatever was he wearing? Could he conceivably have bought those vivid waterproofs purely for this trip? They made him look enormous.

Gower stopped laughing as the boat shot past him, at speed, a hundred feet away. 'Hey, David!' Surely it *was* Gerrard, and surely Gerrard had seen him? The unthinkable had become reality.

Gower gathered his wits. *He can't stop the boat. Now what? If he can't slow it down, what am I supposed to do?*

The launch looped round and came back towards him.

Gower's knuckles whitened on the guardrail. *If he can't control the speed, he might smash into the* Fleur *while attempting to get alongside.*

One mistake would be calamity. Sweat beaded his forehead. He shut his eyes and prayed. When he peeped, Gerrard was close, very close. But the engine's tone had changed. Then it stopped altogether.

Gerrard was ashen. 'This thing's a maniac,' he shouted, dispensing with any other greeting. 'They've hired me a maniac.'

'It'll do,' said Gower, limp after the swing of emotions, glad only that Gerrard was there with a boat, regardless of how treacherous the boat might prove. During the next quarter of an hour he thought they were both going to die.

Gerrard explained why he had shot by, reminding Gower that he had been instructed to keep the *Fleur* between the launch and the shore when he came alongside. Gower said that it had been mystifying but that Gerrard had done the right thing.

Gerrard said: 'I ought to get nearer.'

'No, no,' said Gower rapidly, afraid that if Gerrard started the engine he might career straight through the hull of the yacht. He contrived to get the *Fleur* close to the launch.

'Can you catch this?' Gower held up his canvas bag. 'It's heavy, mind.'

Gerrard adopted the stance of a man about to catch something heavy. Gower threw. The bag hit Gerrard square in the chest and he was knocked off balance, yelping and snatching at a rail. The bag landed heavily on his foot. Only the force with which he kicked it aside revealed his annoyance.

Anger turned to disgust as Gower passed over six dead fish and the line. Gower said: 'Don't turn your nose up, David, you were supposed to have gone fishing, remember? Well, here's your catch.'

Gerrard took the fish. 'Now you, presumably. But just watch where you land, will you, please?'

'Hold on,' said Gower, not bothering to mention that he

was not a long-distance jumper. He threw Gerrard a line. 'Tie that on to that.' He avoided terms Gerrard would not understand and he pointed.

Gerrard tied. Gower gave the knot an untrusting glance.

Gerrard looked up. 'Don't tell me, John, you're going to walk the tightrope.'

Heaving on the rope, Gower could not answer him. He drew the boats closer, until even Gerrard could appreciate the purpose of the line. Then Gower said: 'Grab the guardrail while I come across.'

Gerrard did not enjoy the way the boats scuffed against each other. Gower told him: 'Don't worry, that's what fenders are for.' Gerrard was puzzled and Gower used a hand to indicate the fenders. Then he got into the motor launch.

'Right,' he said. 'Off we go then.' He untied the rope between the boats and drew it into the launch.

'Er . . . yes.' Gerrard tried to restart the engine.

'Shall I?' But Gower could not get it going either.

'This,' said Gerrard with ill-suppressed fury, 'is why I was late. You may have noticed that I was late.'

'Quite.' Gower kept trying the engine.

Gerrard was telling him how it had taken ages to get the thing going before he could leave Cadgwith and how he had finally accepted help from the owner of another boat.

Gower came on deck and watched the widening space between the *Fleur* and the launch. Six feet? There was a current running. The launch was drifting with no means of control. He said calmly: 'What did he do?'

'Got a spanner, shoved me out of the way and attacked the engine in private.'

'Where's the spanner now?' Gower asked.

Eight feet? And the *Fleur* was wheeling away.

Gerrard said: 'It was his. He took it away again.'

Gower bit a lip. He determined to conceal the realities of the situation as long as possible. He said: 'Could you look for one, David. You should find a tool kit somewhere.' He suggested places to search.

With Gerrard in the cabin, Gower snatched up a rope with a grappling hook on the end and swung it at the yacht. It grieved him to hear the clunk as it smashed on to her pristine side, scarring her.

Below, Gerrard sensed something afoot. 'What's going on up there?'

'Nothing. Everything's fine. Just find those tools, will you?' He gathered in the rope, coiled it swiftly, started to swing again.

Twelve feet? And she was still turning away, making herself a smaller target.

Suddenly Gerrard was behind him, head popping out of the cabin like a rabbit from a hole. Gerrard said: 'John, what the hell are you doing?'

'Stay there, *please*.' He was swinging the rope.

Gerrard emerged on deck, bumping against Gower precisely when he released the rope. Gower swore. Gerrard said: 'John, I wish you'd tell me what's – '

The truth hit Gerrard with the impact of a tidal wave. 'Christ! We're drifting, aren't we? That's what all this is about.'

Gower reined in his anger. 'Get that spanner,' he snapped. 'And stay out of my way.' He was recovering the rope, pulling the grappling hook on board.

Fourteen feet? An impossible distance?

Gerrard's voice cracked. 'But that's miles, you'll never do it.'

'It's about twenty feet, and it was a lot less when you interrupted my throw.' That was a wicked overestimate, a lie, but he could not resist it. It neatly plonked the blame for future disaster on Gerrard's shoulders instead of his own.

Unfortunately it also gave Gerrard an exaggerated idea of the speed with which they were drifting. He made a noise that was half whimper, half recrimination. But at least he ran back below and rooted about for a spanner.

For the third time the hook was in the air. Gower clenched his fists, waiting in a state of trembling apprehension as the hook flew, the rope flowed out, the hook achieved the apex of its flight, and it dived and dived and the rope curved after it. And all the while the target ducked and bobbed and tried to avoid the hook.

Please, oh please, let her catch this time. This very last time. There can't be another, and if . . .

The hook snagged on the guardrail of the *Fleur*. Not good, could have been better, but it would have to do. Cautiously, oh so very cautiously, Gower hauled the rope in.

When he was sure it was succeeding, that the hook was not going to slide free, he chanced calling out to Gerrard. 'OK, that's done.' He marvelled at the calm control of his voice, the impression there had never been any doubt that he could reach the yacht and save them from a night adrift.

Gerrard popped out of the rabbit hole again. His face was pink and puffy. Gower saw he had been near to tears. The man had been nervous even thinking about boats and nothing had gone right. Gower said: 'See? I'm taking us back to the *Fleur*. Then you're going to hold the boats again while I board her and get the *Fleur*'s tool kit.'

Gerrard stood rigid beside him. He strained for his languid manner. 'Well, make sure you don't drop that on top of me as well, would you, skipper?'

With the boats alongside, Gower heaved himself on board the yacht and anchored the grappling hook more securely. He told Gerrard where to tie a rope to keep the boats close. This was occupational therapy for the man, rather than practicality. Gower doubted Gerrard's knots would amount to much.

While Gerrard was tying, Gower ransacked the *Fleur* for things that might prove essential if the launch broke down or otherwise misbehaved on the return journey. He tossed over to Gerrard some flares and waterproof clothing and he told him to be ready for the tool box. Gerrard stowed away the flares and clothing and took the tool box.

'What now?' he asked.

'Now me. But don't touch anything, David, the boats can stay tied until the engine is fixed.'

'Yes, all right,' said Gerrard irritably. He leaned back out of Gower's way. There was hardly room to do this and with his vivid waterproofs on he appeared bulkier than ever.

After a few minutes Gerrard asked whether there was anything he could do to help.

'Certainly,' said Gower, struggling with a spanner. 'You can keep watch. Make sure we aren't about to be run down by the QE2.'

Icily Gerrard said: 'I don't believe she comes this way.'

Gower supposed that later on they would have an argument about whose fault it was that Gerrard had been palmed off with an ill-equipped craft with an unreliable engine. The arguments always came later. His and Rob Watson's had never happened actually aboard the *Jumble*. At sea there were always more pressing things to do, like avoiding certain death.

He wrenched at several loose things that ought not to have been, then he tried the engine again. She started. Gower gave a whoop of pleasure and turned in time to catch Gerrard wincing.

When the engine had been running for a while and Gower had fiddled some more and was reasonably content with it, Gerrard said: 'It's remarkable, isn't it, that one needs no licence or insurance to take one of these things on to the high seas but one does apparently require a degree in engineering?'

'David,' said Gower, wiping oil from his hands and replacing the spanner in the yacht's tool box, 'we're going to have to amend the plan.'

'Quite honestly, I don't give much for my chances of getting back to Cadgwith after we've dropped you off at whatever cove it was that you chose.'

'No. It's too dark, apart from anything else. Two journeys are out of the question.'

Gerrard wore the expression of a man reprieved. Gower went on: 'Also the wind's getting up.' As if in response, a wave buffeted the boats. There was a ruthless grinding as they rubbed against each other.

Gower said he was going aboard the *Fleur* again, to release the rope with the grappling hook. Pained, Gerrard asked whether they could not undo it at the launch end and leave it.

'No,' Gower explained. 'It would be as good as putting an announcement in the local paper to say that a boat came alongside and took me off. In fact, it would mean everything we've done so far was useless. Besides, we might need the rope again.'

He boarded the yacht, undid the rope, coiled it and delivered rope and hook to the launch. The swell was increasing, the boats colliding more vigorously. He was glad to get back into the launch.

Gerrard had seized a grabrail with both hands. Gower said: 'Right, let's go. I'll untie the other rope and you can steer.' But he saw Gerrard's lips vanish into a thin line. Gower said: 'Or you could undo the rope, if you prefer, David.'

'Yes. I'll do the rope.'

Gower positioned himself by the wheel. Space was scarce, he wished he had done the rope himself and then taken the wheel but there was a problem about where he put a man of Gerrard's size while he scampered from one position to another. Gower kept the engine idling, ready to move off the second Gerrard called that the rope was free.

Gerrard called that he could not get it undone. Gower opened his mouth to say: 'Tug it.' But before the words were out he knew that would be exactly the wrong thing to say. It was not one of his own knots, it was one of Gerrard's and heaven knew what they were like. Instead, Gower said: 'All right, I'll come. But take hold of this, and if the *Fleur* moves any closer, fend her off with it.'

He saw Gerrard lift the pole, consider which end he should use to shove the yacht. Then Gower inspected the knot. Wet, it had tightened. *A waste of time playing with this*, he thought, and went for a knife to cut it through.

As he sliced the rope, squatting over it, the swell increased but instead of dying back it became a foaming wave that lifted the launch high in the water and then dropped her. Gower's hand reached automatically for a rail. Looking up he saw the mast of the *Fleur*, then the whole yacht tilting above him. The knife spun across the deck as he flung himself full-length to snatch the wheel, frantic to wrench the launch away and prevent her being capsized by the falling yacht.

It took him a full five seconds to register that David Gerrard was overboard.

The pole with which Gerrard had been fending off was like an outsize straw, and Gerrard was clutching it. His mouth was wide in a soundless scream. Water slapped him in the face. A wave obscured him from view. Gower next saw him two yards away.

He remembered the drill without effort: *'Keep your eye on the casualty. Never let him out of your sight.'* But how did you keep him in sight while simultaneously searching an unfamiliar craft for a life belt? And anyway, Gerrard had overtaken the launch, it was not a case of turning back for a man overboard.

Gower chased after him, glimpsing him each time he rose with the swell. Gerrard was afloat but for how long? The water was not warm, how soon would his fingers slacken on the pole? Gower found himself doing a ridiculous sum to calculate the chances of Gerrard's weight being sufficient to let him drag the pole down to the seabed with him.

He got a little ahead of Gerrard, then, conscious that the man might be thrown against the propeller and mutilated, he switched off the engine. He prayed that Gerrard would fetch up against the boat, that nothing else would go awry. Gower had nothing buoyant to throw him, he had seen no life belts on board and had no time to seek one.

Shouting encouragement, he leaned over the side of the launch, a foot securely lodged. Gerrard gaped at him wild-eyed, grotesque, a great man bouncing helplessly through the water in his jolly orange waterproofs, bouffant blond hair slicked to his skull and his fat hands wrapped around a pole.

'Keep hold of the pole,' Gower yelled, fearful that there was no chance for Gerrard if he released it in the hope of a grip on the boat's smooth sides.

Gower lobbed a line over the side, watching the water carry it ahead of Gerrard. If Gower's first manoeuvre failed, there would be a second opportunity with that line.

Gerrard did not fetch up precisely as intended beside the boat. He clouted it with the end of the pole and spun past. Gower leaned overboard further than he would have dared under any other circumstanaces. He reached and he got a hand to the pole. 'Don't let go,' he shouted. 'It's going to be all right, David. We're nearly there.' Again that calm, confidence-inspiring voice that astounded him.

He tugged the pole with Gerrard clamped to it. 'All right,' he said. 'I'm going to get you aboard. But first I'm going to put a line around you.'

Gerrard's eyes had closed. He was not responding. With practised movements Gower made a noose and then dropped this over Gerrard. It hung loosely around his upper body.

Now for the really tricky part, he thought. *I've got to persuade him to put his arms through the loop.*

He yelled at Gerrard to open his eyes if he could hear. There was so much other noise, of wind and water. Gerrard's eyes opened. Gower said at full volume: 'Take your hands off the pole one at a time and slip your arms through the rope. Then put your hands straight back on the pole.'

No reaction. Gower shouted again. There was no time to cajole, he needed instant obedience and Gerrard was not providing it. He tried another approach. 'I'll tighten the rope over your arms. Then I'm going to bring you in.'

The end of the rope was attached to the launch, preventing Gerrard escaping, although the longer he remained in the water the more dangerous it was. And if the pole became an impediment to his rescue, Gower doubted Gerrard would be capable of releasing it. Everything might finally depend on the rope around his upper body but if Gower had to haul him aboard by that, he had to trust it not to travel up until all that was within the noose was David Gerrard's head.

Gower reached for the pole once more, brought Gerrard right up to the launch. He had one final instruction before he began to lift. 'David, don't struggle. If we're both in the water, no one is going to get home.'

With more strength than he knew he possessed, John Gower hoisted David Gerrard aboard the launch. Gerrard was still wedded to the pole.

Leaving Gerrard a huddled orange mass on the deck, Gower restarted the engine. They had drifted south. He raced for the shore, to the west of Lizard Point, cancelling earlier schemes and making for Mullion because, although it was not an easy harbour, it was one he knew.

The seas were heavier now. The sort of wave that had caused their disaster was no longer a rarity. He gave the engine full throttle.

They ought to have been discussing the change of plan but of course discussion was out of the question with Gerrard half-dead on the deck and light dwindling. Once, looking back to check that Gerrard was more or less recovering, he spared a glance for the *Fleur*. The seas made it impossible to see her.

Gower was getting worried about Mullion. *Too far*, he thought. *Settle for somewhere nearer. Anything with a quiet anchorage*.

The sheer cliffs of Kynance loomed to starboard, the craggy coast where quarry owners once transported granite and soapstone, and where the present-day traffic was tourists.

Mullion's too far. But it's a harbour I know. Yes, but it's a difficult one and I haven't been there for years and this isn't the weather for discovering how much I've forgotten. But . . . get in somewhere, anywhere!

He took the launch right inshore, fought his way into a perilously unwelcoming creek, found the remains of a harbour, tossed a line around a stanchion and jumped ashore. Gerrard sat up as Gower secured the launch with ropes at each end.

'Land,' croaked Gerrard in unintentional parody of ship-wrecked sailors everywhere. 'Is this really land?'

'Real land,' confirmed Gower. 'Not heaven. I expect heaven will be cleaner.'

The remark was a comment on the odour of old fish heads and sewer outfall. Gerrard could not have cared less what the place stank of. He staggered to his feet, subsided, succeeded at the second attempt. Gower asked how he felt.

'I believe the phrase is as well as can be expected.'

Gower's inquiry was not mere politeness. People who fall into the sea and suffer as Gerrard had should be taken to hospital for observation.

He could still die, thought Gower. *He could have sea water in his lungs. He must have, I saw his mouth open, the waves smashing into his face.*

He knew what happened to those people. Their bodies pumped their own water into the lungs to dilute the salt water, and the lungs consequently filled with water and drowned the victims. It could occur as late as twenty-four hours after an accident. Gower knew all this. Gerrard did not, and Gower did not tell him.

He only asked whether Gerrard wanted to get to a hospital. Gerrard was put out. 'Certainly not. I have no wish to end up as an accident report in a country hospital log book. What I require, John, is dry clothing and an extremely large brandy. Preferably Courvoisier.'

They were talking with Gower crouching on the quay and Gerrard standing, with wobbly legs, on the deck. Gerrard began to strip off his orange outer casing.

Gower told him: 'I shouldn't do that. The warmer you are, the better.'

'What on earth makes you think I am in the least warm? No, John, I can do without the high profile clothing, if you don't mind.' He shed an acreage of orange stuff.

Gower's jaw dropped. 'Is that a life jacket?'

Gerrard tapped the bulging thing he had strapped beneath the waterproofs. 'To be pedantic, I believe it's a mere buoyancy aid. I understand that's not quite as wonderful as a life jacket but it's what the shop sold me. It did rather well, I think.'

Ruefully Gower agreed that it certainly had. Gerrard went

on: 'I was promised it would keep the head out of the water. Although at the moment when I suspected my skull was about to be pulped between the hull of the yacht and the hull of this frightful launch, I would have given anything to have dropped out of danger.'

He fumbled with the garment, then added: 'Be a good chap and help me get this off. I feel the size of half a house.'

Gower made a mental note that if ever he organized another boat trip he would demand a rundown of what his companion was wearing. If anyone fell overboard in future he would prefer to know whether to bother searching for something buoyant to throw to him, and he would want a clue about how long he had to drag him out.

Gerrard pushed the waterproofs and the buoyancy aid into the cabin and took the hand Gower offered to pull him ashore. Then Gower jumped down and collected his canvas bag and the things from the *Fleur*.

The plot, outlined to David Gerrard on the chalky slopes of Figsbury Rings, was that Gerrard would set Gower ashore along the coast and return the launch to Cadgwith where he had hired it for a week, allegedly for fishing. Gower was to stay concealed until Gerrard drove to collect him. Then Gerrard was to take him to a hideout before making his own way home to London.

Gerrard's ducking had changed things utterly. He was no longer able to fulfil his role. They trudged up the steep track to the open downs above and stopped in the shelter of a wall not far from a farm.

'I'll have to telephone for a taxi,' Gerrard said. He checked his pockets for his car key, grateful it had not been lost while he was in the water. His body was wracked with tremors.

Gower scrutinized him in the growing darkness. If Gerrard was to fall victim to secondary drowning, he would become apathetic first, turn a hideous colour. Gower had not a hope of monitoring his colour in this light, but Gerrard was a long way from apathy.

'You'll have to give the taxi driver an excuse for being wet,' Gower said. 'He won't be keen to take you in that condition.'

'I'm not keen on it myself, but where's the alternative?'

There was a break while they tried to think of another way. Then Gerrard stood up. 'Frankly, I would prefer to endure the snubs of country taxi drivers rather than die of rheumatism. Where's the telephone box?'

He was joking; there would not be one. Gower said: 'You've got a long walk. There's a bridle path that passes the airfield, then you reach a National Trust car park and pick up a metalled road. Follow that until you come to a telephone or a pub.'

Gerrard was flapping his arms about and stamping his feet. 'Where shall we meet?'

'I'll walk as far as the car park with you, then find somewhere to lie low.'

They set off, a silence of collusion settling over them, broken finally as they voiced doubts. Supposing the telephone box was out of order. Supposing the pub was shut. It could be one of those seasonal ones that crop up around the coast in holiday areas that do not provide trade out of season. Supposing the taxi would not come. Supposing the driver would not deliver Gerrard to Cadgwith and his car. Supposing that at Cadgwith Gerrard met the man who had hired him the launch. Supposing this and supposing that.

They stumbled on, tripping over rocks that thrust through the muddy path and clutched by gorse and bramble. At last they reached the car park. Ahead lights flared from windows of two farms that stood sentinel at the end of the track. Gower said: 'I'm not coming any further. I'll wait by this hedge. When you come back, flash your lights. Otherwise I won't be sure it's you.'

'Three times?' Gerrard made a futile effort to comb his hair and make himself presentable.

'Bursts of three.'

Gerrard nodded. He began to walk. After a few paces, he looked back. 'I'll be as fast as I can.'

Gower raised a hand in farewell. He rested against the hedge and stared after Gerrard, the man shrinking into nothingness as he moved towards the farms. Then there was stillness, except for a pale moth exploring the air round the hedge, and the anger of the sea below the cliffs.

Soon there was nothing to look at but all the colours of darkness. Gower tried not to concentrate on the sluggish passage of time. He concentrated instead on Richard Crane.

Crane, he felt, would have handled the day's alarums with more aplomb than he had himself. In fact, Crane's scheming would have been impeccable and the disasters would not have occurred. His hero's face swam into Gower's imagination easily. It was similar to the face of the young man he had stared at in the London hotel the previous week. Similar, but with a tinge more arrogance. Richard Crane was dressed in the same expensive, casual clothes, he was fair-haired and his habitual expression was determination. Crane was not a man at the whim of Fate, nor one to rely on bunglers like David Gerrard. Richard Crane was resolved to conduct his life to his own advantage. John Gower held him in admiration.

He was entranced by the adventures of Crane, part day-dream and part preparation for his novel, when headlights swayed to the end of the road. They blinked three times.

Gower was on his feet and moving after the first flash. Out of the shadow of the hedge, down the track, into the car park and away. Rescue. Escape. The end of one life and the start of another. He was light-headed with exhilaration.

The car door was open. Gower stowed his bag, and the tools and other things from the *Fleur*, in the back before sinking low in the passenger seat.

Gerrard snorted. 'Heavens, no one's going to see you.'

He had changed his clothes. Gone were the sea-soaked, smelly things. Gerrard wore flannels and a chunky sweater. Gower said: 'You've changed!'

Gerrard released the handbrake. 'Yes, John, I never trusted your promise that I wouldn't get wet. Boating has always struck me as a horribly wet pastime.'

Gower laughed. They both laughed. Gower thought: *He's fine. He won't collapse with water in the lungs. How could I ever have thought it? He's a survivor.*

Aloud he said: 'Pity you didn't pack a three-course meal for two in the boot. I'm ravenous.'

'There's a steak and kidney pie behind your seat.'

'Oh?' Gower groped behind. The pie was warm.

'All yours, I've eaten mine.' The lane ended and he drove into Mullion.

With deepening suspicion, Gower asked: 'Where did this come from?'

'A pub.'

Gower's temper rose. 'David, you know we said – '

'Yes, John, I know. But things changed radically, didn't they? And I needed food, we both did.'

'But if anyone in the pub remembers you . . .'

'They won't. I didn't stagger in there drenched in my seafaring clothes. I changed – in the car and with extreme discomfort, I may say – and then I strolled into the pub as cool as you please and asked for two hot pies.'

'But you weren't to go near anyone. You were to avoid human contact at all costs.'

'Not at the cost of my life, we never agreed that.'

'A steak and kidney pie is not a matter of life and death.'

'It was to me. Now eat up, there's a good chap. It'll get cold.'

Sulkily, Gower bit into the pie. Apart from the standard bit of gristle that every pie includes in the recipe, it was the best thing he had ever tasted. Gerrard, meanwhile, pushed home his point that he had been unable to avoid human contact with the taxi driver and that the damage, if any, had been done at that stage. And no, he had not seen the man who had hired him the boat.

Once they were clear of Mullion and on the Helston road, he said: 'I'm going to pull in.'

Gower shot him a look. *Is he ill, after all?*

Gerrard pulled in. 'Two things,' he said. 'First there's some lager.' He reached into a pocket on the side of the car and produced two cans.

'And?'

'And you can drive from here. After all, this is *your* adventure.'

He meant he was exhausted. 'Fine,' said Gower and got out to change places. Sitting in the driving seat, he pulled the ring on his can. He took a deliciously long slow drink.

'You know,' said Gerrard thoughtfully, 'I haven't thanked you for hauling me out.'

'Oooh, it was nothing.' Gower jokily brushed it off.

Gerrard said: 'I'm serious. One minute there I was, thrusting at the *Fleur* with that stick . . .'

'Pole.'

'Yes, pole. And suddenly she leapt away and I tumbled after her.'

Gower did not care to hear this. He wanted to start up the engine and race on as fast as they legally could. But Gerrard needed to say it. Gower understood that. Gerrard needed to say it and there would never be anyone else he could tell. Gower said: 'I guessed that was how it happened. I'm sorry. I should have warned you about tying yourself to the launch, or at least getting your foot anchored around something to prevent you overbalancing.'

Gerrard shook his head. 'No, it wasn't your fault, it was mine.'

'You mustn't blame yourself, you're a novice. Why should you have known what to do?'

Gerrard said: 'Will you shut up, John? I'm trying to thank you for saving my life.'

'Oh.'

'You were fantastic. You had me out of there in around thirty seconds.'

'Eh?' To Gower it had seemed nearer thirty minutes, although rationally neither could be true.

'Yes, I hardly had time to be alarmed.'

A wild laugh. 'Well *I* did. Acutely alarmed.'

'The worst part was seeing the *Fleur* coming down on me and thinking I was going to be flattened. After that I thought it was all pretty plain sailing, so to speak. The buoyancy aid and the stick were going to keep me afloat and you were going to scoop me out. Which you did, with admirable ease.'

Choking, swallowing more lager, Gower made a bid to change the subject. 'We ought to drink a toast.'

Gerrard accepted the topic was closed. 'What shall we drink to?'

They raised their cans. Gower said: 'To the death of John Gower.'

'No,' said Gerrard. 'To the money.'

They drank to the money.

7

Tuesday. Wet and windy. David Gerrard's morning taxi was throbbing in the street outside his flat. He washed down a couple of aspirin with tepid tea and hurried out.

'You don't look well,' his secretary said, taking in the wan face and the highspots of pink on his cheeks.

'Only a cold.' He urged himself to put a spring in his step, ignore the symptoms. 'Did anything interesting happen here yesterday?'

Hazel said not, switched on her caring voice. She often did that, pitying him for living alone, making it up to him by mothering. 'I'll put the coffee on. A hot drink will perk you up.'

Hazel was about thirty, she lived alone too but was not to be pitied for it and had no need of mothering. Gerrard occasionally wondered how it was that women managed so much better than men.

Once she was out of the room, and he heard the rush of water into a kettle, he gingerly raised both hands to his cheeks. Hot. Rather hot. Then he remembered that it was foreheads, fevered brows, that doctors felt. He did not like the implications of 'fevered brows', but he pressed a hand on his forehead. Definitely hot. Inwardly he groaned. What a time to fall sick!

'Won't be long,' promised Hazel coming back. She twined one long leg around the other and got on with her work.

Gerrard gave himself a silent talking to and picked up the telephone. *This will do it*, he thought. *One has to put on an act on the telephone. It's such artifice speaking to people out of a piece of wire that one automatically hams it up.*

There was a time when he would have been meticulous about putting on an act in Hazel's presence, but she had been with him a number of years now and he had let that slip. Out of the blue, waiting for his call to be answered, he remembered his mother's injunction: 'One must always keep up appearances in front of the servants. It brings them up to the mark.'

In the background the automatic kettle's hissing finished with an explosive *click*. Hazel unravelled her legs and rose.

A voice said down the wire: 'Good morning. *Daily Post*. Can I help you?'

'Rain Morgan, please.'

'Just putting you through.'

There was a hiatus, then Rain's voice along the wire.

'David Gerrard here, Rain.'

'David? You sound terrible. What's wrong?'

The act had failed in the first sniffly breath. He confessed to a cold. Rain immediately said they were to postpone their cuff link lunch planned for that day and she recommended whisky and a warm bed. Maddening how solicitous women were.

He said: 'I'm all right, honestly.'

'You don't sound it.'

'One has to bear up, you know.'

Rain said: 'If you're worried about the cuff link, it's absolutely safe. I've kept it close to my person, never let it out of my sight.'

He tried to say that it did not matter. She said: 'Oh but it does, it's not every day I'm entrusted with a diamond cuff link.'

'You weren't exactly entrusted, you wrenched it off me. But listen, I've got something for you.'

'The other cuff link?'

'Something for your column.'

She had been afraid all along he was going to say that. She said ironically: 'As long as it's not too big for me to handle.'

He did not notice her dig. He said, with studied casualness: 'This could make the front page, for all one knows. Just for now it's yours, if you want it.'

146

Rain took up her pen, pulled her notebook forward on the desk top. 'What is it?'

'I've lost an author. It looks as though something has happened to him.'

Hazel crept up beside him with a cup of coffee. She had given him the pretty mug, the one with the cowslip and the bee. She crept back to her desk where she delicately twisted her legs once more. And she as well as Rain Morgan heard him say he had called at Stream Cottage to visit John Gower on Sunday but found no sign of him. They both thought: *So what?* But then they became intrigued as Gerrard skilfully erected a mystery around the unavailability of a writer he described as a byword for reliability, in personal matters as well as in the quality of his novels.

Rain said: 'But what do you want me to do? I can't run a story saying "Reliable Author Goes Missing For Two Days Without Telling Agent". She was puzzled. His efforts to insinuate his authors into her column were generally superior to this.

Gerrard told her: 'I really do have a premonition about this one, Rain. Something odd is going on. If you hear anything, perhaps you'd call me?'

'Er, yes. But what am I likely to hear? "Author Comes Home After A Few Days' Holiday"?'

Gerrard frowned. 'I wish I could find it funny too, Rain, but I'm not happy about it at all. He's been pretty fed up lately. His wife has left him. He's broke . . .'

'I thought all your authors made a fortune. I distinctly remember you saying that once.'

He wished she would stop being flippant. He dragged a handkerchief out of his pocket and rubbed his forehead. If only he did not feel so wretched he would be handling the conversation more adroitly.

Rain reverted to the cuff link saying it would obviously be best if she were to send it round in a taxi to his office. Gerrard said there was no hurry. Then she remembered she would be passing that way later in the day. 'I'll drop it in,' she offered, and he attempted to sound pleased. When she finished the call she and Holly Chase had a good laugh about the whole thing, especially her unexpected escape from having lunch with Gerrard.

What they learned at the morning conference made it far less comical. Riley, the news editor, had added to his list of potential stories for the day the word 'boat'. He told colleagues: 'We've had a call from a stringer in the West Country. Apparently a fishing boat smashed into a small yacht in the fog last night. The yacht was lying where the *Charity* went down and the yachtsman hasn't been found, dead or alive. We'll rake out the *Charity* file and write a mystery story.'

Murmurs of interest assured him this was the correct course. His deputy arrived then, tiptoeing into the room and coming to rest against a filing cabinet as all chairs were taken. He said: 'The story went out on regional radio news programmes this morning and an insurance clerk from Mousehole now says it's his boat. He loaned it to a friend yesterday and only discovered what had become of it when the radio gave the name of the damaged boat.'

People asked whether the friend had been found. 'They're searching,' he said. 'But now they know who they're searching for. John Gower, the novelist.'

Rain went with Riley when the conference ended. She wanted to read exactly what information had come in about the incident. Riley said: 'You can't steal it, it's for news.'

She said she was not in a predatory mood but had promised information to David Gerrard. All she learned that had not been said in the conference was the name of the insurance clerk and his Mousehole address.

David Gerrard was shattered when she passed the news on. Through the thickness of his cold he gave a squeaky gasp and followed up with a number of half-sentences about the horrors of being run down at sea.

Rain attempted to soothe him. 'We don't know that John Gower was aboard at the time.'

Gerrard appeared to clutch at this hope, asking her rather sharply what made her think he had not been.

Rain said: 'I simply mean that we don't know either way. They are searching the area.'

'Oh my God, you mean aircraft and so forth?'

'Helicopters, I imagine. The fog was patchy during the night but it's clear now and they are out there looking.'

Gerrard snuffled. 'How could Hazel have survived such an accident?'

She sought a method, to spare Gerrard's anxiety while official hope for Gower lingered. 'A tender? He might have rowed away.'

Gerrard whimpered. 'How is one to know? The sea . . . the fog . . . Oh, I don't know, Rain, I would like to believe you but I feel . . . I told you I had a premonition.' He ended with a sniff.

She repeated her advice about the warm bed and the whisky and rang off.

David Gerrard writhed in his chair, thinking: *The* Fleur, *smashed up in the fog! It could have happened while we were out there. Or when I was on my own in the murderous craft with the haphazard engine.*

Another groan escaped him. Hazel said: 'You ought to be home in bed, David. You're not at all well.'

He rejected her concern with a wave of the hand, the hand was gripping the handkerchief he kept using to blot his face. 'A mere cold, Hazel. Don't fuss.'

'That looks more like flu to me. David, you must go home. You only had two appointments today, Rain's let you off one and I'll get on the phone and postpone the other.'

He could not think what was in his diary apart from the lunch Rain had all too easily given up. To be precise, he had looked at the page twice but failed to take in what it told him about his plans for the day. He pulled himself together. If Hazel only knew it, the shocking fate of the *Fleur* was upsetting him far more than his illness. He was burdened with a terrible knowledge and he needed to share it, but not with

Hazel. And how could he share it with anyone else while she was there?

An idea presented itself. He said suddenly: 'Rain said whisky and a warm bed.'

Hazel scrutinized him, afraid he was growing delirious. What was original about suggesting whisky and a warm bed? Yet Gerrard was offering up this titbit of conversation as he might a brilliant piece of repartee.

Hazel lifted her telephone. 'I'm scotching that meeting at Pegwoods this afternoon.' He knew that tone of voice, she had used it when she had been bossy about where they sited their Christmas tree.

Gerrard continued while she dialled: 'Would you like to pop out and fetch a bottle of whisky?'

'And a warm bed?'

A voice down the wire asked her: 'What was that?'

Gerrard went to the cloakroom during her call. He splashed cold water on his face, half expecting it to steam. In the mirror over the washbasin he saw a great red face, hair lank and eyes deadened. *Oh God, what a time to be ill!*

'Whisky,' he said as brightly as he knew how, walking back into the office. 'That will perk me up, as you'd put it. Be so good, Hazel, as to slope off to the shops and buy a bottle of whisky.'

He was sorting out cash from his wallet, and shooing her through the door while she inquired what type of whisky he preferred, and whether she ought not to bring a lemon too, and whether a powder from the chemist might not be the best thing. When the door shut behind her, he collapsed into his chair again.

He felt awful. He could not remember a time when he had felt so awful. And it was no time to be feeling like this. At the very minimum, he must succeed in disguising it on the telephone. He checked a number in his diary and then he rang John Gower.

He knew what he was going to say: 'I'm afraid disaster struck the *Fleur*, John. She was crumpled by a passing ship.

Your friend Watson's none too happy, but the good news is that the press are already on to the story of your disappearance near the *Charity*.'

The telephone was ringing out, and went on ringing. Gerrard redialled but it rang and rang again. 'Come on,' he begged. 'Hazel will be back with that damned whisky in a minute. I need to speak to you, John. For heaven's sake, pick up the telephone.'

But John Gower did not pick it up. Pettishly Gerrard slammed his receiver down and beat his fist on the desk. 'The fool. Who does he think is ringing him? After all I've done for him, he can't pick up the telephone when I call.'

Hazel returned with the whisky. He had no other opportunity to ring Gower before lunch. Fairly often Hazel ate sandwiches in the office but fortunately this day she was meeting a friend. Gerrard had dialled again before she reached the street. The ringing tone pealed out. His annoyance grew. Then Gower answered.

'John, why the hell haven't you been answering the telephone?'

'Did you ring earlier? I was out.'

'You were *what*?'

Gower laughed. 'Only in the garden. It's rather nice, isn't it?'

'I hope you weren't seen.'

'Of course not. There's a shed . . .'

'Several, I expect. Listen, John.' And then he got on to the news about the *Fleur*.

But Gower accepted it calmly, even swept it aside, saying: 'It'll be insured.' Then: 'A pity I shan't be allowed newspapers. I'd love to see how the story develops.'

'One can't have everything.' Gerrard would have sounded tart if he had not been muffled.

Gower noticed. 'Are you all right, David?'

'Wonderful, never been better.'

'I haven't forgotten you got wet.'

'Nor me. I'm tired, that's all. Nothing that a good night's – '

'I'll have the radio and television, though. Are they filming the search, do you know?'

Gerrard said he did not. 'I'll call you tomorrow.'

'All right. Just a minute, how will I know when it's you?'

'Nobody else is going to ring you, are they?'

'Wrong numbers? People who don't realize the owners are away?'

Gerrard said very well, they would have a code. He would let the telephone ring four times, then ring off and redial.

After that call he sat quietly thinking of the things he ought to be doing with regard to Gower and deciding they could be delayed without creating problems. Uncharacteristically, he was persuading himself to drop everything and go home. He poured himself another tot of whisky.

When Rain Morgan bounced through his door with nonsense about a cuff link, he had difficulty remembering what it was all about. Rain broke off. 'Good heavens, you look as bad as you sound. Hasn't Hazel tried to send you home?'

'Hazel dedicated herself to it. And I'm giving her best, Rain. I'm waiting for her to return from lunch and then I shall say goodbye and ask her to send for a taxi.'

Rain set the cuff link on the desk in front of him. 'Put that somewhere safe. Leave Hazel a note and come with me.'

He was obtuse. She said: 'My car's outside. If we can get to it before it's clamped, I'm taking you home. I'll be driving past your door, so I might as well. Come on.'

When he continued to stare stupidly, she wrote the note to Hazel herself, laid it on the secretary's desk and then ordered Gerrard into the street. He was still puzzling how he contrived to be surrounded by domineering women when he was in Rain's car again and heading for home.

'What about Pegwoods?' she asked, sliding her small car into what appeared to be an even smaller gap. 'How are they reacting to the disappearance of one of their authors?

Gerrard had not broken the news to the publisher. Rain said: 'I'll be ringing them this afternoon. You were right about the front page, David. We're running a brief news item and

I'm using the rest for my column. Extraordinary, isn't it? Until this happened we wouldn't have wanted to know about him, however accomplished his books. Now that he's, well, *interesting*, we're squabbling over which part of the paper he goes in. Here we are.' She double-parked and let him out.

David Gerrard emerged very carefully, because he wanted no more cuff links torn from his body by her over-enthusiastic seat belts and because of the pain in his head.

'Don't forget,' Rain said in parting. 'A warm bed.'

She did not refer to the whisky again. Gerrard had plainly absorbed that.

He said he would be fine in no time.

Somewhere in the country, John Gower was wondering whether David Gerrard would live.

The afternoon wore on slowly at the *Daily Post* office. Rain and Holly tossed up to decide which of them would attend a party neither of them fancied, and Rain lost. Rosie started tentatively to mention that she might leave her job but the telephone interrupted her. An estate agent was calling Holly to say a young couple had viewed the flat she liked in Hackney and he expected them to make an offer over the weekend.

'Don't believe him,' Rain warned her. 'They might not exist and if they do they might not be especially keen.'

'Cynic,' countered Holly. But she looked bothered and tried to contact Dan to discuss making an offer themselves. Dan could not be reached. He was on a mountain filming a rock climber.

The reporter writing the news story about Gower's disappearance discussed Rain's diary story, making sure overlaps were avoided. They traded: she let him have a line about Gower's wife having left him and the reporter handed her one about Pegwoods' reaction to losing an author. The man she had wanted to speak to at the publishers had been unavailable when she rang and the reporter had been luckier.

To the mystery of Gower's disappearance on Monday, and the mystery surrounding the *Charity* in the past, she added a witty paragraph about the mystery of David Gerrard's sixth sense.

Often, when evening events started early enough, she would work late and go directly from the office. The Dudleys' dog, though, did not like being left alone until late evening, and had pointed this out with displays of doggy bad humour. On that Tuesday, Rain drove from Fleet Street to Islington before the party.

Fred had entertained himself by chewing up the post, including a postcard from his owners. Rain could make out a 'wonderful', a 'marvellous' and a 'superb', the remnant of Marion Dudley's message.

Fred dashed around the back garden while Rain opened his can of brown sludge. *No wonder he couldn't resist eating the post*, she thought. *It looks altogether more delicious than this stuff.*

While Fred slurped over his bowl, she turned on the portable television the Dudleys kept in their kitchen. She was in time for the news, in particular the item about John Gower.

An agitated man called Robin Watson described how he had agreed to lend his yacht but Gower had arrived early and taken her without them meeting. 'I can't understand it,' he said. 'I know John wasn't familiar with the *Fleur*, he'd only been on her once, but he's a good sailor. I wouldn't have been lending him my boat otherwise.'

Out of shot, the interviewer asked whether Gower had ever shown an interest in the wreck of the *Charity*. The camera closed in on Watson's tense face.

'Not particularly,' he said. 'We'd talked about her in the past, in the way everybody does, but he always said the stories were rubbish. I mean the Great Plughole Theory. John scoffed at it.'

'He didn't tell you he was going to investigate her?'

'He hadn't mentioned her for years, and I don't see how he could have been investigating her.'

'Could he have taken your yacht so he could dive down to find her, and the treasure on board, the chest of gold?'

'No, no,' said Watson, getting more worked up. 'I'm sure he didn't do that, John isn't a diver.'

The interviewer put it to him that Gower might have learned to dive during the years when they had not seen each other, but Watson said that whether Gower had taken up diving or not, there was no evidence that he or anyone else had dived on Monday, and that the conditions had been wrong for diving after the wreck.

He said: 'I saw the *Fleur* this afternoon, she'd been towed in. There was no ladder and no line from her. If you're diving, you leave yourself a means of getting back on board, and there wasn't one. Also the waterproof clothes I keep on board are missing from their locker, and the tool box and some flares have gone.'

The interviewer thought of another question. 'But couldn't he have –'

'Look,' said Watson forcibly. 'You don't go diving in waterproofs, and you don't jump overboard taking flares and a tool kit with you.'

'So it's a mystery what's become of John Gower,' said the interviewer and the camera caught the edge of his microphone jabbing towards Watson's face.

'Yes,' said Watson, providing the only quote they had wanted from him all along. 'It's a complete mystery.'

BOOK TWO

Secret Lives

8

John Gower's heart leapt. Someone was walking up to Butlers.

He rose from the table and ran up the first flight of stairs to the half-landing where there was a window in the shadow of the thatch. He saw the garage, or apple store as it had been described to him, a conceit suggesting the pretty thatched outbuilding could be nothing as mundane as a garage. Then he looked the other way, along the curving yellow path. He could hear the grind of gravel beneath shoes.

A man in a Post Office jacket came striding up to the house, envelopes in hand. Gower pressed back against the wall as the man glanced up. He knew he could not be seen, that the diamond panes prevented it, but it was instinct to draw back. For the postman, or any other visitor, it was equally irresistible to look up admiringly at the well-cared-for thatched roof that had been finished with ornament so precise it looked like the hand-sewing of a giant.

In the five weeks he had been hiding at the house, John Gower had watched several people walk up to it. He sat on the middle stair of the next flight up and waited for the postman to go. Unless there was a recorded delivery letter for the owners, a man called Parsons and his wife, who were abroad, the postman would pause only long enough to push the mail through the cast-iron slit in the front door. Other callers had occasionally rung the doorbell and hovered, whiling away time expecting a response that was not forthcoming. Gower usually sat on the stairs until they went.

One day a woman had gone into the apple store and been out of his sight for five minutes, and he had never worked out what she had been doing in there. She had left the gate open too, these callers sometimes did that.

Gower preferred the gate shut. It was helpful to him if visitors were made to open it because it was noisy. There was clanking as the latch was raised. He had good reason to be grateful for that gate to the lane, as Jane Austen had been about her creaking door.

From his perch he heard the clatter of the letter box and the soft, echoing swish of an envelope landing inside the enclosed porch. Then through the window there was the back view of the uniform. Gower watched until the man and the path swerved out of sight.

He opened the door from the living room to the porch, a door rarely used because a side door into a lean-to off the kitchen made a more convenient access to the house. On grey stones lay a brown envelope overprinted with the name of the local council. Gower put it on a shelf in the broom cupboard beneath the stairs, along with all the other mail that had come in the previous five weeks.

He liked them out of sight, not teasing his curiosity. But it was impossible not to be curious about Butlers' owners. Parsons was another of Gerrard's authors but one on close terms, resulting in Gerrard being loaned the cottage as a country retreat while Parsons researched a book abroad for six months. In point of fact, Gerrard had never used it, not staying for as long as one night even after Gower moved in.

'You'll be completely private there,' Gerrard had promised when he had offered it as a hideout. 'It stands in a field, well back from the lane, and the nearest houses are concealed behind high hedges. I guarantee it will be perfect.'

Some things had been awkward at the beginning, such as avoiding electric lights to prevent neighbours spotting activity in an allegedly empty house, but he had quickly adapted. That first night, after Gerrard had driven on to London and left him to settle in, Gower could not tell to what degree Butlers was a children's story-book house oozing charm and picturesque features. Its setting, too, was ideally pretty. Waking in the low square bedroom he had been delighted to see the long humping outline of the Isle of Wight beyond the hedge and a few fields. The field in which the cottage stood was dotted with fruit trees – apple, pear and plum, mainly. Around them the grass was putting on a spurt because of warm damp weather. Gower wondered what arrangements the distant owners had made for it to be cut.

He tried to find out one time Gerrard telephoned him, but Gerrard had considered the matter trivial. Interrupting, he had said: 'John, Pegwoods are thoroughly excited about you. They're forcing copies of the new book on booksellers and the *Sunday Times* is to run an excerpt. Publicity has been everything one dreamed, and now Pegwoods are really capitalizing on it. They've done a deal for a paperback of your last one and that's to be hurried through.' He had bubbled on, the bearer of good tidings.

A shade wistful, Gower had said: 'I wish I could see what's being written.'

'No, you leave it to me. You get on with opus eight. Avarice, the spur of industry, John.'

Indignant, Gower interrupted.

The agent laughed: 'A quotation, John, merely a quotation. A perfectly sound one but, alas, clumsily employed. I apologize for the clumsiness. Perhaps you'd be happier if I'd suggested fame is the spur?'

'At least I'd have understood.'

'Very well. All I meant was you have every incentive to proceed with the next book, and none at all to fret about the publicity. After all, you saw the television with Rob Watson wringing his hands over the crippling of the *Fleur* and you heard your wife on the radio. One would have thought that was sufficient distraction for an author attempting to create a new novel.'

Gower missed the significance of Gerrard's remarks about his eighth book, he was busy thinking that Gerrard was having all the fun and he was doing all the work, and with no legitimate variation except radio and television. There weren't even decent books at Butlers. Parsons was a technical writer and his bookshelf showed it.

Gerrard said: 'Rain Morgan was terrific, did I tell you?'

Gower said he had, when he had telephoned the previous week. Gerrard said: 'I don't mean that, I mean she's been reading your books – well, let's face it, most of the journalists who've been writing about you haven't done that – and she ran another paragraph yesterday about *A Candle Lit*, drawing a parallel between an incident in that and the mystery of your own disappearance at the site of the *Charity* wreck.'

'Oh?' Gower sounded guarded.

Gerrard went on: 'She was making a lighthearted point about life imitating art. You know, the kind of profound statement one can rely on the gossip columns to provide.' He laughed, inviting Gower to laugh too.

Gower did not choose to pursue parallels between the book and real life. There were an uncomfortable number. He said: 'Were you quoted this time?'

He had been niggled at the way Gerrard's name had cropped up as frequently as his own in the coverage he had seen. This was unreasonable and he knew it, but it was an unavoidable resentment. Gerrard was not only having all the fun, he was getting a disproportionate degree of publicity too.

'Yes. Shall I tell you what she said?' The question was put in a rhetorical fashion. Clearly he was going to tell. He said: 'I said that – Oh, just a minute, John. Somebody's coming. I'd better ring you back.'

'How soon can you get some money?' Gower slotted in the question before the receiver went down at the other end. Whenever Gerrard telephoned Butlers, publicity and the publisher's plans took up most of his time, and although he was excited about the money in the pipeline, he had not yet received any. Gower wanted publicity and promotion turned into cash. But he had thrown in the question too late. There was an abrupt resumption of the dialling tone.

The next time the telephone had rung, with its pattern of four rings, a pause and another four, Gerrard had been cautionary. 'They are reliable people, John, they won't fool around. But you must see I can't hurry them up or they'll grow suspicious. You're supposed to be dead and dead writers have no urgent need of funds, and their publishers see no special reason to humour them by paying quickly. Anyway, it's barely a month since you vanished.'

Gower had replied that it felt far, far longer than that.

And now it was five weeks and the heap of mail was mounting on the shelf in Butlers' stair cupboard, the grass was growing in the orchard and the pile of typewritten sheets was rising beside the machine on the table in the living room. Gower shut the stair-cupboard door and sat down at the table. He read through the half-page of writing in the typewriter, found his thread and typed two more sentences. The Richard Crane book was coming smoothly, not so fast as to make him suspect it was facile and no good, but encouragingly well.

He nodded approvingly at the text on the half-completed page and he took up his black pen and scored through a line on a sheet of paper that lay beside the machine. This sheet, of handwritten words, was headed Chapter Three. Beneath that Gower had listed points he intended to cover in the chapter. Altogether he had scored through the first four, measuring Chapter Three's progress.

Gower rewarded himself with a cup of coffee, knowing that if the postman had not intruded he might have clattered on to deal with a further point by this time. One thing that always amused him was to hear non-writers describe with total confidence how, once a fiction writer had reached a certain stage in a story (they generally claimed fifty pages) the characters would 'take over'. He assumed that a professional had once said something like this, and that the idea had caught on. The appeal was obvious. How much easier to believe in magic than in the achingly hard work of creating a novel! And how wonderful his life would be if he could rest his fingers on the keyboard and let Richard Crane dictate the story to him!

In his experience it was sheer concentration on a character that allowed it to build until he knew the way it looked, talked, made love and whether it sliced the top off its breakfast egg or smashed it. Not that he would trouble his readers with all that knowledge. The selectivity, the paring away, was as important to the finished book as the building up had been.

Two elements of the novel came simultaneously. He could not, say, sketch a story line and then choose a character to be the protagonist. Nor could he invent a person, with detailed appearance, life style and foibles, and then cast around for a story to drop him into. When Gower wrote, there was a synthesis between character and plot that was achieved at snail pace and only then through total immersion in the project.

Before character and plot came theme. A fragment remembered from a conversation or broadcast programme, an item in the newspaper or an observation as he went about trivial daily occupations would lead him to look at modern living in a certain way. There was no blinding insight that he had found a theme for his next book. The realization would come gradually, as he found himself reconsidering matters from this new perspective.

In *A Candle Lit*, for example, he had examined independence and the point where it tumbled into selfishness, and the ill-effects of selfishness. Reviewers had called the book 'a story relevant to life in Britain in the eighties', because it was the Thatcher government's stance that people should look after themselves. Gower and his hero had explored what happened to a personality – and by extension to society – when a man took as his text for living the dictum: 'It is better to light one candle than curse the darkness.'

But the Richard Crane novel was coming faster than the earlier seven. Crane thrust himself into Gower's mind in the corners of the day that were not devoted to writing. Over coffee in the kitchen, Crane's face dominated his consciousness, to be superseded by Crane in a field, the back of his sweater as he walked away.

Gower opened his eyes and through the kitchen window saw late apple blossom, long green grass, and a vague path between trees where he walked in the evenings, taking chances that no inquisitive neighbour would trouble about him. As Gower studied the apple tree, he imagined he saw a fair-haired man, moving away. He blinked, discovered that the only actual movement was of grass and florets stirred by a breeze from the Solent.

The confusion of imagination and reality, fact and fiction, pleased him, proving as it did how credible Richard Crane was. If John Gower, the author, could be persuaded of Crane's existence when he knew every second of striving that had gone into his creation, how convincing Crane would be to the reader who met him for the first time on the page. Crane was all the company he had enjoyed for five weeks, except for the briefest of appearances by David Gerrard bearing food parcels.

Taking Gower to the cottage, Gerrard had handed him the door keys and shown him a food cupboard stocked with tins and a freezer full of mysterious frost-encrusted packages. 'Manage with this for a while,' he had said. 'I'll come down and replenish your supplies, but one can't possibly have you wandering about the village buying bread and milk and things.'

Gower had managed. Gerrard had appeared twice at Butlers, delivering a typewriter and paper, clothes and the promised food. Neither the typewriter nor the clothes were Gower's own, because everything he possessed had to be found either at Stream Cottage or else in his car parked near the harbour in Mousehole if an unintentional disappearance was to be at all plausible.

One of the entertaining aspects was that David Gerrard, flashy cuff links and all, had trawled through a branch of Marks and Spencer to buy Gower's new clothes. Gerrard had chucked the carrier bags across to him, saying: 'Don't ever make me do that again, John. One would have believed M and S the perfect place for a spot of incognito shopping, but the girl on the cash desk checked the size of every garment with me before she rang it up. And let me tell you, she had a *very* loud voice. A resting actress, one supposes. Goodness how she captured the audience's attention!'

'She could see they weren't going to fit you.'

'Quite. Eventually I said that it was perfectly all right, that the clothes were for a friend. And then I felt that demanded explanation and I said the friend was too ill to come shopping.'

'And?' Gower had been holding up a thin round-necked sweater with a diamond pattern.

'And a distinct *froideur* settled over the cash desk. I'll swear the queue behind me shuffled back a pace. Simply by the manner in which she accepted the cheque I wrote her, she convinced everyone you were suffering from Aids.'

Before that first visit to Butlers there had been a very worrying fugue. Gerrard had been ill for ten days, too ill to talk sensibly or put any of their plans into action. He had made croaking apologetic telephone calls, blaming his fever on the calamity of falling overboard from the motor launch. Gower had sympathized appropriately and told him not to fret, but he had been increasingly nervous himself. For several days he had been convinced Gerrard was going to die of secondary drowning.

He did not know enough about the condition to tell whether Gerrard's description matched the symptoms of this. Gerrard had stuck to their agreement to tell no one about his dipping, and even though his life could have depended on the truth being confided to his doctor, Gower had not advised him to tell it.

He had pushed the matter to the back of his mind. Richard Crane had been immensely helpful in encouraging him to do this. Gower had found it pleasanter to explore Crane's world than to ponder Gerrard's health.

On the afternoon of the day that the postman brought the letter from the council, Gower had a fright. Without the preamble of the noisy gate and the sound of shoes on gravel, he heard voices right by the house. He scuttled from the living room into the windowless lobby at the foot of the stairs and held his breath.

A young voice, a boy's, came again. 'I won't,' it said crossly. 'You wait there if you're not coming.'

Gentle scrabbling sounds came. Gower identified footsteps by the door into the lean-to. Another voice, an older child's, reached him from further away. 'Danny, *Danny*, you mustn't. Supposing . . .'

'It's all right,' said the first voice.' I told you, no one lives here. Mum was telling Dad, they've gone away.'

Kicks resounded against the outer door. 'Come on,' said the second voice, closer now.

The younger one wailed. 'Ow! Don't do that. Let me go.'

'Danny, come on.'

'Leave me alone. I only want to see.'

'You mustn't. I'll tell Mum.'

More wailing and a scuffle. Then the door to the lean-to sprang open and the pitch of the childish voices changed to alarm.

Danny yelped. The other voice whispered frantically: 'Look what you've done! What if somebody comes?'

Danny recovered his equilibrium. 'From Malta? Mum said they'd gone to Malta. Fancy going to Malta and leaving your back door open.'

Until the lean-to had been tacked on to the cottage, the door linking it to the kitchen had been the back door. There was a stout bolt on it. Gower was across the kitchen and easing the bolt noiselessly into place while the children were getting over the surprise of the latch on the lean-to responding to Danny's jiggling.

Gower stood inside the kitchen and heard Danny on the other side of the door. 'There's a fridge,' the child said.

'A freezer,' the older one corrected.

'And a toilet, with spiders' webs by the tank. Oooh, you could pull the handle and a great big spider could drop on you and – '

'Shut up!' snapped the other voice.

'Look, there's a great big one now.'

More scuffling and shrieks and then the older child's voice

came from the garden. 'I'm going home, Danny. I'm going to tell Mum you've been in Butlers.'

Danny countered. '*I'll* tell her whose idea it was to come into the garden.'

'The gate was open.'

Danny's feet padded outside. Gower heard the child bang the door shut. There was a pause then the older child's voice came from further off. '*Now* what are you doing?'

'I'm looking in.'

'Well mind the rose bush, you'll get scratched. Anyway, you can't see anything, you're too short.'

Feet scraped against the wall as Danny hoisted himself up by one of the living-room windows. 'Chairs, Susan,' he shouted in triumph, and dropped down.

'What do you expect in a house?'

More scraping. 'And a table with a typewriter on it, and a sideboard, and a hunting horn on the beam.'

Susan said: 'Mr Parsons is a writer, of course he'd have a typewriter.' She paused, then: 'I wonder why he didn't take it to Malta to write his book?'

When he was sure he could hear both pairs of feet chasing along the path, Gower went to the landing window and watched the children leave. Danny was about six with reddish hair, his sister two or three years older with paler hair streaming behind her, Danny and Susan, who knew that the house was not locked and that someone was using a typewriter in Butlers. His presence was no longer a secret shared only with David Gerrard. The children would report to their parents and their parents would broadcast it to the village: Butlers' owners were in Malta, but somebody else was in Butlers. How long before one of the villagers decided to investigate the children's story, and discovered him?

He toyed with the idea of taking the typewriter upstairs out of sight of prying visitors, but delayed, locking the door of the lean-to, bolting the kitchen door and returning to the more interesting world of Richard Crane.

By evening he had scored through two more lines on his list

of points to cover in Chapter Three. More than satisfied, he stopped for supper, put a pan of water on to boil for pasta and took from the fridge some sauce he had prepared and partly used a few days earlier. Then he looked out across the grass to where his passage had defined the path through the trees.

Evenings were light and hours must pass before he could risk going to check the gate. He sighed. He wanted very much to saunter openly through the trees, use the other gate that led from the back of Butlers' field to a public footpath running down to the pub. Occasionally, at weekends and on pleasant evenings, he heard cheerful voices from the path as people made that journey.

He wondered, for the hundredth time, what the pub was like, what it was called. If it had not been for the Ordnance Survey map in the sideboard drawer, he would not have known that the cream-coloured building he could see from his bedroom window was actually a pub.

He had come to know the map by heart. On the drive to Butlers he had been aware of flattish country and high hedges. The map showed him that the village, on the outskirts of the New Forest, was a straggle of houses without a centre, a place where it was feasible one rarely saw one's neighbours especially if, as in the case of Butlers, one's house was on the periphery. And unlike the other houses that cropped up spasmodically along the lane, Butlers was set right back in its field.

The map had confirmed that this was not usual, but Butlers was not a usual house. While its thatch and its thick walls and latticed windows gave it the appearance of antiquity, it was in reality a *cottage ornée* of the twentieth century, a rich man's indulgence. Butlers was a sham.

Until he had rummaged in the sideboard drawer one day and come upon the estate agent's details relating to the last sale of the property, Gower had been unable to pinpoint what was amiss. The truth was that Butlers was too good to be true. The leaded lights excluded every gasp of Solent breeze. The interior doors were solid dark oak with wooden latches that owed much to the arts and crafts movement. Everything was perfect and perfectly designed, a signal that Butlers was not what it seemed to be. It was, however, a charming lie, and Gower liked it very much. It was a house with secrets and an ideal place to conceal his own.

He opened the kitchen window a fraction to let steam escape as water reached the boil, and then he went upstairs, for the pleasure of seeing the island. Checking on its colours was one of the rituals he had invented to space the day. He flicked on the radio beside the bed and listened to the news while watching the island creep beneath a shadow. The previous day it had been grey, suggesting a shower was falling there, and it had stayed grey right through the news. The day before that, it had been patchily green and dun during the headlines but at the end of the bulletin sunshine had lit it gloriously.

The water boiled. He cooked the pasta, heated the sauce. Condensation rippled down the window pane and he dried it off with a cloth. Then he closed the window and removed the used pans from the cooker, setting them down out of sight to the left of the window.

The kitchen was too small for him to eat in there. He had to carry everything through to the living room and use the end of the table away from the typewriter and papers. Gower was in the kitchen with the bowl of pasta in one hand and a fork in the other when for the third time that day he discovered he was not alone.

Two strides took him into the lobby. He put the bowl on a stair and the fork into the bowl. Then he strained to hear where the sounds were coming from. But the temptation to look down on the intruder was irresistible. He moved up the lower staircase to the landing window.

His visitors were very near the house. Gower bobbed down, anticipating the man glancing up at the roof. The man was youngish with auburn hair. He had a clear, educated voice with no trace of local Hampshire accent. Trotting ahead of him was an overweight spaniel, and walking beside him was a small boy, pouting. Danny had returned, not with the Mum to whom he was to have been reported but with his father.

'Now then,' said his father as he went out of Gower's sight and close to the lean-to. 'We'll soon see, won't we?'

Gower heard attempts to open the door. The man's voice rose to him. 'Danny! It's locked. You can't have been in there. You were telling stories again.'

'No!' yelled Danny. 'It was open and I went in. Susan too.'

'Susan didn't say that, she said she stayed out here.'

'Well she's telling stories. She came in with me. We were in there. Try the door again. I had to try it and try it before it opened.'

His father tried again. 'No. Danny, it won't open. You made it all up, you know you did.'

'I didn't!' He began to sob. He ran towards the apple store, jumping about in anger and bawling.

His father mocked him, walking over to him and ruffling his hair. 'No good making all this fuss, Danny. The door's locked and it always was, ever since the people went away.'

Danny's noise reduced to a snivelling. His father looked about, asking: 'Where's Twiggy?' He called out: 'Twiggy, Twiggy,' and the spaniel flopped through the grass towards them. 'Come along, you two,' said the man. 'Time to go home.'

He turned to lead the way down the yellow drive. Danny stayed resentful on the spot. He scowled at the house, then the frown faded to perplexity and he rubbed tears from his face with balled fists.

His father called him. Danny was rooted. He said: 'There was a typewriter. I saw it.'

'Like you saw the door open and the freezer and the toilet and the spiders when you were inside the house?' He was ironical, not cross, and resigned to the fantasies of a six year old.

But Danny said: 'No, through the window.' He lunged towards the living-room window.

His father called him away, a shade sterner. Danny knew it.

He wheeled away from the window and ran up to his father saying: 'The man didn't take his typewriter to Malta. He left it in his house.'

'No,' said the father, shaking his head. 'You didn't see a typewriter. Mr Parsons uses a word processor, he told me himself.'

'But I saw it!' Danny was contorted with fury. 'On the table, in there.'

'You know, Danny,' said his father, dropping an affectionate hand on the little shoulder. 'I'm more inclined to believe Mr Parsons than I am to believe you.'

And because that was true, he did not bother to walk back up the drive and peep through the window with its clear view of the typewriter on the table.

Once they had gone, Gower moved the typewriter upstairs to one of the spare bedrooms.

Later on he telephoned Gerrard to report what had happened but in the space between dialling and his agent answering, he changed his mind. A powerful feeling came over him that he did not want to share every detail with Gerrard. Better to let Gerrard concentrate on doing deals and bringing in the money than fret about the insecurity of the hideout.

Gower did not have to explain why he had called, although it was the first time he had done so instead of waiting for Gerrard to ring him. Immediately Gerrard said: 'Hello, John, I was about to call you. Sixth sense or somesuch. Listen, the BBC have been on to me about Linda.'

'*Linda*?'

'Yes, apparently *Woman's Hour* is doing an item about missing people, and as they can't very well have those in the studio they are roping in the desperate relatives instead.'

'And is my wife desperate?' He was deliberately quizzical, although Linda's attitude concerned him deeply. As there had been no way of testing it, he had battled to keep his mind off her.

'One hardly knows,' said Gerrard. 'We'll both have to listen to *Woman's Hour* to find out. She's on tomorrow. You're all right for a radio, are you? Batteries haven't run out?'

'It's on the mains. Everything's fine. But about Linda . . .'

'Yes?'

'How did you know where she was?' Gower himself did not know, all he had was her sister's telephone number. The thought brought back the memory of his telephone conversation with her at her sister's the day he had been in London for lunch with Gerrard, the day he had attempted to persuade her to have dinner and maybe stay the night in the hotel with him, the day before he knew she had written saying she wanted a divorce.

Gerrard said: 'I wheedled the telephone number out of a journalist friend of mine who'd talked to Linda at the time you were front-page news. Today I rang Linda and asked whether she'd mind doing the *Woman's Hour* thing. As a matter of fact, she sounded flattered to be asked.'

Later Gower sifted through this conversation with Gerrard, wishing he had asked more. Gerrard's light manner sometimes made it hard to be certain of his meaning. But as for Linda's feelings, he could get a fair impression of those by tuning in to Radio Four at two p.m. next day. All he had to do, again, was wait.

Glad it was growing dark, he went into the orchard and strolled along his familiar route through the trees. He came up to the hedge that separated Butlers from the path leading to the pub. He opened the narrow gate and stepped out. He had not ventured this far before.

Behind him the path met the lane through the village, ahead it ran straight for roughly six hundred yards and then bent so that the continuation was out of his sight. It was quite wide, the part he could see, a green way rather than the type of path that obliges walkers to go in Indian file.

Gower was tempted to walk as far as the bend and had taken a few tentative paces when a low white bobbing thing appeared at the end of the straight. A dog. He dashed back through the gate and concealed himself among the trees. For a while he lingered until he heard dog and owners, talking in soft voices, go the distance of the path and turn into the lane.

When he was perfectly sure they had gone, he walked to the noisy front gate and found that Danny's father had tidily closed it. After that, Gower went indoors, spent another hour with Richard Crane and then slept. He was so happy with the progress on his book that he fell asleep thinking about it, rather than chewing over what the intrusion of the children might lead to and what his wife might reveal on the radio next day. Both were catastrophic.

'Linda Gower, your husband disappeared in mysterious circumstances five weeks ago. A yacht he'd borrowed was found near the wreck of the *Charity* but John has never been seen since he sailed out of Mousehole harbour the previous morning. His disappearance must have put you under a lot of strain. Could you tell me how you cope with this?'

Gower was sitting by the radio in his bedroom, looking across to the Isle of Wight. The island was a smear, it was an ill-lit day. He heard his wife's voice, coming brightly after the anchorwoman's sympathetic tones.

Yes, said Linda, she could tell. She had received tremendous support from her family, particularly her sister.

'It's not knowing what has happened to John that's so dreadful,' she said. 'I don't actually know what it is I'm being asked to cope with. When somebody close to you dies, you come to terms with it however painful that is because death is something we all understand and, eventually, expect. But when somebody vanishes, he's here one hour and gone without explanation the next, then it's different. You have a hope that he'll come back yet at the same time your intelligence is warning you that as time goes by the likelihood of him being alive diminishes.'

The sympathetic voice came in again: 'And have you any hope now, Linda, after five weeks, that your husband is still alive?'

Linda paused, a heartbreaking pause, before she said

uncertainly: 'I don't know, Jenni. If I say yes of course John's alive, he's had an accident and lost his memory but he's sure to be back, then a voice within me argues: "Don't be ridiculous, how can that be true, someone would have seen him by now, he must be dead." But, you see, if on the other hand I say: "No I've used up all my hope," then the same voice tells me I'm disloyal and it's my duty to go on hoping, that without proof of his death it isn't feasible for me to give up hope.'

'It must have been very distressing for you when people reported sightings of John in various parts of the country and these turned out to be false.'

'Yes it was. There was one report that he'd been spotted in France, suffering from amnesia. He was also noticed in Cumberland and in Norfolk. All untrue, as you say. It does raise my hope when this happens, especially if it comes at a time when that hope needs a boost. But I realized early on I had to be wary of such reports. The police get lots of them when anyone is missing.'

'Linda, the wreck of the *Charity* has a reputation for luring sailors to their deaths. What are your feelings about John taking his friend's yacht out to the site?'

'He isn't a superstitious man and I'm sure he was never impressed by those stories. Actually, I remember him laughing about the Great Plughole Theory when it came up in conversation once.'

'Would you . . . I'm sorry, go on.'

'I was going to say that nobody has ever been able to say precisely where the wreck lies, and John is not a diver. I'm sure he wouldn't have gone looking for her.'

'But that's where the yacht was found.'

'Yes. I'm afraid it's all part of a tragic mystery.'

And that was all the time allotted to Linda Gower. The anchorwoman brought in another guest who ran a support group for the families and friends of missing people. The guest commented on Linda's predicament and offered advice, some specific to Linda's case and some general. Then it was time for an item by a feminist botanist who had travelled up

175

the Amazon in a wheelchair, or that's what Gower understood the introduction to say. He switched off and went downstairs to pour coffee.

Hearing Linda had affected him deeply, he had anticipated that it would. But something had been wrong. He wished he had been able to record the interview, to pick it apart afterwards phrase by phrase, nuance by nuance.

Was it reasonable, he wondered, to expect her to be red-eyed and hand-wringing after five weeks of uncertainty about his fate? What Linda had not volunteered, nor been asked about, was her defection. She was not the little wife who had waited dutifully at home for the husband who never came, she was the one who had walked out. A month and a half before he left Stream Cottage, she had gone herself.

Gower was sorry he had not seen the newspaper stories about the search for him, because he did not know how she had dealt with questions about living at her sister's flat in London instead of at the marital home in Dorset. On television she had not been questioned about that, which was understandable as television compressed every story into a pellet of easily assimilated information and Linda had been on screen rather fewer seconds than Rob Watson. She had little information whereas luckless Rob had plenty.

The telephone rang out, making him jump and splash coffee. He counted. Four rings and it stopped. A gap. Another four rings. He lifted the receiver. 'David?'

'Yes,' said Gerrard. 'Did you hear the radio?'

'Yes.' Gower was trying to assess Gerrard's manner. Not the airy manner, nor the affectedly languid one, something other this time.

'Damn the woman!' said Gerrard.

'What? I thought she did all right.'

'*All right*?' Gerrard sounded like a pressure cooker in full steam.

'Well, er, what was wrong? She had opinions, she answered the questions fluently.'

'John,' said Gerrard in a voice heavy with non-existent

patience, 'how many times did she mention your books? Did either of those silly cows mention once that you are a writer?'

'Um . . .'

'No, they did not.'

'Well, I don't suppose it . . .'

'If the Director-General had handed down an edict that your books were not to be publicized, they could not have avoided them more assiduously.'

Not to be outdone, Gower roused a glimmer of indignation. But it was no use, he truly could not think like Gerrard.

His agent was saying: 'The new book is out in two weeks. Linda could have said so, she could have told millions of listeners it's a mystery story called *The Secret*.'

Gower bridled. 'It's not a mystery story. That's not my type of thing at all.'

'John, a real life mystery about a mystery writer is worth marginally more interest than a mystery about someone who wouldn't know a mystery if it sucked him down a Great Plughole. And take *The Lighted Candle* . . .'

Gower rallied. 'No, David. Let's take *A Candle Lit*. Let's be accurate, shall we?'

Gerrard made cooling-down noises. 'Yes, of course, I'm sorry, she's your wife. Forgive me for blasting off about her, but that interview was a sadly missed opportunity. I got her on to that programme, you know. These things don't drop out of the sky. I had to work for that.'

Gerrard's world was largely obscure to Gower. He did not fritter time asking how Gerrard contrived to have Linda invited on to *Woman's Hour*. He doubted he would have followed the answer and if he had he would have failed to appreciate the brilliance that lay behind it.

He said: 'Did you brief Linda before she went to the studio?'

He heard a humming, musing sound before Gerrard said: 'Not *brief*, exactly. She needed to appear spontaneous and she would probably not have succeeded if she'd been rehearsed. But I did plop into conversation the notion that she ought to speak a sentence or two about the books, especially *The Secret* and its publication date.'

Gower asked what he most wanted to know. 'How was she?'

'Fine on the telephone. We didn't actually meet.'

When Gower had come up with two more questions along those lines, his agent offered to take her to lunch. Gerrard said: 'It will reassure you and it could even be that I will be able to inculcate in her a tendency to refer to your books whenever a microphone is poked her way.'

Gower said quickly: 'David, I'm not sure you should do that. See her, I mean.'

'The jealous husband?'

'No, but she's not stupid.'

'There will be no pointers to the tiresome truth, I promise. And if I don't meet her, how will I be able to report how she's faring and whether she's pining for you or thanking the fates you have stopped cluttering up her life?'

And it was true. Gerrard was his only means of checking on Linda. Oddly, he needed to remind himself that her feelings towards him were the spur for his adventure. To be rich and famous was to win Linda back. Odd too that he had grown less than passionate about winning her back. He blamed Richard Crane for that.

9

Holly Chase and Daniel Marcus were buying the flat in Hackney, the nice flat, the one with the clematis obscuring a first-floor window. In point of fact, Dan was abroad on location with a television crew and Holly was dealing with the purchase by herself. There were problems.

'There are always problems,' said Rain Morgan, partly responding to Holly's latest report from the housing front and partly referring to the difficulty she was experiencing in replacing her secretary, who had resigned. Rosie was off to Wapping, for better money and an introduction to computer technology, and Holly was confronted with a surveyor's report that she did not wish to believe.

Holly said: 'He says there's damp penetration right up the front wall. He says all the rendering has to be replaced. What he doesn't say is that most of the wall does *not* belong to the flat I'm interested in.'

'If it's rising damp, you can't deal only with the top bit of it.' Rain was trying to be reasonable.

Holly huffed and puffed and said perhaps she ought to get another opinion. She passed the surveyor's report over. The man had been depressingly thorough.

Holly said: 'All I wanted was someone who'd say: "Great, Holly. You can really make something of this place." Instead I've got a man who's counted woodworm holes, run around with a meter reading damp levels and tells me he's suspicious what might be behind the tongue and groove pine panelling in the bathroom. I was going to rip that bathroom out anyway. It's green, avocado, and I want turquoise. It's green at Spinney Green too. I've had my fill of green bathrooms.'

Rain looked up from the report. 'He also says the windows don't open fully because of subsidence, he says the roof needs work on the flashing and the chimney stack needs repointing, he says banisters are loose and unsafe, and he says – '

Holly clapped hands over her ears. 'I know, *I know*.'

'And then he says it's a typical London house of its Victorian period.'

'That figures.'

Rain struggled to find hope for the Hackney flat. 'Perhaps that means none of these things actually matter. After all, if this place is typical and if the owners of all the others got their mortgages through safely then you might get yours.'

Holly took the report back. 'Spinney Green was easy. A brand-new house in a decent suburb – there was none of this trouble.'

But Holly was not prepared to stay at Spinney Green. The tiny 'executive home' had been bought as a stepping stone to something nearer the heart of London. She could not afford to stay in Spinney Green any longer because the rise in prices of properties in the centre was outstripping the increase in the value of the Spinney Green house.

The conversation was curtailed by Rosie, sheepish, coming back to her desk and saying, while barely meeting Rain's eye: 'The one called Joan can come for an interview at five-thirty this afternoon. Shall I confirm that?'

Rain said yes. 'What about the others?'

Rosie fluttered a glance in her direction. 'What others?'

'Are you saying nobody else wants to work for me?'

Rosie made amends. 'Oh they do, it's . . .'

'It's what?' She had not meant to be scratchy.

'Well, I don't think they're suitable.' Rosie drew her chair close and whispered confidentially. Some of the secretaries in other departments had inquired after the job on the gossip column but none of them had come up to the standards Rosie was applying to finding her successor. The advertisement in the newspaper had resulted in a deluge of replies of which the personnel department had concluded that very few were worth consideration. Of the few, nearly all had dropped out once they learned the *Daily Post* was so antiquated they would be deprived of word processors. Re-advertising had resulted in a woman called Joan being invited to meet Rain.

'Personnel say she's all right,' said Rosie. Rain resented her secretary's comforting tone. Rosie was, after all, the cause of this humiliation.

They were both saved further embarrassment by the arrival of an ambitious young man from the features department who wanted to lay hands on the Alf Wilson file. Rosie and Rain swore it had been returned to the library weeks ago, but as the library staff had already sworn they had not received it, he did not trust them. Rosie offered to go back to the library with him and hunt.

He sent her on her own and stayed to ask Rain about Wilson, because he was writing a feature about a television actor and Wilson was peripheral to his subject. 'Wasn't there something funny about his death?'

'A rumour that he hadn't committed suicide, but the inquest went ahead without controversy. The pathologist said he'd been hanged, and the other evidence was that he'd been found hanging from the chandelier in his flat. The rumour began with an anonymous telephone call to a newspaper. That's all.'

Rain was tired of the Alf Wilson business. She had felt that the inquest, with its verdict that Wilson had taken his own life, had closed the episode. And she was glad for it to be closed because she needed to forget her own peculiar role in his life and death. Her contribution to the publicity had helped ensure he was fêted in death and now her feelings of guilt about neglecting him were better set aside because she could rectify nothing.

The young feature writer (Rain could never remember his name and it was awkward to keep asking him whenever they spoke) said: 'Wasn't there something fishy about the way the body was discovered?'

She looked on him a mite coldly. She did not want to stir up these unpleasant memories any further. 'You can't possibly mean to write about that in your piece on the actor.'

'No,' he conceded. 'But I wondered whether you'd ever learned why a whole gang of people had been invited to discover the corpse.' Heartlessly he laughed. 'Didn't it remind you of those old novels where the dying man invites a crowd to gather round for a deathbed confession?'

Rosie returned triumphant with the file and the man went away, leaving Rain to meander through memories. She thought of Pat Jarvis, the cousin, appearing at the office to ask for information; of her own search of Wilson's flat and the piece of paper bearing notes indecipherable except for one clear word – Ilkley; of Mr Ratcliffe who had heard Wilson typing and knew he had few visitors; and of Mrs Dobson from the basement going into Wilson's flat on the pretext of borrowing books and choosing, strangely enough, a novel by that other mystery figure, John Gower.

'Oh, I forgot,' said Rosie, breaking into Rain's thoughts. 'This came for you.'

She passed her a copy of a new book, a note poking out of its pages. The literary editor's scrawl asked Rain whether she would care to write a piece about it. The book was called *The Secret*. It was by John Gower. 'As the author is currently so newsworthy it would be more fun,' her colleague wrote, 'if you were to write about the book than if I were to carry a straightforward review.'

Rain read the book that evening, sitting in her roof garden in Kington Square, amid tubs of trumpeting petunias, a waterfall of purple clematis against the wall. She sat there until the early summer sunshine ceased to glint at her through her neighbours' towering trees. Then she went indoors, curling up on the sofa.

The book gripped her, not as a lively thriller might with twists of plot and compelling narrative drive, but because of the quality of the writing, the assurance with which Gower set down his simple tale, and his insight into the human predicament. He told the story in the third person, using a narrator, but this did not distance the subject. Rather it gave the reader two perfectly achieved characters, complementary types who advanced the story.

As a writer awed by anyone's ability to create fiction, Rain was impressed by the talent John Gower brought to his slim passionate novels. She could notice and comment, but she could not ape it. Even as the phrases flew into her head, ready for repetition when she came to write her piece, she knew them to be inadequate and clumsy beside the prose she sought to praise.

And her phrases were changing, were twisting themselves into an obituary. She curbed herself, then questioned whether her instinct had been wholly inappropriate. Gower had been lost at sea for five weeks and his survival would be a miracle. She remembered the last time she had written an obituary, Alf Wilson's. Two writers, unalike except that they had suffered strange deaths, and that she would write about them, and that she had come to know their work only when it was at an end. She wished she had come to Gower's books sooner. Sad to think there would be no more.

As soon as the thought was formed she challenged it. Publishers did not rush into print as soon as a manuscript was delivered. Authors might not offer up a book immediately it was finished. She decided that before she wrote she would check whether a new Gower novel was in the pipeline. David Gerrard, Gower's agent, had been known to ring her late in the evening, and she saw no reason not to disturb him.

'Rain? Have you any idea what time it is?'

'Oh . . . er . . . yes. Sorry, David. I haven't got you out of bed, have I?'

'Not quite. But what's on fire? What can't wait until respectable working hours? Or am I favoured with a social call?'

She cut through his banter. 'I've finished reading *The Secret* and I'd like to know about Gower's next book.'

Gerrard was flummoxed. 'His next one?'

'That's right.'

'Rain, what makes you think there will be another one?'

She explained her reasons. Gerrard grew more chatty. 'Pegwoods don't have a manuscript and nor do I. He told me about the one he was working on. We had lunch in April and he described it then.'

Rain asked whether Gerrard's visit to Gower's home, the weekend before the sea search, was connected with the new book. He did not dissuade her from believing this. They talked around the subject for a while, Rain pushing him to hint at the theme of the book and Gerrard avoiding doing so. She came off the line with her belief in the existence of a new manuscript confirmed.

Gerrard, trying to balance a display of knowledge with a reluctance to share it, had given her the impression that Gower's new book existed, albeit in an unpolished form. He had left her believing they had discussed it in detail over lunch in London and that he had gone to Dorset days later to talk over a big deal, either with Pegwoods or with a rival publisher.

He had been specific that it was to be a better book than anything Gower had done before and it was to make him a fortune. Ignorant of how much he had achieved, Gerrard threw out the cat and went to bed. Rain Morgan, a couple of miles away, was up late, plotting. She thought it would be a fine thing for the *Daily Post* to have access to the unfinished novel of John Gower. And she meant to get it.

Early next day she bounced into the office ready to share her idea with Holly but Holly was delayed. She had left a message with the switchboard operator to say she had gone to Hackney.

'I think,' said Rosie, relaying the message, 'Holly has gone to the flat to see the damp wall for herself. Lucy on the switchboard said she was going to see a clematis she wants to buy but I don't think that can be correct.'

Rain was inclined to agree. She changed the subject. 'Joan was awful.'

Rosie coloured. 'Oh dear, was she?'

Rain pushed curls back from her forehead. 'No, not really. Joan was fine, *I* was awful. I wanted to be sure she knew how dreadful it would be working here. I'm afraid I laid it on a bit thick.'

Rosie looked alarmed. 'It isn't dreadful, it's lovely.'

'Then why are you deserting me?'

Rosie smirked. 'Lots of money. Lots of computers.'

'But look who you'll be working for.'

Rosie's future boss was a pompous philanderer. The smirk faded. 'Every job has its disadvantages,' she said.

Rain yawned. Then: 'Rosie, why don't you ring Joan and tell her she's got the job?'

'But . . .'

'She'll be all right. She was rather sweet, and she'll soon get the hang of it.'

'Oh yes,' said Rosie blithely. 'Any fool could do my job.'

Rain opened her mouth then shut it without speaking. What was the point? Rosie was going and Joan was coming. The column would go on much the same, unfortunately the newspaper would too until a serious buyer emerged, and Rain would settle down to the quirks of a new youngster who would gain her experience as fast as she might and then desert.

She opened a newspaper at a rival's column and compared it critically with her own. Humming softly, not aware she was doing so, she was happy to have beaten the opposition. She skimmed through the other papers and pushed the pile on to Holly's desk for her to read later.

Then, still humming, Rain flicked through her contacts book for a London telephone number she had been given weeks ago. Linda Gower answered. Rain told her the *Post* would like to do a feature about her missing husband, that it especially wanted to concentrate on the difficulties faced by a wife in Linda's position, and that they would prefer to talk to her in Dorset.

Linda warned that she had already been interviewed on that aspect by *Woman's Hour*. Rain, who had not known this, was pleased as it gave credence to her request. Linda, grasping what she took to be the purpose of the Dorset setting, said: 'You'll want photographs of me at the cottage, then?'

Rain said she would. She arranged to drive Linda to Dorset that afternoon. By chance Linda had taken several days' holiday and was free.

Ever since she had met her, Rain had been puzzled who the woman reminded her of. Driving down the M3 it suddenly came to her. The voice lacked the nasal twang but in appearance and manner Linda was reminiscent of a television newsreader. Both were solid women with broad faces and straight fair hair with a fringe.

She did not very much like Linda Gower, although she knew that to be a harsh opinion to hold about a woman she had met under cruel circumstances. Yet she felt there could never be any empathy between them.

Linda was not a great talker but without letting her tongue run to indiscretion, she conveyed that she had been financing Gower's writing and that she had grown resentful. Rain gathered that Linda had no love of David Gerrard and that she was bitter that Pegwoods had treated her husband shabbily. But Rain chose not to take this as a cue to ask Linda whether she believed her husband had been depressed and killed himself. When the story was fresh, Linda had denied that, but after this length of time the answer might have changed. Rain intended to find out later.

Meanwhile, she encouraged Linda to talk about the books. These Linda admired. She expanded and expounded and scattered the names of her husband's books through the conversation with the liberality of a man throwing pebbledash at a wall. Then, turning off the M3 on to the A303, they talked about the scenery and why the Gowers had moved out of London, Rain still bent on saving the meat of the interview until she was at the cottage. The setting where pertinent questions were posed often made all the difference to the answers.

Stream Cottage was pretty. Its grass was shaggy, because Linda had not been to the house for two weeks, but a pink rose around the door was coming into flower, and at a glance the house was as picturesque as any sentimental heart could wish. The unswept path and unwashed windows became apparent on closer inspection.

Surprisingly, the house was cooler inside than out. Linda apologized for this. 'I won't say take your coat off, Rain, you'll need it.'

Rain followed her down a narrow passage, past a newel post with chipped paint. Through an open door she saw a slanting window on to a field. A man was on a tractor in the field, a man wearing a woolly hat. He was shouting, or was it singing?

'Come through,' said Linda. She was in the kitchen. She emptied a bag she had brought and put food in the fridge. A pint of milk she left on the table. Linda planned to stay for a couple of nights.

She was being housewifely, making tea, excusing the minimal untidiness and the unavoidable coldness. She said: 'I'm keeping the car in the garage here, it's no use in London and parking where my sister lives is impossible. They found it at Mousehole but they let me bring it home. The police had a thorough look at it before they handed it over. Milk?' She poured in the milk, gave Rain a mug, saying: 'There you are. That should warm you up.'

Rain was taking in the atmosphere of the cottage, the strange hesitancy in the way Linda Gower found things and replaced them. Rain thought: 'She hasn't lived here for a long time. Or if it's only been a short time, she's cut herself off from it, wanted to forget. She must know I know she'd left him. I wonder whether she'll say so, or wait for me to prompt.'

Linda did not allude to it when they sat and talked in the sitting room, a colder room if that were possible. Rain was having trouble concentrating. She had planned to conduct an incisive interview but was distracted by the need to control her shivering. Cutting short the conversation she suggested they look at the study where Gower's books had been written.

Linda ushered her into the room with the slanting window.

Rain showed an interest in the neat arrangement on the desk, the cheap word processor and its attachments and the precisely arranged piles of paper. She asked whether he had left the desk like that or whether it had been tidied.

His wife was bending down straightening a rug she had rucked up. 'The desk always looks like this at the end of the day. Printed-out pages on one side, word processor in the middle, a pile of paper to the back of the desk and a batch of notes in a paperclip to the other side of the word processor. To look at that I'd never guess he'd . . . well, that he hadn't simply broken off for the evening.'

Rain picked up a sheet of paper. It was blank on the uppermost side, printed on the other. Linda said: 'That will be an earlier book on the back. He reuses the paper from one book by writing an early draft of the next on the other side.'

She also took up a sheet from the pile, turned it over and scanned it. 'Oh yes, that's an early draft of *The Secret*. As a matter of fact the main character wasn't called Tom in the early drafts, he wàs a Steven. I don't know why John changed it.'

Then she lifted a sheet from the pile on the other side of the word processor. 'That's strange. This is *The Secret* again.' She riffled through that pile, confirming that it was more of the same book.

Rain said: 'There's no batch of notes either.' No notes, no new manuscript, just the paper he was meant to be reusing.

Frowning, Linda opened the drawers of the desk. Rain asked: 'Had he reached the stage of writing when he disappeared?'

'Definitely. But don't ask me what the book was about, he didn't say.'

After they had looked in the drawers and cupboards in the study, they checked in the sitting room and then they went upstairs and Linda searched in wardrobes and chests of drawers.

'I don't understand this,' she kept saying. 'I don't understand this at all.'

Back in the study they inspected the desk again. Rain asked:

'When you came here after he'd gone, were the notes and the manuscript here?'

Linda bit a lip, bewildered. 'They can't have been, can they? No one else has been here, no one who'd want to interfere with them. The police nosed around and journalists came. I was photographed in here for one of the newspapers. But I didn't notice there were no notes and I didn't examine the piles of paper to see whether they were what I expected them to be.'

'Would your husband have taken the book away from the cottage?'

'I've never known him do that. When there's only one copy printed out, it's less dangerous to leave it in this room than carry it around. He prints the work out every evening in case something goes wrong with the computer or there's a faulty disk. That way he won't lose everything.'

While she spoke she was rattling through disks in a desk drawer, rejecting those labelled with the names of earlier books. Then she inspected the disk drives of the word processor, but they were empty. 'The print-out *and* the disks,' she said giving up, putting a hand to her face. 'Both gone.' And she had run out of places to suggest looking. 'Anyway,' she said, 'this is ruining your interview. You haven't come all the way to watch me hunt for a mislaid draft. Shall we go back to the sitting room?'

Rain resumed the interview, endeavouring not to shiver, but there was only one clear thought in her mind and Linda's: John Gower's next novel had disappeared as intriguingly as he had.

An hour later Rain was in a call box on the A303. 'I don't believe it, Holly.'

'Nor her?'

Rain said: 'I believe her. She was shaken when she realized it was missing.'

'Manuscripts and computer disks,' said Holly sagely, 'do not borrow boats and leave them near famous wrecks.'

'Eh?'

189

'They don't go off anywhere, Rain. Either somebody removed Gower's after his disappearance or else he took them with him.'

Rain mocked her logic. 'Oh, I see. You think, he took the book with him as reading matter to while away the time as he sat aboard the *Fleur* and dared the Great Plughole to suck him under?'

'No-o,' said Holly. 'But I think you're being invited to believe in coincidence. Personally, I don't trust coincidences.'

'I'll swear Linda Gower wasn't acting this afternoon.'

Rain repeated that to herself as she drove on towards London, the traffic growing heavier, the fields meaner and the houses closer. Linda Gower had not been pretending, she had been genuinely confused and distressed and . . . And *what*? Ah, yes. She had been angry. That was it. Finally, she had been angry. She had not spoken any words to underline this anger, because she was not a woman to let her thoughts tumble out, but she had been angry.

10

Towards the end of the week David Gerrard telephoned
Butlers to say he had taken Linda Gower to lunch.

'I rescued her from a chilly time in Dorset, John. She
intended to stay through the weekend but apparently it was
uncongenial and she fairly leapt at my offer of lunch in
Charlotte Street.'

'How is she?'

'She's looking well and her appetite is unimpaired. Sorry to
disappoint but the lady is not lachrymose. One doesn't wish
to be brutal, yet one has to say she shows all the signs of
relishing being your widow. The attention suits her.'

Gower fought to imagine David Gerrard and Linda across a
table in Charlotte Street. He failed. He said: 'Are you telling
me she would prefer me to disappear permanently?'

'One could hardly offer her a straight choice, but as far as
one could make out, with some judicious probing, she's
perfectly content with the status quo. She intimated that yours
was a timely death as it had saved a lot of bother and lawyers'
fees.'

'Oh.' Gower felt he ought to be wracked with misery at
Linda's heartless rejection, but he did not feel anything.
Nothing, that is, except curiosity at his own lack of feeling. He
said: 'She'll feel differently when I re-emerge.'

Gerrard mocked him with a laugh. 'Yes, John. Livid, I
should think.'

'At being fooled. Yes, I'm afraid she will.'

'Livid at not being free to sell off Stream Cottage – which she
has severely taken against, I may add – and pretty livid about
having to share the rest of the loot.'

Gower provided the question required of him. 'What other
loot?'

And Gerrard reported a coup that would bring many thousands of pounds in foreign sales for the new book. Nonchalantly he added that the earlier books were to be published in paperback in the United States.

'For another impressive figure,' he said, 'but don't pester me for precision, John, you know what havoc currency exchange rates play with income from foreign sales.'

Gower, who had never had occasion to find out, said he was sure they must. He listened to Gerrard elaborating on the new deals, explaining how they worked and what proportion of the foreign earnings Gower could hope to keep. The Japanese, for instance, withheld ten per cent of a writer's money for reasons best known to themselves. Other places had other tricks. Gerrard was attempting to put it in simple terms but repeatedly forgot and treated Gower like an author who had been around the course often enough to understand the benefits and implications of details.

Several times Gower attempted to clarify points, but this was an effort he was loath to make. For him it was enough that Gerrard was talking in long numbers, enough that they were both to reap the rewards of their risky adventure.

Gerrard said: 'You'll have to be canny about the tax, though. Better start giving that some thought. The Chancellor was awfully good to the rich back in March.'

But Gower was not concerned about tax bills or the Budget. His mind was on the next and, in a way, the most hazardous stage of the adventure. 'We have to get the timing right for my resurrection.'

Rapidly Gerrard agreed. 'We must talk about that, John. We bumped you off with indecent haste but we must put serious thought into how we breathe life back into you.'

'Actually I thought it would be best to . . .'

The line was not clear, Gerrard appeared not to have heard. He came in with a heavy quip. 'If you're not going anywhere this weekend, I could call on you for a plotting session.'

'All right. Saturday or Sunday, or will you stop overnight?'

'No, a flying visit. Saturday afternoon and I'll bring supplies again to keep you provided a while longer.'

'Not much longer,' Gower protested. 'It's the launch of *The Secret* in ten days. I'll want to be around for that.'

'We'll talk it all through then, John.'

Gower came away from the telephone with a pricking suspicion about Gerrard's planned visit. He would have liked time to sit down and work through the details of his re-emergence into the real world, to be prepared when Gerrard came, but he was deep in the Richard Crane novel and it was his habit to let his writing take precedence over everything else. He ran upstairs to the spare bedroom where he now worked, a typewriter resting on a dressing table.

Richard Crane had been left stranded outside a nightclub when Gerrard had telephoned. Gower quickly wrote him a taxi home to his lavish Docklands flat overlooking the River Thames. He reinforced Crane's pleasure in his home with an atmospheric scene where Crane stood, drink in hand, on the terrace, listening to the never-ceasing thrum of London, the energy of the city, and looking at one of the most expensive views in the world.

Cornily, but understandably, Crane felt like the monarch of all he surveyed. There was nothing he could not have or do if he wanted it enough. This night there was only one thing he wanted before he went to bed. He wanted a telephone call from Conroy, his partner in a property-development deal. He wanted Conroy to call to say that the way was clear, the counter-bidder had been persuaded to back off and let Crane acquire the site. Crane would not want to know how Conroy had achieved the goal, he wanted only to be told the job was done. Fingers flying over the keys, John Gower wrote the telephone call, wrote what Richard Crane wanted. Crane was a man who got his way.

Then Gower went downstairs, opened a tin of tuna fish and cut in half a bread roll he had earlier defrosted from the freezer. He made his lunch without thinking about it, his mind in Docklands, prowling around Crane's flat, hearing the water churning at the passage of a big ship upriver to Tower Bridge, and overhearing Crane's conversation with Julia, his girlfriend.

Julia? Gower questioned whether the name was apposite, whether he ought not to have picked something harder. No matter, he could change the name later if he liked, when he knew more about her. Steven had become Tom in *The Secret*. Richard Crane had come within an ace of being Mark Caine. What did it matter, so long as it was settled before the book was published? Julia was being shaped as he wrote about her, starting with her feminine appearance, but she was developing into somebody tougher than he had anticipated. 'Julia' sounded altogether too weak, unless he wanted to jolt the reader as he had jolted himself with the unveiling of her steely nature.

He switched on a radio in the sitting room, a room he rarely used now that he worked upstairs. For a minute or two he let the world invade Butlers but after that his concentration lapsed and he was thinking about the next scene, the following day in the riverside flat. He saw Crane pacing about, impatient, which was how Gower liked him to be. He tuned in to the argument, Crane versus Conroy, with Crane building his objections methodically, despite the other character's casual dismissal of them, until Conroy was forced on the defensive and the meeting exploded into ferocity.

Gower gulped his tuna roll and hurried back to the typewriter, getting the exchanges down fast. He was not afraid of forgetting them, merely of not being able to keep pace. Ideas were teeming, he had to discipline himself or else he would be on to another point before he had properly covered the first.

After a page of typing he leaned back in his chair and read through. Then he read it aloud, trying different voices for Crane and Conroy and wishing he were a better actor. But how much was in the acting and how much in the dialogue he had written? He pulled the sheet from the machine and walked around the bedroom, reading the lines again, testing for content and cadence.

Crane's lines seemed to him entirely right. The trouble was Conroy or, more accurately, the trouble was jokes. Conroy was meant to be facetious as the scene began, and facetiousness is treacherous on paper. An actor would get the point but an average reader would not know where the scene was heading and might well accept Conroy's lines as plain statements. So Gower tinkered with Conroy's responses, making them firmer. This inevitably reduced the effect of the climax to the scene because there was more tension from the beginning instead of a creeping ascent.

He wrote the page again, and ripped that up and wrote a third. The crux was his early decision not to qualify speech in the book, to let it speak for itself, as it were. Right from the start, before a word had been typed, Gower had decided he would not write a line to amplify a character's words. There would be 'he said' as required, but there would not be 'he said *glumly*.' Until the scene with Conroy, he had encountered no problems. And now the scheme of the book was foundering on this unlovely minor character. He virtually hated Conroy for the trouble he was giving, and was comically comforted by the secret knowledge that Conroy was destined to meet a bad end.

Grappling with the problem, he wandered through the house. The sun was shining, the garden inviting, but he dared not stride among the trees before dusk. He had to be content with opening a rear window in the sitting room and breathing in the perfume of fields and flowers. Rosebuds below the window were opening. Their pink faces sent his thoughts scudding back to Stream Cottage. He had planted a pink rose by the front door and it ought to be in flower too; this was its best month.

Larksong urged him into the garden. Impulsively he dashed to a cupboard where Butlers' owners had left coats and he pulled one on as a disguise. The coat was of an old-fashioned cut which had recently been revived, although he thought this garment was an original. He wanted to see its effect, and was torn between the outside world of larks and roses and the glimmering of an idea.

Upstairs was a long mirror. Gower burst into the bedroom in the unfamiliar coat. He had the collar turned up, and he shoved his hands in his pockets and posed. Then he tousled his hair, hair that had grown long in his 'missing' weeks, leaving a fashionably untidy effect. Then he posed again. The overall difference was pleasing.

He tried out some Richard Crane lines, in Crane's confident voice. In the mirror his face adapted to the new demeanour, the new style. If he were fairer, he could, in this guise, pass for Richard Crane.

The creak of the gate sent him downstairs to close the window and conceal the kitchen's evidence of his lunch. Then, on the half-landing, he crouched and waited for a visitor to appear on the path.

Danny, the little boy who had been there before, came running into view. Danny was looking back, being pursued. Then Susan, his sister, had a grip on him and was marching him away. Gower strained to hear the closing of the gate. The sound did not reach him.

He forgot about going outside, which was demonstrably too dangerous. He tossed the coat on the spare bed and sat down at the typewriter, its noise diminished by the blanket he had folded beneath it. Leaving the Conroy scene to be resolved later, he skipped to the following one and re-entered the stylish world of Richard Crane.

In the early evening he was astonished by the roar of a tractor starting up close by. Peering from the landing he found an old man riding rhythmically up and down mowing the Butlers' grass. This continued for two and a half hours until most of the garden was shorn except for a deep swathe near the back hedge and another beyond the fruit trees. At that point the engine choked and died. The man failed to restart it and walked off down the path.

Gower opened the kitchen window inviting the heady scent

of cut grass inside. Hastily he made his supper, cleared away every trace from the kitchen and carried his plate upstairs, fearing the old man could return at any time.

When David Gerrard came the next day the man had not been back and the tractor remained abandoned beneath a damson tree. Gower explained its presence.

'Ye-es,' said Gerrard absently. 'I seem to recall Parsons saying something about an old boy in the village who was paid to keep the garden tidy.'

'You might have mentioned it. He frightened the life out of me.'

'You're supposed to be dead already.'

'Not for much longer. Do you think I . . .'

'John, let me fetch the stuff from the car first.'

He went across to the apple store. Arriving, he had driven his car straight in. It did not matter who saw him, as he was entitled to be there, but he preferred not to be noticed.

In seconds he was back with a box of groceries and a brief-case. He put the box down in the kitchen. Gower automatically moved it out of the line of the window, saying: 'I have a habit of keeping things out of sight. No one would see this over here.'

Gerrard approved this level of care. He lifted packages out of the box. 'There are decent restaurants around here but one can't risk it. Alas, we shall have to dine at Butlers this evening.'

He said he had brought a selection of things from his local delicatessen for a first course and was relying on the cottage having a grill for the steaks to follow. Irritatingly, he was chattering about the meal they would eat later, oblivious of Gower's impatience.

Going into the sitting room he paused. 'That thing,' he said, pointing at the hunting horn hanging from a beam that straddled the room, 'does it work?'

Gower thought: *Displacement activity. He's finding things to say and do rather than get down to business.*

Aloud he said: 'Of course it works. Why shouldn't it?' He

showed he could not care less about the state of the hunting horn.

'I don't know, I just thought . . . Oh well, it doesn't matter. Now then.'

'Yes,' said Gower decisively. He sat on one of the fireside chairs, a dark wooden frame and cushion covers that looked like tapestry. Gerrard sat on the matching settee, a small piece of furniture that the man's size further diminished. Gerrard busied himself lighting a cigar.

Gower said: '*The Secret* comes out on the Monday after next. I suggest I walk into the launch party.'

For the first time in his career, Pegwoods were giving a launch party. Gerrard had referred to it in a telephone call. He would be there, so would Linda, so would representatives of national newspapers and magazines and radio and television. The agent planned to use the opportunity to talk about the money the book was earning, enlarging on the statements he had been trickling to the press over the previous weeks as contract had succeeded contract.

Gerrard cleard his throat, tapped his cigar unnecessarily into an ashtray on the low table in front of him. 'John, I think walking into the party needs careful consideration.'

'I've considered. Can you think of anything more dramatic than that?'

'No, but . . . Look, may I get a drink?'

Involuntarily Gower looked at the clock on the sideboard, noting it was only mid-afternoon. 'What would you like?'

'I brought some rather good wine. I'll see to it, you stay there.'

As soon as Gerrard was through the door to the kitchen, Gower's features puckered into a frown. What was wrong with coming to life at the party, with the press there? And why was Gerrard twitchy, because that's what he was?

Hearing the clunk of cupboard doors, Gower called: 'The glasses are in here.'

He took two tulip glasses from the sideboard and set them up on the dining table, then opened a window to disperse the smoke that was steadily filling the room. Gerrard carried in the wine, inspected the glasses, found fault with one and polished them both on a clean napkin from the sideboard drawer. More displacement activity.

Immediately he had poured, Gower took up one of the glasses and walked briskly to his chair, signalling that talk was to resume, interruption was not to be prolonged. Gerrard trailed after him less enthusiastically.

'Timing is crucial now,' Gerrard began. And went on to say that Gower's appearance, alive and well, at the launch would be *un*timely. 'You'd get terrific publicity, no doubt, but you'd jeopardize some of the newer deals I've done. My advice is to wait until those contracts are signed.'

'But that could take for ever!' He had experience of that, of waiting months for a contract and months more for the money payable on signature to materialize.

'No,' said Gerrard. 'They've competed to buy these books, they daren't delay. And I've stipulated that the money comes through quickly too. I'm confident that side of things is taken care of. And I'm not prepared to have you run risks.'

Gower did not care for the bossy way this was being put to him, but he concealed that for the time being. 'All right. I won't do anything to spoil what you've worked for. But I don't understand why my reappearance would do that.'

The agent tried to attain his habitual ironic manner, leaning back, in so far as the tiny settee permitted this, and gesturing airily with his cigar. 'John, one would be less than honest if one were to claim that people are paying huge sums for your books.'

He paused allowing Gower time to raise an eyebrow. Then he continued: 'No, they are not buying your novels at that price. They are purchasing the mystery. Oh, one appreciates that the bulk of the publicity about the sales has centred on the recognition in the publishing world that you are a first-rate writer who has been overlooked and is now to be delivered, winningly packaged, to every home in the land. But the appalling truth is that when it comes to the point – the point of sale, that is – what folk will be manipulated into buying will be those books by that nice young writer who disappeared so peculiarly while diving on to (or not diving on to, here one may take one's pick) the *Charity* and got swirled away into legend by a supernatural effect known as the Giant Plughole. Do you see?'

Gower squirmed. 'You're saying I'll have to stay hidden until all those copies of the books have been sold.'

'Alas, one can't ask you to do that. But no matter. Once the contracts are signed and the books are heading for the bookstalls, you will be safe. We will select a moment and you will pop up, like the sun in the morning.' He drank his wine greedily.

Gower, whose glass was almost full, thought fleetingly of telling Gerrard about the unpleasant pressures of life at Butlers. But that was no good. Frightening Gerrard with worries about children squinting through windows would distract him from his task and, by Gerrard's own account, he was excelling at the task. Why put him off while he was making money?

Gerrard fetched the bottle of wine, offered to top up Gower's glass and then refilled his own. Invited to compliment it, Gower said he liked the wine but had not been giving his mind to it. He drank a couple of mouthfuls and let Gerrard fill the glass up. Tense, on the edge of his chair, he asked what Gerrard proposed would be a good time to reappear.

Unfortunately, Gerrard did not have an answer. Gower's irritation surfaced. 'For heaven's sake, David, I can't hang around here for ever. If I don't come out on publication day, then it's got to be soon after.'

The agent raised a forbidding hand. 'No, John. I've explained. I can't let you do that.'

'You *can't let me*? You can't stop me!' He sprang out of the chair.

Gerrard recoiled, saying: 'That's what worries me, John. If you're wilful about this . . .'

'*Wilful*?'

'Stop echoing, please, and look at the facts.'

Gower pushed past the settee, walked down the room. 'There aren't any facts, David, there are only theories. *Your* theories. You've never been in this position before and neither have I. We don't have any facts. Perhaps my appearance at the launch of *The Secret* would be the most favourable thing. You're just guessing that it might not.'

To see him, Gerrard had to twist round. He was alarmed that Gower was seething, it was out of character. He had never expected the conversation to be easy but he had never expected a shouting match either. 'Believe me, John, I do know the people I'm dealing with. I know the way they think. You must trust me.'

Gower spun, bringing his fist down on the end of the dining table. '*No*, the only person I trust is myself. I haven't known what you've been up to for the past few weeks. You've scarcely ever been here, you've seldom telephoned, you haven't kept . . .'

He stopped, shaken by his own vehemence. He moved about four paces. He needed space. The room did not give him any. Neither did Gerrard.

Gerrard said evenly: 'I want your promise, John, that you will not leave this place until we agree it is wise for you to do so.'

There was no answer and Gerrard persisted, saying: 'If you turn up at the launch you will ruin both of us.'

Gower breathed heavily. Through the diamond-paned leaded lights a cat curled in the grass beneath a pear tree. Roses embowered the cottage, but their scent was withheld. Swallows dipped but he could not hear their mewing. A spider was floating down from the thatch, spooling out its thread. He felt himself cut off from life, figuratively and literally. The house and the predicament were a trap that had sprung on him, and Gerrard refused to help him be free. His ambivalent feelings about Gerrard were crystallizing into mistrust.

Gerrard said: 'You're safe here, John. You have your new

book to work on, and you have as many of the creature comforts as you need. Be patient for a few weeks and then we'll choose a time.'

Bitterly, without turning to face him, Gower asked: 'Won't you be doing any more deals?'

'What do you mean?'

'In a few weeks' time, won't there be other new deals we daren't upset?'

'Oh, I see. Well I'm hoping to sell more rights, it's true. For instance, I expect to hear about the film rights of your second book fairly soon. But none of those things are as sensitive.'

He waited and when Gower was silent, he asked again. 'Please agree to stay here until we settle a time.'

Gower sighed and turned to confront him but Gerrard's head was bowed. There was the sound of wine pouring into a glass. Gower shrugged and walked back down the room. 'Very well,' he said after a long while. 'I'll wait.'

Gerrard's 'good' was almost inaudible. He raised his glass to his pink, full lips. He did not smile but the tension went out of him.

'I can't go to the launch, anyway,' Gower said. 'I don't know where it's being held. You didn't tell me.'

That was interpreted as a joke. Gerrard smiled and said: 'Let's keep it that way, shall we, in case you're tempted?'

And he began to tell Gower how over lunch Linda had become interested that he had been signing contracts on Gower's behalf in his absence.

Gower suggested she had been more interested in the money than the means of claiming it.

'And one can't blame her,' said Gerrard, 'especially as figures have been bandied about in the public prints.'

'Did you tell her how much?'

'As near as I was able. That, I presume, was what you would have wished me to do.'

Gower nodded, doubting whether Gerrard could be relied upon to describe exactly how impressed his wife was with his money-making. But Gerrard said: 'Actually it surprised her it was quite so much. Apparently she'd taken the view that one halved whatever one read in the newspapers and she'd been halving. When I told her she was allowed to double in this instance, she fairly fainted in her soup.'

'When she climbed out of the soup, what did she say?'

The agent scratched the top of his head thoughtfully, searching for her exact words. 'She said she'd had several weeks to grow used to you being famous but it was a shock to discover you were rich too.'

'It will be one hell of a shock when she learns I'm alive.'

'Yes,' agreed Gerrard, and seemed about to amplify, before changing his mind and getting out of his seat to stroll about the room commenting on hunting prints and questioning for a second time the condition of the horn.

'The other thing,' said Gower, splashing wine into his glass, believing it to be reckless to get through a bottle of wine in the afternoon but enjoying the recklessness, 'the other thing is that we must concoct a story to cover my absence.'

Lifting down the horn, Gerrard said: 'Amnesia.' He glanced with distaste at grimy fingertips and wiped them and the dusty horn on a cotton handkerchief.

'That's corny. We can do better than that.'

'It was good enough for Agatha Christie.'

'That's what I mean, David.'

'You will have recovered from it spontaneously, as folk sometimes do, and you will remember nothing about driving to Mousehole or taking the yacht out to sea. Your mind will be a blank until you find yourself on, say, Reading station one Tuesday afternoon, catch the London train and march into Pegwoods office.'

They should be more inventive, Gower argued. As he was banned from putting in an appearance at the launch of *The Secret*, he preferred to come to life in a more startling locale than Reading station.

'Claiming amnesia is all very well,' he said, 'providing there's a convincing explanation for the police and the great

British public failing to spot me. Amnesia doesn't amount to invisibility, you know.'

With lips pursed, Gerrard raised the horn. Then he lowered it without blowing. 'What do you have in mind?'

'Somewhere abroad, somewhere exotic, then my reappearance will increase the mystery.'

The agent's eyes gleamed with interest. He was still holding the horn but he had forgotten about it. 'That would be an excellent twist to the story. The papers would love it.'

Gower said: 'Also, it would skirt around the problem of my reappearing clutching a new manuscript. I'll claim that I travelled a while and then settled down to complete the book.'

The plump face was beaming at him. 'A new book so soon?' Gower generally hated talking about a book in progress and Gerrard had avoided inquiring directly how it was going. He had assumed it would be at least another eighteen months away.

True to form, Gower did not want to talk about it. He merely said that it was going better than anything he had ever written. Then: 'It will help, won't it? Producing a new book at that stage?'

'Of course, John. You couldn't make it America, could you?'

Gower's brain flashed him pictures of wide hats, long shadows, snowy peaks, dust and thirst and sun. 'Mexico?'

'Good Lord, no. I mean the United States. One would find no advantage in being south of the border down Mexico way.'

But Gower dug his heels in. 'Sorry, David. New York and California don't appeal to me.' He knew Gerrard would not have been thinking of anywhere in between.

Before responding, Gerrard leaned the hunting horn against the sideboard and tipped the last of the wine into his glass. 'The United States is terribly parochial, you'd get wonderful coverage if you could say you'd been there rather than in Mexico. And one would court wonderful coverage in the United States, because it's a mammoth market.'

Another image flared in Gower's mind, of surf beating a white shore, palm trees, short dark women with long dark hair, and sun. 'Hawaii.'

Their eyes met over the rim of Gerrard's wine glass. Gower said: 'I'm prepared to compromise and go to Hawaii. It's one of the states and it's exotic enough for my purposes. What do you say, David?'

But he knew the answer. He had read it in Gerrard's eyes. 'Brilliant,' said David Gerrard.

For the rest of their time together they explored the ins and outs of having Gower rediscovered in Hawaii. Eventually Gerrard admitted fearing the plan would flop because they would fail to get Gower out of Britain. His passport was at Stream Cottage and if they recovered it and he attempted to leave through any of the sea or airports he might be identified and stopped.

'I realize that,' Gower said. 'And it would make me look like a common criminal ducking the arm of the law. But there is another way.'

They were in the kitchen. Gerrard was beating steaks, an improvised apron protecting his clothes. He paused. A dreadful suspicion was reflected in his face. 'No, John. I absolutely refuse to take you across the oceans in a small boat. One does one's duty, but my seafaring days are over.'

Gower laughed, clapping him on the back. Gerrard frowned above the bloody steaks. John Gower was not a man to go clapping people on the back. What was happening to him?

'Listen,' said Gower, and told him about the alias he had established, athough withholding the name. 'It exists. All I have to do is apply for a passport in that name. You can sign as a witness to my photograph matching my face.'

The steak hammer was dropped in the sink, the steaks laid to rest until the grill was hot enough. 'Your face,' said Gerrard, 'is a problem. The photograph will be another one of John Gower, the one everybody's been seeing on book covers, in newspapers, on missing person posters and television screens for six weeks.'

'No it won't. I'll look completely different. Well, *adequately* different.'

For a second the enthusiasm died in Gerrard. He untied the knotted tea towels around his girth and hung them on a doorknob. He said ironically: 'John, one draws the line at plastic surgery. It's expensive, not always successful and you are not, to the best of my knowledge, one of the Great Train Robbers.'

The joke amused Gower, especially as it was a joke arising from Gerrard's anxiety. He promised he would resort to nothing as extreme as plastic surgery.

Gerrard said that a beard would be acceptable but false noses were out. He carried on making jokes about available tricks of disguise but revealed an underlying worry that Gower might go too far. Gerrard could not have told himself exactly what he meant by 'too far', except that he was uneasy about the changes in John Gower's personality.

He's been alone too long, he thought. *Isolation isn't healthy. It's not what one's made for. I'll have to watch him, keep control, head him off if his plans grow too outrageous.*

They ate outside, Gerrard insisting that his presence made all the difference because Butlers' owner had told local people that he had the use of the cottage, and therefore it was only while he was absent that a man on the premises was suspicious. Gower acquiesced without demur. To be seated in the sun at a rustic table with the breath of roses around him and finches busy in the fruit trees was heaven.

Gerrard had poured them both sherries, affecting to find their absent host's taste in sherry lamentable but managing to drink the stuff all the same. Everything was pleasantly relaxed until voices alerted him. Plainly, he expected an invasion and Gower had to remind him of the path beside Butlers' hedge and beyond the fields to the pub.

'We're quite safe. That's why I brought the table away from the flower bed and nearer the house. If people are on the path they can't see us here, we're screened by trees.'

'Luckily you've got your back to them too.'

'No, not luckily.'

'Ah.' Gerrard admired the caution. 'You always were the careful type, John. Otherwise I should never have embarked on any of this.'

Presently he grilled the steaks exactly as each of them liked, and served them with salad and bread. Gower had nothing to do but watch and guess that his agent was one of those people who believed that if all other ventures failed he could turn his hand to running a restaurant. Unwittingly, Gerrard enhanced this by talking about food to the exclusion of all else.

Excellent, thought Gower. *He's happy to let me press on with the Hawaii scheme. I'd been ready for him to resist, but he's not going to.*

Gerrard was recalling a meal he had eaten on a visit to France during the winter, *la queue de boeuf des vignerons*. Gower contributed a question, expecting to hear that white grapes were superior to black or vice versa, but Gerrard delved into Burgundian cuisine.

'The essential,' he said, 'is to use *verjus*, the juice of unripe white grapes. Purists would hold out for the juice of a particular variety of grape, but purists, alas, are not in the culinary ascendancy. I was once offered a dish that had been made with sweet Italian grapes, whole ones that glimmered through the sauce like sheep's eyeballs. The cook couldn't have been more pleased with himself than if he'd thought of garnishing it with kiwi fruit.'

Gower had a remark ready, but Gerrard flowed on with other examples of substitution replacing authenticity. He ended with: 'One shudders to see how far people will go.' And in this instance he knew exactly what he meant by too far.

Gower tilted the bottle until the last of the claret ran into their glasses. His agent had come extraordinarily well equipped. He said so.

'Delighted you approve the meals on wheels,' said Gerrard, wiping his lips with a napkin. And when the wine was finished he got up, saying: 'Now don't move, there's more to come.'

Distant voices travelled on the breeze from the direction of the pub. Gower pulled on a sweater. Shadows of trees were long streaks against bristle-short grass. His visitor returned with a gâteau oozing cream and decorated with fresh fruit. Gower had not seen as much food for weeks, he had eaten sparingly and he had drunk nothing alcoholic.

The realization ought to have served as a warning but did not. He indulged, as Gerrard intended he should. They carried on talking about food and wine, and then about the likely merits of the pub over the fields and the changing appearance of the Isle of Wight, visible only from the cottage's first floor and variable according to wind, weather and time of day.

When it was virtually dark they rose to go in, tacitly abandoning the washing up in favour of a pot of strong coffee. Gerrard had brought his favourite blend and also a bottle of brandy. In his own mind, Gower fixed that Gerrard would stay the night and was trying to remember whether either of the spare beds had linen on them or whether one would have to be made up.

But when it came to it Gerrard insisted on driving back to London. 'One is not a country bumpkin, after all. The pleasures of the countryside pall with astonishing rapidity.'

Arguments that he had drunk too much alcohol to be safe at the wheel failed to pierce his confidence. He drove away, promising to telephone more frequently and to shut the gate to the lane. Gower stood on the path, in the space between the cottage and the apple store, and watched the tail lights until they swerved out of sight. Then he ran forward, stopping when he could see as far as the gate. The lights had halted there, before moving ahead and turning left. A shadowy dark shape appeared in their faint glow and there was the noise of the shutting gate. The engine changed gear and the car went away.

Lonely, John Gower stumbled back indoors. He had drunk and eaten to excess, he wanted sleep urgently. Then he was in bed, the time between approaching the cottage and finding himself in bed an unremembered gap. He went to sleep.

The sound that woke him was a shower slashing against the window. He opened his eyes to painful brightness and closed them again, groaning. Snippets of the previous evening came back to him, a random selection of incidents. Drawing himself up, he identified each agonizing manifestation of the classic hangover. It was 10.15 a.m.

Willpower propelled him into the bathroom in search of a cure, although his body wanted to be left to die in whatever peace immobility conferred. The upstairs bathroom cupboard was no help, he had to go downstairs to the bigger bathroom to continue the search.

He dragged himself to the ground floor, reaching the lobby where rooms converged, tried a door and entered the sitting room by mistake. The room was littered with coffee cups, brandy glasses, and Gerrard's ashtray. A window was open and raindrops were speckling the dining table. He went to close it, knocked against the sideboard and sent the hunting horn resoundingly to the floor.

And closing the window he saw the table outside, the crockery he had left, the bottles on the grass, the stub of Gerrard's cigar floating beneath a chair. He groaned again, not pain this time but acknowledgement that the caution of two months had been discarded in one irresponsible evening. Sunday was the day that nosy people strayed from the path to peer through the narrow rear gate on to Butlers' land, it was the most dangerous day of the week, yet he had to go out there and bring the things in.

Wearing an anorak from a cupboard, he shoved his feet into a pair of Wellington boots and went into the kitchen. Again the window was open, raindrops spattered the draining board and the floor. The kitchen door was unbolted, the lean-to door was unlocked. He shuddered at his laxness and went into the wet.

The plates were slimy and the debris of the meal slithered disgustingly as he ferried them indoors. Next he sought out painkillers in the downstairs bathroom, reheated left-over coffee and washed down the tablets. Then he made a fresh pot, scraped off the dirty plates, stacked them and generally forced himself to restore order, his unwilling limbs obeying, sluggishly.

When it was done, he ran through a mental checklist, confirming that the doors were locked, the windows closed, every tell-tale sign of occupation hidden. The only flaw he knew of was the garden table that he had left near the house in preference to carrying it to its usual place near the flower bed. He delayed replacing it until it was dry outside.

The painkillers were wearing off. He took more, drank water to flush away the poison in the system. And then it took hold of him, the anxiety about David Gerrard.

He can't have driven home without being in an accident or being stopped by the police. He drank more than I did; how could he have reached London?

He did what he had hoped not to do, what Gerrard had dissuaded him from doing except in emergency. He rang Gerrard's flat. The lack of answer fed his fears.

If something's happened to David, then I'm stuck. And I won't know what's happened. He's my only link with the outside.

Self-pity surged but was followed by a revival of determination. *There'll be a way round it. If I have to succeed without him then I will.*

He fully intended to try Gerrard's number again, but his thoughts turned to Richard Crane. He hurried to the typewriter and immersed himself in that parallel world.

Conroy was courting trouble because Crane was suspicious of his partner's handling of one of their property deals. Conroy ought not to try and steal the limelight, Crane did not like him doing that. In a bitter exchange Crane accused him of being a mere middleman. Quite soon Conroy would be written out of the story.

John Gower had not resolved what would happen to Conroy. Killing him off was tempting but he was afraid of tipping the novel towards the thriller genre instead of keeping within the bounds of what he knew. Apart from that, killing Conroy would inflate his importance, both in Crane's eyes and in the reader's. Killing was too good for Conroy. Another fate would have to be devised.

Devising, Gower strolled downstairs and realized that most of the day had slipped by. Broken cloud hung overhead and the sheen of water was fast drying from leaf and grass. For a few seconds he listened at an open window and, hearing no human sounds, hurried outside and shifted the table.

Fresh air excited him, he longed to remain there, but the folly of the previous evening chastened him. He punished himself by going straight back inside, shutting the window and putting the kettle on for some tea. The kettle was almost at the boil when a small red head skipped by the window. Gower dropped to the floor.

Danny! That kid again!

He needed to reach up and switch off the kettle before it steamed the room. And he was halfway there, crouching with one arm outstretched, when an equally urgent thought came to him: *The lean-to! Unlocked!*

His fingers flicked the switch and stifled the kettle's steamy breath. On hands and knees he scuffled to the kitchen door. If he had known precisely where Danny was he would have entered the lean-to and locked it, but he did not know and dared not risk coming face to face with the boy. Instead he did what he had been forced to do the previous time. He bolted the kitchen door that led to it.

Keeping low he scuttled to the lobby and up to the landing. The window did not help this time because Danny was already behind the house when his head bobbed past the kitchen. Gower went into the nearest bedroom and looked down. Trees obscured much of what he wanted to see, but in his mind's eye he pictured the child at one of the rear windows.

And in a moment Danny jumped into view, more or less where he had thought he might be. Danny had been close to the house and now he was cavorting on the grass. Gower drew back beside the curtain and looked obliquely at the child. The flushed face was all uncontained excitement. Then the body twisted and the denim legs carried Danny away. Gower shot into the other bedroom, caught a flying figure, then made it to the landing in time to see Danny reach the path and go hurtling to the gate and the lane and home.

Gower understood what Danny would tell them, Susan and his mother and father. He would say the typewriter had gone from the table.

Gower wished there was a way to stop him.

Hazel answered and said Gerrard was on the other line and could she help. Gower said he would call back. He had not given a name and he did not ring again. He had learned as much as he needed to know. His agent was alive and functioning as usual.

Quickly he settled to work but on this Monday morning the writing was not coming easily. His thoughts strayed from time to time to the events of the weekend, and he made a mess of a scene by allowing Conroy's point of view to predominate. Ripping up the pages he did it again, writing more slowly and carefully. Conroy had no right to engage the reader's sympathy, he must be cut down to size. Gower had still not decided what Conroy's sticky end might be.

But the rewrite went no better and he got up with a sigh and started downstairs wondering whether a cup of coffee could perk him up. From the landing window he noticed the dog.

This was a fat spaniel, a pet he remembered was called Twiggy. That's what Danny's father had called out when he was seeking it after proving, to his satisfaction if not his son's, that the door of the lean-to at Butlers was locked and always had been.

Too much to hope Twiggy was alone and, as Gower dismally predicted, Danny's father walked into view. Gower sat down on the stairs and rested his chin in his palm. What a morning! All that time wasted over the weekend because of David Gerrard's visit and its aftermath, and now Richard Crane was behaving feebly and letting Conroy better him, and

Danny's father and the family pet were scouring the grounds of Butlers for clues to the presence of an interloper.

The door of the lean-to was tried. He saw the man wander into the apple store and out again, watched him shake his head over the abandoned tractor and the unfinished grass cutting, heard him moving around close to the cottage. There was no question of it, the man was taking Danny's reports seriously. It seemed an age before he gave up and drifted away down the yellow path, the inaptly named Twiggy bowling ahead of him.

Gower was on edge. Suddenly it was impossible to act naturally and he caught himself hovering in the lobby, keeping out of sight of the window except for darting movements to take a mug from the cupboard and pour his drink. Until now it had not occurred to him that he had already retreated from the sitting room, conceded it to the enemy.

He was ready to hand over the kitchen too, but bullied himself to be less defensive. If the worst happened and he were found at the cottage he would have to extemporize, plead amnesia and let David Gerrard extricate himself as best he might.

But the bullying was not enough, he was deeply disturbed by the visits of the boy and the man. Without further tussle, he carried upstairs to a spare bedroom the electric kettle, a jug, the tin of ground coffee and the remainder of the milk Gerrard had brought. Having protected himself in this way, he was ready to deal with Richard Crane's problem with Conroy.

By mid-afternoon, he had rewritten the sequence for the third time and got it right. Conroy was to be out of the action for a while, Crane could ignore him. Gower allowed him a celebratory meal with Julia, his girlfriend, and then brought him good news about a rival's downfall. The chapter ended on a high note.

Facing up to reality again, Gower's own exhilaration dissipated. He rummaged in the kitchen for leftovers to make a sandwich. While he gleaned he was nervous, one eye on the kitchen window and straining to hear whether anyone was near the cottage.

He ate sitting on the stairs where he was able to watch the path. His habit was to wash up as he went along, not only for tidiness under circumstances where he was forced to be tidy, but also because he did not care to have a job waiting for him when it could be done instantly. In addition to the plate there were four other pieces of crockery that had held oddments of food in the fridge.

Approaching the sink gingerly, he put a plastic bowl in it and ran water. The sound was violent. He imagined it reaching the attention of anyone in the garden, and held his hand beneath the flow to steer it against the side of the bowl so that it ran silently. Everything he did was done with the stealth of a man trying not to awaken a light sleeper.

When the china was washed and draining, he dried it with sketchy wipes of a tea towel and put it away. All the while his eyes were going to the window, his imagination inventing sounds and presences he dreaded coming true.

And when he lifted the bowl to swish the contents down the plughole, he thought of the urgent rush of blue water swirling from a pipe on the back wall into the drain inches below. Instead of pouring, he carried the bowl into the downstairs bathroom and emptied it into the lavatory pan. During the night, when he would be safe, he could flush it away.

Upstairs again he checked from several windows to be sure he was alone. Then he stayed at his bedroom window, staring across to the Isle of Wight. The weather was uninteresting, warm but not sunny, the sky a smudge without defined cloud and the blue parts were a wishy-washy colour. The island was also at its most nondescript.

Yet the island thrilled him, suggesting as it did a sea journey, a separate world, a fresh start. The joy of going there broke upon him, changing his mood as surely as sun, freed from cloud, transforms a landscape.

I'm going to go to the island. I'll get the ferry from Lymington and just go there. Today. No, but tomorrow maybe.

He pressed his forehead against the latticed window, his fingers clawed at the deep, cool, stone windowsill. He wanted to escape, to gain a new place and leave behind him all the pressures that encumbered his life at Butlers.

Once, long ago, he and Rob Watson had sailed near the island. There had been talk of mooring overnight there but something had come up and they had turned for one of the Hampshire harbours.

Gower's body swayed with the remembered movement of the *Jumble*, his ears were full of the slap of the sea and the piteousness of seabirds. He was remembering the time when . . . A swallow dipping by the bedroom window cut the memory away. But Gower went on to think about Rob Watson, Rob as he had last seen him, on television after the *Fleur* was wrecked.

Remorse bit more painfully than it had been able to do earlier. *Poor Rob. The* Fleur *was all he had, and I took her away. But I'll make it up to him. I've got money coming, I'll buy him another boat. As soon as the money comes, it'll be a priority.*

And in the wake of remorse came certainty that something was going tragically awry. Gerrard had promised that a great deal of money was on its way, but Gerrard had also said that Linda was happy to think he was dead. On *Woman's Hour* she had put up a good performance of bewildered hope, but softened with Gerrard's food and drink she had revealed a deeper truth.

The core of his plan had been to make the money to win Linda back. Never, in his most searching moments, had he believed she would not come. Wasn't she the one who had started their 'rich and famous' joke? What had she said in the telephone call, their last one, when he had tried to persuade her to have dinner with him, asked her to talk over her decision to move out of Stream Cottage, and she had refused? He had alluded to their joke: 'You'll be sorry when I'm rich and famous.'

And Linda had replied: 'I might change my mind under those circumstances.'

The probability now appeared remote. Gower felt sick.

His mood swung again, to a savage anger that he was in no position to influence her. He had fooled himself that by hiding for a few weeks he was dodging his problems. In the event, the hideout had become a trap and the problems, although changed, were not reduced.

Without pausing to think it over, he flung himself out of the room and grabbed the telephone. For the second time that day Hazel answered him. This time she put him through.

'David? It's John. I can't – '

'Well hello, Simon! Long time no see.'

'What?'

'Must be years. What are you up to now?'

'David, it's me, John.'

'Yes, I know. Well, what can I do for you?'

'You mean you can't talk now?'

'That's right.'

'Very well, you keep up your Oscar-winning role and I'll tell you what I want you to hear.'

'Yes?'

'I can't go on with this. After what you said about Linda, it's – '

'This evening? Yes, I'll give you a call this evening and we'll discuss it then?'

'David – '

Gower was shouting into the receiver seconds after he knew Gerrard had hung up on him. He seethed.

He's making it worse. He's supposed to be helping, and he's making it worse. Now he won't even let me talk to him.

He paced through the house, a caged creature, helpless. In a while he came to a halt by the typewriter. Richard Crane was sharp in his mind. Crane's penetrating look drew him back into the story. Crane was glad that Conroy had gone, but was suspicious about the reason. He needed to be certain that Conroy would not cause trouble, but that could wait. First, Crane must put out feelers to trace Conroy, but must keep himself aloof from any dirty business. Other people were his tools, it was not necessary to sully himself. The security at the flats where he lived, the extravagant car he drove and all the trappings of the urban rich nicely insulated him from London at large and from the black deeds that were done there.

Around 8 p.m. David Gerrard telephoned. He interrupted a scene where Crane was manoeuvring Julia to betray the confidence of one of her professional colleagues and thus strengthen his own bargaining position. Julia was loyally resisting, although she had no inkling of the value of the information to Crane. Before the scene ended she would capitulate.

Gerrard adopted an admonitory voice, ticking Gower off for ringing him at the office and emphasizing the pitfalls. 'Hazel could so easily recognize your voice.'

'Nonsense. I've hardly ever spoken to her.'

'One's secretary is trained to recognize voices, to weed out the unwanted. She's experienced in this, she used to work for a shady solicitor and there were many unwanted weeds in that particular patch. I would put even money on her identifying you.'

Gower sighed. 'All right. I won't ring your office again, but it was urgent, I mean I urgently needed to talk to someone.'

'And there's only me. Quite so. Well, this is scarcely news, John, is it? You've coped for weeks, why panic now?'

Gower retorted that he was not panicking. Yet when he described his feeling of being besieged by inquisitive neighbours and his despair about Linda, he could not make it sound rational to his own ears.

Gerrard attempted some homespun psychology. 'Under other circumstances I would say you should get out more. It's the isolation that's getting to you.'

Exasperated, Gower said: 'I realize that!'

'Then all I can counsel is that when you suffer these attacks of whatever it is, you close your eyes, lie back and think about the money. "It is pretty to see what money will do." That's Pepys, by the way.'

'That's no answer, David.'

'It's the only one I have for you. And it's useless growing neurotic, there's no immediate respite for either of us. We've got to see it through.'

Gower snorted. 'Thanks for the pep talk.'

Gerrard made a supreme effort, saying he did truly understand and that if there was anything he could do then he would do it. 'For instance, do you want me to see Linda again? Keep an eye on her?'

But Gower said no, he did not want that. He did not explain that if Linda were actually enjoying the illusion of his death he would prefer not to hear any more about it. News of her sparkily coping, planning to sell off the marital home and make a new life for herself would do his morale no good whatsoever.

He said: 'I want to get money to Rob Watson, to repair the *Fleur* or replace her if that's not possible. When the money comes in, that's what I want as a priority.'

The agent said that yes, naturally, that would be the decent thing to do. When Gower asked him how soon there would be sufficient money for it, he hedged and said he would let him know.

Then Gower said: 'When the money comes, will you see that it goes to Rob? You can send it anonymously, can't you?'

'Well certainly your seafaring friend won't be receiving a cheque with my name or yours on it. Yes, one can send things anonymously, through solicitors and banks.'

For some reason Gower assumed Hazel's shady ex-employer would be used. 'Then do it as soon as you can, please.'

He was happier when the call was over. Sheer anticipation of righting his wrong to Rob Watson made him feel as good as if the deed were done. Guilt was assuaged. And he did not regret having told Gerrard about the children and the dog and the man who bothered him. It was to be weeks before he wished with all his heart he had kept his mouth shut about that.

His sense of being besieged was unabated though for the

rest of the week, except for the lengthy periods when he moved out of his Butlers' world into the freedom of Richard Crane's life. But there were no more incidents at the cottage that week, no more visitors and no more telephone calls. Gerrard failed to ring and Gower rang his home number several times without success. Then the jibe about neuroses rose up to taunt him and he was deterred from trying any more.

He banished Gerrard from his thoughts, save when he needed a scapegoat to blame for his predicament. When those moments had passed he took comfort from the knowledge that Gerrard was storing up treasure for him and that before long he would step forward and take the key of the treasure house.

He daydreamed, seeing himself re-entering the world but at a more glamorous level. London, naturally. Hard as it was to admit it, Linda was right about London and he had been wrong about the country. London it would be in future, then. That should please Linda. A smart part of London, not a suburb like the one where she had grown up. His imagination produced a tender scene with himself and Linda, wine glasses in their hands, on the balcony of a flat, watching the tide coming up the Thames.

The Groucho Club in Soho, the first Thursday of the month. The Crime Writers' Association was meeting upstairs, its committee session overrunning and its rank-and-file members hovering, awaiting access to the room. A drunken gossip columnist was spinning in the revolving doors, arguing with a friend on the pavement in Dean Street and with an enemy in the club's foyer.

Rain Morgan walked in through an adjoining door. A man she knew slightly waved to her, not the man she had come to meet for a drink, the one promising to fit the final piece in the jigsaw of an exposé she was working on. No, the man who waved was a crime writer, one who had escaped the turmoil of Fleet Street for a life of murder and mayhem. She liked him. She went over to say hello.

'Glad I saw you,' he said, editing out greetings. 'I've got a titbit that might interest you.'

She noticed a space in the bar, away from the mêlée buying drinks and out of earshot of the rumpus in the foyer. 'Tell me.'

'Everything, for a glass of the Groucho's dry white.'

Rain ordered two glasses, his wine and her mineral water. The space had been taken, but she discovered another, skilfully averting her eyes from the impatience of the other man, the one with whom she had her appointment.

'I'm afraid I haven't long,' she apologized, raising her glass.

'It won't take long. It's this. Did you know Alf Wilson, in whom you have shown yourself to be interested, was negotiating to adapt a novel by John Gower, in whom ditto? I heard it from my agent and he heard it from someone else in the business. You'll need to check it out, of course, but I'll be surprised if it isn't reliable.'

Rain gathered names and telephone numbers from him. 'Did your agent say which Gower novel?'

'No, afraid not. The matter was only mentioned in passing. I was with him to pursue adaptations of my own work, not to bother about dead playwrights and missing authors. He'd have loved a long digression and I wasn't going to let him have one, so I had to let the news flow by.'

Later, when she left the Groucho and snatched a taxi, she was in buoyant mood. The man with the missing piece of jigsaw had been as good as his word and her story was complete. And the crime writer had kindled fascinating speculation about Wilson and about Gower and about whether there was a link.

Back at the office she found Rosie ministering to the giant sweetheart plant on her desk, a 'small appreciation' of a reader's gratitude that had grown into an enormous liability. Holly, watching Rosie spray and polish leaves, said to Rain: 'I do hope you made it clear to Joan that her major responsibility in the role of your secretary will be to look after the jungle.'

Rain gulped that she had forgotten. She had devoted herself to stressing the tedious aspects of the job and assessing Joan's secretarial skills and had overlooked her plant husbandry.

Rosie interrupted, spray in hand. 'Doesn't matter because Joan isn't coming.'

Together Rain and Holly said: 'Huh?'

Rosie coloured. 'I can't think of a nice way of putting this, Rain, but she turned you down.'

'Oh.'

Holly asked: 'Why?'

Rosie shuffled and murmured: 'Computers.'

Rain huffed and whisked up her telephone. But before she had dialled the full number she aborted the call and told Holly the titbit from the crime writer. She said: 'You see, this all comes back to David Gerrard. He's John Gower's agent and he'd have known if there'd been an approach about a Gower novel for television. But he denied any contact with Alf Wilson.'

Holly rested her elbow on her desk and twirled a diminutive plait around her forefinger. 'May I book a ringside seat for when you tackle him? Looks like you're ready to go for the jugular.'

Rain drew a deep calming breath and said: 'I'd better not. I've decided to talk to other people before I ring Gerrard. He's so slippery he'll escape me unless I have a file of incontrovertible proof.'

And Rain avoided ringing him that day altogether. She spoke to the crime writer's agent, whom she knew, and confirmed the story. Then she spoke to the man to whom he referred her and so on and so on until she came to a woman who'd had it first-hand from a man who had wanted to collaborate with Wilson on the adaptation.

Rain did not ring the potential collaborator immediately, because of the time difference. He was in California. His name was Nicholson.

'Yes,' she said to Holly, 'the same Nicholson who broke the news to me that Wilson was finished, that no one would work with him and that anything Wilson told me about a new project was a sham.'

The book in question was *A Candle Lit*. Learning this, Rain detoured on her way home that evening and called at 18 Hunt Road. Mrs Dobson was home, drinking a powerful cup of tea in her basement lair and watching television. Rain was coerced into accepting a cup.

'They've let it, you know,' said Mrs Dobson. 'Didn't take them long, not as long as you might think considering what happened in there.'

Rain asked after the new tenant of Alf Wilson's flat. Mrs Dobson said he was young and noisy and she believed he and the Colonel were not getting on.

'Did the landlord clear all of Alf Wilson's possessions out before reletting?' Rain asked.

But Mrs Dobson could not say. Before going upstairs to inquire, Rain asked after the book that Mrs Dobson had taken from the flat in her presence.

'That book?' said Mrs Dobson. 'Couldn't get through it myself. I like a good read but I couldn't stomach that one. Mind you, it was true what he was saying about being poor in London, you see it everywhere, don't you? Rich and poor, and not much in between. My late husband used to say . . .' Rain's attention drifted. A cushion on Mrs Dobson's chair reminded her of one that had been in the upstairs flat. A vase on her kitchen table, brimming with sweet williams, brought the one on Wilson's mantelpiece forcibly to mind. Rain wondered how much more loot Mrs Dobson had gathered.

The woman heaved herself on to her feet and waddled into the next room, so fat Rain expected her to wedge in the doorway. She came back with two books: the Gower novel and the translation of a Czech novel. She said: 'I should think you'd like to have them both as mementoes, seeing as he was a friend of yours.'

Long ago Rain had given up correcting the mistake. In common perception she would for ever be the friend who had failed him when he needed friendship.

She mounted the stone steps from the garden flat soon after, the Czech translation and the annotated copy of *A Candle Lit* concealed in her shoulder bag. First stop was Ratcliffe's ground-floor flat. As she entered the grim hall, she was doubtful how best to reopen the subject that had petered out in April.

But Ratcliffe was coming down the stairs from the upper floor and they met by chance. He was heated and pleased to have someone to whom he could pour out his anger.

His complaint was the noise from the new tenant. 'Can't have lived in a flat before,' he growled. 'I've been up there a dozen times if I've been up there once but does he take notice? No, he does *not*. Music, you know, loud music and he denies it's excessive although I can hear it from here.'

Ratcliffe seemed older and frailer than when she had last seen him. Anger had reduced his pupils to pinpoints and he was unhealthily pale. There was also a tiredness in the lines about his eyes and a slight stoop in what had previously been a notably erect body. As she took this in, the bass line of a rock band began its distinctive thump, thump, thump over their heads.

The old man rolled his eyes in the direction of the sound. 'Nights, too,' he said. 'Nobody wants to do anything. The landlord isn't interested, the agents managing the property couldn't care less as long as the rent is paid. The other tenants don't bear the brunt of it as I do and they don't want to make a fuss. Afraid of being thrown out, you see. Oh, I've told them they can't be evicted, they have protection under the law, but they say in that case so does the demon drummer.'

At her querying look, Ratcliffe explained: 'He doesn't confine himself to recorded music, he practises his drumming to accompany it.'

Taking his cue, the demon drummer of the first-floor flat began to drum.

Rain offered to speak to him. 'I'll have to pretend I'm your niece or else we'll be sidetracked into discussing what business it is of mine. I think niece will do, don't you?'

Ratcliffe, grateful for this unexpected kindness, agreed it would do perfectly. He plainly supposed she would fly upstairs there and then and confiscate the drum, but Rain was combining her sweetest smile with a confusing hint of ruthlessness.

'First,' she said, 'I'd like you to tell me something about Alf Wilson.'

Ratcliffe was no match for her blend of helpfulness and blackmail. 'What about him?'

'Anything you like, as long as it explains his death and his reason for rounding us all up to discover it.' She laughed, making it clear this was a preposterous demand that could not be met. But the best way to achieve a little was to ask for a lot. Ask for a little and often you got nothing.

Ratcliffe said: 'I had words with Wilson about noise too.' He was sitting in his usual chair, his veined hands on jutting kneecaps clad in lovat tweed. The big room dwarfed him. He was too shrunk for the solid furniture and the long, heavy curtains that were tugged back unevenly at the window.

She coaxed him to say what had happened, and the story dribbled out.

'A week before he died,' he said, 'there were men running up the stairs and shouting and stamping around until all hours. When I complained to Wilson next day that my sleep had been shattered, he denied the noise had been anything to do with him, said it must have been in one of the other flats. He said he didn't have many visitors and certainly not noisy ones. I knew that he didn't have them often, rarely in fact, but I was positive he'd given a party, or whatever it was. We rather locked horns over it. He wasn't being straight with me, and I was furious at being lied to.'

She asked whether this had happened only once. To her mind it was extreme for there to have been an altercation over a unique incident when the two men had lived one above the other for years. Ratcliffe said: 'Yes, only once. Although I did hear people on the stairs late at night on three other occasions.'

'Before or after the one you've described?'

'After. The last time was the night before he died.'

Rain recalled Ratcliffe talking to the police immediately after the body was found, recalled what he had said at the inquest. *Perhaps he's forgetful*, she thought. *Perhaps he isn't aware he's always said he went to bed early the night before we found the body and heard nothing and knew nothing unusual had happened until he came across the note beneath his door next morning.*

Ratcliffe read her mind. 'It wouldn't have made any difference, would it? I don't know whether he was one of the people on the stairs that night or not. It would have meant a lot of idle speculation and it wouldn't have altered the fact that he hanged himself. The fellow was dead, spreading the word that there'd been that unpleasantness between us would have served no useful purpose. Least said, I thought. There's a point where the *whole* truth becomes dispensable. Matter of judgement where you dispense with it, of course.'

She pretended to agree while marvelling at the flexibility of truth. Ratcliffe was claiming he had reserved some of the truth because it would have cast Wilson in a poor light, whereas he was the one whose behaviour would have looked shabby because of what had come after. The dead often have the last word. Privately, she accused him of tempering the truth because of Wilson's fame. If Wilson had been a nobody, or if it had been the lowlier Mrs Dobson in the case, he would probably have told all.

And why, she wondered, was speculation always coupled with idle? In her experience there was nothing useless about it, speculation was what led to discovery. The truly idle minds were the unquestioning ones that accepted what someone wanted them to accept, true or not.

She put more questions, but all he added was that the voices and the footsteps he had heard were definitely male. Rain said: 'I'll go up now and play at being your niece.'

Knocking on the door of what had been Wilson's flat she rehearsed her speech and an attitude of indignant rectitude. When the door opened a very small, very young man stood in front of her. It seemed a pity to shout at him, despite his belligerent stance which she took to be defensive to counter his lack of stature.

Rain told the lie about being Ratcliffe's niece and was letting fly with some neat phrases about lack of consideration for neighbours, when she realized the small young man was looking at her in admiration.

He butted in. 'You're that Rain Morgan, aren't you?'

'So I am.'

'And you're the Colonel's niece?'

She saw Mrs Dobson's influence in this labelling of Ratcliffe. 'Yes.'

'Well. I suppose he's got to be related to someone. I mean, everybody is, aren't they?'

'Very true. Now about – '

'The noise, yeah. Well, the thing is, I've got to practise see.'

'But not in a flat.'

'Where then?'

She shrugged. She did not wish to be bested in an argument about the usual rehearsal arrangements of rock bands. She said: 'I don't know where you can, I'm telling you where you *can't*. The Colonel, er Mr Ratcliffe, er my uncle has pointed this out to you a number of times.'

'Yeah, I know. But I thought it would be all right because all old people are deaf.'

Rain had already noticed she was having to raise her voice to the demon drummer, he was a shade deaf himself, the effect, no doubt, of his own decibels. She gave him a heavy warning, threatening to report him to the pollution officer of the local council and have him prosecuted. The drummer took this in his stride, which suggested he had been down that road before and knew the procedure better than she did.

'Would you put it in the paper?' he asked.

Dismayed, she realized he welcomed prosecution, believing that if he behaved badly enough she would write about the incident.

'You know,' he prompted, ' "Promising Young Drummer in Noise Ban over Gossip Columnist", something like that.'

She could not help laughing. 'You're hoping I'll make you famous?'

'In showbiz,' he said seriously, 'you can never tell which direction the breaks are coming from.'

She laughed again, a wicked idea forming. 'You're already famous in a way, aren't you?'

'Yeah?'

'Renting Alf Wilson's flat. This is a famous address.'

He was all curiosity. 'Who's this Alf Wilson? Oh, yeah – one of the Great Train Robbers!'

She said no, that was Charles Wilson, and Alf, no relation, was a television playwright who had died a couple of months back.

'Oh *him*.' He feigned recognition but suspicion was genuinely dawning. 'Didn't he . . . um . . . ?' He looked around.

'Yes,' she said. 'He killed himself.'

'Didn't he . . . ?' He had his back to her, inspecting his room. She would have sworn the hairs on the back of his neck were standing to attention.

'Yes, that's right. Hanged himself. From the chandelier. Put a rope through the hook above it and hanged himself.'

The demon turned to her a very frightened face. She feared he was going to be sick. Devilment drove her on to say that Alf Wilson had also had complaints from her uncle about noise. The drummer interrupted her again, saying: 'How did he reach, then? Very tall, was he?'

'No, he was your height. You'd have to ask my uncle.'

'How would the Colonel know?'

'You'd be amazed what these old Burma hands know. That's the sort of thing they needed to know for jungle warfare. The Burma Loop and all that. You know, a special kind of noose.'

'Oh yeah,' said the drummer, nodding. 'Yeah, they would.'

Downstairs minutes later she reported that Ratcliffe was unlikely to suffer any more nuisance. 'He's probably packing his drum kit right now. He's not pleased to find his rent includes the company of a ghost.' She cut off Ratcliffe's gratitude with a warning. 'There's just one thing: be prepared to answer questions on the Burma Loop.'

He peered at her. 'Burma, did you say?'

Misgivings flooded in. 'You were in Burma, weren't you?' Surely someone had once said so.

'India, matter of fact.'

'Oh.' Recovering fast she advised him to lay claim to Burma, and to trot out anything halfway convincing about the Burma Loop. 'I've given him to understand you know more about Wilson's end than meets the eye.'

Ratcliffe appeared to have aged five years since this peculiar conversation began. He objected wearily that the Burma Loop sounded like an ice-skating step or a section of British Rail track but that he would try, if pressed, to persuade the demon that it was a particularly effective method of hanging.

They became so enmeshed in this absurdity, that it was a

while before Ratcliffe showed he had been brooding about Wilson during her brief absence upstairs. 'The quarrel was never patched up, you see. I felt he owed me an apology because he'd lied, and I was on my high horse about it. Petty of me, considering what he did. I've felt sorry about it ever since.'

'But you weren't to know.' They had kept themselves to themselves in that house, Ratcliffe had once told her that. She said it was not always apparent when someone was depressed, that victims deliberately concealed their state.

And then she saw they were at cross purposes. Ratcliffe had not meant Wilson was depressed. He looked blankly at her, brimming with memories of something different and unable to grasp her meaning. He ignored her words and said: 'When I went up to complain, he refused at first to open the door. At the time I was exasperated. I mean to say, having to stand out there on the landing shouting through the door while he cowered inside insisting there'd never been any noise!'

She saw the fall from dignity still rankled with him. But the notion that Alf Wilson had been physically scared to face the old soldier was not one she readily accepted, although she betrayed no disbelief.

What Ratcliffe said next put his remarks in a fresh context. 'With hindsight, I'd say he was a frightened man in his last days.'

A pity, Rain thought, as she walked home, *that Ratcliffe had not crystallized his impression about Wilson's fear much earlier. If it was correct, it could hold the key to the suicide.* She wanted to believe it, to believe any alternative to her own responsibility for his misery.

London was enduring a heatwave. The sky was smeared brown because an inversion layer capped the Thames Valley and prevented foul air escaping and clean air coming in. She longed for an excuse to go to the countryside for a few days. Summer smog made people ill-tempered and just plain ill. While she sat in her roof garden and studied Wilson's annotations in his copy of *A Candle Lit*, the world ended in grubby haze a short distance away.

Wilson had written in ballpoint pen and she was able to follow what he intended. Some sections were to be omitted altogether and others were to be dealt with in a new way. The book was a lesson in the difference between the television writer's art and the novelist's, an illustration of the contrasting needs of fiction told in moving pictures and fiction on the printed page. Whole passages of Gower's prose would be encapsulated in one look on the face of an actor, while elsewhere a precise phrase would require an entire scene to be written in.

All this raised the questions that she planned to put to David Gerrard. Why had the adaptation not been agreed? Had Gower resisted this 'butchering' of his story, as novelists were inclined to see it? Or had Wilson failed to find support from a television company willing to set him to work on the script? Or was the failure a matter of cash, of Gerrard seeking too much?

In the meantime she put her other questions to Nicholson, the long-haired television writer she had met the day after Wilson's death. She regretted it needed to be a telephone call because an interviewer learned from an interviewee's demeanour. Did Nicholson pale or stiffen when she raised with him the business of Alf Wilson and the Gower adaptation, and his own role in it? She would never know. Did he tap a toe or nervously increase his rate of blinking, for instance, when she challenged him that he had misled her by claiming Wilson was not involved in any project at all and never would be? She could not tell. Did he look relieved when she moved to other ground with her questions about television companies who might have been interested in him and Wilson collaborating or, conversely, might have refused to deal with Wilson at any remove? Rain tried to guess the answers to the hidden questions, while listening to the verbal replies to the spoken ones.

'You've got the wrong end of the stick, Rain,' Nicholson said. 'To the best of my knowledge, Wilson wasn't working on anything. It was a long shot that he and I would do the Gower script, therefore I didn't bother mentioning it to you.'

'Will you try to go ahead on your own now?'

Across the miles he laughed. 'How can I? Even if that was top priority with me – which it isn't, I'm here working on a bigger thing altogether – I'd never get permission from a guy who's vanished off the face of the earth. John Gower's stuff is on hold until he turns up dead or alive, or until seven years passes and he's declared officially dead. No, I'm glad I wasn't relying on that adaptation, because it isn't likely to happen.'

Rain said that Gower's agent had been pushing out stories about selling rights. Nicholson said sure, Gerrard had, but what happened to those deals if Gower reappeared and did not like them?

She came back with another query about an adaptation: Had Alf Wilson himself approached David Gerrard about *A Candle Lit*?

If only she had been able to watch, she would have seen Nicholson pull a face before he lied to her and said: 'No.'

Yet the lie did not throw her off the scent. She made more telephone calls and amassed information. Nicholson had said no, but she found a television company's production assistant who told her yes, and a director who also did.

Rain delayed the Gerrard call until morning, not wishing to inflate its importance. If Gerrard was, in her own words, slippery, then she was adept at handling him.

Around ten the next morning she rang him to express interest in a story about one of his authors, a story she had pigeonholed as another of his fakes but would pretend to take seriously for the time being. Gerrard oozed charm and complacency, indulged in *badinage* about the superior standards of her column above all others and cheerfully confirmed the improbable tale. He provided the author's telephone number, a sign that this story had the merit of being acceptable to the subject, which was not always the case.

Towards the end of their chat, Rain accused him, in lighthearted fashion, of dissembling when she had wanted his help with Alf Wilson. 'You *did* know him professionally, David. Only weeks before he died he'd been ringing you to ask after an option on one of John Gower's novels.'

Gerrard did not deny it. Like Ratcliffe he had tailored the truth, and like Ratcliffe he justified it. 'He didn't get it, so what does it matter? Besides, I didn't really know him. He was a voice on the telephone, then a brief letter. I wrote back and said no.'

'You mean Gower turned him down?'

'No, I did. He wasn't a good bet, Rain. One didn't want to waste Gower's time thinking about it, because Alf Wilson didn't have pull. The film would never have been made.'

'But what about Nicholson? Is that true of him? If they had collaborated . . .'

'No, Rain. It wouldn't have worked. Nobody wanted to know about Alf Wilson. Tragic, but that's the way of the world.'

'Tragic,' Rain echoed sourly, 'especially as a script by the dead and suddenly famous-again Alf Wilson, based on a work by the missing and suddenly famous-for-the-first-time John Gower, would be a valuable property, wouldn't it, David?'

Gerrard admitted that this was indeed so and mourned that he had not had his crystal ball about him at the time. He went on to say in a self-deprecating way that he had declined to report his connection with Alf Wilson because it was not in his own interests to be associated with failure. 'But should such a script have come to light amongst his possessions one would have been only too happy to have claimed the deepest involvement in its genesis, even down to changing the paper in his typewriter while he knocked it out.'

He was trying to stir up her amusement, but she remarked drily: 'No, you stick to success, David. Although some day, when we both have ample time, you must explain to me what's so very successful about having one writer dead and another missing.'

The last thing she heard before putting down the receiver was the agent's long and appreciative laughter.

She wrote her story about the Wilson–Gower–Gerrard connection. Holly, working on a story that had collapsed through lack of proof, was entertained by it. Unusually, she needed cheering. Dan was rejecting her persuasion to buy the Hackney flat and disregard the condemnation of the surveyor's report.

Holly said: 'If I could talk to Dan face to face, take him right through that report and show him that most of it really is minor stuff . . .' She ended with a sigh. Dan was still away filming.

'Come and have lunch in my garden.'

'And stop moping? Yes, I will. Both.'

Holly and Rain arrived in Kington Square together, Rain nimble up the stairs and Holly, like all visitors, labouring. When Holly walked into the flat Rain had already flung open the french windows and was winding back the tape on her telephone answering machine.

She tossed Holly a cushion to put on a garden chair, and then the taped messages began to fill the sitting room. The first one was short. 'This is Paul, Rain. I can't. Some other time maybe. Bye.' Then there was the builder, followed by a woman who had made some curtains and wanted to know what time would be convenient for her to hang them.

But the only message of interest to Holly was the one from Paul Wickham. She happened to be standing close to the machine when his voice came on and said, as Rain switched the machine off: 'Do you want me to pretend I didn't hear that?'

'You wouldn't be capable of it. Drink?' Rain made spritzers. Holly stood in the kitchen doorway, the cushion hugged to her tummy and her back resting on the door jamb.

Holly said: 'You rang him then?'

'I invited him to a dinner party this weekend.'

Holly was chagrined on Rain's behalf. 'And that's all he said?'

'It doesn't signify. He's laconic with answering machines. You and I, we gabble away. Paul's terse.'

'Hmm,' said Holly and scowled at the offending machine as she and Rain went past it and into the garden.

A couple of love-making sparrows fluttered around a tub of stocks. There was a butterfly on the cascading clematis. 'Well,' said Holly after a sip, as though there had been no pause in the conversation, 'he could have said why he couldn't come.'

'He'd have said work,' said Rain with a rueful smile. 'It's what we both say when we can't or won't, and it's generally true.'

Rain leaned back, soaking in the sun. Holly studied the sparrows. She thought about Rain and Paul Wickham. Wickham was an attractive man, whose physical energy was matched by intellectual vigour. Holly thought he was far better for Rain than the cartoonist, Oliver, had been, but she thought almost any man was.

Rain and Wickham nevertheless seemed an odd match. A leading gossip columnist and a detective chief superintendent gathering promotions in the fast lane were not a natural combination. To begin with, Holly had been agog that a professional defender of the establishment and a natural subversive had found anything to talk about.

Wickham was the type of Englishman Holly could envy for his easy assurance. How neat to be thoroughly English, middle-class, C. of E., safely on the establishment track. To be, in effect, on the side of the angels. Paul Wickham was comfortably on the side of the angels.

He also got his car clamped, had an explosive temper, could be unfairly caustic to stupid colleagues, and had fallen foul of a couple of superiors who resented what they suspected was flamboyance. This flamboyance boiled down to a flashy car and a taste for independent and talented women of striking appearance. Wickham's career had hiccoughed until one of these resentful impediments had been removed by retirement and the other had been outvoted. The further he fell short of perfection, the more Holly liked him.

She said: 'I'm glad you rang him. I couldn't have taken much more of your stubborn refusal.'

Rain opened an eye. 'Oh, I rang. In the end, I always do.'

'Good,' said Holly. 'I was getting worried. I know celibacy is supposed to be fashionable but I hate to see anyone a slave to fashion.'

They burst out laughing. If anyone cared for fashion, Holly Chase did. She would probably never afford a house, even a flat, in an expensive part of London but she magically afforded the most fashionable and flattering clothes each season. Holly's glamour was a byword in Fleet Street.

Holly told Rain about a wonderful new dress shop. 'But beware. Do not venture down that street if you are unwilling to buy, the temptation is insurmountable.'

And she described the décor, the stock, the background music and the informed conversation of the sales staff, ending only at the point where there was nothing left to report except the prices. Holly had years ago adopted the policy that it was of no interest to her to put a price on style.

They ate salads in the garden, happy to be up high and free of the closeness of the streets. Rain's tiny garden was blessed with a breeze, the neighbour's majestic trees sang softly to its rhythm.

'Idyllic,' said Holly. And firmly excluded Hackney and rising damp from her mind because whatever decisions she and Dan faced about their next home, they were not to be made now.

When she reached home that evening the last vestiges of her gloom vanished. An estate agent had posted her another bundle of prospects and she was on the verge of falling in love with the photograph of a garden flat on the borders of Islington and Hackney.

She took the details into the office on Sunday afternoon to show Rain, who had promised to call in at the office although it was Holly's Sunday for editing the column. Rain was reading the details when a call was put through from Pat Jarvis in Yorkshire.

Alf Wilson's cousin had read in Saturday's paper Rain's story about the Wilson–Gower–Gerrard link and had latched on to the suggestion that a fresh manuscript from her dead cousin would have been a valuable commodity.

'It's here, Rain,' she said. 'It's about the only thing I bothered to take away from his flat.'

Rain made encouraging sounds while Pat Jarvis described how she had found the script in the desk, cadged a plastic carrier bag from the old woman in the basement, and carried her prize home to Yorkshire. The coaxing murmurs did not give away that Rain had heard parts of this tale weeks ago.

She asked: 'Is it complete, Pat?'

'I couldn't say really. He's typed it and he's scribbled on what he's typed. I suppose he would have typed a tidy copy afterwards. But as to whether it's all there, well I don't know how to answer you. He hasn't typed "The End", and reading through, which isn't easy what with that scribbling, I didn't find the answer. But you know what drama is these days, they don't always give you an end, do they?'

Rain said she would like to see the script. Pat Jarvis said that was why she was ringing.

'I'd be obliged if you'd take a look at it, as you were more or less a friend of his. Then if there's anything to sell perhaps you could help me go about it.'

Rain asked her to have the script copied, for safety. Mrs Jarvis said she would put that in hand and suggested dropping the copy in the post to Rain.

'Don't do that,' said Rain. 'I'll come up and collect it.' She had her excuse to get out of the steamy heat of London.

Pat Jarvis was not surprised by her response. She had become used to her cousin being treated with more respect than when he was alive. They fixed a day.

'That's one missing script rediscovered,' said Holly, mischievously, 'Now there's only John Gower's new novel to look for. Better ask Pat Jarvis whether she's got that too.'

Rain gave her a withering look, and made plans to go to Yorkshire.

12

Exactly a week after David Gerrard's visit to Butlers, John Gower went out. Although he had teased Gerrard into imagining hilarious attempts at disguise, he had thought of a simple way round the problem of being discovered at the house, a way that prevented him having to admit who he was and claim an unconvincing case of amnesia.

The method was so obvious that he was embarrassed not to have thought of it earlier. All he had to do was wait for a rainy day and then go out.

When he woke on the Saturday and looked automatically towards the Isle of Wight, he could see nothing but rivulets smearing the bedroom window panes. The island was hidden by cloud. Gower's moment had come.

He dressed in the clothes Gerrard had brought him, clothes only the two of them knew he possessed, and he topped them with the waxed raincoat belonging to the owner of the cottage. On his head he put a matching hat with a turned-down brim.

Cheque book and cards in the name of Richard Crane were dropped into a pocket, the Wellington boots were pulled on and the house was locked behind him. He crossed the rear corner of Butlers' land and joined the path, then turned towards the village. The map in the sideboard drawer had allowed him to prepare his route with precision and he calculated on having to walk about three miles to the town.

Cars splashed by him unheeding, no one took any notice of him. Bad weather had set in for the day and people went about their business intent only on getting home again and drying off. Gower was delighted with the weather. He had to spur himself not to meander, admiring hedgerow scents and pretty views, because he was posing as a local and not a bemused outsider.

Even in the deluge, Lymington looked appealing, a well-heeled town rising up a long, low hill above a harbour crammed with pleasure craft. He passed the ferry terminal, noting the cluster of vehicles waiting to embark for Yarmouth, and seeing beyond them the masts of hundreds of yachts. There was no movement but water, it was a bad day to be setting sail.

Saturday was market day in the town, stalls edging the long main street. He pushed through the throng, alert for a bank with a cash machine in its wall. When he found it, he joined a short queue, people as wrapped up as he was or coy beneath umbrellas. He checked the unaltered balance in the account and withdrew cash.

Then he bought a newspaper from one shop, food from another, and from Boots a selection of toiletries including a hair lightener. As the downpour intensified his thoughts turned to the possibility of a bus home. The risks of inquiring about one and travelling alongside people with no occupation other than the study of their fellow passengers put him off. He wrapped the packages more securely in the plastic shopping bag the food shop had supplied and he walked home.

By this time the Wellington boots, a size larger than he took, were chafing and the wet trouser legs in the gap between coat bottom and boot top were clinging unpleasantly to his skin. Yet the return journey was not without its charms. Just to see people moving about as normal was welcome, to rediscover traffic noise and other evidence of busy lives was surprisingly so. With a flicker of regret he approached the first houses of Norleywood. He was nearing his journey's end.

He delayed going to Butlers, nervous about walking directly up to it. At a fork he took a lane to East End, the hamlet visible from the windows of Butlers. When he eventually spotted the pub ahead on the right, he watched keenly for the end of the footpath and then climbed a stile. He believed he got home unseen.

He meant it to be the last time he worried about doing that because that afternoon he bleached his hair from brown to honey blond. The process terrified him. The ammonia was noxious and the results uncertain. But when it was over he was fascinated by his reflection in the bathroom mirror. Whether it was genuinely honey blond he could not say, but he was not disappointed.

The colour was less than evenly distributed and his hair was yellowish instead of the whiter shade he had imagined from the colour chart in the packet. Yet as his hair dried it grew paler and when he ran his fingers through it and shaped it he was elated by the change. There was relief, too. It had been a gamble because, not wishing to draw attention to himself in the chemist's, he had spent minimal time reading the labels on competing products.

The hair cut was quite wrong and he knew it, but also that it would be hopeless to alter it himself. *Easy stages*, he thought. *Clothes next, then the hair cut.*

Sunday he spent with Richard Crane, reaching into his own depths for the character's responses, putting into the story nothing that was not an emotional truth. The work was tough and enervating but left Gower with a contented glow. He had written a passage as fine as anything he had ever done. If there was nothing else of value in the book, this would stand, this evocation of a common instinct that every reader would recognize in his own heart.

On the face of it, Crane was making a move that consolidated his position and blocked a rival developer. A subtle change was hinted at though. Crane's true motive had shifted. He was a man who knew himself and the world too and could control both. Yet his self-knowledge stopped short at a crucial point. Crane was incapable of knowing that he had jumped the gap dividing aspiration and fantasy.

Gower ignored Crane on Monday as he needed to visit Lymington again and the day was conveniently showery. He dressed as for his Saturday outing, left the same way and walked to the town. His goal was a shop selling casual clothes for young men. On Saturday he had noticed the type of customers it attracted. He was setting out to look like one of them.

Monday morning was a bad time because there were few other shoppers and in the shop he entered no others. Assistants were distant, unpacking boxes and talking to each other. He was left to browse.

He paid with a Richard Crane cheque, then bought a newspaper and carried his purchases home. In front of the bedroom mirror the new clothes and the fair hair revealed a man who was obviously no longer John Gower.

For the rest of the day he wore the new clothes, getting used to the way they influenced the movement of the body. When he went out in them he did not want to look like a man in unfamiliar garments.

In the early evening he opened the newspaper to see what was on television. His disguise allowed him to reclaim the sitting room, to be less frightened of unwanted visitors although he still preferred not to be discovered if possible. What he read sent him diving for the television switch, cursing himself for forgetting that this was the day *The Secret* was published. According to the newspaper, Linda was to be on an early-evening chat show talking about it.

Within seconds there she was, coming down the steps to the set as adroitly as if she had been on the chat-show circuit all her life. Gower backed away, keeping an eye on the screen and reaching with one hand into the sideboard. He fumbled for a glass and poured brandy from the bottle Gerrard had brought and which had been untouched since.

Watching Linda, Gower drank a congratulatory toast to himself. She was saying roughly what she had said a couple of weeks ago on *Woman's Hour*, that line about it being disloyal to give up hope and yet painful to go on hoping. Linda hit the right note again, being neither tough nor mawkish. And she looked very pretty. There was a suspicion of curl to her hair, her face was beautifully made up and she was dressed in something blue that flattered her blondeness.

The chat-show host was asking her about the *Charity* and this developed into a discussion involving a second guest who had strong opinions in favour of the Great Plughole Theory. After a few minutes of this, Gower was stirring irritably in his chair.

What about The Secret? *Why the hell doesn't somebody get around to talking about the book?*

In two minutes the item had ended and his book had not been mentioned except for the chat-show host's introductory remarks to explain Linda's presence. Apart from the brief rerun of her *Woman's Hour* interview, it had all been flummery about the power of the *Charity* to lure sailors to their death.

Gower was outraged, bitterly, silently outraged. He understood now why Gerrard had been upset by her performance on the radio, but this was worse. She had not accepted the television invitation to talk about John Gower, she had been there to talk about herself.

While he was still railing against his wife, David Gerrard telephoned to congratulate him on the publication of the book, a compliment Gerrard usually paid his authors. Gerrard commiserated about the television performance. 'But the Sunday papers were wonderful, John, one couldn't flaw them. Inches of it. Several used the publication of *The Secret* as a peg to recap the saga of your disappearance and there were some up-to-date interviews with the unfortunate Rob Watson.'

'The *Fleur*?'

'Scrapped, according to the reports.'

'Have you sent him the money?'

'It's in hand.'

'It will have to cover a new boat. She was a Class – '

'Yes, yes, I know. That was in all the papers yesterday. They quoted the price of replacement too.'

Gower guessed why. 'Because Rob was underinsured?'

'Had he told you that?'

'No, but the *Jumble* always was when we owned that. David, I – '

'I presumed a fellow who sells insurance for a living would be wiser than that.'

Gower did not dissent. Instead he asked whether the critics had liked the new book.

'Patience, John. The papers haven't actually pronounced on it yet. They were so overjoyed at the chance of another crack at the *Charity* story and the mystery surrounding you that they omitted to express an opinion on the quality of the book, although a couple recited the story line.' Gerrard laughed.

Gower did not. He rallied and said that as long as they had mentioned the book that was the main thing. 'And what about the launch party?'

That, reported Gerrard, had been wonderful too. Gower was exasperated that Gerrard was imprecisely finding things wonderful. He prodded, and Gerrard amplified to say that a great many journalists had been present and if Gower were to watch television news programmes he might catch a brief item or two.

Gower watched and he did. There was less rubbish about plugholes and more about him. David Gerrard was interviewed on one channel and successfully played up the new book. Linda was interviewed on another and did not. And each programme flashed up the photograph of the missing John Gower, a photograph Gower believed would no longer be of use to anyone.

He reduced its usefulness yet further the next day by returning to Lymington, dressed in his new clothes, and having his hair cut in a fashionable and more youthful style. The hairdresser, with bleached locks of his own, saw nothing incongruous in the state of his new client's hair and gossiped sympathetically about the merits of various lighteners.

From the hairdresser's Gower went to a newsagent's and was unable to resist buying a paperback of one of his earlier books. All the shops that sold books were today selling his. Two had been issued in paperback to coincide with publication of the hardback edition of *The Secret*, and there were window displays and special racks devoted solely to his books.

He was made to wait before picking up a copy because two women were at the rack ahead of him. While he was paying they came to the checkout, each with a book. He heard them marvelling at his disappearance. They were quoting television items about it.

One said: 'It's that Linda Gower I feel sorry for. I mean, not to know what's happened.'

'Yes, no woman deserves that.'

The first one laughed. 'She's very pretty. I shouldn't think she'll be alone long.'

Gower became conscious that the shop assistant was holding out his coins. He pocketed the change and left, shaken at the easy assumption that Linda would get herself another man. But he knew Linda better than a couple of Lymington shoppers did. She had not left him for another man, neither had she taken up with one since he had gone. Gerrard would have told him if that had been so. He preferred to trust Linda to come back to him once he re-emerged.

With the book in his pocket, he went in search of a booth where he could have his photograph taken. He knew the pose he wanted, he had practised at the mirror in Butlers. What he saw inside the booth was an enormous improvement. The hair cut and the fairness, combined with the casual modern clothes, shed years. He went into the pose, giving the camera the unswerving gaze of a man who knows his own worth.

Afterwards, he called at the post office for a passport application form in preparation for the journey to Hawaii and his subsequent discovery. Forms were available from shelves and he did not have to ask a clerk for them. Crossing the road outside, he caught his reflection in a window. He would not have known himself. He was looking at a stranger, a stranger who was rich and famous but paradoxically unknown. Cherishing that thought he gathered brochures from a travel agent and then caught the bus home.

All went well until he was walking up the curving yellow

drive to Butlers and a middle-aged man stepped away from the front door and confronted him. The man carried a couple of newspapers.

Gower held the key to the lean-to door in his hand. He concealed it, knowing the man had not noticed it. But he presumably had a proprietorial air as well as a hidden key because the man said: 'Good morning. I work for these people.' He held up one of the newspapers, a local freesheet. 'We're conducting a survey to check it's being delivered to all homes in the area.'

'Sorry,' said Gower, 'I don't live here. I'm delivering something. Sorry I can't help you. Excuse me.'

He strode up to the front door, feeling in his pocket for something to push through the letter box. His fingers closed on the passport forms. Through the heavy oak he heard the swish as they skidded across the stones within.

Then he turned away and walked back to the lane, the way the man from the freesheet had done. The man had left the gate ajar for him, and Gower closed it as he entered the lane.

Damn! I don't know which way he went and I've got to walk away and avoid bumping into him again.

The other houses were behind high hedges, the man could be anywhere. Gower tossed up and then went purposefully through the village. It meant a long walk but there was another way home. At the fork he took the lane to East End. Shortly after the pub appeared he came upon the stile and took the footpath.

Picking his way carefully, because the path was muddy and he was wearing his new light-coloured trousers, he neared Butlers. Its trees had been visible most of the way and now he saw fragments of thatched roof, but because he had been dodging puddles, he had not spotted a danger as soon as it arose. With a jolt he realized there was a figure on the track ahead, a man with his back towards him and loitering where the path ran beside Butlers' hedge.

Gower thought he recognized the blouson jacket of the man with the newspapers, but allowed himself the merest glimpse before turning back the way he had come. There was one cheering aspect of the near encounter: it allowed him to visit the pub at last.

Although his bedroom window showed him the roofs of only three buildings, there were several more at East End. The pub was cheerfully indicated by the baskets of lobelia and busy Lizzie hanging from it, but one of the houses near it came as a shock. It was a police house, the occupant's motorcycle standing on the drive ready for action.

Gower gasped and hurried past. None of the fantasies he had woven about what would happen if he went to the pub had included discovery of a police house over the road from it!

Then he was entering the pub, hoping he was not destined to meet the local bobby swilling down pints at the bar. He did not, and neither did the pub live up to any of his other fantasies about it. For one thing, there was a computer game. A trio of lads were playing it and, unaccountably, enjoying its ear-splitting electronic wailing. Every once in a while they were rewarded by a different cacophony, the tumble of coins as the machine paid out on a winning score.

Otherwise there were only two old men in the bar. Gower bought a pint of beer and sat in a corner bowed over his newspaper. One of the things he had missed most about his seclusion was the lack of a newspaper and now when he got hold of one he read it far more thoroughly than he had ever done in the past. He reckoned that by the time he reached the end of this one, whoever had been in the lane would be long gone.

When the man behind the bar was making tidying-up motions and looking wistfully at the clock, ready to announce last orders, the door was flung open and a man marched in. His dog padded directly over to Gower and sniffed his trouser leg.

Gower looked down into the eyes of a spaniel. A fat spaniel. He restrained any alarmed reaction and spoke to the dog. 'What's your name, then?'

He knew it, dammit. The creature was called Twiggy. And

he knew who would be standing at the bar. The newcomer answered the question: 'That's Twiggy. Named her when she was young and skinny.'

The barman and the newcomer laughed. Gower smiled at the joke, the way one would. Danny's father was paying for a pint, getting into conversation with the barman about the shocking effects of the weekend's downpour on the gardens. Gower lowered his head to his newspaper and listened. He learned nothing except local opinion of the weather.

What am I going to do now? If I walk back down the footpath, the chances are that Twiggy and her master will take the same route and see me turn in to Butlers. She doesn't look like a dog who'd want to walk the long way round by road. And if I go the long way, I've got the original problem of entering the garden without being spotted.

The lads at the machine finished their drinks and drifted out into the lane, feigning complaint at winning so little and spending so much. From the corner of his eye Gower saw their shapes through the window. They turned left. That was the way to the path. He gave an inward sigh. His glass was empty, the barman had the towels on the pumps. Without hurry, Gower folded his newspaper and fitted it into his jacket pocket before taking the glass to the bar and saying a general goodbye. The old men were rising to leave. He followed them out.

They went to the right, ungainly on arthritic legs, ambling up the deserted lane. Behind him Gower heard the sounds of Twiggy being coaxed to leave the pub. He walked to the left, the man and dog behind him.

If they go down the path I'll walk on as if I'm going to the fork. If he goes to the fork, I'll take the path.

Danny's father and the dog caught him up. 'Fresh today,' said Danny's father, falling back on the weather as a topic. 'A shade damp underfoot for walking.'

Gower agreed. He looked at the man's shoes, trying to tell whether they were muddy from the path. He wanted to avoid close questioning about where he had himself walked from and cast about for another subject. They were by the police house.

Twiggy was not on a lead, the dog was trotting ahead. She turned right and wriggled beneath the stile. Twiggy had provided the answer. Gower said: 'Knows her way home, does she?'

'Oh yes,' said Danny's father. 'She comes here often, as you might say.'

Gower walked alone down the lane towards the fork. He dawdled, watching through the hedge until the man's figure receded. Very slowly, Gower wandered back and climbed over the stile. He made wretchedly slow progress because he had to guard against coming upon the man by mistake. But when the final stretch of the path came into sight there was no one there and he thankfully entered the garden and fitted the key in the door lock.

Barely was he indoors before the telephone rang. Four rings. A pause. Another four.

'David?'

'Who else? And why have you not been answering? This is the third time I've rung you.'

'Sorry, I was out.'

'*Out?*'

'Yes, to Lymington and then to the pub. But it's all right.'

Gerrard exploded that it could not conceivably be all right and what on earth had possessed Gower to go wandering about and jeopardizing everything?

Gower replied that he was heavily disguised.

'Oh, my God,' groaned Gerrard, with theatrical overemphasis. 'Don't tell me, let me guess. A Mickey Mouse face mask?'

'No, and now I shan't tell you. You'll have to wait and see.'

Gerrard got down to business. He had good news about another contract that would, as he put it, inflate the funds. But also he had some bothersome news.

'Two bits, in fact. The first is that the *Daily Post* is raising awkward questions about your next book.'

'How can it? It isn't written yet.'

With a sigh Gerrard said: 'The perceptive Rain Morgan noticed there was no typescript – and no computer disks either, for that matter – at Stream Cottage.'

'She broke in there?' There was nothing Gower would not believe of journalists.

'No, no,' said Gerrard, placating. 'Linda took her there. They did an interview. You know, sob stuff about the heartbreak of a woman and all that.'

'And?'

'Rain's floating a story that the typescript was stolen. Today she ran a piece on the mysterious disappearance of your next money-making novel, and popped in a quote from the police saying no break-in had been reported at Stream Cottage.'

Gower protested that he had been left way behind and would Gerrard please explain what was threatening about this inaccurate paragraph in a gossip column.

Gerrard drew a deep breath, realizing that this was another of those occasions when he was going to have to spell out to an otherwise educated and intelligent person the art of reading newspapers. 'One, she thinks the book is virtually complete.'

Gower butted in. 'But it isn't, you know that.'

'All right, John, I know that I know that. But I must confess that I did permit myself to convey the impression that another brilliant Gower novel was ready for the publisher.'

'But why?'

'To tickle the interest, John, that's why. It put Pegwoods in a markedly competitive frame of mind when we talked about money for new editions of the earlier books and marketing budgets for *The Secret*. They understood that if they didn't play along, your next book might go elsewhere.'

Gower rolled his eyes. He would never understand David Gerrard and all his works. 'Tell me the rest.'

'Right. Point two, Rain Morgan hints that your typescript was removed from the cottage by someone with legitimate access to the premises. Otherwise its loss would have been reported to the police.'

Gower had a bright idea. 'Well you can scotch this, David. Tell her *you* have the typescript. And the disks.'

'I can't. I'd already told her I hadn't and neither had Pegwoods. She checked with Pegwoods, of course, she didn't take my word for it.'

Gower was thinking aloud. 'And Linda was there when Rain Morgan noticed . . . Look, does Rain Morgan have any idea where the book is?'

'No, how could she? If I'm pressed I shall have to suggest it went to a watery grave, that you refused to be separated from it and you were sucked into the plughole in tandem.'

Tartly Gower remarked that this was not funny. 'The only thing is for you to come clean and admit that there isn't a new novel.'

'No,' said Gerrard. 'One needn't reach those depths. That would be very damaging, to be caught out in an untruth of that kind. Publishers are elephantine, you know, never forget.'

'What else can we do?'

'The obvious, actually. How soon can you let me have a copy of what you've written?'

Gower reeled. 'That's months away. You know that, you know how slowly I have to work.'

'Oh come,' said Gerrard. 'You needn't be quite so precious about it, John. You're a big seller now. You'll be expected to do a book a year in future to keep a hold on that market.'

'Impossible!'

Gerrard said it was not impossible and he was to think it over. Then he changed the subject. 'The other bad news is that Ruby Dobby talked about you on breakfast television this morning.'

The name rang a bell but Gower had to ask who she was.

Gerrard said: 'Oh you know, that fat clairvoyante who dresses like an extra from *Carmen*. All frills and flounces and wobbly chins. I remember telling you about her. It was she who was the conduit for the autobiography of a dead parrot,

249

the book that Pegwoods splurged half their budget on this year.'

Gower admitted this refreshed his memory of Ruby Dobby.

'She told the bleary breakfast-time viewers that she could find no trace of you in the Other World. "John Gower," she intoned, "has not crossed over." And then she gave that awful giggle of hers and added that if you had, you were resisting her. Well, *that* I could understand,' Gerrard continued.

'Nobody believes her nonsense, do they?'

'Doesn't much matter whether they do or they don't. The fact is, the awful Ruby has raised a sneaky little doubt.'

Now who's being neurotic? Gower thought. Aloud he said: 'I'd feel worse if she'd said I *had* crossed over, especially if she went on to publish my posthumous memoirs too.'

Then he brushed Gerrard's concern aside, instructing the agent to pay money into his new account because he was preparing for his trip to Hawaii. He repeated the name of the bank, the branch and the number of the account.

'What's the pseudonym?' asked Gerrard, and not for the first time.

But Gower still refused to tell him. 'Just pay the money in, David. Send money for a new boat to Rob Watson and pay the rest into that account. That's all you need do.'

Gerrard said yes, he would do it straight away, but he smarted at being ordered about. Coming off the telephone he mulled it over for a while and then made another call, to his bank.

On Wednesday afternoon, while Gower was at the typewriter, he heard a car. He was too late to the landing to see what vehicle had driven into the apple store, but fresh tyre marks on the gravel made its route plain. Mystified, he watched David Gerrard walk up to the house and heard the bang of his fist on the lean-to door.

If Gower was taken aback to see his agent, his surprise was nothing compared to Gerrard's pop-eyed gaping when a dyed-blond man, looking ten years younger than usual, opened the door to him.

'Well, come in,' said Gower impatiently. 'Don't stand there staring, I want to shut the door.'

'Er . . . sorry. Um . . .' Gerrard stepped inside and continued to gape. 'This is the disguise? It's incredible.'

Gower nodded. He was amused to see Gerrard at a loss and he looked steadily at him, recording for future use the slack mouth, the rounded eyes, the frequent and failed attempts not to stare, and the way bewilderment confused what the man was attempting to say.

'Coffee,' said Gower firmly, and he boiled a kettle. He had moved the coffee-making things back to the kitchen since his appearance had changed, although he had grown to like working upstairs and the typewriter remained there.

Over coffee Gerrard handed him a wad of cash. 'You sounded urgent, I thought you would prefer to see some of it rather than wait for it all to filter through to that secret account of yours.'

Gower set the money on the sideboard without showing much interest in it. The notes were fifties and there was ample for his immediate needs. He refused to perform the demeaning task of counting it in Gerrard's presence.

'No, you didn't, David,' he said, repeating the straight look that he had learned could make Gerrard lower his eyes. 'You came to see whether it was true about the Mickey Mouse mask. Now you know.'

Gerrard cleared his throat. 'Actually one has to confess it's frightfully good. And, well, different.'

'Yes.' Gower studied Gerrard, pretending he was waiting for the man to say something else but knowing he could not. Gower said: 'You can sign some documents for me while you're here.'

He produced a passport application form and one of the photographs of himself in the booth in Lymington. He pointed out where he wanted Gerrard to sign the form and told him to write on the back of the photograph the words 'I certify this is a true likeness', and then leave a space before adding a signature.

When Gerrard objected, because he was being asked to approve details on a form that had not been filled in yet, Gower retorted that he had not known Gerrard was coming and it would save them both time if he did as he was asked. Grumbling, Gerrard signed the form and the back of the photograph.

Then Gower took the two documents upstairs. When he returned to the sitting room Gerrard's eyes were on the money. Gerrard moved his gaze, guiltily. He began to smooth a well-manicured fingernail.

'John, would you mind telling me what the new book is about?'

Gower stayed on his feet, near the doorway. He was wearing the look Gerrard found formidable. He said quietly: 'I told you, David. I talked to you about it when you gave me lunch, don't you remember?'

'That was a long time ago. No, I don't remember.' And Gower had not told him much because Gower hated talking about unfinished work, but Gerrard was warned off making this point.

Gower's face showed that such negligence was no more than he expected. He moistened his lips. 'I don't think we should talk about the new book, especially as your friend Rain Morgan is already looking for it.'

Gerrard bridled. 'She's not my friend.'

He saw Gower raise an accusing eyebrow. Gerrard knew he presented her as a friend all too often, exaggerated their professional contact because he imagined his authors were impressed by his close relationship with influential journalists. *Trust John Gower*, he thought savagely. *Why can't he keep that acuity for his fiction? Why practise on me?*

The visit was ruined for him, he sought to retreat. He said: 'John, if there's nothing else, I ought to be thinking about driving back.'

This was not what he wanted to say. He had anticipated

staying several hours and perhaps, in view of the excellent disguise, eating out together. He believed there were some decent restaurants in the area.

Gower said nothing. He stepped aside rather than obstruct the doorway. David Gerrard was obliged to get up and leave.

Alone again, Gower snatched the cash, ran upstairs to his bedroom and counted it. He made a note of the exact amount and the date when he had received it, and he put the note and the cash away in his grey canvas bag. Then he went to the next room and resumed writing.

Later, when he broke off for supper, he remembered the photograph and the form Gerrard had signed. He took his own fountain pen and aped Gerrard's handwriting as he added three words to the sentence on the back of the photograph, so that it read: 'I certify that this is a true likeness of Richard Crane.'

Then Gower set the pen down on the table and placed the unsigned photograph beside the one that had been endorsed. There it all was, the fair hair, the jutting jaw, the unrelenting eyes of Richard Crane. And there beside it was the proof, in David Gerrard's hand. 'This is a true likeness of Richard Crane.'

The plan to flit to Hawaii was foundering but Gower could not bear to admit this to Gerrard. He had spotted the flaw on reading the passport application forms. There were two, one for a full passport lasting ten years and the other for a visitor's passport valid for only one year. Gower was unable to use either.

Both relied on birth certificates as evidence of identity, and Richard Crane did not have one. Blocked, Gower had set the problem to one side and worked on his book but Gerrard's visit had brought it to the fore. He paced the sitting room, nibbling at the nail of his little finger as he concentrated on possible and impossible solutions.

Once there was a birth certificate there were two courses of action. Either he posted off the form for the full passport, with Gerrard's endorsement and the two photographs, and waited for it to be processed by the regional passport office at Newport. Or he took the other form, plus two unsigned photographs and an additional identifying document, such as Crane's bank cheque card, to a main post office.

Given a birth certificate and the choice, he preferred to go to Lymington Post Office, for simplicity and speed. But a visitor's passport would not get him to Hawaii. It could be used for up to three months for trips to Europe and Scandinavia, and it could take him to Bermuda. For all other destinations the standard passport was required.

Sidetracked into weighing the merits of Bermuda against Hawaii – well, Bermuda was *near* the United States, wasn't it? – he toyed with going there instead. Then he thought about using Crane's passport as far as France and then, having claimed his own passport from Stream Cottage in the meanwhile, flying on to Hawaii. The schemes were useless, but he thought of them all.

Exhausted by the insoluble, he gave it up and went to the freezer to take on another puzzle, deciphering the labelling on frost-encrusted packages. 'Lucky old Parsons,' he murmured, peering at what was presumably Mrs Parsons's handwriting on a solid block of chicken casserole. 'What wouldn't I give to fly away like you did, to write my book in the sun somewhere.'

He had the wrapper half off the casserole on its way into a saucepan, when he gasped so violently that the block of ice went skidding from his hand, glanced off the edge of the stove and streaked the length of the kitchen floor. Gower barely noticed. He was clutching his head, as if to hold in the stunning idea that had emptied his mind of everything else.

He ran to the sitting room, stepped over the casserole block, took a couple of steps, realized his stupidity and rescued the block by rinsing it under a running tap and then tossing it into the saucepan. In a minute he was tipping the first of the sideboard drawers out on the dining table, hands tremblingly eager. Richard Crane could never have a birth certificate, but Parsons did.

He did not find it in the sideboard. He had to explore a cupboard in the smallest of the three bedrooms before he came upon a file with marriage and birth certificates in it. Gower held the magical piece of paper up, and kissed it. He started to laugh, at his slowness, his obtuseness, his ultimately brilliant answer.

I've been asking the wrong question, asking how I could get a birth certificate for Crane, when all along the real question was whose certificate could I use. There's no reason for me to be Crane except when I'm at the bank.

Yet taking on Parsons's identity was not ideal. Parsons was older than Gower, and therefore older still than Crane. The discrepancy between the youthful figure and the date on the birth certificate ought to make any half-awake counter clerk smell a rat. Gower could see no way to tinker with the certificate, even if he had been unscrupulous enough to do so. He was prepared to gamble everything on the laxity of a clerk.

On the first truly sunny day of the week, Gower treated himself to a morning break in the garden. He walked away behind the house, through trees, until he found a place where he could sit on dry grass and look at sky through branches dotted with embryo apples. A lark was trilling above a fallow field. Goldfinches were investigating a hedge. Gower felt at peace.

This was a peace unkindly shattered by the noise of a tractor. Instantly, he was on his feet and aiming for the house, watching out for the old man who cut the grass, and ready to dodge him around the building until he could get inside.

Fumes emanating from the apple store gave away the man's position, though, and Gower was indoors and locking up by the time the tractor backed on to the path. With a cursory glance around the sitting room and kitchen to ensure nothing was visible that was safer hidden, Gower returned to his first-floor study.

Curiosity brought him out of it in a short while because the tractor that had been cruising up and down, to judge from the sound of it, came to a halt, although the engine was still running. Gower squinted through the landing window. The old man was seated on the tractor, near the drive, and he was speaking to a woman. Despite the weather, she wore an unbelted long raincoat and a blue headscarf pulled forward.

Whatever the old man said to her was sufficient to send her away. She headed for the gate and the mowing resumed. Gower also went back to work.

By lunchtime the man had apparently finished because he put the tractor away. Gower considered lunch in the garden, but the morning's narrow escape deterred him. Better to choose a day when the old man was not around. Disguised, he did not worry about being seen elsewhere but it was still too risky to let it be known anyone was in Butlers.

This was a fortunate decision because in the late afternoon the man came whistling up the drive, fetched a scythe from the apple store and set about some extra long grass in an area he had skipped on his visit weeks ago when the tractor had broken down. The grass had grown too long for the machinery to deal with it. Gower assumed the old chap would go around all the other corners of long grass, and then he put him out of his mind in favour of adventures in Docklands.

But within the hour the doorbell rang. He pressed his face to the usual window but could not see down to the door, and was giving up when a figure stepped back from the porch and looked towards the sitting-room window. It was the woman in the mackintosh.

Her reappearance after the old man had sent her away intrigued him. She rang the bell a second time and then, when there was no response, she began to move away. Gower watched her for a few yards, then went downstairs. He was in the kitchen when she came round the end of the house and peered through the window. The blue scarf had fallen back and blonde hair swung free. Linda!

She darted to the back door but he was there first, unlocking, drawing her in. They stood in the lean-to, the freezer humming to itself, and a big spider slinking into the cubicle that had formerly been an outside lavatory. For an interminable time neither of them spoke. Then he gestured to her to go indoors and she went tentatively through the kitchen, where there was nowhere to sit down, into the sitting room where there was. She did not sit.

Linda took up position in the centre of the room, beneath the beam with the hunting horn hanging from it. She looked him over. He tried to read her expression. His own was determined, daunting.

She said at last: 'I want the truth, John. I've had two months of opinions and guesswork, I want to know the truth.'

'How did you find me?'

She waved a hand as if to say that was unimportant. At her refusal he guessed: 'David Gerrard.'

'Not directly.'

'Ah.' So it was not only Linda who had let slip fragments of the truth during her lunch with Gerrard. 'How long have you known?'

'A while. It wasn't easy finding you.'

'It wasn't meant to be.' A pause. 'So how did you do it?'

'By common sense. If your death was a fake one of two people would almost certainly know: your wife or your agent. I didn't.'

He demanded to know how she had traced him but she was adamant that the details did not matter. He snapped that they did because if she could unearth him then others could. He added a question: Who had she told?

'Nobody,' Linda said. 'David Gerrard doesn't know I was looking. I hired a private detective to follow him.'

Gower swore, saying cuttingly: 'And how long do you think it will be before your detective is selling his story to Fleet Street?'

She said: 'That's a chance I had to take. I couldn't follow Gerrard myself because he would have recognized me. I'm paying the detective half the fee if he traces you and another half if he keeps the news to himself until I tell the world at large that you've been found.'

Gower gave a derisive laugh. 'You're very trusting. He'll make more for himself by selling the story to a newspaper. He's probably negotiating right now.'

Linda shook her head, she was saying that the man had not reported seeing Gower, that he had merely found an address Gerrard had visited and had later visited it to check who lived there, that he had used the ruse of checking deliveries for the circulation department of a local paper.

She was providing more details, about how she had hired her man from a detective agency listed in the Yellow Pages, and Gower ought to have been listening carefully. But his eye was on the hunting horn above her head. *One blow,* he thought, *maybe two. That's all it would take.* He moved forward a step. And then: *But has she told him she was coming here herself?*

He asked her. She said not. As she spoke she turned away from him, shrugging off her mackintosh. *Now,* he thought. *Now! Just one blow.* His hands were rising towards the horn.

Linda did not see. She walked away from him, away from danger, and sat down. 'Now I want your explanation, John. Oh, not why you did it. I can dream up reasons for myself, and the timing tells a lot. After the way everyone went overboard for that playwright who hanged himself, Alf Wilson, I can see the origins of your scheme clearly enough.'

When he replied his voice was calm, cold, belying the tension within. He said it had not been anything to do with Wilson, it had begun with a joke by David Gerrard. He did not want to go into it. All his instincts told him to be wary. Linda had not fully explained why she was there.

He said: 'We haven't finished with you. Why are you here? What are you proposing to do once you leave?' He was relieved to hear himself suggesting she might leave. He pushed his hands into his trouser pockets, kept his eyes away from the horn.

Kill Linda? The inner voice that expressed his thoughts was disbelieving. *Why ever kill her? She's done nothing.* And when that voice mimicked the women in the shop in Lymington, wishing her another man, he was ashamed of his folly. *You can't kill a person because of what somebody else imagined about her! Stop thinking about killing her, listen to what she's saying.*

Linda was looking at him, not speaking. She wore a familiar expression, the one that said he had not been listening. She said: 'John, you haven't heard a word, I wish you'd concentrate on what's being said to you instead of retreating into that dream world of yours.'

'I was listening,' he lied.

'No, you switch off when it's something you don't want to hear. All those times I talked to you about splitting up, all those conversations that ended as monologues, you didn't listen to me once, not really *listen*.'

He shut her up. 'You didn't want to talk about that last time. You refused to meet me when I went up to London.'

She twisted the blue scarf in her hands. Her voice was lower when she next spoke. 'I know, I'm sorry. I guessed you hadn't received my letter. It was obvious you hadn't because you wouldn't have been talking like that. I'd written to you about a divorce and I couldn't face an evening of pretending I hadn't.'

Gower headed her off from reciting the reasons for her letter. He wanted to sweep all that out of the way and discover where they went next. The power, and the future, were in Linda's hands. She could reveal his deception to the world or she could offer to keep his secret and he would have to trust her. Or he could kill her. He looked at the blue silk scarf that she was twisting into a ligature.

He said: 'Does anyone know you're here?'

'I've already told you no. The detective gave me an address and I came. I hid beneath a mackintosh and a scarf and no one saw me come in.'

She was lying. She had called twice and met the gardener. He let it pass. *But what other lies is she telling?*

She said: 'I know what you're thinking but I'm not going to tell anyone. John, I had to know what had become of you.' She nodded towards the television set. 'You know what I've been saying, and it's true. It was hell not knowing what I was dealing with.'

She did not look like a woman who had come through hell. He said: 'You seem to have managed all right.'

She wanted to protest but he said: 'In a while, when the time's right, I'll reappear. That's all in hand. But if the time's wrong, a lot of money will be lost.'

'I had lunch with David Gerrard – he told you? – and he explained about the money. There's a ridiculous amount of it.' She laughed ruefully. 'After all those years of scrimping, there's a fortune piling up and it's no use to either of us. Don't you think that's absurd? We got what we wanted and it's no use to us, being rich and famous.'

He said it was unavoidable and it was only for a short while. Linda's sudden use of 'us' was giving him hope. He said: 'Things will be different when we've got the money. For instance, I'll want to be back in London. Docklands seems to be the place. How about a flat with a balcony over the river?'

'Mmm.' She liked that. 'It would be an improvement to have water running beneath the balcony instead of down the kitchen walls.' She meant Stream Cottage, of course.

Gower said: 'And a boat. You can get flats with moorings, did you know that?'

'I'm not sure I'd feel safe going out in a boat with you. I've heard what you do with boats.'

They laughed. Then her face saddened and she said: 'I was hurt that you confided in David Gerrard and not me. Or was that all his idea too? I've learned a lot about that agent of yours in recent weeks.'

'After your letter,' said Gower, regretting having to refer to it, 'I couldn't be sure you'd co-operate and in any case David was going to have to do all the work.' He drew back from apologizing to her. The confrontation had eased into amiability but he refused to go too far.

'After that letter,' she echoed, 'I was worried how you'd take it. And then when the story broke that you were missing I seriously thought my letter had caused it.'

'A complicated suicide, surely?'

'No, not suicide, I didn't imagine that. But people who are terribly miserable are notoriously careless with their safety.' She paused, searching his face. 'Were you terribly miserable?'

He met her eyes with a long frank look. 'Terribly,' he said softly.

'Oh, John.' Her head bowed and a hand went to her mouth, smothering a sob.

Gower found himself beside her, on the dark wooden settee with the tapestry-style covers. He put his arm around her, her warmth through the summer dress disturbing. He tilted her face to his. Tears were brimming in the blue eyes. 'Don't cry.' He drew her closer, the softness of her breasts against his shirt stirring all the desire he had ever felt for her. Then there was the taste of her lips.

When she murmured, she murmured approval of his movements, of the feel of his skin against hers. They lay on the thick rug before the empty fireplace with its brass screen, and she parted her thighs to accept him, to accept everything he had become.

Gower absorbed the detail of her, the fine blue veins marked on her fair skin, the neat brown mole beneath her left breast, the delicate translucence of her eyelids. Then he closed his eyes and the detail of Linda was lost in an oblivion of joy.

Afterwards they were awkward. The room came harshly into focus as a cramped overfurnished room unsuited to lovemaking. Linda noticed the trio of latticed windows along one side, the lone window on the other, and she reached for her clothes, saying she hoped the cottage did not get many visitors. He saw that her back was reddened by the roughness of the rug. He dressed, reassuring her about his lack of callers, and watched the curve of her buttocks as she stepped into knickers, the deft way she fastened the brassière he had found difficult to undo, the flurry of blue cotton as she shook out her discarded dress, stepped into it, eased it up with a wriggle of her hips and did up the bodice buttons. Then her hands were smoothing the garment, stroking her hair, while her feet slipped themselves into shoes. She was flustered, softened, but striving to be brisk. She was talking about the time, saying she had to go.

Their intimacy had been unpremeditated, perhaps even inappropriate given the circumstances, and Linda was regretting it. Gower did not know why she was, but he did know she had enjoyed it. He said: 'You don't have to go anywhere.'

'I have to get back to London. The office thinks I've got a migraine today, I don't want to have to lie about tomorrow too.'

'You needn't. You can leave early in the morning. The roads will be empty if you go early enough, you can have a quick run.'

Linda sucked her lower lip, wavering. 'There's my sister too. Mary will worry if I'm not back.'

'Phone her and pretend you're at Stream Cottage.' A suspicion reared. 'You didn't tell her where you were going, did you?'

A shake of the head. 'She doesn't know I didn't go to work today.'

He consulted the clock on the sideboard. 'Even if you went immediately you'd be too late to claim you'd gone home normally from work. You're going to have to lie to her, one way or another.'

Linda stayed the night. She manufactured a three-course meal from the contents of the freezer and they opened one of the bottles of wine Gerrard had delivered on a visit. They marvelled at Gower's changed appearance, which she confessed to rather liking, and they talked about her experience of appearing on radio and television, which she also confessed to enjoying once the initial weeks of intense anxiety were over. He told her she was terrific on television, and avoided carping about her failure to plug his books. Linda still held the power, was the key to his future, and he could not afford a falling out.

She said, refilling their glasses: 'My sister says I'm one of the media's nine-day wonders and not to let fame go to my head.'

'I suppose it will rather fizzle out for you once I reappear.'

'Yes, for one thing there's going to be doubt about how much I knew. What Mary calls my "public image" will be dented. So I might as well make the most of it while it lasts.' She raised her glass. 'To fame.'

'Let's hope it doesn't become notoriety.'

Linda gave a wicked smile. 'They're often the same thing these days.'

They drank to fame.

That night they set the alarm for 5 a.m. and made love again in the bed in the room with the view of the Isle of Wight. Linda, sensing a new mood in him, joked that his appearance so changed him that it was excitingly like making love with a stranger. In the companionable warmth that followed she asked him to authorize David Gerrard to let her have some money. There were bills outstanding on Stream Cottage and she was very short. Gower gave her all he had in his bag in the bedroom and said he would speak to Gerrard next day.

She turned away from him to sleep. He moved after her and slid an arm around her.

'I'm glad you came, Linda,' he whispered. 'I shouldn't be, I should be worried that it was easy to find me, but I'm glad you came.' He waited for her reply but she did not answer. He squeezed her. 'It won't be too long, I promise. We've got the money, we'll get a place in London and it will all be different.'

'You already are different,' she said drowsily. She removed his arm and drifted off.

Gower felt ecstatically carefree. He had dreamed a beautiful dream and it was coming true. Gerrard had misinterpreted Linda over lunch, she had been putting on a brave face and disguising her vulnerability, and Gerrard had believed she did not care that her husband was missing and probably dead. Now Linda had explained it all. And she had promised that tomorrow she would tell her detective that the man at Butlers was not John Gower and she would send him to search elsewhere.

It appalled him that he had thought of killing her, but he recognized his panic as a manifestation of fear that she had come to spoil everything. Instead, Linda had become part of the conspiracy. He loved her and he was sure she loved him.

13

Rain Morgan walked through the gate marked PRIVATE and along a footpath at the bottom of the strips of garden in Cragg View. Pat Jarvis lived at the end one, number twelve. Her slender garden was ablaze with flowers. After the half-hearted efforts of the owners of the other houses, it was an oasis of pleasure.

Her front door stood open. Knocking, Rain looked into a tasteful, uncluttered room.

Pat Jarvis appeared through a door, smoothing the skirt of her powder-blue dress as she walked forward. 'Rain, you're early. Good. Come in.'

Rain stepped on to the pale floorboards, then a rug. The room was light, a backward glance giving her the colour of the garden and then the stepped rooftops of grey-stone Addingham houses before a hilltop and then a blue sky. A typical Dales-scape, in fact.

'This is it,' said Pat Jarvis, pointing to a pile of ribbon-bound papers on a table to the left of the door. 'You take a look while I fetch some tea.'

At home, the woman had none of the inhibition she had shown in London. She was livelier, more forthcoming. Although she had invited Rain to examine the script, she called through to her from the kitchen a number of times, asking after the journey and generally displaying pleasure in having a visitor.

Rain broke a nail on the ribbon and gave up. When Pat Jarvis brought the tray, Rain admitted defeat and a pair of kitchen scissors was produced.

They talked of this and that, meaning to concentrate on the relevance of the script but straying to reminisce about Alf Wilson and to say what they had each felt about the stream of news stories and the re-establishment of his reputation. Then a neighbour popped in, creating another distraction.

'I've kept it all together,' said Pat Jarvis once they were alone again.

At the back of the bundle, several inches thick, were different papers, not all full sheets and not all of the same kind of paper. Rain looked at a few.

'Notes,' said Pat Jarvis.

'For the play, I presume.' Rain made out a list of points to incorporate in Scene Two and several underlined words relating to names that she took to be the names of characters in the story.

The woman said: 'I was going to chuck the notes away when I realized that's all they were, but then I thought well, what with Alf being famous perhaps one of those American universities will come begging for them one day so I'd better find houseroom for them.'

Rain asked what she had intended to do with the script when she carried it away from London. Mrs Jarvis said she had not really thought, she had only known it ought to be kept.

'To tell you the truth, Rain, I was very disappointed when I read it. It's not a patch on that *Dead and Alive* they all go on about. Even I can see that. And so I thought, well, if this isn't finished and I offer it to, say, the BBC and it goes out, well, perhaps that would damage his reputation. I could picture all those heads shaking and saying he wasn't that good after all.'

They did not pursue the point but it was apparently David Gerrard, as quoted in the *Daily Post*, who had swayed her by dreaming of the huge amount of money a Wilson adaptation of a Gower novel could have netted. And why should she not be swayed? Pat Jarvis lived in a pretty place but it was no palace and she had her own future to pay for.

'Before I was divorced,' she was saying, coincidentally catching Rain's train of thought, 'I lived in a big house near Grassington. You could walk straight out on to the moor. I'm afraid I've had to pull my horns in a bit since those days, and there's only part-time shop work to be had around here.'

Rain nodded understandingly. 'I'll read the script and then we'll see what we can do.'

The woman rubbed her hands, feigning glee. 'That David Gerrard, in the paper the other day, he was almost begging for this play, wasn't he? Will you be showing it to him?'

'Probably.'

'Well, I'll not get too excited about it until we know exactly what we've got. I've already told you my reservations.'

Rain agreed to the wisdom of waiting and seeing. There was too much scope for false hope for her to take any other line, but in her heart she was more thrilled than she cared to admit. If the play proved to be finished, or as near finished as made no difference, then she would be able to perform a satisfying service for Alf Wilson by getting it produced and she would be able to help Pat Jarvis by making sure it sold for the highest figure attainable. If anybody would be willing to assist in this, then David Gerrard was the man. She smothered her excitement with silent warnings about the number of slips between cup and lip, and the risk of counting unhatched chickens, and she cut confidence down to modest hope. But she was thrilled.

'One other thing,' she said, taking a sheet of paper from her bag, 'can you read this handwriting?'

Mrs Jarvis put on her gilt-rimmed reading glasses and patted her skirt and pored over the paper. 'Oooh, Alf. What a scrawl!'

'My guess is that they were notes taken during telephone calls.'

'Very likely. Well, the easy bits are the names.' She read out Ilkley, that was the clearest, and added London, Brighton and Sussex. Then she hesitated before Birmingham and then foundering.

Rain said: 'Assuming they are all place names, is there anywhere called Bibey? Or Slaborne? Or Gomer?'

As soon as it was spoken, the word assumed another shape.

'Gower!' they said together. Rain rattled out that John Gower lived near Sherborne and that this could be the origin of Slaborne.

'Yes,' said Pat Jarvis. 'It's plain as you like now you've said it. And isn't there a village called Bibury? Is that near Sherborne?'

Regretfully, Rain said not. They spent more time attempting to unravel the notes but were only ever confident about the place names and Gower's. Resisting temptation to twist the rest of the squiggles into logic, they had to retire defeated.

Pat Jarvis said: 'He could have meant this place when he said Ilkley, it's part of the address.' She was gathering tea things and had carried the tray to the door when she stopped, cocked her head on one side and gave Rain a quizzical look. 'How would it be if I told you there's a farm at Ilkley called Bibury Farm?'

Rain followed to the kitchen, avid for the rest. Pat Jarvis put the tray on the draining board and stayed there, framed by the window's view of a green-painted garage with flowering shrubs beside it. She said: 'They're people from away, at Bibury Farm. They bought it five years back, around the time I moved here. I remember there was a bit of upset because local farmers had their minds on it, but it wasn't to be. They came from London and they bought it up right under their noses. Outbid them at auction.'

She said it was a hill farm, running sheep on the moor, but its buildings were good and it was an attractive and desirable property in every way. 'They don't fit with the local people, they never will. I've a friend lives near by and my tittle-tattle comes from her, but it's sure to be right. Coming in like that and living the way they do, never a care about how they spend, posh holidays and expensive horses, well, it's no wonder if they don't rub along with their neighbours.'

When Rain prodded she heard that the tittle-tattle extended to stories of well-meaning folk being snubbed and kept away. Pat Jarvis said: 'The rumour, once they'd got their hands on the farm, was that it wouldn't be long before they were moving on, probably bankrupt. They don't understand the local way of farming, but what can you say? They seem to be making a better go of it than most.'

Over the washing up, Rain learned more about the Benton family of Bibury Farm. What use it was to her, she could not imagine. Except that Bibury and Ilkley appeared in close proximity in Alf Wilson's notes, and he had asked his cousin whether he could stay with her while he did research in Yorkshire. On impulse, Rain decided to take a look at Bibury Farm. She did not tell Pat Jarvis this, but when she left Cragg View she booked a room for the night at the Devonshire Arms at Bolton Abbey, two miles away, and then she drove up on to Ilkley Moor.

Cloud descended before she got there. Her enthusiasm waned with the sunshine, but she had nothing better to do than go on. A couple of times she stopped her car and pondered the map. Finally she came to a track that seemed promising. No house was in sight, but the lie of the land cut short her view. The only buildings were field barns that had so far escaped being changed into expensive houses.

About a half-mile along the track, she came upon it, a big limestone house with the characteristic arched doorway of an integral barn. Around it lay outbuildings and a yard in which three vehicles were visible. Good horses raised their heads from a paddock to look her way. Sheep were tufts of wool on hillsides, their cries varying from the pitiful to expressions of disgust. But there was no human being in sight.

She reversed her car to a field gateway and went back the way she had come. Although the map suggested the track continued past the house, she preferred not to be caught snooping. An ordinary motorist, posing as a meandering tourist, would get away with it, but a face that appeared daily in a national newspaper and cropped up repeatedly on television panel games and chat shows had no chance.

By the time she saw the Range Rover bounding towards her she was well on her way to the road. Passing it was a matter of forcing her car within a whisker of a jagged stone wall and praying the other vehicle was slimmer than it looked. There were two men in the Range Rover and they each took a very close look at her.

When the manoeuvre was complete, she pelted forward but in no doubt that she had been recognized. In her rear-view mirror she saw the Range Rover stationary, one of the men on the track looking after her. Cursing her nosiness, she rushed recklessly up to the junction, skidded and barely avoided sliding beneath the wheels of a horsebox. Her annoyance at her bad driving was compounded by the certainty that the horsebox driver would also have reason to remember her. Altogether, the snooping had been a mistake.

Eating alone at the hotel that evening, she mulled over the day's events, Pat Jarvis's helpfulness and hopes and her own unhelpful curiosity. But no matter how severely she chided herself, she came back to the same justification for her jaunt to the moor: whatever Alf Wilson had been researching had led him to plan a visit to Ilkley and possibly to that farm.

She could not see what this had to do with the John Gower novel. Having read it with immense care, while considering Alf Wilson's proposed adaptation and with his annotations to guide her, she believed she knew the story as well as anyone, and there was nothing in it to prompt a journey to Ilkley, nothing about farms or farmers, nor about sheep or horses. *A Candle Lit* was an urban tale about a man faced with the worst of bad luck but refusing to buckle. John Gower's hero had set out to take charge of his life, change his luck, and he had done it.

After supper, Rain continued to brood for a time, watching from her room as light altered the contours of sheepy fields on the banks of the Wharfe. Then she summoned fresh energy and hurried out, to take the path along the river until she came to the ruins of the Abbey.

KEEP OUT, the signs said. DANGEROUS, they said. It had not been like this when she had been here years ago, but nothing else in her life had been the same either. *Things change*, she reminded herself. *Whether you want them to or not, that's what they do.*

Disobedient, she went in, defying the masonry to crash on to her. There was a plan to repair the ruin, but only, of course, to the stage where it was a safer ruin. Somewhere, she supposed, there were guidelines about that sort of thing. Someone, but more likely a committee, must decide how far was far enough, must determine which hunks of redundant stonework must be preserved and which the countryside could well do without. She wondered whether there was not something unhealthy about a society that could always find money to hang on to decrepit and unremarkable relics but scorned to build homes for its homeless.

For a while she prowled around the graveyard and then took a different route back to the hotel. The hotel had altered too, since her aunt had brought her there in her girlhood. It had grown, smartened, and, according to the hotel literature, a duchess had taken charge of its interior design. It amused her that the designer's husband's parentage should be regarded as an attraction. She had liked the hotel years ago, before the duchess had picked the pretty colour schemes, and she liked it now. She believed Paul Wickham would like it too.

But when she telephoned there was no answer. Untrue, there was an answering machine but she did not wish to speak to it. She listened to his recorded voice and then hung up.

It would have been nice to have spoken to him. Just that, to have spoken to him.

Later, when she went to bed in the double bed that was all the hotel had been able to offer her, she reflected that it would have been nicer still if he could have been there. But in the months she had lived alone she had learned to protect herself from the lonely moods, the spasms of alarming inner emptiness. Lacking anything else to read this night, she had saved up the Alf Wilson script.

She untied the ribbon and the sheets slid over the duvet. Rain gathered up a handful and began to read. She was hooked, but after a few minutes questions arose and she skipped to a later scene and started reading from there.

And then she went back to the beginning, resolved to read from start to end. As she did so, her puzzled look became a frown that turned into tight-lipped resignation.

Alf Wilson's script was *not* based on *A Candle Lit*. It had nothing to do with John Gower and his work. Only at one point did the stories collide. Gower had written about the plight of the poor in London but he had only touched on the subject in a glancing way. Alf Wilson's script was a ferocious indictment of people who exploited the desperation of the poor.

Rain got out of bed, cleared the dressing table of obstacles and used it as a desk, going through the script deciphering handwritten corrections and changes. This was easier than dealing with Wilson's telephone notes and she made heartening progress.

This script was not a final version and possibly only a first. Probably no producer would wish to consider it in this form. Wilson himself had noted numerous points to check. Rain was writing herself a list of them. If what Wilson proposed in this play were true, then he had a powerful story to tell.

Coupled with the notes Pat Jarvis had bundled in with the script, Rain had enough pointers to investigate the story. What she did not have was the free time, because she dared not tell the *Daily Post* about it yet. Doing that would inevitably result in the newsdesk staff scrambling together a story based on one aspect of the whole while she wanted to look at it thoroughly. The problem was not purely one of professional judgements or expediency. Not for the first time, her motives were different.

The night was wearing away. She went to bed, her mind too stimulated with plots and plans to wind down into sleepiness. *I'll take some holiday*, she thought, *and come up here and* . . .

With that decided, she turned over and made herself comfortable. Unfortunately another thought raised the subject of Paul Wickham, and her treatment of him raised guilt, and this in turn resurrected her negligence of Alf Wilson.

Spiralling through the familiar topics, she slowed to the point of sleep.

And she was on the very edge of sleep when an idea stung her into full wakefulness. *Alf Wilson wouldn't have killed himself when he was deep in a play as important as this one. He had too many plans and too many hopes. What if the rumour were true, that he was killed? And what if he were killed because he was researching at Ilkley?*

There was a major flaw in this, and she was relieved to spot it. Alf Wilson's play was about London, Yorkshire did not feature in it. Nor did it feature in his margin notes. He referred to it only on the sheet of telephone conversation scribbles, and he had a cousin living there.

She sighed crossly, turning over in search of sleep. 'And that's another thing. Paul is very good to talk things over with.'

She frowned at the ragged grammar of that, then shrugged and went to sleep.

'You might find cuttings on housing charities, for instance,' Rain said to Rosie next day. 'Anything related to the subject will do.'

Rosie took a deep breath and said: 'Quite honestly, I'm not going to have time.'

Rain thought this a shade mean. Rosie had arrived for work late, with her hair freshly cut and with an eye-catching new outfit. She was apparently not in the mood for work, especially not for tucking herself away in the library to trace stories relating to corrupt housing officials and the exploitation of down-and-outs.

'There's no hurry,' Rain said. 'Next week would do.'

'Oh dear,' said Rosie. 'You've forgotten today's my last day.'

'Today?' Rain clapped a hand to her forehead. 'What am I going to do?'

'Personnel are sending Sylvia down from advertising until you get someone permanent. I did tell you.'

Rain ignored the censure. She said: 'Advertising!' in the derogatory tone peculiar to journalists referring to advertising.

Fortunately for Rosie, her telephone purred and she was called away. Holly appeared in time for Rain to round on her and demand whether she knew this was Rosie's last day.

'Cheer up,' said Holly. 'She's not going to be shot at dawn. I expect she'll ring us up from time to time and tell us about the wonderful world of computers.'

Rain snorted. She wanted to blame somebody, *anybody*, for her failure to remember Rosie's departure. Holly leaned over and whispered: 'Don't worry. I put a huge donation on your behalf into the collection for her present.'

Rain smiled through gritted teeth and asked whether that was supposed to make her feel better.

At Rosie's farewell she met Sylvia. The wine bar was disgustingly hot, a subterranean place that was cosy in winter but needed superior air-conditioning to get its clients through crowded heatwave lunchtimes. Sylvia was unexceptional, she could have been any one of half a dozen young women Rain had encountered about the newspaper building. There was nothing to like or dislike.

Once the presentation and the kind words were over, Rain slipped away. She had noticed Linda Gower at the other end of the bar, her dress was striking both in colour and brevity. She was with a man, a television producer.

There had been rumours that the missing writer's wife had been sufficiently interesting during her flurry of television and radio performances to find a niche in the business. Seeing Linda drinking with a producer working on afternoon talk shows made Rain suspect she had discovered where Linda Gower was heading next.

She had only to pause at their table and say hello for the producer's demeanour and teasing denials to strengthen the rumour to the point where it was unbreakable. Linda Gower smiled at her without joining in. Rain read a great deal into that caution too.

At work again, she set Holly to test, through their television contacts, whether it was true that a job for Linda Gower was in the offing. Holly could not prove it and the story remained a rumour.

'It'll keep,' said Rain philosophically. She meant to return to it another day when there was more to be had. She did, but not in the way she predicted.

14

Richard Crane had misjudged Julia. He had doubted her loyalty, believing a titbit of gossip Conroy had dropped. His behaviour towards his girlfriend had reflected that, and now he had discovered that Conroy had been malicious. There had been no substance in the accusation, and Crane's relationship with Julia had suffered unnecessarily. He meant to get even with Conroy.

John Gower pecked away at the story, the pile of paper to the left of his typewriter growing taller as chapter succeeded chapter. He arranged to have Crane and the estranged Julia meet up at a country house, by chance. He wrote them a tender scene where, in flurry of passion, they made love on the hearthrug. He wrote that there was a log fire, but it was the wrong time of year for one and he typed a row of x's through the phrase and substituted an empty grate behind a fire screen. That pleased him, alluding as it did to the hollowness of their relationship and the various ways in which they masked the truth. The hearthrug pleased him less, with its shades of Elinor Glyn, but he let it stand.

Engrossed in the novel, Gower resented David Gerrard's interrupting telephone call. Gerrard said: 'Linda came to see me today.'

Gower had to shuffle his thoughts into order. 'What did she want?'

'Money. And one hardly knows how to refuse. There's oodles of it and it's tough on her knowing that and being broke.'

Gower frowned. Surely he remembered . . . He was about to comment that he had given her a couple of thousand pounds only days before, but in the nick of time he recalled that he and Linda had agreed to keep it secret from Gerrard.

'Better,' she had suggested, 'if he doesn't know I've found you.' They had agreed on that too.

He asked Gerrard: 'Did you give her anything?'

'No, of course not. Not without your authority. I said I'd have to think it over and I'd ring her tomorrow.'

'All right,' said Gower. 'Find out what she needs it for and give her what seems reasonable. Don't overdo it.'

At the end of the line Gerrard's face objected to the peremptory tone. There was the faintest sneer as he asked: 'Can I provide *you* with anything? More cash, more hair dye? Any little errands to be run?'

Gower declined to notice the sneer. He said: 'Did you transfer the money to my new account?'

'Immediately, John. It won't have reached your bank by now, there was a weekend intervening.'

'Oh yes, I'd forgotten.'

'What do you want it for? Roistering in the local pub behind the safety of your new exterior?'

Testily, Gower said: 'Hawaii. There's a ticket to buy, more clothes, all sorts of things.' His conversations with Gerrard were becoming repetitive, as though Gerrard utterly forgot the details of their plan each time he put the telephone down and had to be reminded over and over.

'You can't have a passport yet. They take for ever, and there's another delay at the passport offices. It was in the paper this morning.' Gerrard did not sound fed up about the delay.

He reported on the latest publicity and on the excellent sales figures for the new book, cautioning that those figures referred to the numbers bookshops had taken rather than the numbers the public had bought. What remained unsold would be returned to Pegwoods in due course.

When they had exhausted that topic, Gower asked whether there had been news of Rob Watson's reaction to the anonymous gift covering the cost of a replacement yacht. Gerrard said there had not.

Gower came away disappointed. He had hoped to hear that

Rob was happy, but perhaps Rob had been advised to keep the gift secret. Offhand Gower could not think of a reason, but for all he knew there might be one.

Linda's approach to Gerrard was more puzzling. She had not rung Butlers since her visit, although she had said she would try to do so if she could ever be certain of making an absolutely private call. That was impossible at work and equally at her sister's home where the only telephone was in the living room. Public call boxes were unreliable and using one would involve making excuses to leave the house.

Half an hour after Gerrard's call, Gower was dragged away from the Crane–Julia scene by Linda. 'Mary's gone to the cinema,' she explained. 'How are you?'

'Fine. I hoped you'd ring.'

'I imagine you've heard from David Gerrard this evening.'

'Yes.'

'He pretended he had to think it over but I knew he'd report to you. John, I must have some more cash. I've paid the bills on Stream Cottage and I've paid what I owe Mary, but now the car's packed up.'

The car was very old and the news not unexpected. He said: 'It would be best to replace it.'

'Well, if you're sure. The garage has a list of essential repairs as long as my arm. It's failed the MOT, you see, and the gear box has tied itself in a knot.'

Gower saved her giving a catalogue of the car's defects. He knew them well. 'Don't worry about it. Trade it in for a new one and I'll tell Gerrard to meet the bill.'

'Thanks, John. I won't go mad. It won't be a Rolls Royce or a Porsche, just something small and reliable.'

'I know,' he said, and he did. 'If you do anything extravagant people will wonder how you can afford it.'

The call ended with them saying that they missed each other and Gower hoping Mary would develop a serious commitment to cinema. Before he returned to the tangle of Richard Crane's life, he squandered five minutes asking himself whether he trusted Linda. On balance he did, but she had never been as scrupulous about money as he had and it was odd how she had run through a couple of thousand pounds within days.

That week he steeled himself to take Brian Parsons's birth certificate and the photographs of himself into Lymington Post Office. He picked a busy morning, when pensions were being collected, and the staff were rushed.

He had three photographs and David Gerrard had signed the back of one. But the type of passport issued at post offices did not require this signature and it was the unmarked pair that Gower presented. To support the birth certificate he had to offer one other piece of identification, but if he was to be Brian Parsons the Crane bank book was useless. Gower took the Parsons's gas bill from the pile of mail in the stair cupboard. The application form specified that a gas bill would do.

The queue was slow and resigned, and he strove to look as bored as the rest of them, denying the fright that was chanting a refrain in his head telling him to get out of there while he had time to do so. He knew by heart the words above the Parsons signature at the end of the form: *I know that it is a criminal offence knowingly to make a false statement in this application.*

David Gerrard had jibbed before signing the other form with its similar warning. Gower knew he ought to tell the man that the form had not been used, that he had not after all been involved in criminality, but he knew too that he would not tell him. The time might come when the threat would be sufficient to ensure he got his way against Gerrard's opposition.

He reached the counter, and pushed across the form, certificate, photographs, gas bill and cash. The clerk reached for a rubber stamp. Within minutes he was back in the street with a passport in his pocket. It would not get him to Hawaii, but it would get him away. He was going to have to think very hard about the necessity of Hawaii.

As the weeks wore on Gerrard reported that Linda had bought a modest Renault and he had paid the bill. The old car had fetched a pittance at trade-in, which was what Gower had expected. Later, Gerrard relayed that Linda wanted more money.

'I was charming,' he said, 'and told her I would have to sleep on it. I said that should you ever turn up alive you might not approve of the money having been spent on the things she deems essential and I am prepared to sanction. I said my position was a shade delicate.'

Gower asked drily: 'How did she react to this ill-concealed snub?'

'John, she said I was not the only one in a delicate situation. One assumes she means her own life is sadly unresolved.'

Gower suspected she had been referring to the predicaments of all three of them. He asked what she wanted money for this time.

'Nothing ludicrous,' said Gerrard. 'She wants to smarten up Stream Cottage. I'm prepared to concede her a point when she says it needs damp treatment and central heating. As for a modern kitchen and bathroom, I couldn't say. I was far too cold the time I was there to notice such facilities.'

'But you told me way back that she was keen to sell the house.'

'I know, but if you want my opinion, whether you two live in it again, together or singly, or whether it's put up for sale, improving it would be money well spent. However, I would advise care because if Linda is seen to be splashing money around then the journalists, who take an unrelenting interest in her, will demand to know where she acquires it. Although you and I know my doling it out is legitimate, I don't want Fleet Street challenging me. Linda, of course, never will because it's in her interests to get her hands on it.'

Gower swallowed a protest at Gerrard expressing it like that, making Linda sound a gold-digger and not a wife. But Gerrard had never appreciated the sacrifices Linda had made in the name of modern fiction and he would consequently not understand Gower's wish to indulge her now he was in a position to do so. He told Gerrard to encourage the Stream Cottage improvement scheme.

'Very well,' said Gerrard. 'But if that's your instruction I propose to treat her like an adult instead of a child who has to beg for pocket money. I'll ask her for an estimate for the work and I'll give her a sum to cover it.'

Gower was pleased. He stayed pleased even after Linda rang Butlers another day to say that the builder from Sherborne, not one he had heard of, had found a problem with the roof and this would add another thousand pounds to the overall bill. He approved the extra work.

She said, her enthusiasm endearing: 'I'm surrounded by brochures. Kitchens, bathrooms, wallpapers . . .'

'What are you thinking of doing with the kitchen?'

She described a range of solid oak units that would look good, and some green wall and floor tiling. 'I want it to echo the scene through the window, the trees and the fields. Does that sound mad?'

'No, it sounds perfect. Especially if you can find a window blind with a picture of Jed Mullen in his bobble hat riding by on his tractor.'

The conversation ended in laughter.

Another time she discussed the builder's progress on the roof. Gower said: 'Hold on, I thought he was going to start on the damp proofing.' He was certain she told him that.

'The weather was fine, he decided to get the roof done instead.' And she asked his advice on the merits of different types of mixer taps for the kitchen sink.

Her calls never became frequent but they were full of the minutiae of refurbishment of Stream Cottage. Linda, who had never cared for the place, was now enchanted with it. He teased her about this and she said that a country cottage was only fun if one lived in town. She was going there at weekends, after her work in London, but they had vowed not to use the telephone there for fear of being overheard by her workmen who were busy there at weekends too. Her calls to him came generally on Tuesdays. Tuesday was when her sister went to the cinema with the new man in her life.

'I'm getting jealous of Stream Cottage,' Gower bemoaned

one Tuesday. 'If you weren't supervising that each weekend you could come here. You could drive over on Sunday evenings and travel to London on Mondays from Butlers.'

'Oh no, I'm busy right through Sundays washing down and clearing up. You've no idea what a mess builders make and I'm trying to keep it under control. I'm fit for nothing by Sunday evenings.'

And so Linda never did drive to the New Forest on a Sunday.

Meanwhile, Gerrard kept up a parallel commentary, unaware that Linda had discovered her husband. Although Gerrard had presented her with a lump sum for the builder, he received pleas for additional cheques for decorating. He told Gower: 'I'll be on holiday next week, therefore I paid what Linda asked. I trust that was in order.'

'Yes, of course.'

'Oh dear, you sound doubtful.'

'Surprised,' said Gower, 'That wallpaper appears to have gone on with a rush. I expected the new plaster to take far longer to dry out.'

Gerrard pleaded total ignorance of the practices of the building and decorating trades. 'But don't they use huge blow driers these days?'

'Not usually in people's homes.'

'I'm prepared to believe Stream Cottage may be a special case when it comes to drying out,' said Gerrard.

Gower did not want to joke about it. 'Look, David, I'm afraid Linda might have been taken in by a cowboy firm. It's not a name I know.'

'Oh I don't think there's any problem,' said Gerrard quickly, and went on to promise a postcard from Barbados. 'It will be addressed to Mr Parsons, the rightful occupant of Butlers, but it will be for you.'

Gower permitted himself a fleeting jealousy of his agent's freedom to fly off for an expensive holiday in the sun, fleeting because his own flit was drawing near. He had his passport, he needed his ticket and he needed to choose his destination.

He took out the travel agent's brochures and thought hard about Hawaii.

He could get there in two hops. The visitor's passport in the name of Parsons would serve to get him out of Britain and then his own passport, with its American visa, would take him the rest of the way. Should he ask Gerrard or Linda to fetch the passport? Linda, he thought, if only because he did not want Gerrard to know how flimsy the Hawaii plan had been all along. Yes, Linda, but he would not ask her until the last minute. The fewer people who knew the detail of his plans, and the shorter the time they knew them, the better.

Waikiki? Maui? Kauai? Or the big island, Hawaii? He browsed, weighing brilliant nightlife against scenic splendour, cosmopolitan crowds against tranquillity. Would he tangle with tourists or duck out of their sight? How long would he stay before letting himself be discovered? Daydreaming was a fine game.

He put the travel brochures away and went to the spare room where he typed a line about Crane's Hawaii plans. Crane ought to be searching London for Conroy, but instead he was going to Hawaii. Julia, reconciled with Crane after the misunderstanding caused by Conroy's lies about her, was to join him in Hawaii after a few weeks but she had responsibilities that would then draw her back to London. Gower encapsulated the newer, deeper relationship between Crane and Julia in a few well-judged phrases.

Then he stopped and went to the mirror in his bedroom. The dark roots of his hair were increasingly visible, but as he was rarely out of the cottage, he had delayed bleaching them. Now, with the passport to hand, he wanted to visit the travel agent. He had already bought another packet of honey-blond hair dye. He took it into the downstairs bathroom and began the tiresome business of touching up his roots.

This was messy, smelly and awkward because he did not have a hand mirror to show him the back of his head and he had no means of telling whether the lotion was being applied correctly. The instructions made much of the need to apply it evenly and he doubted whether he was doing so.

And then there was the wait, a dreary phase where the foul-smelling potion remained on his head and the colour developed. He wandered through to the sitting room during this phase and put on the radio, wiping a trickle of lotion from his neck. A news bulletin was coming up. He heard a minute or two of a tedious consumer affairs programme, then the programme's irritating jingle, and finally the news.

The main items among the headlines were a summit meeting of heads of government, the latest twist in a financial scandal and an armed robbery at a London warehouse. By the end of the bulletin the gravity of the robbery had magnified because a security guard initially reported wounded during the attack had died in hospital.

During his time at Butlers the real world, as conveyed by radio, television or the occasional newspaper, had become distanced. He had been obliged to narrow his vision to concentrate on the trivia of his existence, because that was the natural way to survive isolation. He had not understood this to begin with, and had at times been ashamed of his involvement with nugatory detail.

A man of his intelligence and education ought not, he had thought, to wrap his small world around him and exclude the rest. But, as he had come to realize, the attitude was a mechanism for survival. If he could not be part of the outside world, then he would not taunt himself by fascination with it. The days when he had devoured newspapers bought on his trips to Lymington had proved this. They had resulted in restless days of dissatisfaction and stress.

The useful trick of the mind that rejected the larger world had another practical advantage: it allowed him to bury himself in Richard Crane's world and to write about a fictional character with more authority than he had ever done. And so it was that John Gower conjured no interest in the summit meeting that might have settled a war, or the financial scandal that would change a law, or the dead security guard whose killing was also to have repercussions.

He returned to the bathroom and rinsed the evil mixture off his hair, quelling panic by recalling the difference that wetness and dryness made to colour. His hair looked yellower, even while wet, and yet he was basically pleased with the result. The dark roots had gone. He wished the rest were not so patchily corn-coloured, but it was unimportant. He would never have to perform this chore again because soon he was going abroad and then his natural colour would reassert itself.

A preliminary telephone call to the travel agent to ask about flights, prices and frequency brought no immediate answers and he arranged to call in. 'First class,' he told the agent. And his inner voice grumbled: *I'll draw attention to myself. I'll be one of a bunch instead of an easily overlooked face among hundreds.* But the more powerful thought was the one that went: *Do it in style. What's the point of being rich if I can't enjoy spending?*

Leaving the agent to unravel any complications wrought by a customer who wanted to fly first to France and then to Hawaii, Gower worked for an hour before setting out to Lymington, this time on the bus. He had other equally important business in the town. He had to check up on the balance in his bank account. Gerrard had been instructed to pay in substantial sums and now Gower wanted to start drawing out sizeable amounts. Apart from the bills at the travel agent's, he wanted to buy luggage and clothes, and he wanted to take with him a lot of traveller's cheques and cash. Going abroad for an indefinite period was expensive.

After some whirring and wheezing, the cash machine spewed out a slip of faintly lettered paper. Gower had to hold it close to his face to read it. When he read it he did not believe it. He called his card back from the machine and began the process a second time. Then a third. But each time the machine produced the same figure: the Richard Crane account held less than £200.

He went into the bank, ready to question this. At once he

saw how foolish that would be and, pretending to be put off by the length of the queue, he walked back out. He strode up the street, looking as though he had business somewhere. In truth his business had come to an end. Useless to present himself at the travel agent's when there was no money to pay for the Hawaiian trip. If he could not reach David Gerrard immediately he would have to wait until after the Barbados holiday to learn what had become of the money.

What I mustn't do, he thought, *is make a fuss at the bank. Lymington would refer me to Dorchester where the account is held. I can't write to them at Dorchester because I can't give Butlers' address to anyone. And I can't visit them because they knew me as Richard Crane before my disguise.*

The missing money was frustrating but not unduly worrying. It was easy to imagine Gerrard writing down a wrong number and the money being paid into another account by mistake.

Gower returned to Butlers but failed to get through to Gerrard on the telephone. He was angry, especially, that he had torn himself away from the novel when the writing had been going extraordinarily smoothly. With luck he could slip easily back into the mood to write.

As was his practice after a break, he read through the last scene he had written. He read aloud, to pick up the inadvertent repetition of words or phrases, or the clumsy sentence construction that his eye could miss. Part-way down the first page he faltered and dried up. He felt a tingling apprehension.

It's good. It's very good. But why have I done this?

The page trembled in his hand. *How could I have done this without noticing?*

He laid the page on the makeshift desk and stepped back as though it were a wild thing. And in a way it was, for what Gower had proposed was not written on that sheet, another will had intervened and overruled him.

He snatched up successive sheets, scanning them but knowing what he would find. The mode of telling the story had changed, fundamentally. John Gower was no longer writing the story of Richard Crane. The novel had transmuted into a first-person story. Richard Crane was telling it himself.

Gower flung the sheets on the dressing table, letting them fall where they would, not caring about the usual meticulous arrangement of his papers. He flounced out of the room, into the bedroom that he slept in. He pressed his forehead against the cold window. The island was green, humping above the hedges of the mainland.

An argument was raging in his mind. *How could I have failed to notice? To do a thing like that, at this stage of the book! But it doesn't matter. It's exceptionally good. It flows from what's gone before. A natural progression. It's all right. No, it's impossible!*

Aloud he said: 'I'll write it again, in the third person. Then I'll compare and decide.'

Doing so occupied the rest of the afternoon. There were three pages typed with double spacing, and the total was around nine hundred words. This was rather more than he ordinarily produced in a day, but the work had been going excitingly well. He coaxed himself to rewrite and eventually had a third-person version to set alongside the first. The choice was easy. Although the second try had been painstaking, it lacked the tension and vitality of the original, and Richard Crane was a man suited to tension and vitality. John Gower tore up the afternoon's work.

He went into the garden, exhausted, winding through the trees and agonizing about the book. Only that morning he had been dreaming of completing his first draft within a couple of weeks of his arrival in Hawaii, providing he found a good place to work. Yet now he was confronted with an almost empty bank account that ruled out a expensive journey, and the suspicion that he ought all along to have allowed Crane to speak for himself.

The grind of footsteps on the drive chased him indoors seconds before the tractor in the apple store rasped into life. Grass-mowing time was round again. Gower stayed upstairs, fugitive, unhappy. But the mood passed long before the tractor engine spluttered to a stop.

I'll go on in the first person. I'll follow the instinct that let me put the story into Crane's mouth. It's not unique for a writer to bring a character forward into the first person, all that's upsetting me is that it's not what I planned. No, worse, it's that I didn't notice I'd done it.

He remained at the window until a cloud crept the length of the island. Just as he was moving away, movement below caught his eye. The ginger head of the boy, Danny, was bobbing near the kitchen window. Gower went into his study, put a new sheet of paper in the typewriter and entered Richard Crane's mind. He did not bother about the noise of the typewriter because Danny could not hear it above the sound of the tractor that, at this time, was crawling up and down the long swathe of grass beside the drive.

As the July evening cooled, hunger urged Gower to stop work. Crane's words were tumbling out in an elating fashion. The story had been nudged away from what Gower had envisaged because Crane was let down about his Hawaii holiday and had been obliged to delay it. This allowed him time to seek out Conroy. Crane was about to embark on that when Gower went to the kitchen.

Food was to be the simplest this evening. He had only to reheat what he had cooked the previous day. With the pan on the stove, he strayed into the garden and the scent of freshly cut grass. Roses were tangled around the sitting-room window and it was annoying not to be able to tidy them, nor interfere with weeds the gardener was overlooking in the flower bed. He breathed the scent of a red rose, and wondered about eating at the outside table as he had done on one of Gerrard's visits but not since.

The table was in the worst position for a man hoping to avoid being seen. He thought of moving it over to the trees, and walked towards them looking for a good spot. Each tree stood on an island of long grass, where the tractor skirted. In the grass around one tree he noticed something red. He picked up a child's sandal.

His impulse was to look about in case young Danny was peeping round a tree trunk at him. The sandal was well worn and the buckle had been ripped free of the leather and was fastened now only to the strap. Gower turned it over in his hand. He was certain it had not been in the garden when he was out there earlier, but felt that a man who could fail to see a switch from third person to first could presumably fail to see a shoe in deep grass. He fiddled with the thing, questioning whether it was the right size for Danny's foot. He had made an instant connection between the inquisitive youngster and the lost shoe, but actually had never noticed what Danny wore on his feet.

He pictured the child dashing into hiding when the door of the lean-to had opened and Gower had come out. He imagined the stumble, the wrench on the side of the sandal, the buckle pulling away and the foot leaping free for Danny to reach safety.

But where was safety? Gower continued through the trees, taking no clue from the position of the sandal because, if his theory was correct, that had gone flying into the air as it had been discarded. No, what led him this way was the knowledge that one far corner of the field had never been mown in the three months he had been there. The tractor had broken down the first time and missed it, the gardener had ignored it when he had returned one day with a scythe and cleared other areas of extra long grass, and the neglect had persisted. Either Danny knew a secret way through the rear hedge into the fields, or else he was seeking refuge in the wilderness of weeds in the corner beyond the fruit trees.

Gower came upon a giveaway sign of flattened grass where someone had recently forced a way. He hesitated, knowing the stupidity of revealing himself to the child if Danny were actually hiding there now, but fully expecting him to have slipped out of the garden by a secret route. He stroked the sandal, guessing whether it would have been warmer if it had been wrenched off within the past three minutes or whether it would have cooled more rapidly to its current temperature.

He thrust caution away. There had been no movement from the vegetation in the corner all the time he had stood there and he believed Danny incapable of maintaining that degree of stillness. Gower made up his mind to follow the route of flattened grass and satisfy his curiosity. Either he would find a quivering boy, which would not be a total disaster now his appearance was altered; or he would find a secret hideout, the type of fantasy he had himself indulged in as a boy; or he would find an alternative entrance to Butlers and he needed to know of such things.

There was another alternative. He did not think of it, until he found Danny lying dead.

Danny was on his back, his clothes disordered, his face discoloured and distorted. A red sandal was missing from his left foot.

Gower took in the horror at a blink and dropped the sandal. Immediately he snatched it up. Danny would be missed, was probably already missed, and he would be found rapidly once a search began.

Gower's brain ran a sequence of imaginary scenes. The police would call at Butlers. He would have to answer their questions. Danny's father would say the boy had played around the cottage, so would Danny's sister, so would the gardener. Gower's fingerprints would be found all over the sandal, incriminating him. And within hours Gower's true identity would be revealed with all the dreadful consequences. Worst of all, Linda would be lost to him.

While the sequence was playing he was inside the cottage hiding evidence of his occupation and putting his typescript and notes for the novel into his canvas bag where the computer disks had stayed ever since he had left Stream Cottage. He squashed his essential personal items, plus the Parsons passport, in on top of them. Deep in the stair cupboard he hid the typewriter Gerrard had loaned him.

For a moment he was also going to hide in the cupboard his older clothes and the few things that had travelled with him from the day he was on the *Fleur*, but he did not entirely trust

David Gerrard to rescue them without drawing attention. Instead, he packed them into a plastic shopping bag and took them with him. Within ten minutes of the disaster he was walking down the footpath towards the pub. Once he knew he was out of sight he crouched by a hedge, scooped soil, wiped the red sandal with a handkerchief and buried it.

He kept on walking, anywhere, trying to remember the map. Then he was in the forest, following a ride he hoped would bring him out on a road leading him in the direction of Brockenhurst.

As night fell the forest enfolded him, dark and protective. He wanted to find the blackest shadow and hide there. But his brain insisted: *I've got to get away. I'll walk all night if I have to but I must get away.*

Walking all night was not feasible, not in forest without the aid of moon or torch. When he came to a clearing he saw distant car lights sweeping an open road, and he made for that road, taking a track that, after a long time, led him there.

On the metalled road he expected at any time to be overtaken by a police car. The wild sequence of imaginary scenes resumed, showing him the car slowing to disgorge questioning figures in uniform who were not satisfied until he was in a police station and confessing he was the missing yachtsman, John Gower, not gulped down by a giant plughole but deceiving his publishers and readers while hiding in a New Forest cottage where a boy had been murdered.

He tried to blank out the escalating sequence, to be practical instead of fanciful. Already he had discarded in the forest some of the things from the plastic bag, things he hoped would be as well concealed in daylight as they had seemed to him in the darkness. He dropped into a ditch beside the road and got rid of some more. Before long the plastic bag was empty and in his pocket. Everything he wished to keep was in the canvas bag. He was pleased with his practicality.

In reality, no police car came for him. A man in a beaten-up van stopped and offered a lift, guessing he was the luckless driver of a car broken down at the roadside a mile before

Gower joined this road. Gower let him continue in this mistake. The man deposited him near a garage in Brockenhurst.

He went to the railway station, caught a train, then another, walked, caught a bus or two, then he walked. Each time exhaustion swamped him, fear spurred him on. Each time he neared despair, obstacles were swept aside and the journey continued. Each stage carried him nearer his goal: Stream Cottage.

He knew nowhere else to go. *It's not just that I can get my passport there, it's homing instinct,* he thought, unresisting. *There's the rest of the country to choose from, but I want to go home.*

He saw it clearly in his mind: the difficult gate from the lane; the shed that was used as a garage and had a door that swung dangerously; the rose, the pink one, he had planted beside the front door; the narrow cold passage leading to the square damp rooms; his study with the slanting window; and the kitchen with . . .

He pulled himself up. *No, it's all changed. I know that, of course I do. Probably there'll be builder's rubble in the front garden. There'll be green tiles on the kitchen floor and oak cupboards. There'll be radiators and central heating pipes everywhere. There'll be a smart new line to the roof. The bathroom will be . . . What did Linda decide about the bathroom? I remember she asked whether I preferred pink or green for the suite and I said what was wrong with white?*

And then he was in the lane leading to Stream Cottage. He had a little moon and the gurgle of the ditch they called a stream to lead him. The cottage was a black hulk on his right, others up the lane invisible. The whiteness of the gate urged him forward, lightness where there was darkness.

He reached out a hand and touched the iron of the gate. Cold. Dew damp. He felt for the latch and moved it noiselessly. With care he took the path to the front door. After the sweep of the drive to Butlers in its great plot of land everything at Stream Cottage appeared mean.

Gower felt in their secret hiding place for the spare key to the front door. It was there, he had never paused to doubt that it would be. His fingers sought the lock on the door, he jiggled the key into it and turned.

Months at Butlers had schooled him not to switch on the electric light. He stepped inside, pushing the door back as he did so. It resisted. Something soft was preventing it moving freely. He squeezed through the gap, his feet on loose, shifting papers.

The house felt colder than ever, unwelcoming, although the night was mild. He entered the kitchen, a torch in mind but unsure how to locate one now the kitchen had been modernized. *The drawer by the sink. We used to have one in there. Perhaps Linda has kept the same arrangement in the new kitchen.*

The faintest natural light guided him across to the sink. She had never mentioned moving that, believing it best to have it in full light in front of the window. Gower reached the sink and felt for the knob or handle of a drawer. His fingers closed around the torch exactly where he had hoped it might be.

Pointing it downwards, rather than flash a beam out over the fields, he clicked it on. The disc of yellow light revealed a black splodgy pattern around his feet. He started, rubbed his eyes and moved the beam. The pattern was real, he had not imagined it.

With a cry he swung the beam around the room, picking out the old kitchen furniture, the original damp-stained walls, and again and again the pattern of the tatty linoleum on the floor. Then he disregarded the danger of signalling his presence and turned the beam full on the sink. No mixer tap, just the twin taps there had always been and the twin stains on the old enamel.

He ran from the room, streaking the blade of light along the hall that was not redecorated, the walls where no radiators hung and down to the mass of papers behind the front door. He would deal with them later, first he needed to know the extent of his discovery. He lunged into the sitting room with its frayed carpet and furniture. Soot from last winter's fires had fallen into the hearth and over the rug. The faded wallpaper had not been replaced.

Gower wheeled into the study. Exactly as he had left it. Upstairs, past the chipped newel post, it was the same. No builder or decorator had been near Stream Cottage. Whatever Linda had done with the thousands of pounds she had begged, she had not spent a penny on their cottage.

Nausea seized him and he made for the bathroom. The spider in the bath was dead. Gower heaved, then took a grip on his emotions. *It's only money. It doesn't matter.*

But it wasn't, and it did.

He left the pile of papers in the passage until daylight but he was in no doubt what they would tell him. After a few hours' fragile sleep he went downstairs, gathered them up and carried them into the sitting room where he spread them on the floor and examined them. Bills had come and not been paid. Banks and electricity boards and so forth had protested. A few free newspapers had been delivered, although thankfully the Gowers' cottage was, in its relative isolation, spared most trash of that kind. The *Reader's Digest*, and other senders of unsolicited junk, had kept up the pressure.

Gower sifted out the few things of importance, and kicked the others into a heap. From the dates, it was plain that Linda had not been near the place for months. Wherever she had been spending the weekends that left her too weary to visit him on Sundays, it was not here.

Desperate, he rang her at her sister's before she left for work, to demand an explanation. Mary Green's breathless voice answered him. Gower faked an Irish accent, not a good one but enough, he prayed, to fool his sister-in-law.

'Is Linda there, please?'

'My sister? No, she isn't.'

'What time will she be there?'

'If she's coming, you know more than I do.'

Gower recognized his familiar feeling of being at cross purposes with Mary Green. He tried again: 'What time will Linda be home from work?'

'I couldn't tell you.'

'Well, what time does she normally get home?' He had an

idea he'd had exactly this discussion with her once before and wished he could remember the answer.

'I really couldn't say, seeing as she doesn't live here any more.'

Gower recovered and asked for Linda's address or telephone number, even the name of the company she worked for.

Mary Green said: 'I'm not to say, she's asked me not to. But I could tell her you rang. Who shall I say called?'

Gower hung up on her.

15

'When you say he's not in, Hazel, you mean he's being questioned by the police, I suppose?' Rain Morgan winked at Holly Chase who was listening to her conversation with David Gerrard's secretary.

'I expect he'll be back soon,' said the secretary, wishing neither to confirm nor deny.

Rain asked her to tell Gerrard she had called.

The news coming into the office was that the discovery of the body of a six-year-old boy in the grounds of the home of one of Gerrard's authors, a technical writer called Parsons, had been made during the weekend. The lad had been missed by his family, who had believed him to be playing at a friend's house. They had searched the village, going to an empty thatched house that had fascinated the child for months.

Holly had skipped the morning conference because she was house-hunting, and so she had missed some of the details. Rain explained that Parsons had told people in the village that his agent would have the use of the place while he was away and they had noticed a man there from time to time.

Holly giggled. 'I'm looking foward to seeing David Gerrard on the television news protesting his innocence. He'll look so shady no one will believe him.'

Rain disappointed her. 'They won't be able to pin it on him, even I can give him an alibi for the evening the boy was killed. We were at the same party.'

'Shame,' said Holly.

Gerrard returned Rain's call late in the morning. He hoped for sympathy and she endeavoured to provide it. He had been about to leave for the airport and Barbados when the police had come for him. Worse than the lost holiday was the ensuing indignity.

'One doesn't,' he complained, 'expect the generous loan of a country cottage to involve one in such depravity. But there I was, having to justify my visits to the satisfaction of a bunch of provincial police officers.'

Rain knew how deeply he resented their provincialism. She asked whether he had ever noticed the boy, who was reported to have played around the cottage.

'Oh God, Rain, don't you start all that too. No, I never saw the boy, and I've hardly been there. Of course, it was awfully kind of Parsons and his wife to lend me their house, yet one is no country bumpkin. I dropped in a few times for the novelty as much as anything, but really the world ceases at Richmond. Why should those provincial Plods assume I'd be out there nabbing small boys?'

Rain simmered with laughter as Gerrard's lament revealed the way his interview with the police had gone. However much he despised them, they despised him more.

She said: 'Now pull yourself together, David, you know you can rely on me for an alibi for that evening. All I require in exchange is a pithy quote for tomorrow's column.'

'Oh, Rain, my pith is at a low ebb. I really don't feel one has anything to say.'

'And you the one that's usually so keen to get into print!'

'Must you be heartless?'

She said yes. In the end he did tell her what she wanted to hear. She wrote the story, a brief paragraph that she meant to run in the gossip column but which, by mid-afternoon, had been stolen by Riley the news editor to stretch the news story. Little Danny had been the darling of the village and the villagers had pressed forward to say as much, but most of it was repetition and David Gerrard's line about his difficulty in contacting Butlers' owner who was abroad was at least different.

Merriment at Gerrard's predicament was a very small part of Rain's day. She was able to confirm that Linda Gower was to be co-presenter of a series produced by the man seen with her in the wine bar on the day Rosie left the *Daily Post*. This fact was accompanied by tantalizing hints about Mrs Gower's precise relationship to her producer, and by straightforward pique from several professionals who had been tipped for the job.

Then Rain took a call from a man who worked for a charity helping London's homeless. She had been seeking him, because his name surfaced in a handful of newspaper cuttings about exploitation of the homeless, and those news stories tallied with the situations illustrated in Alf Wilson's unfinished play.

The man, who had been away from London while she was searching for him, agreed to meet her immediately. She drove to a scruffy south London high street where the charity was housed in a room above an unprepossessing café. As she feared, the meeting took place in the café.

The coffee was insipid with scum forming within seconds of it being poured. The glaze of the thick white cups was scarred grey around the rims and the spoons were misshapen and stained. Rain chided herself for minding, for living such a clean and cosseted life that she had forgotten such cafés persisted. A cigarette burn had punctured a neat round hole in the red-and-white-checked plastic tablecloth. She moved the rickety tin ashtray, with its residue of ash trapped in corners, and began to speak.

Her companion, a streetwise young man with lank hair and a drab sweatshirt that had started life white, lit a cigarette and blew smoke in her face. He dragged the ashtray back to its original position.

'What do you want to know?' he asked in a flat voice.

She mentioned the news stories, his name in them, the general drift of events they described. He took another drag. 'What do you expect, with this government? That's what we do here,' he cocked an eye at the ceiling, at the charity office overhead, 'try to make people aware what's going on. The regulations, they hurt people who haven't got a voice. We try to be that voice. We speak up for them.'

He clamped his mouth around the cigarette again, his eyes

small and mean. The eyes accused her. He had mentally labelled her and pigeonholed her on arrival. The eyes condemned her for wasting his time, for resisting his view of society and, when it came to the point back in her cosy office, of choosing not to write about it.

Rain said: 'Did you know a playwright called Alf Wilson?'

The eyes responded to the name seconds before the cigarette was delicately removed and laid to rest in the ashtray. Smoke squirmed around a dribbled sauce bottle. The man nodded. 'Yeah. *He* was interested. I thought he was interested, but he didn't write anything. He talked about doing something for television, but it didn't happen.'

Rain tossed up whether to tell him outright that Wilson had been working on the play when he died. *Heads I raise Alf a notch or two in his estimation and give him one less writer to sneer at, tails I don't.* Tails won.

She asked him: 'Did you provide contacts for his research or did he have all his information from you?'

'Contacts. I suppose you're going to ask who they were?'

'That's right.'

He cascaded sugar into his coffee, the scum splintering and sinking and resurfacing. He said: 'He went to squats, he went on the patrols at night with the vans taking food to people sleeping rough. It's all there for anyone to see, if they open their eyes and look around. That's all it takes.'

Rain said: 'Did he say – '

'Look, what is this? You want to talk to me about our setup, or you want to talk about this Alf Wilson? He's dead. He didn't do anything for us, not for anybody. So what is this?'

Heads had won after all.

The young man heard her out. Then he said: 'You've seen what he wrote?'

When she didn't instantly reply he said: 'Of course you have, or you wouldn't have made that speech. Tell me what he wrote.'

She said he had set his story in a house that was being squatted, that it was a strong piece but that it was apparent

Wilson had intended substantial changes. All this encouraged the young man to grind out his cigarette and order her: 'Take this down.'

Then he dictated three names and telephone numbers that would put her in touch with the people who had helped Wilson. He said: 'I started him off, last year. I don't know exactly who he contacted afterwards, but these are the people I sent him to. If you want, you'll be able to follow his route, find out what you want to know, if not . . .' He shrugged. If not, she would be just one more writer who had wasted his time and written nothing to further his cause.

Rain paid for the disgusting coffee and left.

She drove to a call box some streets away and rang the first number on the list. To her surprise the telephone was answered by a receptionist announcing a council office. Rain asked for a name and another woman came on the line. Rain got the feeling the woman would not have talked if she had not recognized Rain's name, or if Rain had not mentioned Alf Wilson. In fifteen minutes Rain was in another café waiting for the woman, then learning about the conversation with Wilson in that same place a year before, and the pointers he had been given.

But she stuck at that. The squats the councillor referred Wilson to had been ended and the houses restored to normal occupation, and the two other names on Rain's list did not answer their telephones. She went home, telling herself she had done all she could for the day, while knowing perfectly well that if she were to pursue Wilson's trail through the city's homeless, she should be going out again that night and prowling the notorious South Bank and Charing Cross areas where the down-and-outs were most in evidence.

She was arguing with herself about the relevance versus the futility of dogging Wilson's steps, when she entered her flat and was greeted by the bright light on her answering machine announcing a recorded message. Paul Wickham had rung, sorry to have missed her again and asking her to call him.

There were days when she would have snatched up the

receiver and done it, but this was not one of them. She opened a fresh bottle of Perrier water, clattered ice cubes into a long glass, sliced a semi-circle from a cut lemon and thoughtfully sipped. How long was it since they had met? Months rather than weeks, unless she admitted a brief encounter when they had coincidentally been at the same place at the same time. But there had been telephone calls regretting that they could not get together, and there had been messages making further attempts.

She showered and changed, then returned to her drink and her thoughts of Wickham. Better, she decided, not to tell him about her renewed interest in Alf Wilson. She would relate the other events of her day, but she would not refer to Wilson. *If* she spoke to him at all.

She got his answering machine, joked that they could not go on not meeting like this, said she would be home for the rest of the evening and hoped he would ring back. She sent her love. Rang off.

Unwittingly he had given her the excuse she hankered for not to brave the South Bank or Charing Cross. She had to wait home for a telephone call, didn't she?

She finished reading a novel, titivated her garden, and ate a late supper while refusing to confess she had delayed in case Wickham had invited her to eat out. She put off half a dozen telephone calls she had planned to fit into the evening, so that the line would be free, and slumped in front of the television with another glass of Perrier to hand. It was not her favourite kind of evening.

The murder of the little Hampshire boy was one of the main news items on the television. Rain was intrigued to see for herself the fairytale thatched cottage where one of David Gerrard's authors had invited him to weekend and where Gerrard, somewhat churlishly in her opinion, had declined to put in more than a couple of appearances.

Then Gerrard himself filled the screen, telling that part of the story and describing efforts to locate Brian Parsons, the owner of Butlers. Naturally, Gerrard emphasized his denial of seeing the boy or anyone else near the premises, and he managed to plug two of Parsons's books. Then a trio of villagers took his place on screen to say that some local people were of the view that the house had been occupied during the owner's absence.

'Did you see anyone there yourself?' asked the reporter, out of shot except for a shoulder pad and an earring.

'No,' said the man, 'but the story's going round that a thin young man was seen skulking there on and off for the last few months.'

The police officer in charge of the case confirmed that they were looking into these reports but there was as yet no evidence to support them. Rain jiggled the ice cubes in her glass and considered that sightings of a thin young man let David Gerrard off the hook. No one could confuse him with thinness.

Towards the end of the bulletin came news of a development in the police search for the men who had killed a security guard at a London warehouse. Premises had been raided, men had been taken to police stations. Wickham was not filmed but Rain knew he was engaged in the search for the killer. The 'latest developments' suggested he was unlikely to have time to ring her again that day.

When her phone did ring, she pounced. But it was Holly Chase, eager to share her hilarity at David Gerrard's performance as murder suspect. Holly said: 'He'll hate it but the police will have to grill him again now to see what he knows of "the thin man". If anybody was there, then he could hardly avoid knowing, could he?'

Rain agreed wholeheartedly, adding that if the villagers thought a man had been there, then it was probable one had. She expanded on Holly's suggestion that Gerrard had known, and she and Holly dreamed up preposterous clues that Gerrard, however intermittent his visits to the house, ought to have spotted.

And all the while Rain was covering up that she had never noticed the implications for Gerrard at all, that she had been so preoccupied with sitting by her telephone that she had overlooked the obvious.

Holly summed up: 'Either he was stupid enough not to notice he was sharing the cottage, or he's protecting someone whom he knows was there, perhaps even invited to stay there.'

Not to be outdone, Rain enlarged the point. 'He must be convinced the man is innocent. I don't think Gerrard would shield a murderer.'

Holly agreed, a mite reluctantly. Rain went on: 'And then you have to ask yourself why, now that something so dreadful has happened, he's preventing the man's identity becoming known.'

Holly said: 'Hmm,' and that she could not guess at that. 'If he's stashed one of his authors away down there for peace and quiet while a masterpiece is created, I'd expect him to own up in a case of murder.' She laughed and said: 'I wonder whether we should recommend the police to do a head count of his authors, to make sure they're all accounted for.'

'They're not. You're forgetting John Gower.'

There was a pause in which Holly caught her breath. 'Are you serious?'

'No, but it would explain months of odd behaviour by Gerrard. And you've got to admit that as an explanation for Gower's disappearance – plus, remember, the manuscript he was working on – it makes more sense than the Great Plughole Theory.'

Holly leapt at the idea, half serious and half joking. Rain killed it, saying: 'It's an entertaining theory but it won't do. The man the villagers saw is young, thin and fair-haired. We all know what John Gower looks like, and it isn't that.'

Yet when she sat alone thinking about it, her joke provided a neater explanation than any other she had heard since that rumour-laden week when the *Fleur* was smashed up in fog near the *Charity* and John Gower had suddenly become famous.

BOOK THREE

Victims

16

John Gower stood by a newsagent's window, pretending to read the advertisements pinned there. 'English taught to foreigners.' 'Cleaner required, four hours a week, light work only.' 'Pram for sale, as new.' 'Wedding dress, bargain, worn only once.' Etcetera.

His mind was on the telephone kiosk and the black youths who had been crammed into it for a quarter of an hour and showed no signs of shifting. Across the road was a bookshop. Gower could make out his own books, a large photograph of himself as he used to be. He was thinner now, fairer except where the dark roots were pushing up, but he had found a hat on his travels, a cotton hat that suited the casualness of his new clothes, and he wore the hat nearly all the time.

The youths spun out of the call box, chattering noisily, shambling away down the pavement in their loose-limbed way. Gower ran forward, cut in front of a woman who had appeared from nowhere and thought the next call was hers. He dragged the door behind him, shutting out her indignant curses. His hand shook as he tried David Gerrard's number.

'Tell him it's Richard,' he said when Gerrard's secretary asked for a name.

A puzzled Gerrard came on the line. 'Richard?' The way he said it proved he numbered no Richards among his acquaintance.

'It's me – John. I want to know what's going on, what's *been* going on.'

'*You* want to know! Just a minute . . .' Silence as Gerrard cupped a hand over the receiver, then: 'I've sent my secretary to make coffee. John, where are you?'

'London. We've got to meet. There are a lot of things . . . And I need money.'

Gerrard was whispering. 'They're looking for you. The police.'

'You haven't told them?'

'Nothing. They don't know it's you they're looking for, but they've convinced themselves there was a man at Butlers and that he killed that boy. One can see their point, it appears a wholly reasonable hypothesis.'

Gower bridled. 'And you, David? What do you believe?'

He resented the delay before Gerrard carefully replied that, of course, he did not suspect any of his authors of child murder but that it was no healthy position for an agent to be in, having to lie to the police while not actually being in full possession of the facts.

Gower snapped that he did not have time for Gerrard's sensibilities, he was in a call box, his money would run out. What he wanted was a meeting to sort out a great many matters, not least the whereabouts of the money that ought to have been paid into the bank account for him to reach Hawaii; and the huge expenditure on Stream Cottage while the property had not benefited from so much as a smear of paint.

He heard Gerrard croak and he pushed on, demanding, challenging, accusing and not letting Gerrard speak had he been capable of it. Then it came true, the call box money ran out. 'Tonight,' Gower shouted, voice high with urgency. 'The concourse at Euston Station. Eight o'clock.'

'But I – '

'Be there. And bring money.'

A click. The dialling tone. He could not say who had achieved the last word. He stood, receiver in hand, then became conscious of the fuming woman waiting outside. She tore at the door and shouldered past him, with fresh complaints. Gower drifted down the street.

Euston Station had been a spur of the moment notion, perhaps a bad one. It was spacious, there was nowhere to sit, it was . . . He shook his head. Whatever it was like, it was where they were to meet.

That was most of a day away. He walked to the nearest

Underground station, got out at Charing Cross and mingled with tourists in Trafalgar Square, then mounted the steps to the National Gallery. It had never occurred to him not to come to London. When he had rallied from the shock of finding that Linda, and probably Gerrard too, had cheated him over the renovation of the cottage, he had headed for London. He had cadged lifts from lorry drivers, and he had walked, and he had made it to London and a cheap hotel.

The hotel had thick white paint on the stucco and a stunted tree in the front garden. But the corridors upstairs were dingy and the rooms dank. He told them he wanted to stay for a week, but meant it to be less, just as long as it took Gerrard to fix him a new hideaway.

From the steps of the gallery he looked at the Square, at the fountains teased by a summer breeze, at children braving pigeons for the sake of family snapshots, at young men conquering Landseer's lions, at demonstrators outside the South African Embassy condemning the brutality of apartheid, at traffic racketing round and round, and at buildings coming down and others rising up. He turned his back on it and went into the gallery.

They had stopped searching bags and scrutinizing faces, given up playing 'Spot the Bomber'. He was glad of that. As John Gower his face was in shop windows, on book covers and in advertisements. As 'the thin man', sought in connection with the Butlers' murder, his face was transformed into a photofit picture on posters in the streets and outside police stations. So far, no one had made the fit. He was glad of that too.

The day trickled away. He invented methods of squandering time. He learned where the security staff hung around and he learned not to hang around there. He discovered how to blend into crowds around lecturers. As he meandered among the galleries he broadened Richard Crane's knowledge of art, explored his taste, earmarked certain artists Crane might hang on the walls of his penthouse. Crane was not to be merely a modern man, the choice of a few paintings from other centuries would give him depth. Gower frittered the afternoon, first as the hireling who would seek out pictures for Crane, then as Crane himself browsing among the miraculously attainable.

As the hireling, he picked out *Belshazzar's Feast*, seeking to flatter Crane with a Rembrandt of this scale, and then rejecting it as the script, *Mene Mene Tekel Upharsin*, impressed itself on his mind. Crane would not wish to be reminded he had been weighed in the balance and found wanting. He replaced it with Holbein's *Ambassadors*, with the oblique skull in the foreground at the feet of the illustrious subjects and their paraphernalia. Crane and his guests could marvel at the perspective of this intrusion into the portrait and feel free to ignore the significance of the *memento mori* – 'Remember you must die.'

As Crane, he bought a passive Corot, depicting a horseman in a wood, and a fourteenth-century triptych by Memling. Then he spent lavishly on the sensuous expanse of flesh and silk in a Velasquez, *The Toilet of Venus*, excusing the whimsy of the pink ribbon around the wrist of the winged cherub. And then he wavered about reselling it to pay for another Venus, Botticelli's *Venus with Mars*. He would not have wall space for both, especially as he fancied a Rubens, *Samson and Delilah*, too.

Finally he found a fifteenth-century portrait of an unknown woman by an unknown Swabian hand, a woman holding forget-me-nots and oblivious of a fly on her creamy linen headdress. But it was the warmth in the humorous brown eyes that caught him, her tranquillity with a ripple of mischievousness running through it. As she was nobody, he span stories to fill her years, credited her with family, friends, lover, attributed to her an enigmatic relationship with her painter, and wanted her for himself.

Gower took the Northern line on the Underground from Charing Cross straight to Euston, ages too early for the appointment but happy to while away the time in the bookshop and the snack bar. The newspaper he bought had a paragraph about Linda and her new job, the first he had heard of it.

He hunched over the page, reading and rereading, trying to make it mean something other than what it said. How was it possible that she had abandoned the career she had left him to pursue? Chucked it away because of a whim that she might earn a living from television? What was this producer to her? Could they really be paying her that much?

The words blurred into meaninglessness. He passed a hand over his eyes, accusing the world of going mad. Nothing was what he had understood it to be. All the attitudes and values he had been used to had been changed. People had tinkered with them behind his back and he had been left to discover the changes by chance.

He attempted once more to decode the story about Linda. Then he savagely folded the paper and crammed it into his pocket. He was being trapped. The few weeks' disappearance to stir interest in his books had resulted in threats he could not evade. Emerge as John Gower and people would want to know where he had been, admit the place was Butlers and he would be accused of killing the boy.

His feeling was encapsulated in the image of a man whose leisurely swim across a gentle river was transformed into a struggle with a whirlpool. Gower sensed the dangers dragging him closer to disaster, every effort he made to shake them off induced greater hazard. He was being sucked inexorably forward. Under.

An elbow jostling him banished the moment's horror. He edged along the bench to give a portly commuter extra space. He hated the closeness of people, their antlike purposefulness and numbers, but he craved it too. The ants' nest was the finest place to hide. He soothed himself with thoughts of the money his books were earning, with confidence about the future of the Richard Crane book and with preparation for his confrontation with Gerrard.

Eight o'clock came and went. Gower paraded the concourse, on the lookout for him. There was a scattering of travellers waiting beneath the indicator boards for information about trains, hundreds of figures coming and going, clutches of drunks and drug addicts pestering people for money or slumped senseless, and there were snake-eyed men who offered dubious friendship to confused youngsters taking their first steps in the capital. But there was no Gerrard.

Gower tried his flat but the calls went unanswered. When it was nearly ten he headed for the hotel.

The tramps who had hovered around the concourse or lain on the grass outside during the day had tucked themselves into right angles and convenient doorways near the station, claiming their sleeping spaces for when sleep came. Some had pitched down already, the paper-stuffed plastic bags they used as pillows flashing white in car headlamps to give the only clue to their owners' presence among the shadows.

Away from the station their numbers diminished, Gower was no longer torn between interested glances or averting his eyes out of delicacy. He shrugged himself free of the disgust and the guilt these people aroused in him, and he quickened his pace. Then he made a mistake.

Although traffic was sparse, he used an underpass to cross a major road. The body he fell over groaned, accompanying Gower's sharp alarm. In dimmest light he made out other figures, crouching or lying full-length by the foul-smelling walls.

He backtracked, thinking to flee up the steps to the safety of street lamps and passing vehicles. But the way was blocked. A man stood there, a pathetic importuning man, young but looking old, a frightening man.

Gower jerked away from the clawing hands, from the bleating incantations. He tripped into the hands of others. Three men? Four? His lungs fought against their odour as they pushed him against the wall and hands thrust into his pockets. Throughout, the whining pleas ran on without pause. Even when the robbery was done, and Gower was hurled painfully on the steps, the man droned the same 'give-me, give-me'.

Feeling bludgeoned, defiled, and physically hurt from his fall and the frantic scrabbling to regain street level, he staggered into the road. A car racing from traffic lights swerved around him and a horn blasted. On the pavement, he tried to run. They might come after him. Anything might happen. He must get away. He could not afford to be beaten up and taken to hospital or a police station. He did not give a damn about the money or the false Parsons passport they had taken, he cared only that he be allowed to escape.

His legs could not co-operate, they were leaden and slow. He forced them on, resisting the need to sag and sit. All he wanted was to be back at the hotel, safe in the stuffy room. His aspirations had shrunk to that one wish.

Finally, he was there. He locked the door behind him and he counted the damage. His shoes were scuffed, his trousers torn, his leg was bleeding and his hands grazed. But the rest was serviceable. He washed, staunched the cut with paper tissues and opened a can of beer. Then he checked his bag in the wardrobe, feeling into the envelope that housed his typescript and notes, until his fingers touched the smooth hardness of Richard Crane's bank cards. In the morning he would have to find a cash machine.

He slept badly, a row in an adjacent room – or possibly a television set – interweaving with a dream until he imagined himself in a fight, a garbled replay of the incident in the underpass. Then he lay awake, concocting improbable schemes to locate Linda, concentrating on them rather than on the accumulating evidence that Linda would never return to him. And when that thought intruded, a daunting realization followed it: Linda might believe him guilty of killing Danny. Not killing him deliberately, of course, she knew him too well to entertain that, but she might assume an accident – the boy snooping, an attempt to restrain him, something of that nature. Children were vulnerable, accidents happened. And, as far as he knew, the press had not reported the detail he knew, the disarranged clothing, the evidence of sexual interference. 'Strangled', they had said, and left it at that. Danny had been strangled.

Early in the morning, Gower left the hotel for the nearest call box and rang David Gerrard's flat. 'I waited. You didn't come.'

Gerrard's voice was thick, he was roused from sleep. 'I tried to say it was impossible, but you wouldn't listen.'

They argued but Gower cut it off. 'I'm in a call box. I'm using the last of my change. I was mugged last night. You meet me at lunchtime today, David, with the money or I walk into your office this afternoon. Is that clear?'

Gerrard squirmed then capitulated. Gower was being authoritarian again, he ought to have got used to that by now but it always came as an unpleasant surprise. 'Where? Euston?'

'No, Holland Park. The café. One o'clock.'

'Oh, well, grab a table, will you?'

'*Outside* the café, David. No money, remember? Until you come, that is.'

Gower hung up on him, beating the pips by a fraction. He felt ridiculously good about that.

At one he was positioned some way off, looking towards the café. People ambled contentedly about, enjoying the sunshine or loitering while their children, who had loitering down to a fine art, inspected each individual blade of grass as they passed. Then Gerrard marched into view, chin up, chest out. He paced up and down in front of the cafés, looking at his watch, showing every manifestation of a man who wanted to turn tail. Gower closed in on him before thought became deed.

'We'll walk,' said Gower.

'I'm starving.'

'Then we'd better get the business over quickly. We'll walk this way.' He took him along a path, not into the wider spaces of the park but between shrubs and trees.

'One doesn't wish to cavil,' drawled Gerrard, 'but that is an absolutely hideous hat.'

'It's wonderful. It didn't fall off when I was mugged.'

'God, you sound like a character in a Western. You know, when there's a terrific brawl and the piano keeps on playing and none of the heroes' hats fall off.'

'The money,' said Gower. And his brained chanted: '*Give-me, give-me.*'

'A hundred and fifty, give or take a pound or two.' He darted a worried look at Gower, and then his worry increased a degree. 'John, one doesn't carry a fortune around. You've got everything I could lay hands on this morning.'

'Cheques,' said Gower, speaking slowly as he might to a dim-witted child. 'You could have brought me an enormous cheque. There's a bank account, I could pay it in. You know all this, David. Why am I having to explain it again?' He was very quiet, very intense.

Gerrard was flushed, a big red-faced man taking a lunch-time airing in a park and scared stiff every step of the way.

Gower said: 'No money has been paid into the account. Why not?'

The fat man mumbled that perhaps the bank had made an error, perhaps he had filled in the wrong number on the paying-in slip. 'You refused to give me your alias, remember.' He was eager to share blame.

Gower said: 'All right, then. I'll give you the number again.' His expression denied that he believed Gerrard's excuse. Gower said: 'And the alias is Richard Crane. Remember that, it could be important.'

Writing down the name and the account number, Gerrard cleared his throat and geared himself up for a speech. 'John, things are getting out of hand. No, they've been out of hand for weeks. What we intended, well, it hasn't worked out, has it?'

Gower believed it had worked superbly but it had not stopped where they had planned. It had gone careering out of control. He did not say this. He said: 'The publicity, the sales . . . Exactly what we hoped.'

'Yes, but . . .' Gerrard could not think how to finish. Rehearsing on the way to the park he had prepared a decisive speech about the time having arrived for the play-acting to cease. Gower's manner precluded him making it.

Gower said: 'You prevented me going to Hawaii. You didn't give me the money. Why not?'

More unnecessary throat-clearing. At last Gerrard said: 'Well, the truth is that I didn't think Hawaii such a good idea after all.' And when Gower protested, he held up a hand and continued: 'I wasn't sure what you might do, John. It seemed less trouble all round to keep you here.'

'To be trapped at Butlers and suspected of murder?' He expressed his contempt for Gerrard's reasoning with eye-rolling disbelief. And he asked sarcastically whether Gerrard had an equally sound reason for putting thousands of pounds into Linda's hands for work that had never been carried out.

When he prodded further about this, and the apologies and excuses had begun, Gower leapt at an unspoken truth. 'She blackmailed you, didn't she? I can't bel—'

They were facing each other on the path. A grey squirrel was watching them from an overhead branch. No one was in sight, but they would not have cared who had come by, they would not have noticed. Gerrard admitted bitingly: 'You can't believe it, John? Oh, yes you can. Your wife blackmailed me – no, *us* – she blackmailed *us*. She forced us to give her money because if we didn't she would reveal that you were not killed on the *Fleur* but were deceiving your publishers and the public to promote your books.'

There was a pause while Gower assimilated the extent of Linda's treachery and fumbled to understand his agent's role in it. Connivance? Or had he been truly blackmailed?

Gerrard grasped this. He said: 'You needn't doubt me, John. I'm enmeshed as deeply as you are, and she knows it. I was in no position to resist the lady's blandishments.'

Gower burst out: 'You could have said! If I'd known what she was up to – '

'She was canny. She didn't bounce into my office and introduce herself as the friendly neighbourhood blackmailer, you know. It was a while before I twigged something was wrong, and by then she'd had thousands. I judged it best to let you finish the book in peace and sort it out afterwards. I mean to say, once the book was done you were to reappear anyway and that would put an end to her tricks.'

Gower leaned against the tree, eyes closed, a deep and agonized sigh reaching up from the depths of his suffering. 'Tell me the rest, David. Tell me how much she got.'

The agent said the figure quietly, trusting low volume to reduce the sum. Gower did not react. His eyes were still shut, his face impassive, the tree bearing his weight.

Gerrard said tentatively: 'John? Look, I know it's one hell of a lot of money but you're a very rich man now.'

Gower swallowed. 'Not if this goes on.'

A choking laugh. 'It won't go on. Now you've fled from Butlers the safest thing to do is declare yourself alive and well and that will automatically end Linda's game.'

Gower could have hit him, wanted to. Through gritted teeth he reminded him, in the talking-to-a-child voice: 'David, I would be arrested for murder. I can't pop up again, not until they've arrested somebody else.' And when Gerrard studied the ground and drew shapes in the dust with an expensive shoe, Gower accused him of holding back on the money to coerce him.

The agent's jaw tightened. 'Yes. If you have the cash and a free rein, one has no idea what you might do. You'd be risking everything *I* have as well as what you have.' He was on the verge of the play-acting speech, but pulled back. He shook his head, softening a shade: 'It's for your own good, John. In the long run, it really is.'

Gower controlled his anger, just. 'You talked once about getting the timing right. You wanted me to stay concealed until it suited your idea of rightness. Now I'll tell you mine. The right time for me to emerge is when someone has been arrested. I used to watch that boy, you know. In the garden. He used to run in and out. I didn't know him, not really, but he was one of few people I saw for months and he was a lively, impulsive little chap. I found him dead. That was, how would you like me to put it? Distressing? Threatening, anyway. I had to run away because of it. And now I'm going to stay out of sight until my hair has grown back to its normal colour. If I don't wait, the moment I reappear, someone, somewhere is bound to connect me to the photofit of the wanted man. I'm not asking you to take responsibility for anything, except giving me the money I need. *My* money. Not yours or Linda's, but *mine*.'

Through nearly all of it, the longest speech he had ever heard him make, Gerrard had avoided meeting his eye. The squirrel ran down the trunk beside them and delved into undergrowth. Neither of the men was free to escape so simply. Gerrard said, eyes on the tree trunk, somewhere to the left of Gower's head: 'Think it over, John.' And when Gower did not speak: 'I've got to get back. It's a busy week.' He shot a cuff to look at a slim gold watch.

'When did you last see Linda, David?'

'Er . . . a few weeks ago.'

'In that case I doubt if you'll hear from her again.'

Gerrard questioned with a look. Gower said: 'Since I disappeared from Butlers, she hasn't any proof, has she? All she can offer in support of a story that I was alive and living in Hampshire, is evidence that you paid her money to shut her up about it.'

Relief transformed Gerrard. Gower concluded: 'She's no fool. She won't hawk her story around Fleet Street and ruin her career in television.'

He smiled, but it was a hard, glinting smile without warmth or comfort.

At the nearest bank he paid the cash from Gerrard's envelope into the Richard Crane account. It was not a hundred and fifty pounds, it was a hundred and thirty-eight, a pittance compared to what he had demanded but too much to carry around with him. From the bank he went to Kensington Gardens where he sat for a while and attempted to organize his future. Obviously he was going to have to manage without Gerrard's help, any hope that the man would have provided a new hideout had been ill-founded. Gerrard might not even dole out his money.

He banished thoughts of Linda's duplicity. There would be time to dwell on that later, in fact he would be unable to avoid it. The more pressing need was to arrange a place to work. By late afternoon he was in Holborn Library, approving the subdued atmosphere of concentration in the reference section and prepared to be there early next day to lay claim to a desk. He would have to write by hand but that was no impediment. Richard Crane's story was begging to be written, anywhere, by any means. He found a space, scrounged paper from a student and wrote some disjointed paragraphs to feed later into the flow of the text.

Gower's last words to his agent had been to insist on a meeting the next day, a meeting at which Gerrard should produce a cheque for £10,000. He had picked Holland Park again because it was reasonably convenient for Gerrard although, as it was turning out, it would be awkward for Gower himself.

In Theobald's Road he ate a bowl of pasta in an Italian café and lingered over coffee from an espresso machine that repeatedly drowned conversation and traffic noise. He was rearranging his future again.

The hotel's in the wrong place. I'll move to another one. No, a room. Then I can work there too. But as the suggestions surfaced in his mind he knew they were futile unless Gerrard paid up. A room would be expensive, he did not look like a reliable tenant with his two-tone hair and damaged, untidy clothes. In any case, a room would involve payment of a deposit and he could not spare the money.

Back at the hotel, his mind was a flurry of plans, some to carry out if Gerrard paid and others to fall back on if he did not. And intercepting him all the time was Richard Crane, the worldly-wise, handsome young property developer who commanded admiration and respect, had an enviable way with women, filled his Thames-side flat with luxurious things, was cultured besides, and reaped rewards from exploiting the financial opportunities that came his way.

Crane had only one problem, Conroy. Conroy had treated Crane's woman, Julia, badly. Worse, Conroy had switched his allegiance and disappeared bearing information about Crane's most recent business deal, information that could be presented in an unfavourable light if Conroy chose. Conroy was the weak stave in the structure of Crane's empire. He could bring it crashing. Conroy had disappeared and Crane was going to have to go and look for him.

Gower wrote in his hotel room that evening, against the noise of televisions through the walls and brawling in the street. He struggled on while his room was lit by the blue flare of police cars called to quell the fighters. In the early hours relative peace was restored and he was able to work on and on, letting Crane tell his story in his own words. The space between author and character was closing tighter, tighter.

Exhilarated with the night's work, Gower woke early next day and left the hotel carrying his bag containing the typescript, notes, and all the handwritten material he had subsequently produced. Among the items was the green and gold notebook he had bought at the stationer's in Sherborne when he was occupied with establishing the Richard Crane alias. Gower went to Euston Station and deposited a parcel containing almost everything with the left luggage office. He kept the notebook with him. Then he went to Holborn and wrote in the notebook until it was time to set off from the library for the meeting with Gerrard.

The agent did not turn up. Gower rang his office, adopted the incompetent Irish accent he had once inflicted on Linda's sister, and gave the name of a well-known Irish author. The secretary put him on to Gerrard who came on the line with an effusive welcome that petered out as soon as he learned his caller's true identity. Again, the secretary was dispatched on an errand.

Gower attacked, promising to storm into Gerrard's office

within the hour if there was no good excuse for his failure to appear with the £10,000.

Truculent, petulant and not at all apologetic, Gerrard shouted him down. 'Well there is, a thoroughly good explanation. I have every reason to suppose I would have been followed.'

'Followed?' Gower's rage subsided in stupefied repetition.

'Yes, followed. One has no inclination to overdramatize, but I assure you, John, I was followed home last night, I was followed to my office this morning and I have no doubt I would have been followed to the park.'

'Who by?' asked Gower, intent on information rather than grammar.

'Not the police, or not as far as I know. Fleet Street sleuths, which is possibly more threatening.'

'Ring me back,' said Gower and gave him the call box number before the money ran out.

Immediately, Gerrard obeyed. 'John? Well, as I was saying, I believe Fleet Street is on my tail.'

'Why?' Gower expected a yarn about a Gerrard plot to promote one or other of his authors. Gerrard was always teasing Fleet Street into taking an interest. Gower was unprepared for the answer.

'Because of you. Rain Morgan has an idea I secreted you away and that business with the *Fleur* was an elaborate publicity stunt. It was with the utmost difficulty I managed to laugh it off, but that isn't to say she'll drop the idea.'

'And now she's following you?'

'Not the young lady herself, a minion or two from the *Daily Post*, I should say. You see, John, jaunts to the park are entirely out.'

Gower said that he did not see, that he frankly could not accept what Gerrard had claimed, that unless she was blessed with second sight there was no means by which Rain Morgan could know the truth.

'Oh, come,' said Gerrard. 'One need not be quite so guileless. You and I are not the only guardians of the truth.'

'Linda?'

'The very same.'

Gower repeated what he had said the previous day about Linda's inevitable reluctance to give him away as her only proof was evidence that she was a blackmailer. Gerrard concurred, saying he believed that argument held good but that Rain Morgan might not have been told, she might merely have seen through Linda. Gower, who had never seen through Linda, heard him out but did not know what to think.

He nudged the conversation away from Gerrard's difficulties to his own. Money. They agreed Gerrard should pay the £10,000 into the Richard Crane account, and Gower repeated the number of it, yet again. He had no option but to trust Gerrard, although it would be several days before he could check whether Gerrard had complied this time or not. After the call he went back to the library and wrote in the notebook.

The change from big sheets of paper to the small pages of the notebook, coinciding with the passage where Crane started in pursuit of Conroy, led him into writing the section as a diary. He used the real dates of the days he was making the entries, an added touch of authenticity.

August 2, Crane follows a tip that Conroy has gone to ground in north London. August 3, Crane lays plans to follow him there. August 4 and 5, Crane makes several business telephone calls but is otherwise fully engaged in tracking down his man. So on.

Gower could not later fix the point in the day when he decided what he himself would do next. On the face of it, it came in the late afternoon but with hindsight he guessed the decision had been taken earlier, at a subconscious level. The obvious, but challengeable, reason for his move was the arrival of the police.

They were in the lobby as he ran up the hotel steps. Two of them were standing by the reception desk. One had his back to him, the other was sideways on and talking to the hotel owner. The register was lying on the counter top between them.

Outwardly calm, insides heaving, Gower wheeled away. *Supposing I'd walked into them?* What he supposed was that they would have known him, for one reason or another. One might have collared him as 'the thin man', the other as the missing John Gower. The thought brought a spluttering laugh to his lips, and a street-sweeper looked nervously at him.

Walking, carrying on walking. In his imagination the policemen were by now in his hotel room, riffling through his possessions. They would not learn much from a few clothes and toiletries. *Thank God the book's safe.* Bank cards and other things with Crane's name on them were in his pockets, the notebook and the rest in the grey canvas bag on his arm.

Don't ever go back, just vanish.

On the Underground he aimed for Euston, urgently wanting to confirm the safety of the typescript and notes in the luggage office. But during the journey he decided he was being foolish, that it was impossible for the police to know about the parcel, and he stayed on the train a stop further and got out at King's Cross. Only that morning he had written about Richard Crane scouring the seedy streets near the station hunting for Conroy.

Wandering those same streets, Gower sought a hotel. Bed-and-breakfast signs proliferated, but he was wary. The people coming and going from them were bitter-eyed, eager to miss nothing, they needed to grab every chance that came their way. Suddenly he wished he was in an area with tourists, because tourists are preoccupied about other matters than whether a newcomer is worth robbing. But he did not move to a different area, he carried on searching.

Settling for one of the slightly more salubrious places he took a room for the night. The bathroom was down the passage and he was asked to pay in advance. There was no chair in his room, just a bed with a chipped headboard, a matching single wardrobe that learned forward when he opened the door, and a shelf beneath a mottled mirror. He tried the window because the room smelled sourly of the previous occupant, but it was jammed with paint and unmovable.

Gower sat on the bed and wrote in his notebook. At least there were no police sirens, no street fighters, no bawling television sets. After a time a different quality of noise pierced the wall, the rhythmic strain of a bed. He pocketed his notebook, took up his bag containing everything except a newspaper and a paperback novel that he left on the bed. Out he went, to eat and to shop for replacements for the toiletries left behind at the other hotel.

A young woman was opening the door of the next room but one, a man following her in. Gower dropped his gaze, miming looking for something in his jacket pocket, until he heard the door close and he was able to get past without them having a clear sight of him. His shopping was quickly done at the railway station, he ate at a hamburger bar, and he returned to the hotel.

In the passage a man came out of the room the couple had entered. It was not the man Gower had noticed going in. Gower avoided his eye, reached his own room. The newspaper had gone, the book too. The door of the rickety wardrobe hung ajar.

He hesitated a minute, the beat of bedsprings through the wall as regular as his bloodbeat. Then he went into the street, crossing Euston Road and leaving King's Cross behind. He did not know where the streets led but dreamed that not too far afield there was certain to be an ordinary hotel. He no longer had faith in terrace houses with bed-and-breakfast signs. He trudged on.

The journey became entangled with the search for Conroy. Gower turned off Caledonian Road as the drizzle began. The run of mean houses was broken by smarter ones. The number of smart ones increased. Streets varied, each with its own variation of architectural detail and its independent flavour. Some houses flaunted ranks of doorbells, indicating bedsitters or flats. Others aspired to no more than one bell and displayed curtains and window boxes. There were no hotels.

Sheltering beneath a tree, he assessed the drizzle, but saw no benefit in going back. Surely he would find somewhere to stay, a room in a pub, anything? But he was not regretting bypassing the terrace houses down the hill at King's Cross. Conroy had gone to ground in the warren of Georgian and Victorian streets, he had to find him.

While he was taking a steep narrow street of slender prettified houses, the shower developed into a downpour. He darted forward, seeking a doorway but the houses stood back from the pavements. Ahead the road widened and there were trees on the kerbside. He raced for them. And standing there, catching his breath, he saw the alleyway between two houses and knew, for no discernible reason at all he positively *knew*, that there was shelter to be had down there.

Water swilled around his feet as he hastened down the alley to meet disappointment. A dead end. Only a locked garden gate on one side and on the other a similar . . . He pushed back a broken gate and entered a garden. A rough path crushed a way through wilderness and he took it, heading for a shed. This was small but sound, wooden and fairly new, more or less empty except for a lawnmower.

John Gower shook water from his hat, hung it on a nail, sat down on the curved metal casing of the mower, took out his green and gold notebook and wrote up Richard Crane's entry for 6 August.

Conroy is near. I feel it. I don't care what lengths I go to, I'll find him. I've checked out King's Cross today, came upon a disgusting hotel he'd stayed in (I've never cared for that sleazy side to his nature) but all the leads directed me towards the Angel. He'll be involved in a racket around here, I don't doubt it. I've found a place to camp tonight, a shed in a derelict garden. Julia would have a fit, she wouldn't understand, but I couldn't care less about comfort tonight. I'm going to sit it out. I feel he's almost in my sights.

His pen hovered momentarily, then he finished the entry.

'He's let me down. I won't take that. When I find him, I'm going to kill him.'

Whispering awoke Gower. He stirred, harsh contact with the floor of the shed reminding him where he had slept, if he could call it sleep, so disjointed and uncomfortable had it been.

He sat up on one elbow and blinked into full wakefulness. The door of the shed was open a couple of inches. Two faces squinted through the gap. With a lurch he was back in the underpass, cornered, attacked, a victim again.

'What do you want?' His voice was thick, the tone formidable, incongruously so for a man who had trespassed in somebody's garden, spent the night without permission in a shed.

The gap widened. The faces belonged to two tousled young men, teenagers. They were short, with spiky hair and earrings. One shoved a hand in the pocket of greasy jeans and leaned the other hand nonchalantly on the door jamb. 'What do we want? It's what *you* want, that's the thing, isn't it?'

The other nodded his bristling head. 'Yeah.'

'I mean,' said the nonchalant one, 'it's like our shed, isn't it?'

Gower spoke, coughed, tried again. 'I needed somewhere and it was late. I didn't know it was your house.'

An inexplicable smirk spread over the two faces. Then the hand dropped from the door jamb. 'Don't do it much, do you?'

'Eh?'

The other one enlarged. 'Sleeping out. You haven't got the look of it, see.'

Gower said: 'Oh.' He was thankful he had not. He clambered to his knees, to his feet. The lads seemed benign enough, the memories of the underpass faded.

'I'd better go.'

'No, it's all right with us, you stay here.'

'Yeah,' said the other one.

Tiredness made Gower weak, disoriented. He leaned against the side of the shed. 'Well, if you're sure.' It had stopped raining but was proposing to start again, an unwelcoming day.

'Sure,' they said together and retreated, then, after taking a couple of steps, called back: 'See you.'

After that they were past the apple tree and out of view. Gower sank to the floor of the shed, meaning to leave once he had gathered his wits. His watch had stopped and he wished he had asked the time, that and directions to the nearest main road. He wanted to locate a cash machine, although he would not have told them that.

It won't be there yet, you know that, he reasoned. *A cheque takes several days to get from one account to another, and he might not have started the transaction yesterday.*

But it was no help, he wanted to be standing outside a bank, punching out his questions and reading the balance in the Crane account, reading that it was the richer by ten thousand pounds.

His only clue to the time was the range of drawn curtains in the backs of houses that reared up beyond the garden. *Not yet, you can't go anywhere yet.* He lay down again, his head once more on his canvas bag, and fell asleep.

The second awakening was rougher. A voice shouted close by: 'Hey, we want to show you something.'

Nervously he started up. The pair of youths were back.

'Oh sorry, didn't know you were asleep.' The one with the nonchalance and the greasy jeans was still doing most of the talking.

Gower asked: 'What?' He got up, picked up his bag. Definitely it was time for him to be going.

'Our house.' The youths exchanged grins. 'Come on.'

Gower was suddenly overwhelmed with a desire for a cup of coffee, breakfast, anything at all. 'Thanks.' He went with them through the garden.

Wet plants, overgrown and gone to seed and largely unidentifiable, swished around their legs as they went beneath the apple tree and neared the building. Gower looked up at the back of the house. No drawn curtains. No window cleaner, either, in a long while.

'Oh, I'm Joe,' said the one with the jeans and the chat. 'And this is Rod. I call him Hot Rod 'cos he's not so smart.'

'Shut up,' said Rod without rancour, and aimed a careless kick in Joe's direction.

As it appeared to be first names only, Gower said he was Richard.

They were close to the back door but Joe jinked away to the left of it and leapt with ease on to the windowsill of a downstairs room and threw up the sash. Rod and Gower went after him.

They were in a dirty, disused, unmodernized kitchen. Gower took in the lack of coffee, food, hygiene, anything promising. Joe said: 'Come on.'

Down a passage, floorboards whipping beneath their feet, he swung the door of an empty front room with peeling paper, a brass light fitting and a magnificent marble fireplace. Then he ran lightly upstairs where a room at the back was revealed as another kitchen. There was a kettle, a primus stove, two beakers, a jar of instant coffee and a packet of unopened biscuits.

'Breakfast,' said Joe grandly, and waved Rod forward to make it, which he did by boiling the kettle, shaking coffee into the beakers and stirring the drink with a knife from his belt.

Gower was grateful he had not noticed the knife earlier, he would have been uneasy. He squeezed out words of appreciation, managed a smile or two, accepted a beaker of scalding coffee and a custard cream. Rod was saying the obvious: that the house had been divided into two flats and this was the kitchen of the upper flat.

Joe said: 'It's all right, Richard, isn't it?'

Gower dredged up a compliment for the coffee, although in truth it tasted vile without his usual complement of milk and sugar.

'No,' said Joe. 'I mean the house. It's good, isn't it?'

Gower nodded appreciatively. He wondered whether he had added burglary to trespass. He did not like to ask outright who owned it. Instead he asked how long Rod and Joe had been there.

Joe said: 'Couple of months.'

Rod, the one who was doing without coffee because there were only two beakers, crunched into a biscuit and replied with a spray of crumbs that he thought it was a bit longer than that.

'Anyway,' said Joe. 'We were around the area, looking for this and that, and we found it. Funny nobody had been in before, but there it was, overlooked like.'

Rod sprayed more crumbs in agreement. Joe said: 'Come on, let's show you the rest.'

The rest was a big first-floor room across the front of the house. Two full-length windows took up most of the wall and looked on to grand houses on the other side of the street, although trees broke up the view. Like the others, the room was virtually bare. In this one was a stool, a floor cushion and a discoloured carpet. A couple of sleeping bags were chucked in a corner. The floor above was an attic room, with nothing in it. On landings were two old-fashioned bathrooms.

The skies opened as they were going downstairs from the attic. Gower had been on the point of saying he had to leave, but the weather forced him to hold back. He sat on the floor of the big room with Rod and Joe, and fielded questions about himself but not the questions he feared.

For instance, he was not made to justify his arrival in the garden shed, nor his need for a free roof over his head, nor asked to give details of where he had come from, or how he had come to such a low ebb. All those things, they took for granted. Nor, of course, was he asked what his job was or whether he had one. They did ask what benefits office he used and whether he had found the payments had run out and left him stranded.

Rod said to Joe: 'But you could go back to your mum, they told you that.'

Joe scoffed. 'Yes, but they never asked her. She wouldn't have me back and I don't want to go.'

'Yeah,' said Rod. 'And then there's the train fare to find if you did want to go.'

Little by little, in ways of which they were unaware, they were opening up for John Gower a seam of underlife of which he knew nothing apart from the occasional newspaper story. He was fascinated by them. Long after the shower had stopped and the sun was winking through the grimy window-panes, he sat there listening, squirrelling away information about the subculture of which they were part, learning what it was to travel to London to seek work and instead to live on your wits. He felt privileged that they trusted him sufficiently to share this with him.

His trust of them was not unqualified. Rod's knife did not threaten him, Joe's tough talk was not aimed at intimidating him, but he kept his bag with him at all times, slung over his shoulder, his few possessions safe.

'The thing is,' said Joe, when they had talked for an hour or more, 'nobody knows about this place. We could get some furniture in, do it up a bit, but we've got to keep quiet about it.'

'There's owners somewhere,' put in Rod. 'There's always owners.'

'Yeah,' said Joe, deflated.

Gower guessed that the house, on the market in its present state, would fetch hundreds of thousands of pounds. It was basically sound, it was in a street of fine properties. And it was a mystery how any owner could abandon it to the likes of Rod and Joe.

He was glad of that negligence, though, because Joe and Rod were apparently willing to let him stay under their roof for a few nights and he wanted to do that. He wanted to experience what would normally be beyond his reach. By a fluke he had crossed the gulf between one society and another, and he wanted a thorough critical look with his writer's eye before he crossed back again.

Joe got to his feet and stretched. 'Got to meet somebody,' he said.

'Oh, yeah,' said Rod, remembering and getting up too.

Joe said: 'You going to be around tonight, Richard?'

Gower said yes.

The three of them walked up the street together, then Gower accepted their directions to the main road and they parted on a corner. Mid-morning, the sun had won and there was a corresponding lightness in the steps of passers-by. Gower located a bank and joined a queue at the machine in the wall. The woman in front of him edged away. He accepted that he looked a mess and did not blame her. A window reflection confirmed it. His hat was battered, his jacket misshapen and blotched with dust, the trousers were torn around the knees and the shoes were scuffed. Oh, and his face was dirty. In the accommodating presence of Joe and Rod all this had been *de rigueur*, outside the bank at Islington Green it scared respectable middle-class women. He wanted to laugh.

After withdrawing a small amount, and confirming that the cheque for £10,000 had not arrived, he went to a café a few yards away, a French-styled Dôme with walls made of doors that opened on to the sunny pavement. In the tiny basin in the men's lavatory he washed his face and hands, then sat in shirtsleeves in a shady corner of the bar, his dirty jacket folded beside him and the hat in his bag. Without incident he ate croissants, drank coffee and read the selection of newspapers provided.

The main news, in the more sedate newspapers, was tension in the Middle East, a squabble over EEC regulations, and more about the arrest of several men in a bungled raid that should have netted the killer of a London security guard. Gower searched the Rain Morgan column but there was nothing about David Gerrard or about himself.

When the café became busy towards lunchtime, and he could no longer hog a table, he found a street market, Chapel Market, and bought food to carry back to the house. Beneath the apple tree he ate some of it, keeping the rest for later. Then he took out the notebook and set down what Richard Crane had been doing. He was finishing this when Joe and Rod entered the garden. He confessed he was keeping a diary.

Rod said: 'My sister used to keep one of those. Until my mum read it.' And that was all anyone said on the topic of diaries.

They climbed through the window into the house. Rod produced another packet of custard creams from his pocket.

'Bloody custard creams!' said Joe, half disappointed, half laughing.

'Yeah, well, they're at the front, aren't they?' Rod came close to a pout. 'You needn't eat them if you don't want them.' Rod put them on the cupboard beside the primus and the kettle. From another pocket he took a pot of powdered milk substitute and a packet of kippers.

'Great,' said Joe.

Gower opened his bag and drew out a slab of Cheddar cheese, some bread rolls and apples. Rod and Joe looked at the food, inscrutable. Clearly, his was of a different order from Rod's shopping.

'Help yourself,' he said. 'I'll fill the kettle.'

They laughed then, seeing him twist the tap above the sink and realize that the water no longer ran from it.

Joe said: 'It's behind the shed. The supply to the house is disconnected.'

'All right.' Gower set off with the kettle. He regretted being so obliging. It meant leaving his bag behind because it would have been insultingly obvious to have taken it with him. When he returned he was convinced they had examined it.

He made an effort not to let his eyes fall on it, concentrating instead on the primus and the performance of coffee-making. The other two were talking in a desultory way. It seemed they had been to meet someone but he had not given them what they hoped for.

Joe was resigned. 'Yeah, well, it's the money, isn't it?'

He probably sighed but the sound of the kettle reaching boiling point covered it. Rod pushed the dirty beakers forward to be filled. Gower balked, stood them in the sink, splashed hot water over them as a gesture towards hygiene, tipped them out, then tilted coffee in from the screw-top jar.

'Sorry,' said Rod. 'We should get another mug.'

Gower said he would have his coffee once they had finished. No one argued. They had given up playing hosts with a visitor, they were too concerned with their disappointment. Their demeanour was altogether less perky than when they had childishly shown off their house to him that morning. He passed the coffee mugs over, Rod contributing to the extent of stirring in the powder with the blade of his knife that he then wiped dry, if not clean, against his trouser leg.

I could give them the money for another mug, thought Gower. *I could give them the money for whatever it is they wanted this morning and couldn't afford. I could put my hand in my pocket and I could change the nature of their lives for a few hours. But I won't do it. It would alter our relationship, they would no longer have the advantage. I won't do it.*

They carried the beakers into the big room and the three of them sat on the floor, as they had done before, and talked. Then Joe said he had to go out, to see someone else. Rod and Gower stayed at the house.

Rod confided that he wanted to take some stuff to sell but that Joe would not countenance it.

'Sell what?' Gower could see nothing of any value.

'I'll show you,' said Rod.

In the downstairs front room he slapped a hand on the marble fireplace. 'You could get hundreds for that.'

Gower fought back a gasp of disapproval. 'Ye-es,' he said. 'I suppose you could.'

'And this,' said Rod, pointing at the brass light fitting. 'I reckon that's worth a bit.' He waited for and got Gower's reluctant assent. 'Trouble is,' said Rod, 'Joe doesn't like to do it. And the fireplace especially, it takes two, a job like that.'

Gower realized Rod was weighing him up. Hot Rod, not-so-smart-Rod knew exactly how to get the wherewithal and was waiting to see whether he had found an accomplice. Gower chose not to understand. He strolled to the window, as if drawn there by the sound of an expensive car rolling out of a garage at a house opposite.

Rod said: 'There's plenty of places to sell it. All round here there's shops selling fireplaces like this, some specialize like. I've seen them. People buy them to put them in houses where they were ripped out.'

'Houses like this,' said Gower.

Rod missed the irony and beamed. 'Yeah, that's right. All these houses round here and not enough fireplaces! Stands to reason, a good one fetches hundreds.'

He gave Gower a look which plainly said: 'What about it then? Shall we?'

Gower studied the curving white marble, the unscathed stone that had stood there for around a hundred and seventy years. He shook his head, smiling. 'I think it looks pretty good where it belongs.'

Rod did not argue, but the light went out inside him.

They went into the garden. The rest of the afternoon passed in an aimless way that was habit to Rod. Joe returned with a thin plastic beaker that bellied the first time they poured boiling water into it. But at least Gower had a mug of his own now.

For two nights he slept in the ground-floor front room, not a scrap more comfortable than if he had been in the shed and wishing there were better arrangements than a cold tap down the garden and bowls of water to pour down the lavatories. He got into a routine. Each day he walked to the cash machine at the Green and asked it whether David Gerrard's cheque had percolated through the system. Each day it said not. Then he went into the Dôme and ate breakfast and drank real coffee and squandered the morning. He shopped for food in the street market, went back to the house and at various points throughout the day he jotted entries in Richard Crane's diary.

Gower did not always bother to fictionalize, knowing that he could later sift out the true events he did not want and substitute others more in keeping with the story line. So he wrote about Rod's designs on the fireplace and Joe's hold over Rod, although Rod appeared to be more efficient as a getter of food. And he did not set down the reason Crane chose to camp out with these two instead of chasing after Conroy. Crane still thought obsessively about the man, but was confusingly biding his time. Gower left all that to be cleared up later.

On the third day he grew anxious about the absent cheque and telephoned David Gerrard, but Gerrard was away. At the house again, he came upon Rod and Joe having a row about the fireplace. Rod had his back to it and was waving a metal bar, not attacking his friend as Gower instantly thought but illustrating what a fine tool it was for wrenching out fireplaces.

Joe was shouting that Rod was such a fool he would break the thing up and then it would be of no value to anybody, and besides, why would Rod not get it into his thick skull that they could not hawk a fireplace around the dealers because they had no vehicle?

Gower calmed them down, with a distribution of chocolate bars from a market stall. 'That's right,' he said firmly. 'You can't shift it even if you get if off the wall.'

Rod cursed, then threw down his metal bar and stamped out into the garden.

'He's all right,' said Joe fondly. 'But he doesn't think.'

Gower said, rather primly, that it would be better all round if the fireplace were intact when the owner, whoever that might be, reclaimed the house.

Joe stuffed chocolate into his mouth and said nothing.

Before conversation resumed, there was a shout from the garden. Joe dashed to a window, Gower close behind. They could not see Rod, but the shout came again.

All at once, Rod appeared from behind the apple tree, the long grass and overgrown shrubs quivering behind him. He did not see Gower and Joe, he was talking to someone else.

Joe's tension slackened. 'Oh, it's nothing,' he said. 'I thought somebody had come, but it's all right.'

Gower saw a large black dog with a fanned tail lolloping

around Rod, the youth bowing to pet it. They ran nearer, Rod muddling the dog because between pats he was ordering it to go away but in a tone of voice the dog interpreted as encouragement.

Rod noticed the others. 'It's Fred,' he called over.

'Yeah,' said Joe wearily. 'And where Fred goes, his owner follows. You'd better come indoors.'

Rod joined them in the house and with some difficulty they shut out the overaffectionate dog. He whined by the back door only turning his head to the broken gate when a woman called: 'Fred? Fred? Where are you?'

Gower, Rod and Joe went upstairs, to be out of sight in case the woman tracked Fred as far as the back of the house. Joe pointed up the street. 'She lives over there.'

'Yeah,' said Rod, whose good humour was recovered. 'But Fred prefers it over here. What you might call a regular visitor.'

'The only one,' said Joe, stretched out on the carpet, twiddling an earring.

They laughed at that, and laughed again when Gower corrected them, saying: 'Except for me.'

That night when they were asleep there was a dramatic change. The crash of the front door being forced woke them. Gower, who was nearest, grabbed his bag and his jacket and poised, uncertain what was happening, which way to run. Then the door was closed, there were voices in the hall, the door to his room was pushed back and a torch whisked around it.

'Shame,' said a voice without pity. 'You're about to be evicted.'

Another man in the hall chuckled at this. He joined his companion behind the torch. 'How many of you are there?'

Gower wanted them to lower the beam. He stammered that there were two people upstairs.

The man with the torch said: 'I reckon we can handle three.' And his companion laughed again.

They left Gower where he was and he heard the sound of a

screw driver on the door, the clattering of a chunk of metal being dropped to the floor, and some rattling sounds. Gower guessed what was happening in the hall. He wondered what Rod and Joe were going to do about it, and wished he could be sure it was nothing violent.

Joe's voice cut the air, challenging from the staircase. There was an altercation, but no scuffling. Gower grew less fearful, especially when he heard Joe fiercely ordering Rod to put that thing down. He knew for sure that Rod was brandishing his iron bar again.

'All right,' said a voice in the passage. 'I'll tell you what we're going to do. There are three of you, right?'

Three voices said yes.

The man said: 'Well, you can stay here and have company or you can get out. What you can't do is have a place this size to yourselves. OK?'

The yesses were less certain.

The man went on: 'We've changed the lock on the front door, now we're going to do the back one. It'll be secure but only people with a right to be in here will be let in. All right?'

Silence.

Then the other man went through the passage with the springy floorboards and set to work on the back door. The voice started up again: 'They'll be round in the morning.'

'Who?' demanded Joe.

'They'll get the place fixed up, it'll be better.'

Gower said: 'You've been in here before.' The knowledge was a blow. Men had been in and the three of them had remained ignorant.

'Yes, this morning when it was empty. We didn't touch anything of yours.'

Nobody objected. The man said: 'They'll bring their stuff round and they'll make it better. Like I said, you can stay or if you don't like it you can get out. It's up to you.'

Minutes went by. The other man came back. The torch snapped off. The front door opened and closed. There was the sound of a car. The two men had gone but the hierarchy had changed. The house was no longer in the control of the spiky-haired youths, Rod and Joe, who had discovered it.

'Christ!' said Joe.

Rod said 'Yeah!'

Gower said: 'Who were they?'

'I don't like it,' said Joe. 'I mean, it's our place, after all. Sort of.'

Rod said: 'You should have told him, Joe.'

But Joe snorted and Gower muttered that it would not have made any difference. They sat around worrying about it until it was getting light outside. Joe and Rod were going to have to stay, no question of it, they had no option. The chance of finding another empty house they could move into was negligible. But Gower meant to go. He said so.

'Where to?' asked Joe, showing a keener interest in Gower's affairs than at any time to date.

Gower admitted he did not know.

Joe said: 'Well, then, better stay. Move on later if you have to, but see how it works out.'

Rod said what he usually said.

The squatters arrived before it was properly daylight. They had a dilapidated Ford estate car crammed full and with bulky items strapped to the roof rack.

Gower, Joe and Rod huddled at the front of the stairs and watched them unload. There were four of them, all men. Introductions were brief and polite without risking friendliness. An armchair was lifted off the roof rack and carried up to the big room. A small refrigerator appeared. There was bedding and more furniture, and boxes that clinked with concealed crockery and pots. There were rugs and an electric kettle. It looked like the result of furnishing a house from a jumble sale. But there were surprises. Gower stared in disbelief as a standard lamp was taken up.

Rod giggled nervously after the lamp. 'Wait until they find there's no electricity.'

Joe gave him a pitying look. Within hours the electricity was connected and the fridge buzzing in the upstairs kitchen.

Water was no problem, either. One of the last things to be taken from the car was a waterboard key that was pushed down a hole beneath an iron cover in the front path and used to turn the water on.

Urban gypsies, thought Gower. *They're always on the move. They've done this so often they don't have to discuss where to put things or who should do what.* Curiosity vied with furtive admiration.

But he felt sad about Joe and Rod. Younger, gauche, unskilled, they were abruptly outranked, made into outsiders in what for months had been their home. He watched Joe's chirpiness become guarded, his attempts to ingratiate himself rebuffed, his role of leader switched to that of mere observer. Rod did not help. By goading Joe to make pointless gestures of independence and protest, he irritated him. Barked at by Joe, Rod became sullen. Gower prayed somebody would confiscate Rod's iron bar. All his worries centred on that, that there could yet be violence.

For himself, he was interested to see how things progressed and to negotiate for an adequate space to write without disturbance. George, a courteous man with glittering eyes, told him: 'We live as a commune. We don't have personal space.'

Nonplussed, Gower planned then to use the garden shed, a space too small for sharing, except with a garden gnome.

'Excuse me,' said George, and went into the downstairs kitchen with a hammer and nails. Gower followed him, wondering whether getting information out of a commune meant perpetual committee meetings, or whether individual members were empowered to speak.

'I've got to go out,' Gower said. 'How do I get back in?'

George slammed two nails into the window frame before saying: 'Bang the front door, somebody will look out of the upstairs window and go down and let you in.' The conversation ended with more nails thudding into the frame.

At Islington Green the cash machine still said no, and Gower went through his daily routine at the Dôme and market. On the way back to the house suspicion mounted about what a commune might do with his food. He turned into public gardens and ate some, burying the rest in the bottom of his bag.

They let him in. Joe and Rod were out and no one knew where. Gower did not like to ask directly whether they had left for good, and was kept in suspense. He saw that more furniture and blankets had appeared. More faces, too, including the two who had changed the locks the night before. Assuming the four who had come with the estate car were still resident, that made seven. Plus himself and perhaps Rod and Joe.

The house felt overcrowded. There would be no quiet corners, except the shed, to think and write and sleep. However, he intended to stay until his money announced itself in the Crane account. Resigned to a miserable existence for another day or two, he showed willing by helping where help was needed.

Joe and Rod arrived during the evening. Gower wanted to hear whether they had been scouting for another bolthole, but private conversation was impossible. Too many people around, and it got worse. A ringing at the doorbell brought cheers as men on the first floor recognized a man called Murray who was carrying a television set. What they did not cry out was that Murray had brought his dog, a threadbare Alsatian.

Instinctively, Gower drew the line at Murray. Murray was slightly drunk, he was not polite, his dog was boisterous and evil-tempered, and they both smelled rank. Gower put what distance he could between himself and them.

And his instinct was correct. Murray it was whom he discovered that night stooped over the grey canvas bag, feeling into it, clamping a black-nailed hand around some toiletries. Murray was unabashed, looking up at him with a twisted smile. 'Where'd you nick this stuff?'

'Put that back.'

Murray straightened. 'Only asking.' But Murray did not

care. He was not apologetic. His dog growled warnings at Gower throughout the exchange.

Gower forced himself to thrust past the beast and pick up the bag. He carried it away to another room where he went through the contents. Everything seemed to be there.

The incident persuaded him that come what may he would leave the house at first light. He could get just a few more pounds from the Crane account before it ran dry but he would not wait for that to happen, he would take himself to David Gerrard's flat and demand cash.

That night was worse than any other he had spent. He was in the ground-floor room with the fireplace again, but he had company and one of the men snored. There had been a lot of beer drunk and people were making trips to the bathrooms. The plumbing was noisy. In addition, there was coming and going at the front door and footsteps running on the stairs. He had no difficulty in waking up early, he had been awake most of the night.

Stealthily, he got up and reached the door of the room, opened it as far as he could without bumping it against a sleeper, and squeezed through to the hall. When he stepped into the street fresh air hit him like a douche of cold water. George had nailed boards over the downstairs windows to prevent anyone breaking in but he had banished air as well as light.

Gower pulled the door shut behind him, the angry snap of the new lock stirring Murray's dog into watchful growls. He felt free, relieved of the pressure of people. Slowly he walked along his regular route, stopping off at gardens to sit on a bench and make up the diary.

Then on, into the main road, a long way down it, meandering because there was time to kill and nothing else to do. The café would not open for a long while. He jingled coins in his pocket, dawdling, window shopping. These shops were not particularly good for window shoppers. There were too many restaurants and a disproportionate number of estate agents for variety.

Schoolchildren were on their paper rounds. A tramp slept in a doorway and the pavement outside a pub was streaked with vomit. Gower reached a newsagent's, the owner crouching low, marking up papers. He bought one, asking for it by name, not picking and choosing among the alluring headlines.

Litter lay thick near the bank, the wind electing to swirl the detritus of take-away food shops away from the offenders' premises. He crushed a carton underfoot as he homed in on the cash machine.

Please insert your card.

Please enter your account number.

Please wait, your card is being processed.

What service would you like?

Please enter the amount.

He held his breath as the computer counted Richard Crane's wealth. Then he released it with an inhibited moan. No £10,000. Next to nothing, in fact. He drew the next to nothing.

Resigned he thought: *So that's it, I'll present myself at David Gerrard's office this morning. Either he thinks of something fast, or the deception's over. If he's not there, or he won't help, I'll go straight to one of the newspapers.*

He put the cash away, along with the Richard Crane cash card that he might never use again. And then he thought: *A hair cut first, to get rid of the blond. Any hairdresser will do, as long as he'll cut it short enough.* And then he amended that too. *No, I don't want a hairdresser going to the press with a story about my disguise. I'll get scissors and a mirror in Woolworths in Chapel Market and I'll cut it myself.*

Over the road was a triangular garden, a wedge bounded by roads. He sat there and opened his newspaper. And he looked into his own face. On page three a journalist asked in tall letters 'Is John Gower Alive?' and in a four-column story below drummed up reasons to doubt his death. The photograph was the one everybody used, the one on the book covers.

In itself, the story had nothing new except for some updated quotes from his wife and his agent. But it was the juxtaposition that was frightening. On the same page was a story labelled 'Danny Search'. This was about the police hunt for the killer of the boy in the New Forest. Alongside the copy was the photofit picture created from villagers' sightings of 'the thin man' at Butlers.

Even Gower, who was regularly mystified by the press, understood that somebody in the newspaper office had chosen to run those two stories close together to draw attention to the similarity of the images. The positioning also drew attention to the fact that the man who featured as Gower's agent in the first story was also the man who appeared in the second as a legitimate visitor to Butlers, but a visitor who denied, against the local evidence, that another man had been there.

And as if all this was not plain enough, the second story underlined the point by quoting a villager as saying Butlers' owner had bought the house because it was a good place for a writer to get away from it all and work undisturbed. Parsons had meant himself but the newspaper's readers could not fail to understand that the *Daily Post* meant John Gower too.

17

'He said it was going to be like *Cathy Come Home*, only bigger,' the woman said.

She was sitting on the side of a single bed, her two-year-old daughter sucking the fringe of a grubby counterpane. Rain Morgan stood at the end of the bed, there was no room for a visitor to sit down. Anyway, the woman was not allowed visitors. Rain had been smuggled in.

Rain defended Alf Wilson, with an assurance that he had been working on the play when he died, but the woman's words were not accusation. She was impassive, young with the voice of a woman that life had kicked around, the eyes that looked into Rain's were dulled.

She said: 'He told me he'd written a play once and it had been really successful and it had changed the law.'

'That was *Dead and Alive*,' Rain said confirming, still justifying.

The woman leaned over the child and drew the cloth from its mouth. 'Sharon, that's dirty.'

The child did not protest, she had been denied too often. The mother said: 'He got my name through a friend of mine, only she wouldn't talk herself. She said to him: "You want to ask Dawn, she'll tell you, she's been in ever so many places – hostels, bed-and-breakfast hotels, short-life housing, everything that's going." That's why he came.'

Rain pictured Wilson standing where she was standing, at the foot of a bed in an inadequate hotel room that was home for Dawn and Sharon. On the floor beneath the bed, a bag spewed out clothes. The cot had to be moved to reach the wardrobe, and in any case there was no room in the wardrobe for clothes. Everything else Dawn owned was packed in there, including the food she cooked clandestinely for her daughter. The hotel did not allow cooking in the rooms.

Statistics rattled around in Rain's memory. They had not substantially changed since Alf Wilson had talked to Dawn. One hundred thousand homeless families in Britain, 23,000 families in temporary accommodation, at least 30,000 people in bed-and-breakfast hotels. The statistics of misery.

She listened with sympathy to Dawn's story: her husband's redundancy, his depression, domestic violence, debt, desertion, a mortgage foreclosed, homelessness, over-optimistic schemes to stay with overcrowded friends, help from the local council who could offer a few weeks in a flat with cockroaches before it was demolished for an office block to go up, then a hostel, and then the cruelty of existence in one of the hotels given over to providing bed and breakfast for the homeless.

Dawn said: 'I told Alf the hotel charges the council seventy pounds a night for me and Sharon to have this room, and I showed him what we get for it. He said somebody was making a pile, because there are two hundred rooms here and this is one of the smallest ones. He was going to see the owners about it.'

And so Rain also went to see the owners, following in Alf Wilson's wake, being shocked where he had been shocked, outraged where he had been outraged. She found the company's office straight away and untangled threads of information that showed it owned three similar big hotels. Pinning down the owner was trickier. A secretary tried to keep her out and then a paunchy man with a glib manner met her questions with minimum response, intent on dissuading her with his opinion that a private company's affairs were private and the company was acting within the law.

Rain stuck to her guns. Public money was involved and it was being spent badly, that gave the public the right to know.

But it was futile, she was left stranded in his office when he left the premises pleading a meeting. Later, she learned he was not the owner, only a manager.

Companies House failed to provide her with helpful names.

Businesses were owned by other businesses, the path to the true owner dauntingly obscure. The truth could be reached, but it would take more time than she had to spare. She was meeting Paul Wickham that evening.

They were to see a film, at the Renoir cinema in Bloomsbury, meeting in the foyer, Rain on tenterhooks in case he could not come after all.

'If I can't make it, I'll get a message to the box office for you,' he had promised.

And all the other waiting individuals were paired and disappeared downstairs during the clock's countdown for the film to begin, and she was alone. Accepting the disappointment, she decided to go in alone when there he was, running up the steps and through the doors.

Even then she did not know whether he would stay until the end or be sought out by the manager because of a telephone call from his office. It was an unsettling way to spend an evening.

There were no interruptions of that kind, but the outing was not an unqualified success. The audience kept up an irritating commentary of reaction. *Babette's Feast* contrasted the self-inflicted pain of the lean puritan existence of Jutland villagers with the exuberance of a French refugee who, when a fortune comes her way, splurges the money on a Parisian dinner for them. Shudders at the Danish diet of mulched bread and ale gave way to ooohs of appreciation as the boats came in from France with the produce for the feast, and the audience risked ecstasy as Babette created the dishes that had made her name at a classy Paris restaurant. That the dishes were actually the creation of Roger Verges, whose restaurant at Mougins few if any of them would ever visit in real life, enhanced their pleasure.

Directly in front of Rain, a woman excitedly named the dishes for her companion, together with their principal ingredients. And while the audience drooled, the villagers affected not to notice that they were eating anything superior to their habitual mulch and thus protected themselves from the sins of gluttony and having a good time.

The film was amusing and not a little sad. Rain had approached it in the wrong mood, her feelings about Dawn and Sharon too raw for the sumptuousness on screen to be other than grossly inappropriate. Afterwards, in the restaurant, she did not say that, she argued that the audience had been facile in their response, that they had been eagerly seduced into mocking the frugal and applauding excess.

She said: 'The community had held itself together through its chosen way of life. Babette was there because she had escaped from a revolution, and I don't think . . .'

Paul interrupted her seriousness saying, lightly: 'Me, I was admiring the camera work. There wasn't an ugly frame in the entire film.'

She granted him that. Then: 'I'm sorry, but it's my day for realities, not fantasy. The film was so superbly beautiful that Babette's dress was made by Karl Lagerfeld, did you see that among the credits?'

He laughed, saying she should eat up, saying all his working days were concerned with realities, that he deserved some beauty and fantasy in his time off.

'Besides,' he said, 'you're wrong. The story was about love. *That's* what the villagers excised from their lives, and it's what Babette celebrated.'

He watched her put another forkful to her mouth. He said: 'Rejecting love is always a mistake. Haven't you noticed?'

She ducked it, giving him a look that said: 'Not *here*!' And earning in return his most boyish smile.

Over coffee she asked: 'Can you talk about your day?'

'Not much.'

There was always that barrier. Her natural curiosity, heightened by the journalist's propensity for questioning, was repeatedly frustrated. Too often he would only tell her things after they had already appeared in the press. She understood the reason perfectly. If she was in no position to leak information by mistake, he need never suspect her. His silence prevented a tension that might otherwise have existed between them.

But the silence meant that he eluded her. Sometimes she had to wait until he was on television with a microphone in his face before she knew the reason for a cancelled evening, or his preoccupied moments when, with anyone else, she would have asked: 'What's on your mind?' and would probably have received a truthful answer.

She stirred her coffee, conscious that they were making a mess of this, their first time together for months, unable to reach a topic about which they were both prepared to speak fully without arguing. While her own work was not secret, except from rival journalists, she did not want to bring it up. Dawn and the bed-and-breakfast hotels would make a dreary topic, and she was afraid she would grow impassioned about it. Deeper than that, she had no wish to explain that she was harbouring doubts that Alf Wilson had killed himself and that she was, in a tentative manner, groping towards another explanation for his death.

Paul misinterpreted her quietness. He said, placating: 'I'm not denying you much. It's the warehouse shooting.'

'But the police raided a house and people were arrested. It said so on the news.'

They both laughed at the absurdity of Rain citing news reports as an authority on his case. Then he said: 'Well, yes, we took people in. Four of them. Since then we've had to let them go. Not enough evidence to hold them. No one was charged.'

She struggled not to pester him with questions, fell back on quoting the press again. 'Our crime reporter said he understood the Goad gang were thought to be involved.'

Wickham was ironic. 'Wouldn't it be easy if they had a monopoly of armed robberies? Then we'd be able to go to them straight away instead of tiring ourselves out with all that surveillance and detection.'

'You'd hate it,' she said happily. 'You'd miss the thrill of the chase. And you wouldn't know what to do with all that spare time.'

'I'd have a hobby,' he said. 'I'd take pretty blondes to dinner. Or I'd conduct serious research into why Fleet Street glamorizes certain criminals. First call would be the *Daily Post* to ask the editor why it describes the warehouse robbery as "daring". Or why it refers to Goad as the "mastermind behind a series of brilliantly planned raids that netted millions of pounds".'

Rain grunted, unable to erect a defence of editor or crime reporter.

Wickham said: 'And I'd take up writing letters to the newspapers, saying it isn't daring to arm yourself to the teeth and shoot a security guard because he happens not to have the key your incompetent planning suggested he might carry.'

Rain held up her hands in surrender. 'It wasn't me, Chief Superintendent. I wasn't even there. I've got one of those cast-iron alibis – I was on the gossip column at the time.'

He signalled the waiter and paid the bill.

'What next, Paul?' she asked.

'A taxi to Chelsea?'

'Yes, but I mean in the case? Or have we reached the bit you can't talk about?'

'Oh, it's easy not to talk,' he said. 'Especially as I haven't a clue what comes next.'

She did not take that literally but let the subject fall, after a final remark that Fleet Street did rather enjoy its characters and Goad had become one of them.

They went to her flat. He put some Mozart flute concertos on her tape player while she switched on her coffee filter machine. Vanessa Kyle's painting still hung on her sitting-room wall. Rain had toyed with moving it, but there was nowhere to move it to and taking it down would have been tactlessly pointed.

When he first visited the flat after their acquaintance was renewed, during his investigation into a murder at the *Daily Post*, the painting had come as a painful surprise. The wounds of his failed marriage to Vanessa had been tender. Rain had seen the look of hurt, the tightening of his jaw, the determined turning away.

Later, they had been able to discuss the painting, as they might the merits and appeal of any other picture. In truth, it held a unique significance for both of them. Rain had first met Paul Wickham at the private viewing where she had bought it. He had bought a similar one. For the next year Rain had seen him socially, on and off. And at the end of the year, he had married Vanessa, cutting himself out of Rain's life until he walked into her office one day to investigate murder.

As Rain carried in the coffee he said: 'I thought you might have changed the room when you had the decorators in.'

'No imagination. I couldn't think what else to do with it.' She was being unfair to herself, she had considered half a dozen possibilities only to remember how satisfactory the cool whiteness of the original was and, save for moving a door a few feet along a wall, she had recreated the room exactly as it looked before the damp came through and the plaster came off.

Wickham had taken up the John Gower novel from her table. He started to speak about the story and then noticed the jottings.

Rain explained. 'Alf Wilson wanted to adapt the book for television. Those are his notes.'

He flippantly asked whether she was plotting to steal Wilson's ideas and write the dramatization herself. 'Or you could pass the results off as Wilson's work which, if David Gerrard as quoted in your column is to be believed, would be worth a great deal more money.'

Rain feigned interest in doing this. 'But if it was thought to be by Wilson, how would I make sure of getting the money myself?'

'Easily. You'd have to be in cahoots with his next of kin, that cousin from Yorkshire. I don't see why she shouldn't help out, for a cut of the profits.'

'I wonder what would be a reasonable cut?'

'Offer her fifty per cent. That should do.'

'Seems a lot.'

'Not from her point of view, as the property would ostensibly belong to her.'

Rain raised an objection to involving Pat Jarvis. 'It won't do, Paul. She's too honest to get involved in a trick of that nature.'

Wickham said that if that were the case Rain would have to use David Gerrard. 'Now there's a man who appears not to let scruples stand in his way when it comes to making money. Or handing it out.'

Her puzzlement showed he had left her behind. He said: 'You're not the only gossip columnist in town. Didn't you read what John Wainfleet had to say today? About Gerrard letting Linda Gower tap into her husband's account in a fairly unrestrained fashion while Gower is still officially missing and not yet presumed dead?'

'Holly checked that paper, she didn't report anything of interest.'

'Maybe Wainfleet made it up, but it was padded with details about a deposit on a flat, the cost of renovations, hire of fashionable interior designers, expensive clothes-shopping trips for her television job, etcetera.'

'Weren't Gerrard and Linda quoted?'

'They told Wainfleet to mind his own business.' Wickham passed her the Gower novel and she put it on a shelf.

She thought: *Silly to have left that lying around, as I don't want to be drawn into telling him my theories about Gower and Wilson.* And she was glad to continue talking about Gerrard and Linda and John Wainfleet, and let Wilson slip out of the conversation altogether.

Mozart came to an end. They talked a short while longer and then Wickham got up to go, as she knew he would. He was letting her set the pace, wary perhaps of her backing away as she had already done once.

When he was gone, she regretted letting him go and stood alone at her bedroom window watching the lights of his taxi swing around Kington Square. A conversation with Holly, in

351

the spring, haunted her. Holly had been prodding her not to leave the question of her relationship with Wickham undecided, and she had told Holly: 'Paul understands.' Holly had demonstrated a space between finger and thumb and retorted: 'A man's understanding is so big.'

Rain jerked the curtains across, thinking: 'But it's Holly who doesn't understand. I'm relishing not being responsible to or responsible for anybody.'

The thought sustained her as she undressed and prepared for bed. She lay there thinking about Wickham and, when the distinctive sound of a black cab drove into the square, she indulged in the unreasonable expectation that he had come back.

Rain did not know how long it might be in reality before he came back, as it was even more difficult to foretell his future than her own. But the warehouse case threatened to occupy him solidly for a while.

'A curse on Goad and all his gang,' she grumbled, snuggling the duvet around her and settling to sleep. 'He's netted millions from his brilliantly planned raids, so why doesn't he retire?' And a minute or so later, more drowsily: '*Do* gang leaders retire? Well, anyway, it's high time Goad went.'

The unexpressed thought was that if he were not chasing Goad and his cohorts, Detective Chief Superintendent Paul Wickham would be available to chase round to Kington Square more often.

Holly Chase had news for Rain. Holly had a buyer for her semi-detached house in Spinney Green, but a Stoke Newington flat she had been tempted to buy had been sold under her nose; Rosie was hating her new job at Wapping and had hinted that she would like to return; and David Gerrard had been on the telephone to the editor complaining that he was being persecuted by the *Daily Post*.

The item about David Gerrard gave Rain her first smile of the day. 'He's getting paranoid. He's already accused me of setting a watch on him, having reporters tail him wherever he goes.'

Her secretary, another temporary helper filling the job until a permanent one was recruited, interrupted to say that the editor would like to see Rain.

'Oh-oh,' said Holly.

Rain turned down the corners of her mouth. 'Gerrard,' she said.

When she reached the editor's office she could hear the Irish tones of the news editor coming through the open door. Riley's lean form was lounging against a bookcase. He broke off speaking as Rain entered. On the editor's desk lay the page with the stories about the search for the killer of the Hampshire child and the possibility that John Gower was alive.

'David Gerrard,' said Rain, eager to skip preliminaries and get the matter out of the way.

The editor nodded. He removed his glasses and laid them down on the page. He was an insignificant man, more so without them. All one ever noticed of him was his flamboyant ties. Today he wore the blue and yellow one. He said: 'This emanated from you, Rain?'

She agreed, tacitly damning Riley who had been content to take credit for the theory up until the point where Gerrard had complained. Then she went over the ground, reciting how she had tackled Gerrard and how his rebuttals had convinced her he was hiding the truth.

'And then there was Linda Gower,' she went on. 'She took me to her cottage once, told me everything I wanted to know about John and his disappearance but now she clams up when I want a word. Seems nervous.'

Riley tried to help. 'So she should be. If Gower's alive, she's up to her neck in a rather nasty deception. That wouldn't do her any good at TV PM. They like their presenters to give the appearance of honesty and fair dealing. A scandal would destroy her.'

'If he's alive . . .' Rain began.

'*If,*' said the editor. 'Let's find out for sure, shall we? The two people most likely to be involved in the deception, if such a deception does exist, are behaving nervously and guiltily. The reporters who checked Rain's story and wrote these . . .' He tapped the page with his glasses. '. . . well, they confirmed what she'd found. But if we're going to get into trouble with Gerrard's lawyers or the Press Council, I'd like us to have something harder.'

Riley and Rain exchanged glances at this understatement. The editor asked her: 'What have you got on?'

She mentioned several stories for the column, adding that there was nothing she could not hand over to Holly to free herself for the Gower inquiry. And then, impulsively, she brought in Alf Wilson, saying there was a link with Gower.

'Wilson approached David Gerrard about an option on Gower's book, *A Candle Lit*. But Gerrard says he didn't tell Gower about it because he thought it would come to nothing. Instead, Wilson researched his own story about homelessness, although he used material in the Gower novel as a starting point. I've read the play and it's clear Wilson was going to make major changes. He had come by fresh information that was going to give him a stronger angle.'

She told them about the charity office in south London and the trail she had taken from there, ending in the bed-and-breakfast hotel in Bayswater and Companies House. She faltered. Itemizing the points the story sounded weak, whereas in her own mind the connection between Wilson and Gower had developed into fact.

The editor tapped the page again. 'We'll concentrate on this. If you find John Gower alive, Rain, he can tell you himself whether there was a link between him and Wilson.'

Rain returned his smile. 'This looks like a nice day for a trip to Cornwall,' she said.

She went on the sleeper, hanging around Penzance until she could hire a car. At Mousehole she drove to the harbour and asked until she met someone who knew Rob Watson. Rob was at work in an insurance office and came out, puzzled by news of a visitor, to see who she was and what she wanted.

'No, I don't have a boat now,' he said. 'I sail with a friend but I don't have a boat of my own. The *Fleur* took all I had, and the bills outstripped the insurance cover. One day I'll buy another one, but not yet.'

He begged time off and took her to the harbour to show her where the *Fleur* had been berthed the last time he had seen her, and indicated the route Gower had taken when he had snatched the boat one Monday morning. The tragedy was painfully apparent in his face, twin losses, of his friend and of his boat.

Rain did some probing, but Rob Watson's story was unchanged since April when he was in the news as the bewildered owner of the unmanned yacht that a fishing boat had run down in fog off the Lizard. He reminisced about the old days, when he and Gower had been students and co-owners of a patched-together craft called the *Jumble*, but recalling the good times did not turn the tide of sadness in him. Only a new boat and definite news of his friend would do that.

'Are you surprised,' she asked, 'that John's body hasn't been washed ashore?'

They were on the pier. He was staring out to where a yacht tossed on the swell near St Clement's Isle. 'No,' he said. 'It could have come up anywhere along the coast. The tides are such that it's unpredictable and we've had some rough seas since he went down. But a man could go over the side out there and never be seen again at all. If a body gets into the shipping lanes it can be hacked up by propellers, or it can be smashed to pieces on rocks in a storm. Anything could happen.'

Squeamish, Rain controlled a shudder at his matter-of-fact detail. But the fate of the body was not the only unpleasant question she had for him. 'Have you seen this, Rob?' She held out a newspaper cutting of the police photofit of the man sought in the murder inquiry.

Not a *Daily Post* reader, Rob Watson had not seen the juxtaposition of photographs in the newspaper. This was the first occasion he had been asked to say whether there was not a likeness to John Gower. Rob shook his head. 'Now you mention it, I should say there's a bit of a resemblance but John was quite an ordinary-looking chap. And these things never really look like anybody, do they?'

It was hard to argue with that. She got him to show her a map of the coastline, a map she had seen herself repeatedly but which Rob with his seaman's knowledge would be able to interpret for her. Where, she wanted to know, might someone come ashore if they left a boat at the putative site of the *Charity*?

'You mean John?' he asked superfluously.

'Yes.' He had done months of hypothesizing himself, she did not jib at inviting him to do a little for her. 'Supposing he got off the *Fleur* and came ashore, either swimming or in another boat, where would be the best place for him to land?'

Rob Watson scoffed, shaking his head. 'He wouldn't swim that far, it's a long way. And a boat could come in at any of these bays.' He ran a finger along a few inches of map. 'There's no shortage of choice.'

A small frown puckered Rain Morgan's forehead. 'What would be best? If you were doing it, what would you do?'

Fortunately, he had no aversion to this kind of game. 'Given the weather and the time of day – we know what time he left here and we know what time the *Fleur* was seen near the *Charity* – well, if it were me out there, I'd want to get ashore at Cadgwith. There, see?' His finger alighted on a fishing village not far from Lizard Point, on the east coast of the headland.

'Why, Rob? What makes this more favourable than all these other places?'

'I know it. So did John. I could be sure of getting in there and I know I could leave a car there ready for me to get away.' He gave her a smile of triumph. Gower getting safely ashore and going into hiding had been one of his fantasies too.

He admitted it. 'I used to think about it and wish it could be true, but I knew all along I was dreaming. John couldn't have come ashore, Rain. He died out there, I know he did.' And when her expression queried that certainty, Rob Watson said: 'I knew John Gower, Rain. He would never have risked my boat like that. He understood how much she meant to me.'

Any thoughts Rain had nurtured of taking him along with her on her quest, were abandoned. Her certainties were different from his. Rob Watson was a simple, good man but John Gower had shown himself to be more complicated. She did not wish to be the person who offered Rob Watson the proof that in the years between the carefree sailing trips on the *Jumble* and the sacrifice of the *Fleur*, Gower had become a different creature.

An inch or two on the map caused her a long and tiring drive, trapped in holiday traffic and fretting that the journey was not entirely with point. The folk of Cadgwith had been asked when the incident was news whether they had seen Gower in April, hopeless to believe they might help her now. Yet if she was to search for Gower she had to go where he had definitely gone and then pursue the probabilities.

The fishing village was quiet at midday, especially the harbour. Two somnolent men pottered by beached boats and three gulls sliced the air, but otherwise the harbour was at rest. The pub had half a dozen patrons in rubber boots.

They let her buy herself a fruit juice before telling her what her name was and waiting to hear what she wanted in their part of the world. Sometimes her face, made famous in television panel games and in her byline picture in the newspaper, was a help, other times a hindrance. This time it was helping.

One man said, before she could explain herself: 'If it's a boat you're wanting, then that's the man to hire you one.'

His companion brushed beer froth off his upper lip with the back of a weathered hand. 'He's right there. Best boats in Cornwall, isn't that so?'

The men jokingly agreed. Rain said no, she did not want to hire but just to talk about boats, about whether a boat had come into harbour one particular Monday evening in April.

'Ah,' said the man with the boats for hire. 'You mean when

357

the *Fleur* was wrecked and that writer fellow – what was his name? – yes, Gower, well you mean the night he died?'

A third man said: 'They'll never get the truth of that one, the police won't. And nor will the newspapers. If you ask me, he's at the bottom and the *Charity*'s at the bottom of it.'

He admired that phrasing and repeated it. But the others shuffled their feet, impatient with superstition. Rain had to keep a hold on the conversation before it degenerated into yarns about past incidents, and most of those based on hearsay.

Then the man with excess froth licked a trace from his moustache and asked her: 'You'll be wanting me to take you out there then?'

She said she would.

His boat was fast and clean, they were circling the scene of the *Fleur*'s disaster within the hour. On the way, they had talked, shouting above the engine, recounting the story of the *Fleur* and Gower, comparing police information with local rumour. And he had pointed out landmarks: Whale Rock, the Devil's Frying Pan, Black Head, Housel Bay, and Lizard Point.

He cut the engine, the quietness leaving them with only the slap of the sea against the boat's hull, and an aeroplane high overhead. The slightest of breezes lifted her curls playfully.

'Well, now,' he said. 'I don't know what you hoped to see, but this is all I can show you.'

Secretly, she was amused. Back at the pub he had been pressing her to make the trip, afraid she might change her mind about it, and anxious about losing the afternoon's hire. He could never have believed in the value of it as a means of understanding the fate of John Gower.

She was looking at the long line of the shore, the bare cliffs, the wooded hillsides, the meagre distribution of buildings, and she was thinking. She bit her lower lip, remembering something Rob Watson had said. *A pity*, she thought, *not to have come in the evening instead*.

The boatman might have been a mind reader. He said: 'The *Fleur* was here in the evening, you know. Things would have appeared different then. She was seen around here in the late afternoon and on into the early evening, but it got dark early.'

Rain took the folded map from her pocket. 'Which is Cadgwith?'

His arm shot out. 'There. You can just make it out.' He told her what to look for.

She said: 'If someone took a boat in there in the evening, could he rely on being able to beach it?'

'No. You've seen what little space there is.'

She bit the lip again, considering. If Gower had gone ashore at the likeliest point, he would either have struck lucky or else he had made prior plans with one of the local boat owners to bring him in. She dismissed the second thought as fast as it came to her. Gower would not have trusted any aspect of a carefully planned disappearance to a local boat owner. That was the last thing he would have done.

The boatman said: 'He didn't come ashore there. No stranger did. Of that you may be sure. We wouldn't have missed a thing like that.'

This declaration persuaded her that she had too easily adopted Rob Watson's theory. Rob would have got himself ashore at Cadgwith and jumped into a waiting car if he had been endeavouring to vanish in mysterious circumstances. But Rob was not the type to attempt the underhand. And he would have failed if he had tried, for the very reasons the boatman was giving her. Cadgwith was a thoroughly bad place for a disappearing act, because everyone knew what went on there.

Rain referred to her map once more, asking about coves and bays near by and their suitability as escape routes where a boat would not be noticed. There was a glut. The boatman could offer no theories, soon tired of the conversation and revealed a restless need to go home. He started up the engine, letting it idle until Rain gave the word to set off for Cadgwith. Having made his money for the trip, he was determinedly cutting it short and she had no plausible reason for delaying him.

Rather than travel in what threatened to be a disagreeable

silence, she shouted across a question about the success or otherwise of the summer season in the boat-hiring business. Apparently it was not a good year. The summer had been warm, although the heatwave that had held London in its grip had missed the south west, but many people were too poor to afford extra holidays and the West Country tourist industry as a whole was suffering.

The boatman himself had suffered late cancellations from holidaymakers, one of his regulars who usually fished on summer weekends had let him down by dying, and there had been unusual expense on two of his motor boats. One had been smashed up by a careless hirer and the engine of another had needed replacement.

She commiserated with him, then there was a long spell when they did not speak and watched a sailing boat beating upwind with feather-like vulnerability. Nearing the harbour, the boatman said, as though conversation had never lapsed: 'Yes, it was a trial, that engine. Never was right but I kept it running for years, putting off the big job, if you like. It always catches you up in the end, though.'

'Could you risk hiring it out, if it wasn't reliable?' She knew perfectly well he had done so, that holidaymakers had borne the frustration and the boatman had taken the money. Sympathetically voiced, the question remained a criticism.

He pulled at his moustache before saying: 'She was out that day in April we were talking about.'

'Before the season?'

'Yes, a man came and he wanted that boat, no other would do for him. I only had two and I offered him the bigger one for the same price, but he had set his mind to having the *Pintail*. Paid me for a week and away he went.'

Rain asked whether the boat had given the man trouble. The boatman laughed: 'He couldn't bring her back in because of it. Phoned me near the end of the week and said she was in a creek up the other side of the Lizard, and refusing to start. He'd left her there and called me when he got home.'

They entered the harbour, a mix of white and grey-stone

buildings, of thatch and tin roofs, of holidaymakers and fishermen. The same men with sleepy movements were by their boats but now there were also people strolling about.

Rain caught sight of the *Pintail*. The man said: 'She's going to be fully refitted for next summer. Of course, I offered that man a refund.'

She seriously doubted that. She said nothing. The boatman said: 'But he wasn't interested. Said he'd been up and down the coast a good way, she only gave trouble on the homeward run.'

Rain flinched as the boat aimed for a gap between two others. He said: 'To be truthful. I never thought he was much of a sailor. He didn't look right, but you can't be sure. Came from London. We get all sorts.'

He was ashore and tying up. He held out a hand and Rain slid hers into it. His grasp was warm, the skin toughened by the constant touch of ropes and salt spray and harsh things. She got ashore, sensing that he held her fingers a fraction of a second too long.

Then she thanked him for the trip and waited to see whether they would walk away from the harbour together, but he lingered with one of the pottering men and she moved on. The windscreen of her car was glinting, beckoning her. She needed to book into a hotel for the night and she had given no thought to it until now. Perched on a wall she unfolded the map on her knee. Suddenly a shadow fell over the map.

'There,' said the boatman. 'That's the creek where the *Pintail* was left. And in my opinion, she'd been there a while by the time I got to her.'

Rain wondered how he could tell, but she only half listened to his explanation about tides, weather and the way the *Pintail* had settled at low tide. She was bursting with more important questions, the relevance of the *Pintail* story belatedly striking her.

'What was he like, the man who hired her?'

He had a clear memory, although his vocabulary was

imprecise. 'A Londoner, like I said. Heavy. Not a seafaring type, of that I'm sure. And I'd say there was money there. Why do you want to know?'

Rain gave him her warmest smile. 'Tell me something else and I'll answer that.'

And so she traded her nosiness against his, knowing how keen he was to have another good tale to entertain them in the pub that evening about how he had taken a beautiful young gossip columnist out to the scene of the mystery and become invaluable to her inquiries.

He said: 'What's that, then?'

'Tell me his name.'

But he had to tug the moustache and admit April was a while ago and he no longer remembered. Rain said: 'You keep records, surely?'

'Well, yes, up at the house.' He was very doubtful about taking her there but she did a bit more smiling and cajoling and then they walked up the hill. In a cupboard, in a cottage front room that he called his office, he put his hand on a file containing information about the previous year's hires. He opened it on the dining table, saying that his income-tax point was at the end of April so the details were not in the current file.

Rain contained her impatience. The records were in a muddle. He flopped papers to and fro and tweaked his moustache. Rain could not resist going to stand by his shoulder. Letters from hirers, and the jottings from telephone conversations, produced names and addresses and several times she saw the word *Pintail* scrawled.

A woman poked her head in, ignoring Rain and asking the man to go to the back door and speak to a man who had called on business. Rain seized the chance and went rapidly through the file, wishing she had time to write down all the names relating to *Pintail*.

She was not quick enough. The door swung, the boatman came into the room. He was cross at her temerity. 'You shouldn't be looking in there, that's private,' he said, and repeated this in variations of anger.

Rain apologized, but it was no use. He was upset and, she suspected, afraid. She hoped to allay that fear, saying she had been purely interested in the name, nothing else.

He closed the file and stood with his hand on it. 'Well, we couldn't find it, could we?'

She was relieved to be going. Embarrassed by letting her inquisitiveness get the better of her manners, and by being foolishly caught snooping, and at the way her name would figure in his story in the pub that night, she dashed for her car. Every step of the way she imagined the deprecating eyes of everyone in the village following her.

Rain drove the length of the long steep hill and pulled the car into the first convenient gateway. Then she banged her fist down on the steering wheel, gave a shout of glee and let her joy be unconfined. If there had been anyone with her, she would have hugged them. Alone, she laughed and congratulated herself aloud.

'I've done it! I've *done* it!' And she looked at her watch and wondered who she could ring who would say well done and want to listen to her relive her success. She ought to share it with Riley, it was a news story after all, but somehow Riley was not her choice. She drove to the nearest call box away from Cadgwith and rang Holly Chase at home.

Holly's gasp was exactly what she wanted to hear. 'Wow!' said Holly. And could not go on.

Rain babbled about her discovery, then begged Holly to keep it to herself until she was ready to tell the editor and Riley. 'I don't want them to send a team out to spoil things, just when everything's going my way.'

Holly promised she was sworn to secrecy. Then: 'Wow!' she said again.

Rain laughed, ringing off, setting out to find a hotel. She no longer needed to worry which direction to take. She was going to examine the creek the boatman had pointed out on the map and then she would take a road inland and head for hotels in an area she knew.

Ponderous holiday traffic could not mar her cheerfulness. She sang to herself as she bowled slowly along to join a main road that she left a short distance later to take the Mullion turn. At Mullion she picked up a minor road, going as far as it went to the south, before walking to reach the creek. There were no boats. As the waves thudded against rocks at the entrance and sucked greedily at decaying stanchions she asked herself how it had been on a rough night in April when the *Pintail* had sought a hiding place.

She knew enough to tell that a good seaman would make it, but a poor one could not. Rain turned her back on the swirling water and walked up the track. She went into the first pub she reached. What did they remember, she asked the couple behind the bar, about a boat called the *Pintail* that had tied up in the creek back in April.

They remembered, or said they remembered, little. Their unvoiced remark was that it was none of her business. Each of her subsequent questions about specific points was wasted on their blank-faced mistrustfulness. She went away, just getting into her car when a man walked up to the pub. She waylaid him on his way to the door. Was he local? Did he know about the *Pintail*? Well, as he had been in the pub the evening before she was spotted in the creek, had he noticed a stranger in the area that evening? Oh, a man called at the pub and telephoned for a taxi? And he was wet through? Well, now, whose taxi came for him?

The pub door closed between them. Rain drove back to Mullion and caught the taxi driver, in front of his television set and waiting for business. Did he remember picking up a wet man in the pub near the creek? Did he notice what type of car the man got into when he dropped him off at Cadgwith?

She got a clean run of yesses and a London-registered BMW. Things were still going her way.

But it was harder than she anticipated, claiming a room for the night. At last a small hotel way off her route took her in, providing an uninteresting room with a view of the back of somebody's house. The plumbing sounded like Concorde taking off and as it was 9 p.m. she was too late for food. With no alternatives in the vicinity, she negotiated until they relented and sent up to her room a microwaved pasty and a tomato, also microwaved and consequently disintegrated within its skin.

But it had been a fruitful day and her good humour flourished. Her hunch had been sound and the deception should soon be over. Ideally, she would like to produce John Gower, so far all she could produce was the accomplice who had helped him get away from the *Fleur*. That Gower had reached land was beyond doubt. David Gerrard, palpably no hand with a boat, could not have brought the *Pintail* into the creek that night. But John Gower could.

Rain mulled over the next stage of her investigation, wanting more detail before she confronted Gerrard, more than that before she shared her discoveries with Riley and the editor. She had made the luckiest start, but experience warned her to be cautious and not rush into confrontation until the facts were incontrovertible. Coincidence could play havoc, and life abounded with coincidences. She meant to tread softly.

Before getting into bed, she rang her own London number to listen to any messages left on her answering machine that day. A friend asked whether she would like to go to an art exhibition with her. A contact wanted to tell her about a scandal brewing at a fashion house. An American friend wanted to sleep on her sofa when she came to London in a month's time. And then there was a savage, educated voice that she did not know.

It said: 'This is a warning, Rain Morgan. Don't interfere in things that don't concern you. You could, as they say, meet with a very nasty accident.'

She slammed the receiver down. Her breath was short, her body weak.

Words, she thought. *That's all, just words. They can't hurt me.*

But they already had. They had shocked her, forced her to

face her vulnerability. She lived alone, for her work she went into strange places alone. She believed that she had that very day discovered a truth that John Gower and David Gerrard wanted buried and now she had been threatened.

She filled a glass of water, her nervous hand slopping it on its way to her lips. Gulping the water, she made her mind rest on actualities instead of panicking through a blur of detail. The nub of the matter surfaced and she faced it bravely.

Among the people she had spoken to that day was at least one who knew more than he – or, possibly, she – admitted. That was not the person who had left the message, someone else without a regional accent had done that.

All the people she had met since walking into the pub in Cadgwith became vignettes viewed through her filter of suspicion. Each became a danger, because one of them had reported her to the man who had acquired her home telephone number.

Gower himself? She had never heard his voice. Despite her worry, she forced a wry smile. *If that was John Gower, I've got absolute proof that he's alive.* But her smile twisted into an expression of frustration as another thought overtook her. *I'm no nearer finding him.*

Hazy about what could and could not be done in the way of tracing telephone calls, she decided to consult a higher authority and telephoned Paul Wickham. But they did not speak. She left a message on his machine saying she would call later in the week.

So there was after all no one with whom she shared the irony that she had this day resurrected John Gower and simultaneously put her own life at risk.

Linda Gower had used a key from beneath a stone behind the shed when they had entered the cottage together. Rain Morgan located the key and let herself in, going about it openly on the premise that furtive creeping was likelier to arouse doubts in local minds about her right to be there.

The narrow passage swam into view, a scattering of junk

mail behind the door was pushed against the wall and then she was inside. Cold. Damp. Inhospitable. She wondered afresh what life had been like for the Gowers in such a place, John deeply involved in his books and not noticing or caring, and Linda feeling her talents and ambition snuffed out as year succeeded year.

The hints had been plain, when Rain had interviewed Linda early in the summer. The proof had been glaring: in London, independent of her husband and the constraints of the writing life, Linda had bloomed. She had a new career, a well-paid one that exercised skills that had lain dormant and, at Stream Cottage, would have continued to do so.

Rain turned the knob of the sitting-room door. A mound of letters was heaped in the centre of the floor. She knelt and peered at them, noticing that the pile was not entirely haphazard. Someone had arranged it roughly in order of arrival, oldest things on top.

Back in the hall, she meant to continue past the stairs to Gower's study, which was what she had actually come to see. But the things on the floor behind the door attracted her and she picked them up, examining postmarks. They were all, as she had presumed, more recent than the envelopes in the sitting room. Rain wrote down in her notebook the dates of the newest mail in the sitting room and the oldest in the passage. Between those dates someone had been into the cottage, probably Linda but perhaps Gower himself.

In the study she looked through the desk where Linda had in her presence searched for the typescript, notes and possibly computer disks of the book Gower was working on when he disappeared. Rain no longer set much store by the absence of disks, having learned enough about the slowness of his writing to guess it was improbable he had written much, apart from notes, before he vanished. She searched again, for anything that would provide a clue to where he had gone after he came ashore from the *Fleur*. She dismissed his copy of J. B. Mullen's book, *The Wreck of the Charity*, as a well-placed red herring, and spent longer leafing through a road atlas because of the slender chance that he had marked it. He had not.

But she was not only looking for the things he had left behind, she was checking on the things he ought not to have taken away. His passport, for instance. She found all the other personal documents she would have expected in somebody's house, but she did not find John Gower's passport.

That's what I'd do, if I was going to vanish deliberately, I'd go abroad, she thought. And she knew he must have a passport because Linda had mentioned holidays abroad, in the optimistic days before she had come to believe that only penury lay ahead if they continued to live in Dorset. *I think John Gower intended to go abroad, but something went wrong and he stayed in this country, in hiding.*

She was sitting in his chair, her fingers drumming lightly on his desk as she wondered where to search next, when the telephone on the desk rang. She sprang up in shock.

Perhaps she ought to have ignored it, waited for the caller to give up and go away. Perhaps. Instead she lifted the receiver after the third ring. Hesitantly, a man's voice said: 'John?'

Rain was rigid. She neither spoke nor let her breath escape. Her fingers whitened on the receiver and she prayed for the voice to speak again. It did not. There was a click and the resumption of the dialling tone.

Abruptly she became afraid of sitting in Gower's chair, gripping his telephone. She retreated to the window, her eyes on fields ready for harvest, her thoughts whirling.

If only the man had spoken again. If only he'd said more. How can I say whether it was David Gerrard or not?

She ran fingers through her hair, pushing back a lock from her forehead, counting the alternative possibilities. *Either it was Gerrard or somebody else who knows Gower is meant to be dead but is really alive. Or it was somebody who doesn't know about his disappearance. Or it was a straightforward wrong number, a coincidence because John is a very common name.*

She chose to put her faith in the wrong number. Then the telephone rang again. Rain flattened herself against the wall by the window and let it ring. Once. She fought a battle in her mind.

Listen to the voice more carefully this time.

Twice.

No, if it's somebody seeking Gower it's better if they don't get an answer.

Three times.

If I don't answer I'll never hear the voice again.

Four times.

She lunged for the receiver. And waited. This time she and the caller listened to each other's silences, until he returned his receiver to its cradle.

Rain left the house. She had been supposing this and supposing that when it dawned on her that the caller could be close, a man who had seen her car by the gate and knew Gower was alive. If he called round and discovered her, what then? A nasty accident?

She stalled the car, got it moving at the second attempt, made an incompetent three-point turn that nearly put her back wheel in the ditch after which the cottage was named, and then she shot away down the lane, putting the miles between herself and that wretched house. Crossing the county boundary, she realized that she had brought with her the key to Stream Cottage. The next person who went there really would have to break in!

Driving fast, south then east, she joined the road to Bournemouth. Destination undecided. Flight essential. *This is crazy. I must slow down. No one's chasing me.*

But they were, not driving up the road after her, but in other ways, with telephoned threats. Threats *plural*? Had there been another? She had not checked her home telephone, had chosen not to. She put her foot down, kept up her speed.

She needed somebody. A friend. A friend to share the moment, a friend who could take the sting out of it. All her friends were busy people, with problems of their own.

Bournemouth. Mary. Haven't seen her for a while but she'd be pleased. I'll ring her, go straight over to Westbourne. I could be there

*in half an hour. Mary. So much to catch up on. Oh . . . that husband
of hers. Freelance journalist. Hmm. Better not. Don't want him filing
tips to other newspapers about my story. Oh well, forget Mary. But
why do my friends marry such awful men? Law of nature, or
somesuch.*

Rain Morgan skirted Bournemouth, pressed on east.

Butlers looked deliciously pretty, its setting charming. She
parked in the road, opened the noisy gate and walked up the
long and curving yellow drive. A car stood outside a thatched
garage to the right of the house. Birds played along hedges,
grass had been cut and perfumed the air, and the orchard was
burdened with fruit. Bliss.

Rain made for the porch with its darkened oak door, but a
man, the type that looks old when he is years from it, came out
of a different door to greet her. Brian Parsons knew her at
once.

'You're Rain Morgan?'

'So I am.'

'I thought I'd finished with the press.'

She donned a sympathetic smile. 'I'm sorry.' She wasn't, it
was what one said.

She told him she was gathering background information,
for use later when there was a conviction for the murder of
Danny. For all she knew, it might be true.

'Drink?' asked Parsons.

'Thanks.'

They sat among blowzy roses at the back of the house, bees
fussing in lavender and house martins commuting from fields
to nests below the eaves. More bliss.

Parsons told her he had bought the house because it was an
ideal place to write. His wife took temporary jobs as a
secretary in Lymington and they had organized their lives to
allow stretches of time abroad each year. His wife was still on
Gozo. It had been a pity to give up the farmhouse they had
rented, and he was planning to rejoin her in a fortnight.

Rain felt a prickle of interest in this unexceptional story. She
encouraged him to chat about his time on Gozo and learned

about afternoons typing on a vine-shaded terrace while his wife and several lizards basked in the Mediterranean sun. She heard about climbs up barren hills topped with ancient fortifications, tussles with unreliable electricity supplies, wonderful parcels of books from England, and the vagaries of a car that passed as roadworthy on the island but would qualify as a museum exhibit in Britain. When he paused to offer more drinks, fetch more ice, she had made up her mind. Somebody was not telling the truth.

Parsons came back, the hiatus a natural point to switch from the pleasantly chatty to the business of her visit. He gestured with a glass in his hand. 'It was over there,' he said, meaning the child's body.

Rain glanced but there was nothing to be seen except apples and pears on the bough. With a twinge of revulsion she realized she would be taken to see the exact spot. She delayed. Parsons sat down again, swatting at an investigative wasp.

He said: 'The police had taken a thorough look at the house by the time I came home and they raised no objection to me moving back in. After all, the thing happened outside. Two yards further and it would have been in the farmer's field and not on my land at all.'

Rain savoured the touch of ice on her tongue. Then: 'There was the business of the man who was believed to have stayed in the house.'

Parsons shook his greying head. 'Quite honestly, I don't believe it. David Gerrard didn't see anything and the police found nothing that wasn't attributable to David. When you think about it, nobody in the village claims to have seen signs of a man *inside* the house. All right, so somebody was hanging around, but what does that prove? There was no break-in and I've had people hanging around while I've been here myself.'

He pointed across to a spot beyond the concealing trees. 'There's a gate there. It takes you on to a path over fields to a back road where there's a pub. People use the path all the time and every so often there's a nosy parker who thinks Butlers looks interesting and they slip in through that gate for a closer look. I'm sure that's all that happened.'

'And unfortunately for the little boy, he was playing nosy parker at the same time?'

'So it would seem.'

'But,' Rain objected, 'the man was spotted here by a number of people on a number of different occasions. Here, but nowhere else.'

Parsons contradicted. 'Oh, that's not true. For instance, he was seen walking through the village one wet Saturday towards Lymington, and in the pub one lunchtime by Danny's father, as well as the landlord and some of the regulars. There were a number of sightings away from Butlers.'

Rain said that as the man was apparently frequently in the area, he must have been staying there and if not at Butlers, then where?

Parsons laughed that off. 'There's a whole forest for him to choose from. He could have made a den anywhere he liked.'

She let him have the last word, although all reports of the thin man suggested he was neatly and fashionably dressed and took great care of his appearance. That did not chime with nights spent in a woodland bower.

Parsons showed her around the house, coped with her relentless questioning, led her to the site of the murder, said he would introduce her to Danny's parents and, when she failed to book a local hotel room for the night, offered her a bed at Butlers. Ordinarily, she would have declined such an offer, preferring independence, but her previous night in the wretched Cornish hotel weighed in his favour.

The talk with the parents elicited nothing Rain had not already read. Danny had not described a man in or near the house, in fact he had reported only what Parsons had denied anyone had seen – *signs* of occupation: an open door, a typewriter on the dining table and later the lack of it.

Parsons, who was with Rain throughout the talk, gave a start at one stage and they all looked inquiringly at him. He apologized for interrupting, said it was nothing, made them disregard him and continue.

Later, walking back up the village lane, Rain asked him: 'What was it, Brian? The typewriter?'

'Yes, I hadn't heard that part before. But, of course, the kid was wrong. You know what his father said: at that age they live in a mix of fantasy and fiction, it's hard to tell when to believe them.'

There was a distressing silence while they reflected that Danny might be alive if his parents had made the right guess and trusted him when he had insisted there was something odd happening at Butlers.

Rain said: 'What if the boy was right, and there was a typewriter?'

But Parsons would not have it. 'I've got one, and it was in Gozo with me.'

'And your wife?'

'The same. I do a draft and scribble over it, she types a clean version for me. It helps if we have two machines. When I'm here I use a word processor, but the electricity supply on Gozo is dangerously erratic, so I didn't take it. I loaned it to a friend in Lymington while I was away.'

They opened the noisy gate, breathed the mown grass. Shadows were stretching out beneath the trees. The front of the house had gone from creamy-white to grey. Rain had promised supper in Lymington in exchange for the bed and breakfast. She wanted to urge him to do something first, but a table was booked and time was against her. And besides, how far should she go? Somebody was lying, but who?

Brian Parsons was a pleasant companion over supper although, in the restaurant on The Quay, the sloping cobbled lane down to the harbour, he talked inordinately about the complicatedly scientific subject on which he was writing a book. He was intelligent, highly qualified and had some of the unworldliness that sometimes went with this. And he was, once he got on to his own subject, extraordinarily boring except, she hoped for the sake of his books, to other professionals. Rain preferred it when they were gossiping about David Gerrard.

The wine was finished, the brandies had been brought, and he grew usefully confidential. 'Actually, I did push David about the rumour there'd been another man at the cottage. He might have had a friend there, and wanted to conceal the fact. The police thought so too. They asked me whether his taste ran to young men. I had to admit I didn't know. We're friendly enough, but he doesn't confess to me about his sexual activity.'

Rain supplied the information that she did not know either, that Gerrard was either supremely discreet about his sex life or else did without one.

She left the car in the harbour car park and they took a taxi to Butlers. Providing a treat for Brian Parsons had pushed her well above the legal driving limit, she had eaten and drunk far more than usual. London with its small, light meals and its fancy mineral waters seemed a foreign country.

Parsons, too, did not normally indulge to this degree. A necessarily economical well-ordered life permitted few excesses. He yawned and fumbled his key in the lock of the lean-to.

Rain hoped he would just be tired and go to bed, that alcohol would not encourage him to mistake her motives for staying the night. He had swayed against her in the back of the taxi and she doubted whether the camber of the road was entirely to blame.

But Parsons was the epitome of politeness, furnishing her with towels, thanking her and the *Daily Post* for the evening and sending her upstairs to a picturesque room with long views silvery beneath a moon. She sat on the edge of the bed with a relieved and self-mocking smile.

If I hadn't been so stupid as to think he fancied me, I could have asked him what I wanted to ask. Now I'll have to leave it to the morning when he might be a deal less mellow. If he's hung over and irritable, he's going to say no.

She washed her face and slid into bed. The day's events

374

blended pleasantly in her memory, each scene scented with those symbols of English high summer, cut grass and roses.

The rumpus awoke her with a terrifying jolt. Before she recollected where she was, there was a hand against her bedroom door, a man's voice calling her. Urgently.

Her own voice came weakly. 'Yes?'

'Can I come in?'

She said yes, reached for a lamp, sat up. Parsons entered. He was wearing what he had worn all evening, and he was agitated.

He was saying: 'I've found it, Rain. It was all true. All along, it was true.'

Rain rubbed her eyes. He said: 'Sorry, you're in bed. I didn't think you would be yet.'

She looked at her watch. No more than ten minutes had passed since she had come up to the room. Her mind was slowly focusing, her voice firmer, 'What have you found, Brian?'

He was thrilled. 'The typewriter! The one Danny said he saw. I mean, it must be the one. It's not mine, nor my wife's. It's, well, I don't know whose it is.'

Rain smoothed hair back from her face. 'Where was it?'

'Under the stairs. Oh, do come and look.'

She said she would follow him down. With her linen jacket over her nightdress as a nod to modesty, she tramped barefoot to the living room. Parsons was fiddling around with a typewriter, a portable. He was running his fingers over the keys.

'It's practically out of the ark,' he said, scarcely looking up as she appeared in the doorway. 'Fancy anyone using one of these things today.'

'Is there a ribbon in it?'

'Yes.' He typed a few words straight on to the platen. 'It's in full working order.'

He had the typewriter on the dining table. A grubby duster was lying beside it. He picked that up and rubbed it over all the keys, then over the frame. 'The case was dusty. It was at the back of the stair cupboard, tucked round a corner behind some boxes of junk and vacuum cleaners and so on. No wonder the police didn't find it.'

'I imagine they did but assumed it was yours.'

'Oh, yes. They could have done.'

Rain watched dismayed as he chattered about his sudden whim to look for the mysterious typewriter, his inspiration that if there had been a man with a typewriter and he had fled hurriedly on foot, he would not have carried it with him. She popped in words of admiration for his reasoning, but all the while she blamed herself for not asking him to search the minute they had returned from Danny's parents' house, or at any rate once they had come in from the restaurant, instead of postponing her request until morning.

The damage was done. Brian Parsons had found the typewriter, and he had wiped it clean of clues to the identity of the fingertips that had last struck those keys, clutched that handle and pushed the case into the deepest hiding place Butlers afforded. He was an educated, intelligent man and she had failed to prevent him behaving like a fool.

'The police, first thing in the morning,' Parsons was saying.

She agreed with all the enthusiasm she could muster. Then she yawned a little and went back upstairs. There was a pale sky. Her latticed window looked over a monochrome wheat-field to the lambent outline of the Isle of Wight.

Rain lowered her gaze, looked at apples blue and silver among night-black leaves. Through those fruit trees was the place Parsons had taken her to see before they had gone out. The spot had been sunny and not of itself disturbing, but she could tell that at this time of night the shadow of the hedge fell across it and that the bunch of flowers Danny's sister had laid there would now be leached of all colour, spectral.

18

Gower heard the news about the finding of the typewriter on Murray's television set. The man had taken his Alsatian and gone out, determined to claim a pitch outside the local supermarket before any other hopefuls got there. Murray was said to be successful at begging, although those members of the squat who disliked him attributed his success to the appeal of his dog. Behind his back there were lively discussions about it.

'Would *you* give anything to an old boozer like Murray?' one would say.

'Course not. But you've got to feel sorry for that dog, haven't you?'

'Well, there you are. That's what I said. The dog's the one that brings the money in.'

And someone else would mutter that it was tough luck on the dog that the money got spent on beer instead of pet food.

Behind his back they also watched his television. When he was at the house, Murray was in control of whether it was switched on or off. When he was out, they did as they liked. They liked the news.

The New Forest murder was one of the main items on breakfast television that day, partly because of the intriguing development that appeared to prove what the victim had told his parents, about a typewriter being at the cottage, and partly because the television companies had film of Butlers that they were able to re-use to produce a lengthy story. An interviewer battled to develop a further line, by accusing the police of negligence in failing to locate the mystery typewriter sooner, but the senior officer defended his men without flinching.

He said they had seen the typewriter in the cupboard at the start of the inquiry but as they were searching the house of a writer the machine did not seem out of place and the writer's agent, who had borrowed the cottage, had identified it as Brian Parsons's property. When Parsons returned home he was asked to check that there was nothing on the premises except what he owned, and he had not reported an extra typewriter.

Gower sat through a couple of repeats of this item, revealing no more than the casual interest of his companions, and pretending to be waiting, as they were, for the succeeding story, about a London drugs case. Gower was fascinated to see Brian Parsons. So *that* was the man whose home and possessions he had made free with for all those weeks, the man he had claimed to be when he had braved Lymington Post Office and tricked the clerk into giving him a passport. Not only was Parsons older than him, but Parsons looked older than he really was, premature greyness and hollow cheeks contributing to the effect.

The purpose of pushing Parsons in front of the camera was to have him explain that he used a word processor when he worked at Butlers but took a manual typewriter abroad, because of the difficulties with electricity supply. He said he had not heard of Danny's claim about a typewriter at the cottage until shortly before he searched for and found it.

Gower was calculating his diminishing chances of escaping without having his name linked with Butlers and the murder. *Fingerprints on the keys*, he thought. *Did they take my prints from Stream Cottage when they were searching for me? God, I wish I knew that*.

Then: *David Gerrard. He might know. And if he doesn't, he's still the only person I can ask*.

He transferred the charge and rang Gerrard from a telephone outside the post office, catching him at home before he left for work.

Gerrard was sharp: 'Where are you, John?'

'That doesn't matter, David. It's best if you don't know.'

'I disagree. You put me in an intolerable position. They've found the typewriter I loaned you.'

378

'That's why I'm ringing. I need to know, did they take my fingerprints from Stream Cottage? And have they checked the rooms at Butlers for prints?'

Gerrard sighed. 'How should I know? One isn't privy to everything the police get up to. Good Lord, I'm not even privy to what you get up to any longer.'

'Never mind that . . .'

'John, I do mind. You don't appreciate what trouble you're causing me. I really do think it's time to stop play-acting and come into the open. Do it now and I'll tie it in with a profitable tour to promote your American paperback.'

'Damn the American paperback! This is serious. If they match my fingerprints from Butlers with some from my house, then I'm going to get arrested for murder.'

'All the more reason,' said Gerrard, 'for coming forward now instead of waiting for them to make you appear utterly guilty.'

Gower said: 'You don't believe I killed that boy, do you?'

'No, certainly not.' But Gerrard failed to sound confident.

Gower groaned. 'You see? You can't put your hand on your heart and say it wasn't me. What chance would I have of persuading the police?'

Gerrard started reiterating his plea for Gower to abandon pretence, but Gower interrupted him to demand what had happened to the £10,000 he had requested.

Gerrard said: 'I never promised to pay it, John. You've got to come into the open and face up to things. It was never intended to go on as long as this, and the longer it does, the more complicated and difficult it all becomes.'

They wrangled about whose fault it was, Gower making sound points about Gerrard having persuaded him to keep out of sight longer than he wanted because it suited the money-making process. And Gerrard equally accurate in his accusations that Gower himself had spun the escapade out when it would have pleased Gerrard to have had him back in the world, on tour and on television, and signing contracts for future books.

The acrimony was forced to end when a man hovered close to Gower to await use of the telephone. Gower concluded with an insistent demand for the money. Gerrard concluded with a refusal.

Habit made Gower walk on towards the cash machine, although he did not bother to use it because he had drawn out the last of the cash. Then he went to the Dôme. Through the run of open doors he saw people at tables, reading newspapers or talking, although most of them were alone. Several of the regulars were there, such as the young busker in the cowboy hat and jeans with his guitar resting against the marble-topped table, or the elderly American writer in the tattered straw hat and cream linen jacket over yellow trousers. The table where Gower usually sat was unoccupied. He hesitated, but did not go in.

What cash he had was going to have to last him a long time, and there were cheaper cafés. He walked on in the general direction of the street market, taking his time because it did not get going until about 10 a.m. Another estate agent was setting up an office in the street. Another restaurant was opening, offering cheap foreign food expensively but doubtless sure of custom. He sauntered on, window shopping, watching office workers hurrying into glassy modern banks and building societies.

Eventually he reached Chapel Market and killed time by wandering to the end of the street while vans unloaded and stalls were erected. Around corners tramps were awakening, poised to seize whatever scraps came their way. A white-haired, mentally confused woman, so short that her hessian shopping bag brushed the floor as she trudged along, was already seeking plunder.

She was barked at by a brawny man with a parade-ground voice as she lifted a nectarine from a box. Mumbling a dribbling apology, she let the fruit fall back into its nestling place and shuffled on.

The man shouted after her, not abuse but commentary for the benefit of his peers. He ended with a raucous laugh. Gower passed by, on the other side, avoiding his eye.

He bought a bun in a baker's, the cheapest kind they had, and ate this outside a shop window, looking at the higgledy-piggledy arrangement of inexpensive clothes, mock leather belts, cut-price shoes. In a while, when the stallholders were marking prices on cards to stick among the fruit and vegetables, and the vans were emptying the street of traffic, he walked back down between the twin rows of stalls, seeing what was good on the market this day, comparing prices.

He bought bananas – not a cheap item but filling and nutritious – and oranges, dropping them into the grey canvas bag over his shoulder. A stall selling tinned goods had a special offer of sardines, so he bought three cans. Most of the bargains came like that: buy three or four of something, or two pounds instead of one pound and you got a bargain. If you could afford only the smallest amount in the first place, you did not.

Setting up the stalls, the men had discarded damaged fruit and vegetables, tossing them into boxes beneath the stalls or sometimes missing and letting them lie on the ground. Behind a fruit stall, Gower saw the old woman with her hessian bag, picking her way through a box of rejects.

He went up to her, said hello, gave her a banana. She looked at it, not at him once. She sniffed it, regarded it suspiciously and then flung it into the gutter. Stooping over the box again she chose a cucumber, liquified at one end. The stallholder, looking round from serving a customer, saw her and yelled for her to go away. She carefully put the rotten cucumber into her bag and with a touching remnant of dignity, stuck her nose in the air and left.

Gower bent to the gutter and retrieved his banana.

Back at the squat, changes were taking place. When he saw the car parked by the kerb, a long-nosed and flashy model, he feared the owners had come to claim their property. The reality was more dangerous than that. For the second time control of the house had been seized by outsiders, the hierarchy had changed again. First, Joe and Rod in charge, then the polite George and his commune, but now something more menacing.

Two men wearing designer jeans and well-cut leather blousons were in the doorway and about to leave. They let Gower in. The atmosphere told him at once that something bad had taken place. Finding out precisely what was not easy. People averted their eyes to dodge his questions.

Only half the squatters were present, the others being out and about until later in the day, but there were more new faces. One in particular impressed him. This was a florid youth whose arms were bare except for tattoos, bulged with muscles. He wore leathers, a smattering of chains and a malign expression. Despite his aggressive stance, he went by the cosy name of Mel, a name that was tattooed on to his left arm.

No one actually called him that, or anything else. Mel, Gower heard, in a series of whispered out-of-the-corner-of-the-mouth exchanges, was the rent collector. Gower would have laughed at this nonsense, except that he now identified the atmosphere in the house. It was fear. And he knew it could have been no simple matter to scare the squatters, most of whom were rather tough themselves.

Mel was not tough, he was ferocious. 'Right,' he snarled. 'You heard what they said. It's ten quid a week, and I mean from all of you. You can pay me tomorrow for this week and I'll be back for next week's.'

This meant they would be charged a full week's rent for a week that was already half spent, but nobody cared to fight Mel. Their silence was acquiescence.

Mel hung about until the end of the day, spelling out the situation to each of the returning squatters. 'So as nobody can say they weren't warned,' as he put it.

The spiky-haired lads who had found the house in the first instance and invited Gower to share it with them, were shocked by the arrival of Mel. Rod was prepared to argue but Joe, who was brighter, jabbed him with an elbow to shut him up. Gower was relieved.

Later on, Mel left. But the new faces that he and the men with the flashy car had brought with them in the morning were still there and it was unclear where their allegiance lay. Criticisms of Mel and the pair with the car, and the enforced payment of rent, were necessarily muted.

Joe, his role as leader usurped since the first wave of squatters arrived, gave up all pretence of being able to cope with circumstances. He caught Gower's eye across the big upstairs room, tipped his tousled head meaningfully and went outside.

Gower felt sorry for Joe whose little bit of freedom and authority had been so decisively snuffed out. He could look back with almost affection on his first days at the house when Joe had run things and laughed a lot. Joe had given up laughing. Gower counted to one hundred and left the room too. He could not see Joe in the upstairs kitchen and started down stairs when Joe hissed to him from around the door of the bathroom on the landing. Gower joined him and Joe locked the door.

There was a stained bath, a cracked washbasin, an unhealthy-looking lavatory pan, peeling paint, an old geyser hanging off the wall, but Gower had long ceased to notice the degraded state of the house. It was a roof over his head and until now it had been free.

Joe tweaked an earring, a tic he had when he was worried. 'What do you reckon, Richard?'

Gower shrugged. 'If there isn't any money, then he can't take any, can he?'

Joe gasped. 'Are you serious? Somebody got killed at a squat for saying no. Mel said it was a lesson to the rest.'

Gower did not want to believe he was hearing this. 'But he knows people don't have money. Why else would they be here?'

'Yeah, all right, he knows. Those guys he works for, they know. But people make sure they get the money for Mel, don't they? Otherwise the racket wouldn't work. They're leeches, we won't be able to shake them off. They'll bleed us dry.'

Gower grew curious. This did not sound like Joe speaking. 'Who told you all this?'

Joe said he had got it from George, the man with the glittering eyes and an inclination to run a squat like a commune. Perhaps if Joe had named any of the others, Gower would have been less troubled. But George's opinion carried weight with him. George was not a drinker, nor a drug user, nor a beggar, nor a scaremonger. For a mixture of social and political reasons George believed in direct action to make homes for the homeless. He lived by a personal code, and Gower held him in greater respect than the rest of the crowd.

Joe was still feeling responsible, for Rod if for no one else. He was worrying the earring. 'I've told Rod, but I don't reckon he took it in. Maybe it's just as well. I don't want him setting on Mel with his iron bar or anything crazy.'

'All right,' said Gower, surprised at his own resolution. 'You just keep Rod out of trouble, and leave the rest to me.'

He sought out George. 'Have you got a minute, George?'

'Certainly.' George excused himself from the friends he was speaking to and he and Gower went into the downstairs front room. It was dark as the windows were boarded up, and the light bulb was broken, and it was airless. The whiteness of the marble fireplace loomed and smelly bedding was piled in a corner.

'What are we going to do about this?' Gower asked.

'We're a peaceful commune, not an army. There isn't anything we can do. They've put their locks on the doors now, so they can come and go as they choose.'

'You don't mean you're going to pay up, without a struggle?' Gower thought 'struggle' was a key word, political jargon that featured frequently in George's conversation.

'We're in retreat,' said George. 'Tomorrow we'll pack and go to another house. There's somewhere close. I know the people there, they'll make room for us.'

'Just a minute,' said Gower. 'By "us" you don't mean all of us in this house, do you?'

'No, I mean the people I brought here. The commune.

There wouldn't be enough space at the other place for everyone.'

Gower's face hardened. He enjoyed seeing George recoil. 'So you and your chums will bolt and those of us that are left will have to handle Mel. What was all that you were saying the other night about the essential solidarity of the underprivileged?'

George winced. 'Look, Richard,' he said, 'I don't like any of this. All right? I find empty houses and I get people in so they've got somewhere to stay. Until we get moved on. Moving on's part of the scene. Sometimes it's the police, sometimes it's the council and sometimes it's people like Mel and the men he works for. So what? We move on. Now, if you want some practical advice, from a man with a bit of experience – move on. This squat is finished.'

Bitterly Gower said: 'I look forward to hearing you announce that your solidarity speech was eyewash.'

'*They* know you can't fight Mel and his outfit. He's a psychopath. He killed a man for refusing . . .'

'I've heard.'

'. . . and he's carved people up. There's no room for negotiation.'

'There must be something we can do.'

George said ironically: 'Call the police?' He excused himself and went back upstairs.

The police came, but not for the reason George had joked about. They came that night and raided the house for drugs. Two of the commune were arrested and taken away. Murray, who was dead drunk and asleep, was the only one to escape being searched because his dog held the police at bay and, besides, he was a well-known local figure and they did not suspect him.

After they had gone and people stood around, humiliated and angry, they talked about the way the police had made a beeline for certain individuals. 'It was a tip-off,' said someone.

A name was sifted out as the conversation went along. One

of the squatters had been away for a day or two without explanation, could he have been picked up by the police and told them about the drugs in exchange for his own sins being overlooked?

Gower wanted to know why the police had taken no action about the house being squatted. Someone assured him they could not, there had been no complaint from the owner because the man did not know it was occupied. He had inherited the property from his mother, but he lived in West Germany and had taken no interest in it.

Next day Mel called for his money. Gower kept out of the way, wandering about the streets and sitting in public gardens until very late, and hoping that Mel would assume he had moved out. Several people had said they were going to sleep rough or move into other squats, rather than let Mel get his hooks into them. During the afternoon Gower met one of George's commune by chance and learned that they were not able to squeeze into the other squat, as George had intended, because an eviction was pending. George had decided they should pay Mel until they could find a new home.

As he stood on the doorstep that night, waiting for a face to peer down from the first floor and sanction the opening of the door, Gower heard a commotion inside the house. He feared another raid or worse, but the face that opened the door told him to come in, it was all right.

It did not sound all right. 'Come in here,' said the man on doorkeeper duty, meaning the downstairs front room. But Gower ran upstairs. The row was coming from the attic.

On the upper landing a few people were nervously smoking. Murray was crouched on the stairs with a lager can to his lips. His dog growled as Gower pushed by. Voices tried to deter him but he went up to the attic regardless.

Three men were beating up a youth. Gobs of blood flew through the air. The victim's face was indistinguishable through blood, and he was screaming: 'Don't kill me! Don't kill me!'

They were swearing they were going to.

Without thought for the consequences, Gower plunged into the mêlée, roaring at them to stop. He got an arm between the pulped face and someone's boot and he ignored the savagery of the blows that pounded until his unexpected authority established itself. It was not that he appealed to any lurking sense of decency in the attackers, purely that he astonished them by the bravery of his intervention and the reasonableness of his claims that the fight could be heard in the street and they would have a neighbour sending for the police.

He lingered until other people had dared to come up and the three assailants had gone. Then he left the beaten youth to be patched up by his friends. He locked himself in the bathroom and inspected his own damage. Despite the throbbing there was only a reddening that he knew would become massive bruising.

Minor though the incident was, it had far-reaching effects. Gower was imbued with a respect he had never commanded before. He was no longer an oddity who liked to be alone, thinking and occasionally writing in a green and gold notebook, or interrupting their debates with awkward questions. He was braver than most of them, as well as more intelligent and better educated.

Though the pain in his arm endured and stung him to secret tears, he had become a hero of sorts. A leader, anyway. He was allowed to decide what was to be done with the injured youth, whom he discovered to be the squatter suspected of tipping off the police about the drugs. Gower dispatched him to the casualty department of the hospital at Archway, with instructions to say he had been beaten up by unknown attackers outside a pub in Holloway.

Gower's view was sought on all the everyday matters that arose. People did things for him instead of overlooking him. The three attackers, friends of the pair arrested for possession of drugs, kept a respectful distance from him. He was both alarmed and flattered to hear that they had given a fanciful version of his exploit in the attic, crediting him with single-handedly battering each of them into submission.

He wrote their version into Richard Crane's diary with the comment: 'I've got a hold on them now. They'll do whatever I want, and what I want is to get Conroy.'

But the days flowed by and it was the rent collector, Mel, that Gower had to think about, not Conroy. Gower believed that if they all stood up to him, Mel was nothing. But he knew they could not all be trusted to do that. The teenagers, Joe and Rod, would copy anything Gower did himself, a half-dozen of the rest would too, but he could not rely on more. The stage where one person capitulated was, as George had once said in one of his dissertations on the class war, the stage where the principle was lost and they all became victims.

George and Gower had long talks about resisting Mel, or rather they started off with that but went tangentially into the socio-economic failures of the British political system.

George said: 'You see, Richard, Mel and his bosses are a result of the system. They're actually a manifestation of it.'

'Fine,' said Gower, goading. 'And you're committed to fighting the system. Right?'

He was half sure George and his group would be with him.

Half sure was not enough. He fretted and schemed, he counted his support and worried. Mel's next weekly visit was drawing nearer. Discussion erupted into violence as factions could not agree what to do. Those who were receiving state benefits were prepared to pay up, those with nothing felt themselves left exposed. Gower quelled the rows.

He went for a walk. The morning routine of cash machine, café and market was at an end. He had no money, a few pounds in his trouser pocket and that was all. He walked through residential streets, avoiding tantalizing restaurants, food shops and clothes shops. By now his dreams revolved around meals, and in his waking life he gratefully accepted what George and the commune provided, refusing to wonder how much of it was honestly or decently come by. No one else spared time to wonder.

The streets of Georgian houses had basements a passer-by could see into. They were kitchens with comfortable country-style pine furnishings, or they were dining rooms with lace tablecloths sweeping to the floor, or they were bedrooms with thick pile carpets and seductively plump duvets, or they were sitting rooms with rich fabrics.

The kitchens were most interesting, as unintentional guides to foodie fashion. Coffee-making machines, pasta-making machines, food processors, machines he could not name, and wine racks, everywhere wine racks. People were seldom in these kitchens. There were no women up to their elbows in panchions and bread-making, or reducing wine in small saucepans and clouds of steam, or pounding ingredients for the stuffing of ravioli. The people were elsewhere, at work, and the kitchens were for hurried evening meals although they came into their own at weekends when it was often the men he saw in them, and the front doors of the houses opened and shut, opened and shut, as giggling friends bearing wine bottles arrived for lunchtime parties that generally took place in the gardens. He lived in the midst of this world, and he lived a world away from it.

In a garden square he sat on the grass, nursing his painful arm and watching children playing near by. He drew off his jacket sleeve, rolled back his shirt. The arm was swollen and blackened, it ached the whole time and was agony to the touch. A woman stepped out of the shadow of a tree and drew the children away, sending a censorious look Gower's way.

I've had enough, he realized suddenly. *I've got the Richard Crane story. I won't learn any more by hanging out in the squat. Time to go home.*

And by home he meant also that it was time to go to a hospital and find out the true extent of the damage to his arm. Flinching, he got the arm back into the jacket sleeve, rose, and joined the path. The woman was moving down it, children toddling ahead of her, like geese before a goose girl. She saw him over her shoulder and frowned. Darting forward, she clutched at two of the children and called to the others. By the time Gower passed, the gaggle were close around her, safe from him.

He walked down Caledonian Road towards King's Cross. As he went, his idea of going to Fleet Street and the *Daily Post* faded because of the experience in the garden. He preferred to be cleaned up and to have his hair cut first. It was shaggy and the dark roots were a couple of inches long at least. Also, his hat had been mislaid during the weeks at the squat and his clothes and shoes were filthy and ragged. He did not wish to appear in the nation's media looking like a character from Fagin's kitchen.

Because of the zoning system, he could save a few coppers on the price of an Underground ticket by walking to King's Cross. Once there he could take a train to a stop close to David Gerrard's flat and wait outside until Gerrard came home from work.

It was quite a long walk to King's Cross, and on the way a better plan occurred to him. *Why don't I carry on up the road to Euston Station and collect the typescript and other things I left there, then I'll have something to show David?*

He invented the publicity as he walked along. Gerrard would organize press conferences to announce the wonderful new book about the iniquitous contrasts of London life, a story about a powerful character called Richard Crane and based on the author's research into the drab subculture of the homeless.

Then Gower invented Linda's reaction. She would be overwhelmed, thrilled to have him back, proud of the book and penitent about her deceit and blackmail. He would forgive her. They would buy a penthouse with a balcony over the river. He pictured them on that balcony, champagne glasses in their hands, planning lavish parties and extravagant holidays.

And he dreamed about their reconciliation, sweeter even than that tender coming together when she had traced him to Butlers. Imagining, his body responded to the very thought of her.

One of the first things, he decided, *when I get to Gerrard's flat, is to find out exactly how much money there is. Oh yes, and whether he was serious about that American paperback tour. Linda would enjoy coming on that.*

With a flicker of surprise, he realized he had not been interested enough to ask Gerrard which of his books was appearing in paperback for the American market. Then he thought about the money again. *I'm immediately going to make him transfer every penny of mine into my proper bank account.*

He kicked a beer can into a gutter. *And what's more, I'm not going to let him get away with claiming his ten per cent on the money he paid as blackmail.* Truculently he marched on, to end the adventure on his terms, to meet his fate.

The evening newspaper billboard outside King's Cross Station stopped him dead. Two words, and his future disintegrated. 'Gower Found.'

He dropped coins into the vendor's palm and took a paper. He was the front-page story. 'The body of the missing author John Gower has been washed up on a West Country beach five months after he disappeared. His widow, Mrs Linda Gower, now a presenter with TV PM, travelled to Devon this morning and identified the body. It is understood that clothes and a medallion were shown to Mrs Gower and she was able to confirm that they belonged to her husband. Mrs Gower told reporters: "This is what I've been dreading ever since John vanished." She appeared upset and was driven away in a police car.

The remainder recounted events surrounding Gower's disappearance, all that was new was a line from a police officer who said that a body might take months to come ashore.

Inserted in the text was a very small photograph of John Gower. And alongside it a big one of Linda, grim on her way from the mortuary.

19

Holly Chase's face was solemn beneath the perky braids of her Caribbean hairstyle. 'A body changes everything.'

Rain ducked as her temporary secretary misjudged the spray and doused Rain instead of the giant sweetheart plant on Rain's desk.

'Oops,' said Sylvia. She was not really Sylvia, but Rain called them all after Rosie's original stand-in. There had been too many of them for her to bother to get it right. They all stayed a week or two and then went. This one would have to go, she was no hand at the office gardening.

Rain rubbed her face with a paper tissue. 'I think you've twisted the nozzle the wrong way.'

'Oh, yes,' said Sylvia. And sprayed Holly at the adjoining desk.

Rain passed over the tissue for Holly to dab at her hair.

Rain said to Holly: 'A body brings my inquiry to an abrupt end, but it doesn't change the fact that David Gerrard hired a boat at Cadgwith and left it in a secluded creek the other side of the Lizard. It doesn't alter the way he behaved after the murder at Butlers, giving credence to local opinion that Brian Parsons was in Malta and difficult to contact when all along he had the telephone number of the Gozo farmhouse where Parsons was staying.' She gave a sigh that was almost a growl.

'About now,' she said, looking at her watch, 'a coroner in the West Country is recording an inquest verdict on John Gower. Gower will be officially dead and tomorrow the remains will be cremated. His friend, Rob Watson, is to scatter the ashes on the sea. Linda Gower asked him to do that. And that will be an end of it.'

Holly said. 'You'll never get the truth from Gerrard. Whatever he had to hide about that boat trip, he's hidden it for so long and so well, he won't let you winkle it out of him now.'

'He has the answers,' said Rain. 'He and Linda, they both know more about John Gower's fate than they're saying. I'm convinced of it.'

Holly mocked her certainty. 'Unless you contrive to get them into deep hypnosis, I don't see any way of tearing the facts from them. Whatever was attempted ended in tragedy. Perhaps it *was* an elaborate publicity stunt to begin with, and Gower drowned by accident. David Gerrard wouldn't have killed him because Gower was the goose that was going to lay the golden eggs. Whatever else we accuse Gerrard of, we can't say he's a fool.'

'No, not where money's concerned.'

Rain was equivocal about the end to her inquiry because it also meant an end to the threat to cause her a nasty accident. She had kept that to herself, rather than be pressured into dropping the investigation, but now that it was safely in the past tense she was tempted to tell Holly.

Before she could speak, her telephone rang. Marion Dudley, inviting Rain to dinner at the house she had looked after in Islington during the Dudleys' spring holiday in France. Marion said teasingly that she had interesting news about developments at the art gallery where she worked part-time, but would breathe not a word until they met. They talked only briefly because in the background was a crescendo of noise being caused by the Dudleys' dog, Fred.

'See you on Tuesday week,' said Marion. 'You won't forget?'

'I promise.'

'I'll tell all then. Oh, I'm so glad you can come, Rain. It's getting quite impossible to keep up with our friends. I seem to be either in the country, or else getting the French house into order, never in London. Do you think I shall turn completely into a gypsy?'

Rain said she rather thought not.

Sylvia had put the spray away and was tidying her desk.

This particular Sylvia was always tidying up. She said: 'Oh dear, I forgot to give you this, Rain.' This particular Sylvia was also absent-minded. She produced a sheet of paper with a message she had taken from a caller the previous day while Rain was out.

Rain did not recognize the name or the telephone number. She dialled and asked for Gerry. A man told her to hold on, then a female voice came on. This was Gerry.

'I'm ringing for Dawn,' said Gerry.

'Dawn?' Rain was having trouble disconnecting from Marion Dudley's milieu to that of the homeless stuffed into bed-and-breakfast hotels. 'Ah, yes, Dawn.'

Her mind was back in the single bedroom with the cot wedged in front of the wardrobe and no visitors allowed, with the dull-eyed mother and toddler, and a hotel owner in the background making his fortune out of unfortunates. Yes, Dawn.

Gerry said: 'She says to watch out for Drummond.'

'Who's he?'

'Sorry, she thought you knew. She was worried after she talked to you, scared you'd go to Drummond and she doesn't want him on to her.'

Rain was at a loss. She had encountered no Drummonds on the trail Alf Wilson had taken. 'I'd better talk to her again.'

'No, she doesn't want that. Like I said, she's worried. But I could meet you. Can you come over here lunchtime? Make it late, and be prepared to waste time. I might be busy.'

Rain said all right and took down an address. A public house. In the East End.

Gerry was a young woman who cleaned the pub in the morning and washed up at lunchtime. She had the chapped hands to prove it. Luckily, it was a quiet day. She and Rain talked in a passage outside the kitchen, Gerry wishing to avoid anybody in the bar seeing her with a journalist. It was one of those occasions that Rain's famous face was a hindrance.

'Drummond,' said Gerry, drying off suds on the damp apron she wore, 'was Dawn's brother-in-law, her husband's brother. When her old man went off, she and the baby moved in with Drummond and his girlfriend. It was supposed to be temporary, but it dragged on a while and the girlfriend got jealous of Dawn and Drummond being together so much. The girlfriend worked in a nightclub, see.'

Rain strove to look riveted by the Drummond ménage. What it had to do with Alf Wilson and her own inquiries she could not imagine.

Gerry said: 'Well, in the end the inevitable happened and then the girlfriend walked out. Dawn says she'd never have let him, only he was threatening he'd put her and the baby out if she didn't. So that's how she took up with Drummond and got to know something of what's going on.'

'I see.' She did not.

'He was involved in a racket, to do with housing. She'd heard there was an agency where you could go if you wanted somewhere to live and they'd find it for you. Of course, she was desperate to get away from him so she went to the agency and the girl there told her she'd have to bring a forty-pound registration fee and then her name and requirements would be put on a list and they'd find her somewhere.'

Gerry was wearing an expression that made Rain feel stupid that she could not grasp what was coming. Gerry said: 'It was daft really. She had to borrow the money from Drummond, lying that it was to buy stuff for the kid, and then when she went back to the office to see the girl, Drummond was there too. A manager or something, he was.'

Rain tried to fathom it. 'And he was cross because Dawn was looking for somewhere to go, so that she could get away from him?'

'No, he was mad she was going to spend his forty quid on it. He said to her: "Those lists we print, we just send them round to landlords, that's all. They won't get you a flat".'

'But that's illegal, to take money just for registering people.'

Gerry beamed. 'You've got it.'

'The Accommodation Agencies Act, I think it's called.'

'Drummond got fined. He was in it with two others, but they did a flit. I never heard whether they got caught in the end. Anyway, it gave Dawn a fright. She'd never crossed the law and she didn't want to start. That's when she walked out on him and told the council they had to find somewhere for her and Sharon. But Drummond, he reckoned she'd talked too much. Like I said, she's scared of him.'

'The names,' said Rain. 'What were the names of the other two men?'

Gerry said she could not remember.

Rain drove straight to Bayswater and parked near the hotel. She waited longer than an hour before Dawn and the toddler came listlessly up the street. Rain opened the car door. 'Get in, Dawn.'

A few streets away she parked again. 'Dawn, I want to hear the rest of what you told Alf Wilson.'

Dawn wriggled in her seat. 'I told you, everything I could remember.'

'You didn't tell me about Drummond. Did you tell Alf about him, and the agency fiddle?'

'Yes. I forgot when I was speaking to you. Then I couldn't remember whether I'd told you or not. That's why I asked Gerry to ring you for me.'

Rain only half believed this. She said: 'Where's Drummond now?'

'In London. He's always in London.'

'And what's he doing?'

Dawn hesitated. 'He works for somebody that runs squats. He goes around on a motorbike looking for likely houses, empty ones or ones where they can throw the squatters out and put new people in.'

'When did you see him?'

Dawn dithered some more, finally said sulkily that she had seen him in the last few days. 'He was drunk, he was showing off about a big house he'd found.'

'You're frightened of him?'

'He's all right, but sometimes . . . Well, he likes to think he's hard.'

So hard it had been necessary to warn Rain about him. Rain said: 'Does he know I've been asking about Alf Wilson and his research?'

'No,' said Dawn too quickly.

'Did he meet Alf Wilson?'

'No,' she said. Then: 'I don't know.' Then: 'He might have done.'

'One more question,' said Rain. 'What are the names of the two men he was involved with in the agency fraud?'

Dawn jiggled her daughter on her knee and pouted. At last the names came, barely audible. 'Shelbourn. Roy and Tony Shelbourn. Brothers.'

Before starting the engine, Rain reached for her bag, ripped apart an envelope containing a month's expenses from the *Daily Post* and held out the wad of notes. Dawn took them and buried them in her coat pocket. Neither spoke. Rain dropped Dawn and Sharon off near the hotel, telling Dawn to take care. She knew it was a waste of breath.

She believed Dawn had been seeing Drummond regularly and had recklessly told him about Rain's investigation. Rain shrugged and drove to Fleet Street.

She completed a story for the following day's paper and then checked on Shelbourns in the London telephone directory. There were two, but not with the initials Dawn had given her. In the library she found the court case in which Drummond had been sentenced but his accomplices were not named, only the spurious accommodation agency. Rain dared to hope for a file of the same name. She was lucky.

Inefficient filing had kept stories about the agency separate from the bulk of stories about exploitation of the homeless, therefore they had not been among those dug out by the original Sylvia when Rain's interest in Alf Wilson and his project had begun.

The agency fraud was bigger than Rain had supposed from Gerry's description. It had operated simultaneously in several parts of the country. The news stories were accounts of pathetic people, usually youngsters, who had been conned into handing over their money. Sometimes the youngsters had complained to the press or the authorities and sometimes the stories had come from landlords who wanted to draw attention to the fraud and thus warn people off. The names of the Shelbourn brothers did not appear in any of these stories, nor did Drummond's.

She could not approach the Shelbourns but Dawn had given her ample clues to Drummond's whereabouts. He liked to use a nightclub, near the river. It was not one of Rain's common haunts but she was willing to go there that night.

Just as she was leaving the office to go home, Holly came rapidly through from the newsroom to stop her. 'There's been drama at the Gower inquest, a clash of evidence and an outburst. Riley's running it on the front page tomorrow.'

As she spoke, they were hurrying towards the news editor's desk. Riley was on the telephone but, seeing Rain, he lifted a sheet of paper from one of his trays and offered it to her. She mimed her thanks.

The story had been filed by the newspaper's West Country reporter, an old and lazy individual who treated the job as a hobby to be fitted in around his gardening. Rumours abounded about his propensity to be spreading muck on his tomatoes while news was happening unattended. There had been moves to oust him, or at least shunt him on to the gardening column, but he was rooted in the job. Riley, on a short-tempered day, had once accused him of being otiose. The man mistakenly believed this to be a compliment, being too idle to look it up in the dictionary.

Rain ploughed through some dense sentences that it would be a subeditor's duty to rewrite, and then came to the drama.

Linda Gower had given her evidence of identification, based on clothing and a medallion found on the body, and she was treated with sympathetic courtesy by the coroner. A fisherman described how the body had come ashore at a South Devon cove on the morning tide and how he had summoned the police. The trouble began with the pathologist.

This pathologist was a young man eager to display his knowledge and the coroner was an old man who believed the less said about certain matters the better. Interrupting the pathologist to ask him to confine his evidence to a recital of a few salient facts leading to his conclusion about the cause of death, the coroner became embattled.

After each intervention, the pathologist resumed at the exact stage where he had left off. The jury heard the details of his examination of the corpse, and there was nothing the coroner could do to protect them.

They were obliged to learn that the hands and half a leg were missing, that the features of the face were obliterated due to damage caused after death, but that much of the body was preserved in an adipocerous condition. He gave out the details of adipocere like a student reading from a textbook: an effect of damp on a body that is immersed; the natural body fats solidify and form a white waxy substance; it adheres to bone and therefore retains the shape of the body; it forms slowly over a period of months as neutral body fats are hydrolysed into fatty acids and soap; once formed it remains stable for many years.

'The body I examined was a typical example of the adipocerous state in that the condition affected chiefly the chest wall and the limbs, although the face and the hands were, as I have said . . .'

'Yes, yes,' said the coroner testily. 'Perhaps you could move on to possible evidence of drowning.'

The pathologist saw his sentence to its end: '. . . the face and the hands were missing. There was no clear indication as to the cause of this mutilation.'

'Doctor, was there evidence of drowning?'

After more of the unpalatable facts of death, the pathologist addressed the evidence of drowning. 'Extracts of body tissues yielded diatoms. The presence of these microscopic algae, that are found in both sea water and fresh water, is a positive indication that the man was alive when he entered the water. Diatoms would have been swallowed and entered the bloodstream before death.'

The coroner latched on to this and attempted to force an end. 'Therefore, doctor, you reached the conclusion that the man met his death by drowning?'

'Yes, sir.'

'And were you able to form an opinion as to the length of time the body had been in the water?'

The short answer was no, but the pathologist gave the long one. This involved more textbook stuff about relative rates of decomposition in water versus dry conditions. The jury were nauseated. One man held a handkerchief to his nose.

After further ill-tempered prods from the coroner, the pathologist wound up his evidence and sat down. People in the room – police, officials, jury, witnesses, family and press – gave a collective sigh of relief as the contest, and their ordeal, ended.

The coroner called Rob Watson, to give evidence about John Gower's state of mind when he had asked to borrow the *Fleur* and to answer questions about Gower's competence as a sailor. Rob Watson was willing to be led the shortest route to a simple statement and was soon back in his seat.

A police officer followed him to the witness stand to detail reports of the *Fleur* being near the site of the *Charity* during the late afternoon and evening of the day Gower disappeared. The coroner was encouraging him to say that the evidence pointed to Gower having gone overboard from the *Fleur* off the Lizard, when the pathologist shocked everybody with a contradiction.

'No, sir,' he said. 'The evidence gathered at the post-mortem does not support that view.' He got to his feet while speaking, the gleam of the zealot in his eye.

The coroner stuttered and looked at the police officer who stared at the pathologist. The pathologist said: 'If I may make this point, sir, the diatoms discovered in the body tissues appear to be of a different variety from those located in the area where the *Fleur* was seen.'

Doubtless the coroner wanted to tell the tiresome man to sit down and be quiet, but a room full of people were avid for an explanation. The coroner invited the pathologist to return to the witness stand and resume giving evidence.

What it came down to was that there were over fifteen thousand species of diatoms and the young pathologist happened to know, as a result of reading up reports of examinations of other bodies found on that stretch of coast, that a particular type of diatom occurred there. This type had not been found in the body he had examined.

The man produced copies of the reports. The coroner skimmed them, sucked on his teeth and embarked on a series of questions about diatoms and their movements. The answers he received were scarcely scientific but the pathologist appeared to be hinting that the inquest ought properly to be adjourned until samples of water from the area where Gower was thought to have gone overboard could be examined.

At this point came the outburst. Linda Gower shouted hysterically and collapsed in noisy tears. Her solicitor and the coroner's officer failed to calm her, and her solicitor respectfully begged the coroner to allow the inquest to proceed to a speedy conclusion as his client had been under incalculable stress for a very long time and was demonstrably unable to withstand more.

The pathologist was courteously thanked by the coroner for his thoroughness and sent back to his seat. Linda Gower would not leave the room and her sobbing was a pitiful undercurrent as the coroner swiftly summed up and invited the jury to consider its verdict. Within a very few minutes he recorded a verdict of death by misadventure on John Gower.

Rain did not learn all this from the news story itself. She telephoned the reporter whose wife brought him in from the garden to describe the event in all the minutiae he and his shorthand notes could recapture. The full story deepened her conviction that the mystery about John Gower remained, and that Linda as well as David Gerrard was concealing some part of the truth.

The *Daily Post* front page next day was going to carry a three-column picture of 'tragic Linda Gower' leaving the courtroom with her solicitor. Inside would be a background feature, prepared in advance of the verdict and hauling together all the strands of the story. Then the file on John Gower would be laid to rest in the library.

'But the story ends with almost as many questions as we began with,' Rain grumbled to Holly as they walked across the foyer from the lift and faced the Fleet Street traffic.

Holly said: 'If you could have only one of them answered, what would it be?'

Rain cunningly said she would start with the one that arose last, in the hope that an honest answer to that would force an unravelling of the whole mystery. 'I'd like to know the significance of Linda Gower's outburst.'

For three nights Rain went to the nightclub, an accommodating barmaid promising to point out Drummond. On the third night he came. Rain had infiltrated herself into a group of acquaintances, but she had not enjoyed the evenings on the fringe of the jollity while watching out for the woman's hint. Seeing Drummond was a relief.

She had worked out a fancy cover story, about keeping watch for a missing heiress, the kind of flim-flammery a gossip columnist ought to be concerned with. When it came to it, she sensed that this would not do. Drummond had to be confronted head on.

As his woman companion headed for the cloakroom, Rain went to his table. She got quickly to the heart of it: had he known Alf Wilson, and did he know where the Shelbourn brothers were?

Drummond was supercilious. 'You want to put them in your column, do you? My, my they'll love that. Fame at last. Can I be in it too?'

She was grateful for the low lighting that prevented him seeing how her colour rose at his taunts. She tried again, coming at it in different ways, but Drummond did not want to talk, except to sneer at her impertinence in expecting him to.

She could have made him do it, she was actually very good at that, but she was not given time. The door to the cloakroom moved and the girlfriend was coming back, swaying on dagger-thin high heels. The look the woman gave Rain was one to kill. Getting closer and identifying her competition, the woman addressed Drummond instead of Rain: 'What's she want with you?'

Drummond switched on a lazy smile. 'She wants to know where she can see Roy and Tony.'

'Well, you'll need a telescope, won't you?' said the woman to Rain. 'They go up north for the weekend, don't they?' And she sat down, put an elbow on the table and made her long hair fall like a curtain between Rain and Drummond. Rain pulled a face at the woman's back view and returned to her own table.

It was time to go, but she did not want to step outside alone. For another three-quarters of an hour she joined in a party and when it broke up she wandered to her car surrounded by protective, happy, slightly drunken company. Locking the car door immediately she got in, she drove off. Was it her imagination that Drummond was standing in the shadows near the exit? She had seen him and the woman leave earlier. They had not stayed long after she spoke to him.

Rain yawned, wishing people who envied her the glamorous life of a coveted Fleet Street job understood what it was like to spend three abstemious evenings drinking mineral water alongside everybody's else's champagne in a second-rate nightclub and faking pleasure. And what for? Not for high-quality information from a criminal who might know about Alf Wilson's last days but for a vague remark from a jealous woman, a remark that might mean everything or nothing.

The stairs to her top-floor flat seemed further up than ever.

She was worn out with insincere smiling and desperate for sleep. There would be time enough in the morning to test the usefulness of the woman's remark.

Rain let herself into her flat, thankful for a warm secure base to return to, unlike the deprivation endured by Dawn and all those with nowhere to call home. She was going to make cocoa – an occasional comforter when she needed comforting – and she was going to set her alarm clock an hour later than usual.

Rain took two steps into the flat before it hit her. The flat had been ransacked. Furniture was overturned, papers from her desk were flung about, ornaments had been swept from resting places, walls stripped of pictures. At her feet lay the remains of the sinuous white vase she had bought in Antibes, the one Alf Wilson had admired on his sole visit to her home.

Through the blur of tears she surveyed the extent of the damage. Even the contents of the fridge were thrown to the floor. In lipstick on the bathroom mirror a hand had written: 'No more warnings. Next time, you're dead.'

Rain gripped the edge of the washbasin, nausea rising. Through the words she saw her own face, pale, the lipstick like streaks of blood over her.

Gulping she swung away. The police. Of course, she must ring the police. And, of course, they would not find anything to show who was to blame.

They would ask: 'Do you have any idea who could have done this, or why?' Because the door was not damaged and nothing had been taken.

And she would have to say yes, she could guess. And he had done it because she was asking too many questions.

Rain stood in the doorway to the sitting room, taut with anger, impotent. And also feeling very, very foolish.

That threat on the answering machine, it was because I was asking about Alf Wilson, not John Gower. If only I'd realized, I'd have been much more careful.

If only.

Then she knelt amidst the wreckage of her home and wept.

Her doorbell rang. Rain spoke into the entryphone, her voice thick and unnatural. Paul Wickham answered her. 'I saw your light. Can I come up?'

He did this from time to time, driving home late and spotting her light. By the time he was up the stairs she had dried her eyes, blown her nose and forced herself into a less self-pitying mood. She greeted him with sham formality, saying: 'Forgive the mess, I didn't know you were coming.'

Wickham looked from her fragile smile to the upheaval behind her. He assessed it with a glance. It had not been searching, it had been wrecking. He put his arms around her and held her tight not, thank heavens, saying that it did not matter and it would be all right, saying instead that it was dreadful but she would be able to cope with it.

Then he asked her when she had discovered it and whether she had called the police. She said she had just come in, and she said no.

She said: 'There's no point calling them. They'll never find out who did it. I'd better clear it up and do my best to forget it.'

'Your insurance company will be happier if you've reported it.'

She had forgotten that. 'All right, then. But in the morning.'

He moved further into the room, stepping over things. There was barely a clear space to walk. 'Is the bedroom the same?'

'Yes, kitchen and bathroom too.' Wildly she spun round and hurried, careless of what she trod on, to reach the french window.

'Oh no!' With her outside light on she could see the shrubs, wrenched out by the roots, the earth spilled from the tumbled tubs, the tangle of her ripped down clematis outside the door, the total destruction of the garden it had taken her years to create. She clamped hands to her face, too shocked for tears.

And she sensed Wickham close to her. Quietly he said: 'I think, Rain, you should tell me what this is all about.'

She did. They righted a couple of dining chairs and sat amid the debris while she poured out everything she knew or imagined about Alf Wilson and John Gower and David Gerrard. She ended, a shade defensively. 'I know you'll accuse me of guesswork, and think there's nothing behind it . . .'

He cut her off with a gesture at the turmoil around them. 'After this? Whoever did this got into the building and into the flat without difficulty or damage, and destroyed most of what you own. No, I'm not going to dismiss your theories. But I do think for your own safety you should stop investigating them yourself. You've had a telephoned threat, and now a break-in and a death threat. What do you suppose the people behind this might do next time?'

She wrapped her arms around herself for comfort. She did not actually promise him she would drop her inquiry, her words were too vague for that, but she did encourage him to hope she had been warned off.

'Tomorrow,' he said, 'ring the police and the insurance company and then go through the rooms and establish whether anything's been removed.'

'I'm going to make a start now.'

'No, you're coming home with me. You can't stay here.'

She demurred, saying lightning did not strike twice and the perpetrators would not be back. He insisted. She said there were friends near by she could go to. He said not at that time of night. She still demurred. He insisted. She gave in.

Somewhere in the chaos was her shoulder bag, dropped from her arm as she had come upon the calamity. They hunted for it, found it at last near the shattered contents of a shelf. Beside it lay the painting by Vanessa, Paul's ex-wife. Someone's knife had ripped through the canvas and the frame had been smashed. Paul pushed it aside with his foot, handed Rain her bag and followed her out of the flat.

In his car they listened to a radio news bulletin which is how Rain learned he had also endured a bad day. He flicked the radio off once it was over and played a tape. Sibelius. Soothing.

'Goad,' he said, knowing her mind was on the news story,

'has gone to ground. We ought to have netted some of his gang today but we let them escape. They were planning another raid and we thought we knew a great deal about it. But we were wrong. Weeks of surveillance, and we were wrong.'

He slowed at traffic lights. In a shop doorway a dark-coated figure crouched in a foetal position, its head on a white plastic bag of possessions.

Wickham continued to speak in the same measured way, concealing all the frustration and disappointment, embarrassment too, that the failure was causing him. 'We assumed they were going to raid a security depot on an industrial estate. And we had good reason because one of the handymen employed there was meeting them and passing on information. So we kept following them around and today they were joined by the pair we want for the warehouse job and we thought: this is it, this is where we catch the lot of them redhanded. But we didn't.'

The lights changed to green and he pulled away, finishing the story. 'We were positioned to close in as they left the security depot with the gold, but they didn't do that. Just after they entered the industrial estate, we lost sight of them. They raided a factory on the access road and by the time we realized they weren't coming to the depot, they had done the job and were away. We were, literally, looking the other way at the time.'

Rain asked whether they had all got away, and what was the explanation for the handyman's involvement.

Wickham gave a disbelieving laugh. 'He used to work at the factory, that's why he was helpful to them. We missed that. No, they didn't all run off. We've got the handyman answering some pertinent questions and we've caught two of Goad's small fry who will, if they run true to form, refuse to talk. And meanwhile there's an armed gang, who've already shot dead one man, on the loose in London.'

He sighed and reversed into a parking space near his flat. 'I was going to ask whether you had a nice quiet job for me on the *Daily Post*, but after what I've seen tonight I'm not sure I could handle the pressure.'

His flat was bigger than Rain's. Vanessa had needed a huge room for her painting although in the event she hated working from home and had rented a separate studio where she had gone to work each day. Since she had left him, he had switched the rooms round and now the big room was a sitting room and the small sitting room had become a spare bedroom.

Rain did not care for the flat, not because of its traces of Vanessa that were everywhere but because she was disturbed that two people who were deeply aware of visual things should have bothered so little to make it pleasing. It was Holly who had suggested that they had made nothing of their home because they could make nothing of their marriage.

Rain had often thought that if it were hers she would have cheered up that gloomy great room with a lively wallpaper of rich roses, added delicate touches like china fingerplates to the doors, stripped the painted fireplace in the hope that it was marble underneath, and if it turned out not to be, she would have replaced it with one that was. She would have hung swagged drapes to emphasize the attractive feature of the long window and . . . Well, everything that would transform it from a depressing room into one she looked forward to entering.

Rain entered the room. Gloomy, as always. And yet Paul was not conscious of it. He picked up his post from the table where the Filipino woman who cleaned the flat left it for him. There was only one envelope he wanted to open. Doing so, he dropped a carefully casual remark about the spare bed being already made up for visitors if she would like to use that room.

While she listened to answering machine messages and telephoned a colleague, she washed. The spare room was next to the bathroom. Afterwards she went in there, put her bag on a chair and sat on the green-covered single bed, thinking: *He's being no help at all, dammit. He's leaving it up to me. Whatever happens between us will be of my choosing.*

She heard the telephone call ending, footsteps along the

passage, the sound of the bathroom door. Then she rose, smoothed the green cover, and went to the other bedroom. She undressed and then lay in his bed, waiting for him to come and make love to her.

It was the nicest thing that had happened to either of them that day.

Afterwards she said to him: 'I wish I could find Goad for you, then we'd have more time for this.'

He said he preferred to find Goad himself. 'And for the wrong reasons. It would do my career no harm at all to put the Goad gang behind bars. Arrogance, you see, to imagine that I can do it when Goad's eluded better detectives for years. Ambition, yes. Vanity, no doubt. I want to catch them and I want it to be known I caught them. Pretty unworthy, wouldn't you say?'

Rain did not say. She went to sleep.

Next morning he left her early, telling her to sleep on. She did not but lay awake wondering to what extent she had let events push her into resuming her affair with Wickham. Those faltering reasons she had once offered him for not going on had been disregarded when circumstances had left her with an uncomplicated choice of this bed or that.

She sighed, rueful. *So much for me giving up recklessness, taking a solemn decision, needing a relationship based on serious commitment. Huh!*

Rain got out of bed, wandered through the rooms, seeking nothing in particular unless it were the truth about her night in Paul Wickham's bed. In her mind she tried out snippets of the conversation she felt obliged to have with him soon, to explain the thing away as the outcome of her hurt and his kindness.

The phrases were idiotic and impossible to speak without inferring that she rejected or undervalued him. Some attempts were so hilarious that she burst out laughing. She gave it up, as something to be thought about later. The words would come, if any needed to be said. It was her business never to be short of words.

Carrying a mug of coffee, Rain went into the bathroom

opting to bath rather than shower. *I'm delaying getting home to that mess*, she admitted. Unexpectedly, she was relaxed about what she would confront at Kington Square. The sting had been drawn.

She soaked herself for a long time, planning her telephone calls to police and insurance company, and also to a friend she hoped would be free to help her clear up. It was after eight when she dried herself, tossed the towel into a linen basket, walked naked out of the room and came face to face with a Filipino woman carrying a duster.

The police were sympathetic and efficient. The insurance company was efficient without the sympathy. Rain's friend who came to help was horrified and reduced to feebleness. Rain summoned reinforcements. By the end of the day bags of rubbish were lined up for disposal. Rain had written an arm's-length list of things to replace and she was planning shopping expeditions. The practical effort deflected her nicely from the underlying nastiness.

Holly called in after work. Rain was shovelling earth back into her tubs by then. 'This one might survive,' she told Holly, and they looked pleadingly at a replanted azalea, willing it to make the effort.

'Who,' demanded Holly, 'could have done all this?'

Earlier, when Rain had made her excuses for taking a day off, Holly had not been offered an answer to that question. In the garden Rain told her.

'Paul's right,' said Holly. 'You've got to drop this Wilson–Gower business. If you push on, you could be killed.'

Rain flung down a trowel. 'Alf Wilson *was* killed, I'm sure of it.'

Holly scratched her tourniquet-tight braids, before saying: 'As sure as somebody with no evidence can be?'

Hot, exhausted and confused Rain agreed. 'Yes, if you like. I don't have the kind of evidence Paul would need to bring a charge against anyone, but I'm not short of the other type. Alf was killed because he found out something during his research for his play, and I'm being threatened because I'm following in his footsteps. Not only might I discover what he unearthed, but I might also find proof that he was killed.'

Holly was extremely worried. 'Rain, I don't like the tense. You're talking as though you're going ahead with it.'

Rain sighed and went to stand at the end of the garden, looking over her parapet wall and into the great green mass of summer trees. Pigeons were moaning softly among the foliage.

'There's more,' she said after a minute or two. 'I couldn't know until the chaos was straightened but something was stolen last night.' She leaned with her back to the wall and watched Holly's face before going on. 'The draft of Alf Wilson's play was stolen.'

Holly's dark eyes widened momentarily then shrank to pinpoints of anxiety. She drew in her breath sharply.

Rain said: 'It was in a folder, with his notes and with my notes. They've all gone.'

'Then you must tell the police that too, and let them chase after Drummond and ask him about it.' Holly was bossy.

'Yes. I shall do that.'

Down below, in another garden, people were sitting around a table and eating and drinking. Their happiness rose, echoed against sun-baked walls. Holly remembered she had brought a bottle of wine.

'And these,' she said producing a pack of plastic beakers, 'in case you haven't any glasses left.'

'I haven't,' Rain admitted. 'But I know exactly which ones I'm going to buy as replacements. Marion Dudley has some I've always coveted and I'm going to buy some like those.'

'That's the spirit,' said Holly, pouring liquid sunlight into clear plastic.

In a while they put the bottle in the fridge and decided to head for Rain's favourite local restaurant and supper. 'You know,' said Holly, lamenting the ravaged sitting room, 'I used to envy you this flat. But not today.'

As they went downstairs, discussing the merits of the new

lock Rain had just had fitted, the street door opened and an elderly woman came in. Other people in the flats had denied letting anyone inside the previous evening and there was only this neighbour left to quiz.

The woman took a ridiculous time for it to dawn on her that there was anything amiss. 'Yes, Rain,' she said, 'a young man, well, young to me, that is. Older than you, I expect. He said he was from the *Daily Post*, one of your reporter colleagues. Apparently he had been ringing your bell for ten minutes and could not make you hear. He said you'd been having trouble with your entryphone. And as you were expecting him, I let him go up.' She blinked through pebble glasses first at Rain and then at Holly, before a nervous hand flew to her lips and she whispered: 'Oh dear, did I do wrong?'

And when answered with a pitying smile, she moaned: 'Oh dear, I was only trying to help.'

'Can you describe him?'

But the description was poor because the conversation had taken place over the woman's entryphone and she had only looked out of her door for a second to make sure he was safely inside after she had released the front door by her remote control.

'The voice, then,' Rain asked. 'What was that like?'

'Oh dear, Rain, I was sure he was from the paper. Well, he sounded educated. No accent.' And that was virtually all she had to say about him, except that, over and over, she was sorry and had believed she was helping.

As Rain and Holly extricated themselves, she added a question: 'Was much stolen?'

'Very little,' said Rain.

The woman brightened. 'Oh good, that's all right then.'

'If she only knew,' breathed Holly.

Inexplicably the restaurant had closed for renovations. Rain exclaimed, to the surprise of passers-by, that she could not take any more. 'My whole world is collapsing. All the anchor points are being swept away. Now even this place has let me down.'

Holly dragged her away, Rain looking backwards at the CLOSED sign as she went, unwilling to accept what her eyes told her. Holly said: 'Don't worry, there are plenty of other places for supper.'

'That's beside the point,' Rain wailed. 'I like that place, I'm used to it, and I want to go there.'

'You must have been an awful child,' said Holly, laughing.

The pub they went to was more fashionable and busier. Among the first people they recognized in there was David Gerrard.

'Who's the po-faced man with him?' Holly whispered.

'One of his authors. Not a famous one. Can't remember the name.'

Gerrard was seated where it was impossible to avoid him. Rain greeted him as though there had never been any trouble between them, no complaint to the editor about the juxta-posed stories and no paranoid invention that she had set reporters to trail him.

'David, I didn't know this was one of your haunts.' Rain switched her smile to acknowledge the author.

'One prefers to flaunt rather than haunt, Rain. And this isn't a bad location for a spot of flaunting.' He waved a hand to indicate the kind of people available to admire any flaunting that was going on. Media people and moneyed people, the well-connected and the influential.

He said: 'Do you know Gordon? He writes very fat novels under female pseudonyms, sells a great many copies and is never reviewed. Wouldn't you say that puts Fleet Street rather in its place?'

Rain held out a hand to Gordon and said hello. Across the room she could see Holly winding her way to the bar. She said to Gerrard: 'I've never been sure what Fleet Street's place is.'

For the benefit of his author, Gerrard persisted in his banter with Rain, each word underlining the friendly familiarity he wanted the world to know he enjoyed with her. None of this was new, for years it had entertained her that he was compelled to do it.

Quite unexpectedly she felt irritated by it. She pulled up a chair and made all the motions of settling in for a long and companionable chat. 'Your agent,' she said to Gordon, who had remained impassive throughout, 'is a man of wide interests. Did you know that? Well, he is. Tell us about your boating adventures, David.'

Gerrard's face was extraordinary. The mouth kept smiling but the eyes registered alarm. He did not speak.

Rain said: 'You know, David, your week boating around the Cornish coast. You can't have forgotten it. Wasn't it at the time that . . .'

'Look,' said Gerrard, leaping to his feet and toppling his chair. 'I'm sorry, but we really have to leave now.' He appealed to Gordon.

But instead of seeing the agent's supplication, Gordon was comparing his wrist-watch with the clock on the wall. 'Not yet, David,' he said. 'We ought to give them a bit longer.'

A woman behind Gerrard set his chair back on its feet. He was ignorant of her action. He repeated to Gordon that they must leave. Gordon repeated his refusal.

It seemed Gordon was expecting to meet two women from a publishing house, and later to be taken to dinner by Gerrard. He was not to be deterred. While Gerrard loomed over him, a bulky man on the verge of panic, Gordon was both literally and figuratively unmoved.

Rain spoke to Gordon. 'I'll say this, it surprised me that David had taken up boating. I'd always seen him as a sedentary townie.'

Gordon might have murmured agreement at this, but there was other noise and it was hard to tell. Recklessly, Rain plunged on. 'And the Cornish coast is demanding, not at all like pottering up the Thames to Boulter's Lock on a Sunday afternoon. Yet David was sufficiently intrepid to set out alone, in an eggshell of a boat with a faulty engine and . . .'

Gerrard dropped back into his chair, denying everything, speaking loudly to drown whatever else Rain had to say. 'This is all nonsense. Life is adequately rich and varied without

414

having to take up boating. And especially not boating in Cornwall. I can't remember the last time I was on board a boat.'

She said: 'Probably April the – '

Gerrard said: 'And I would be neither competent nor rash enough to set forth single-handed into the sea.'

Rain said: 'Who was with you, then, David?'

He forced a laugh, telling Gordon: 'One must take care never to get up to one half of the things of which Fleet Street accuses one.'

Rain repeated: 'Who was it, David?'

His panic had been muted to anger. Anger was boiling to fury. He tried to mask it, saying: 'Rain this is sheer invention, a joke that I fear has miserably failed to amuse.'

She said: 'Shall I make a stab at a name?'

Gerrard babbled, to shut her up.

She found a gap. 'Shall I say John Gower?'

Holly arrived and stood behind Gerrard with two glasses in her hands. She saw the group around the table freeze, Rain leaning forward inquiringly with a sweet and not-to-be-trusted smile on her face, and she saw the hairs rampant on David Gerrard's neck. Gordon, stirred to life at last, looked from Rain to Gerrard and then said: 'Wasn't Gower the fellow who drowned?'

'Quite,' said Rain.

Gerrard was on his feet again, the chair was nudged off balance again. Pivoting, he caught Holly a glancing blow with his arm. One of the glasses was knocked from her hand and smashed on the falling chair. Gerrard charged through the crowd and into the street, people clearing a space for him rather than be mown down.

Gordon half rose to gape after the departing figure. He turned back to Rain in anguish. 'He's gone!'

'Yes.' She was tight-lipped.

Gordon swallowed, resumed his normal state of passivity and asked: 'Would you recognize Dulcie Martin and Jonquil

Bray of Pegwoods if they came in? It would be such a shame if I weren't to meet them after all.'

'Yes,' she said. 'I'll introduce you.'

They came. She did.

'We saw David Gerrard across the street, striding along like a great bear,' said Dulcie Martin, puzzled.

'He looked as though he were being pursued by a swarm of invisible bees,' said Jonquil Bray, equally baffled.

'No, not bees,' said Rain Morgan. 'Only by questions he can't shake off.'

Stream Cottage was in Hardy country. So was the hotel where Rain and Wickham spent a weekend. John Gower was frequently on the fringe of her thoughts.

Goad and his gang were more obviously taking Wickham's attention. 'I'll be glad to forget them for a couple of days,' he said as they drove westwards from London early on the Saturday morning.

She smiled a knowing smile. He would not be able to. The search for the killers of the security guard at the warehouse dominated his life. As soon as they reached the hotel he was on the telephone to his office.

Rain sat on the lawn alone with a glass of wine and calculated the odds on being forced back to London before their weekend was more than a few hours old. The odds were not in her favour.

She and Wickham had stayed in this hotel before, and been happy there. Hardy, in his days as an architect, had worked on the house, although there was nothing that could be confidently pointed out as his contribution. She suspected he had been better at poetry and novels anyway.

A butterfly settled on the edge of her table, so still was she. Its wings had lost the clear brightness of youth and their outline was no longer crisp. Damaged by life, it would die before winter. Unknowing, it floated away, an orange speck becoming a black one above a blue swimming pool. And then it was gone.

Rain took another mouthful of wine, noting how the sun had warmed it and released its perfume. An elderly couple walked distantly beside a hedge. A car hissed along the village road. Nothing else was happening, except that in one of the pretty bedrooms with bamboo furniture and flowery fabrics, Wickham was on the telephone deciding whether to spoil it.

She watched the elderly couple through half-closed eyes. *What would it be like to be half of an elderly couple? Will I ever know?*

She closed her eyes completely, seeing instead the red glow of sun on her eyelids. Of course, she had never said to Wickham any of those foolish things to explain away her choice of his bed instead of the spare room. She had come not to believe in any of them.

Commitment? No, not that either. She could not offer him, nor offer herself, that. She would like to be the kind of person who could do so, for whom loving was long-term, who would be nourished by marriage. She was sure she was not.

Recovered from the débâcle of the four years with Oliver West in her flat, she had not after all opted for seriousness and solemn intent. Her nature had denied her. It was enough for her to be happy in the short term, she could not face up to anything other.

If Wickham had asked her whether she had found the commitment that had kept her from his bed for months, she would have given him a true answer. But, knowing the truth, he did not ask.

She could not answer all of her own questions, or settle the doubts that sprang at her in unguarded moments. At a recent art exhibition with her friend, Jane, she had lingered by the squared-off orderliness of brownish Dutch interiors, liking their assurance, the steadiness of the figures depicted in those rooms where shadows were warm and not threatening.

Jane had dismissed them with a remark: 'Studies in perspective, and dingy. Perhaps if they were cleaned up a bit . . .'

Rain had echoed the phrase in her head. *Studies in perspective.* Yes, paintings were that all right. A choice of viewing on any given day offered a perspective on her own feelings: the frothy beauty of Impressionists for her lighter moods, the challenge of Surrealism when she was feeling strong, and the contained solidity of Dutch interiors when her life was a mess. As her notebook doodles varied from flowers skipping across the page during her happy times, to complicated rectangular structures when she was tense, so her feeling for paintings changed.

And it was in this Dutch mood that she had taken up again with Wickham. Did this mean she found in him the protection she currently needed? Had she always chosen her men to meet temporary needs? Would she need to escape from the relationship once the other areas of her life were straightened and she was fit for Surrealism and Impressionists again? Would he care much if she did? How much did he care for her anyway? In her heart the questions multiplied, unanswered.

For encouragement, she repeatedly asked herself, sitting there in the sun, a question that had nothing to do with her past or her future. 'Am I happy *now*?' And the answer was always yes.

When Rain lazily opened her eyes again, Wickham was striding towards her. He kept her in suspense, giving nothing away by his expression, only when he was sitting opposite her admitting that his colleagues had persuaded him he was surplus to requirements and should stay in Evershot and enjoy himself.

They strolled through the street, on raised pavements outside bow-windowed houses of yellow and grey stone. The last time they had been there they had poked around in the Victorian church looking for an ancient brass the guidebooks considered worth a mention. He appreciated Victorian, she did not.

This time they went down the hill instead, to watch the River Frome gurgle and set forth on its journey to Poole harbour. There was nothing more demanding for them to do. They both appreciated that.

And so the afternoon was spun out, in woody shade and sunlight, talking and relishing time squandered in a way that was too rare in both their lives. When they went back across the lawn to the hotel, a breeze caught the cascading notes of Schubert from an open window.

Rain said gravely: 'I used not to believe in perfection.'

He kissed her lightly on the mouth. They went indoors.

The shot that killed the constable was fired at two in the morning and at close range. Wickham was informed at six. Perfection had been short-lived.

The telephone, on Rain's side of the bed, tore into her dreams. She woke to find him leaning over her, not this time for the pleasure of closeness but because her body was an obstacle between him and his work. He lifted the receiver, put an end to the electronic warble. Rain feigned sleep, listening to his words, his indrawn breath, his terse assurance that he would return to London straight away.

As he replaced the receiver she opened her eyes. The previous night she had cultivated a superstition that if she slept on the side by the telephone there would be no calls for him. But the joke she was going to make about having got the spell wrong died unspoken as she saw his face.

He did not linger, he was out of bed and on his way to the bathroom while she was registering his shock. After that she felt uselessly in the way.

Although it was she who organized the coffee and rolls that were sent to their room so they could snatch at them while packing, and she who paid the bill while he telephoned London, she felt herself unnecessary to him, excluded. He was not seeing her. She caught mild surprise on his face when she asked the occasional question, not that they were idiotic questions but his mind was engaged elsewhere and he had forgotten her.

His effort at kindness was clumsy. 'You needn't come,' he said. 'It's a lovely day, why don't you get the train up this evening?'

Rain picked up her shoulder bag and walked outside. Grass glistened, there was the breath of dew on the green roof of his car.

Casually she said: 'I might as well come now.' She could not face the awful emptiness of abandonment.

She drove the first part of the way, loving the smooth power of his car after the quirkiness of her little red runabout. The radio news in the hotel room had told her about the shooting but Wickham had told her nothing. He put the car radio on very low, ready to turn it up when the next bulletin came.

As they swished away through oversleeping Sunday lanes, she said: 'Before you tell me about it, I'll tell you something. It wouldn't have made a scrap of difference if you'd been there.'

He did not reply, but it was apparent he did not agree either. In a minute he turned up the radio and they heard again the formula of words that equally revealed and concealed tragedy.

'A policeman was shot dead in London last night during the hunt for an armed gang. Detective Constable Roger Fleet was one of a team of police officers who were searching an area of north London. A police spokesman said this morning that Constable Fleet disturbed a man at lock-up garages near King's Cross Railway Station. The officer died shortly afterwards. A major search is under way to trace his killer who escaped in a van after the shooting.'

Rain switched the radio off. She wanted to talk. 'What was Roger Fleet like?'

Some things, surely, he could tell her.

He said: 'Single. Twenty-three. A Londoner who knew his London.'

He paused so long she thought that was all she was going to be given. But as she started to speak, he began again. 'He was the keen type. Impetuous. Always wanted to be a policeman, ever since he was a kid. And he was sure he was going to be a good one.'

There was a hint in the way he spoke the last words that made her say: 'But you weren't so sure?'

'He was an accident going somewhere to happen. Bloody dangerous, but unfortunately not everyone thought so.' He swivelled to look at her. 'You were wrong. You can't tell me anything about what happened last night. If I'd been there, Roger Fleet would have been alive today. I'd have had him recklessly counting paperclips, not charging into gunfire.'

She approached a roundabout, changed down, let a massive Continental juggernaut go by and pulled on to the roundabout. The chalk downs were curved seductively, the road ahead empty for a clear run home. To murder.

He said: 'I didn't want Roger Fleet on the Goad case, he was dumped on me.'

'Paul, you can't be there all the time. This Goad thing has gone on for months, you said yourself this was the first weekend you've taken off.'

The conversation, *any* conversation, was irksome to him now. She said something else. He snapped that it was the stupidity that appalled him, that plans had been overturned and someone had given Roger Fleet his head, with the result that Fleet was dead and still no one had been arrested, either for that killing or the one at the warehouse.

She allowed him the last bitter quiet words on the subject. 'Roger Fleet was always playing the hero, by lunchtime the press will have made him one.'

The road dipped and swayed, a sprinkling of traffic joined them on the route to London. Rain tried out some cheerful remarks about the beauties of Hardy country, adding that as far as Hardy himself went she found the work too dark. 'All that stuff about the seed of destruction deep inside people, much too bleak.'

Wickham replied that he experienced that side of human nature all the time.

She said: 'John Gower lived in Hardy country. At Stream Cottage, in a village over that way.' She lifted a hand from the steering wheel, waggled it towards the south. 'I wonder whether he read Hardy.'

'They didn't write about the same kinds of things. You're not proposing a Hardy influence on Gower's novels, are you?'

'Oh, no. Gower was more positive. He believed people could change their lives if they didn't like them. And things had gone so badly wrong in his own life – his career in the doldrums, his wife running off – I suspect he might have been trying to change it.'

Wickham raised an ironic eyebrow. 'And he died. There you are then. That rather proves Hardy's case, doesn't it?'

She tutted and said she had not meant to do that but he was laughing at her, not listening to her protestations. Then he was teasing her about her obsession with Gower. 'Now that we know he's finished with this world, it's only fair for Fleet Street to finish with him too.'

Despite her intentions, she was growing passionate. 'How, when the questions are increasing instead of diminishing? Look what happened at the inquest. When the pathologist was arguing that the body might not have drowned near the *Fleur*, the widow had hysterics and the inquest was wrapped up quickly. All we know is that the only professional who considered the point decided the body did not come from the area everyone had assumed it came from.'

Wickham was amused by her frustration. 'If you think Linda Gower staged that scene to distract attention from a quibble about the exact place where her husband fell in, why don't you ask her? You know her.'

'Yes, but . . .'

He completed her sentence. '. . . but it's a damn silly question.'

'No sillier than many I've asked.' She moved out to pass a van with a canoe on its roof rack. Then she adopted a comically patient voice as she said: 'If those diatoms mean anything, it was either that John Gower did not drown from the *Fleur* or else that the body they found was not his. If it was Gower's, then we don't know where he was between leaving the *Fleur* and being washed up five months later in the next county. And if it wasn't, then we are entitled to wonder about the identification, and about the outburst that effectively stopped the questions surfacing at the inquest.'

Wickham ruffled her hair affectionately. 'You certainly put your faith in those diatoms.'

'I spoke to the pathologist. He was very persuasive.'

'Pity he made an ass of himself at the inquest and upset the coroner.'

Rain excused the man. 'He's new at it, too young and too keen and he made a mess of it.' This echoed the earlier conversation about Roger Fleet. Not wishing to resurrect that topic yet, she hurried on. 'He's learned his lesson. Next time he has something important to say, he'll say it to the police before the inquest and not try to make a name for himself by wrong-footing everybody in public.'

There was a pause while Wickham thought about the implications of it having been the wrong body. 'Linda Gower could have made an honest mistake. She needn't be culpable.'

'The ashes have been scattered over the sea. Whoever that really was, there's nothing left of him now.'

He gave her a sidelong glance to see whether she was joking. It was plain she was not. He shrugged, thinking that a preoccupation with John Gower's fate was not dangerous. Had she been harping on Alf Wilson, it would have been serious.

He drove for the latter part of the journey, Rain regretting the increasing pressure of traffic, the way the countryside was engulfed by brick and tarmac as the capital drew nearer. Usually she found London stimulating but her weekend of Dorset greenery had been too brief and she resented the early return. Besides, she had turned down all other invitations for the weekend and what was left of it promised to be a dull affair.

The recognition, at first gloomy, cheered her. She would not have to fake sociability. Her telephone would not ring because her friends believed she was away, and she would enjoy the solitary pleasures of reading and letter writing. Yes, she meant to make the most of her enforced solitude.

She took a taxi the final part of the way home, there being no point in asking Wickham to go out of his way to drop her off. He vanished before she had finished giving the driver directions and entered the cab. The driver was the chatty type. He told her about the weather, and about the roads being more potholed than in living memory because of the cut in expenditure on maintenance and how much harder this made his job. And he told her what a terrible thing it was, that young policeman being shot.

'They want to bring back hanging,' he said.

She made a noncommittal grunt, having long ago learned the futility of argument with cab drivers. He yelped with ironic laughter and said: 'Of course, they've got to catch them first! They don't seem much good at that, do they? Look at this fellow, Goad. They can't get their hands on him. He's the Mastermind, he is. Head of all the crimes in London. I read it in the paper . . .'

The trees of Kington Square came in sight, and she already had her cash in her hand, poised to escape.

Within the hour Holly Chase was on the telephone, having guessed the shooting would have brought Wickham back to town. 'Hi! I'm ringing to commiserate about the ruined weekend and to offer you lunch. A barbecue in the garden and a few friends. What do you say?'

Rain said yes.

'Come early,' said Holly, who had to be in the office by late afternoon.

'Anything new for tomorrow's column?'

'Yes. One of our sneaks at the BBC rang me this morning. Guess what? Linda Gower is going to marry her producer.'

BOOK FOUR

Heroes

20

John Gower did not read the Rain Morgan column's story about his wife's plans to remarry. Neither did he read the reports of his inquest. No newspapers came to the squatted house, only fat property magazines crammed with photographs of stylish interiors in houses and flats for sale at exorbitant prices.

One of the squatters had a radio but it was permanently tuned to Capital Radio and Gower received only the constant thrum of music. The other source of news, the television set owned by the evil-smelling Murray, had been stolen.

Murray appealed to Gower, as a power in the squat, to bring the thief to book, but nobody confessed and there were any number of suspects who might have wanted to sell it for the few pounds it would raise. Gower's own unvoiced opinion was that Joe and his dimmer-witted companion Rod, who had once had the run of the house to themselves and resented the company forced on them, had made off with the set.

There had been a spate of thefts, including some things from his own bag. He did not make a fuss about it because it did not suit him to seem anybody's victim. Especially not Rod's or Joe's. He was going to use them. In fact, they had already been useful. Apart from stealing *from* him they eagerly demonstrated their loyalty by stealing *for* him. A mere hint about the green and gold notebook being full had resulted in a fresh book appearing in his bag.

Neither had Rod lost the knack for obtaining custard cream biscuits and other odds and ends to eke out their meals. Joe continued to object to the fare. 'Hot Rod strikes again! I've told you I don't like custard creams. Can't you bring Bourbons, or those squashed fly things?'

'It's what's to hand, isn't it?'

'Gawd!' said Joe. 'I wish that Paki would rearrange his shop.'

Whenever Mel, the murderous rent collector, was due to pay a call Gower went into hiding, sometimes no further than the garden shed. Since the water supply to the house had been reconnected, making the garden standpipe superfluous, no one troubled to go down the garden.

He had other reasons for wanting to spend time alone. Writing the diary was one, examining his painful arm another. The kicks had left it dark and puffy and it throbbed without pause. Only in the relative security of the shed did he dare strip off the jacket and shirt and examine it.

One sultry afternoon he crouched in the shed and wrote that Richard Crane had suffered the ultimate betrayal at the hands of Julia. She had hired someone to kill him. In this he saw collusion with the despicable Conroy who had double-crossed him in business and also over Julia. In a searing passage, Crane recorded his determination to kill them both. Conroy was easier to reach, he would do for him first. Then it would be Julia's turn.

He stuffed the diary back in his bag, pulled on his jacket and left the shed. Vegetation that had been high and rising was past its peak and the garden was yellowish. Bees and cats found it pleasant and once he saw a lean brown toad, but the best was over. Scaly misshapen fruit hung from the apple tree. Roses flowered, but the flowers were incomplete because the buds had been entered by creeping things and destroyed from within. Everywhere plants fought and strangled each other. Where there had been untamed beauty, there was now corruption.

Gower brushed poppy seeds from a trouser leg and walked back to the house, specks of withering leaves or seeds of lovage and lupins attaching themselves to him until he arrived at the back door fairly speckled. He stamped about by the back step, rubbing the flecks away.

An anxious face beneath a cowboy hat appeared through

the hole in the back door. Originally there had been glass, then it had been secured with stout boarding, but in one noisy incident the door had been broken in and no one had fixed it.

Fright disappeared from the face. 'It's you, Richard,' said Cowboy. 'I thought it was Conlon. Gave me a scare, that did.'

Gower gaped at him. *He thought I was Conroy?*

He said aloud: 'You thought I was *who*?' His voice was involuntarily high, excited.

'The rent collector. There was a message to say he's coming today.'

'Mel?'

'Yeah. Mel Conlon. That's his name.'

So that was it, the resolution of a problem that had been nagging at him. Richard Crane had been in the house for weeks, knowing he was close to Conroy but not making contact, swearing vengeance but not taking it. Yet his instinct had been right. Conroy was to be found there, nowhere else. Crane's fault had been to miss the disguise but at last Conroy had been delivered to him. Conroy could not know that, he would think he was protected by the slight alteration of his own name (and how often people chose pseudonyms very like their own names, fearing to part entirely with their identities).

Gower went indoors, evolving a plan. There was no one else there, the man who had admitted him being the guard for the day. George, the polite politico who led the first wave of squatters, had insisted it was legally necessary to maintain a presence at the house if they were to avoid eviction. Gower had used his own influence to reinforce that.

He sent Cowboy to keep watch at the front upstairs window, and then prowled the house scheming. After a time he discovered one of the things he was looking for. It was concealed in a lavatory cistern. As he lifted it out, it dripped. He wiped the floor, to prevent the owner knowing it had been disturbed. Then he carried it to the downstairs front room and, in the near dark created by the boarded window, he hid the thing in the chimney above the marble fireplace. Checking that there was no bulb in the heavy brass light fitting in the centre of the ceiling, he closed the door and went upstairs.

He asked Cowboy what time the rent collector was due. Cowboy said: 'He's late. We heard he was coming early because he realized some people have been staying out in the evening to dodge him.' Gower felt himself included in this.

He said: 'Some people don't have any money to give him.'

'There are ways, Richard. Everybody's got ways of getting it. I mean, you can't exist without any, so you're entitled to go and get it.'

Cowboy's way was busking. Unoriginal – there were several other men with cowboy hats singing country and western songs in the streets round about, including the smarter man Gower had seen regularly drinking coffee in the Dôme. Cowboy busked at the bottom of escalators on the Underground. His singing was terrible and his guitar playing was terrible. He did not earn much.

Gower sent him to make a cup of tea. The milk and the tea were not Gower's but what he wanted people allowed him. He liked seeing Cowboy spring into action at his whim.

Will he be the one to help? He might. Somebody will have to. But it ought to be Rod or Joe, I have the measure of them.

While the kettle in the first-floor kitchen hissed, Gower ran downstairs and paced from the front room to the back door. About fifteen normal-sized steps. He calculated the distance from the back door to the shed. Perhaps a further forty. A long way. Probably too far.

He turned to walk back down the passage, automatically stepping over the creaking, uneven floorboard. A few steps on, he stopped and looked back, as the state of the floor assumed a fresh significance.

With his fingernails, he peeled back the edges of decrepit linoleum. Then, using a rusted cooking utensil from the wall of the ground-floor kitchen, he jabbed at the crumbling wood until he could reach down into the gap below. Eighteen inches, or thereabouts.

Steps at the front of the house and steps at the back. A good space underneath, and if I'm lucky . . . I won't need help, after all.

He unscrewed a light bulb from its socket, inserted it in the brass fitting in the front room and explored. Finding what he hoped for, he returned the light bulb to its usual place and sauntered into the upstairs kitchen where Cowboy had his tea ready.

Mel Conlon did not come. The change of time had been either an ill-founded rumour or else a deliberate piece of harassment. Opinions divided. Gower did not regret the delay. It offered him the opportunity to sound out George once more about means of ending the extortion.

George continued to favour paying up until a safer berth could be found. Gower said he had endured enough of it and was going to take Mel on. Mindful of Gower's alleged attack on the pair beating up the youth believed to have inspired the police raid, George advised caution.

Gower said: 'I want everybody out of this house when he comes round next, everybody except me. It's time he and his bosses learned they can't intimidate us.'

George coughed politely and said: 'Unfortunately, they do.'

'Not me. Not any longer. You take your crowd and look for another squat or something, anything to keep them away. I'll meet you in the evening, in the gardens in Thornhill Square, and tell you when it's safe to come back.'

He brushed aside George's misgivings and ended with the man's consent. George went so far as to make a speech to the other squatters who were not part of his original contingent, telling them about the rent strike and insisting on their solidarity.

'It's part of the struggle,' George said. 'These parasites are a manifestation of the capitalist system, and we've got to struggle against them.'

Two days later they got word that Mel Conlon was on his way. The house emptied. The rent collector had a great number of properties to visit and word went round when he arrived in an area. If he was reported east of Essex Road, where he had a handful of houses, he would be in Barnsbury not much later.

Gower locked the front door behind the drunken Murray and his dog, the last of the tribe to clear out. He fanned the air in the passage. Murray and the dog were equally disgusting.

Then Gower took up position at the first-floor window and awaited the rent collector. Mel came on a very powerful motorcycle, ideal for snaking through city traffic and disappearing at speed. Gower watched him, leather-clad, bullet head encased in shiny black plastic, astride the great metal machine. The power of the one was indistinguishable from the power of the other.

Gower let him ring twice before he opened the door. Mel pushed inside without a word. He tore off his helmet and gloves, looking beyond Gower, anticipating the cowed figures who usually waited to pay him to go away and leave them in peace.

Gower said: 'There's nobody here.'

Mel stared at him, his florid face uncertain. He made an open-mouthed grunt.

Gower said: 'In here.' He pushed the door of the front room and Mel, bemused by authority where he expected cringing, stepped into the room. Gower closed the door. There was only the sound of Mel's leathers creaking, the chains decorating them jingling as he rubbed his eyes.

In the time between seeing Mel arrive and opening the front door to him, Gower had waited in the darkness of this room to get his eyes accustomed to the lack of light. For Mel, coming in from the sunny street, the effect was extreme.

Gower said: 'They've asked me to speak to you, on their behalf.'

'All I've come for is the money,' said Mel. 'I'm not interested in talking about it.'

'You'd better hear this. Sit down, Mel.'

Caught unawares by the transference of initiative, Mel sat. There was only one chair in the room, angled away from the fireplace. Gower had put it there. He affected to lean on the marble mantelpiece as he said they wanted Mel to take a message to his bosses. But although his words were unhurried, his speed was lightning.

From the fireplace he snatched up an iron bar and smashed Mel on the back of the head. Mel and the chair collapsed. Gower stood above him, breath tearing at his throat, waiting for Mel to rise, prepared to whack him again, and as many more times as it took.

Richard Crane was poised above Conroy's body. He had outwitted him, lured him, dispatched him with one blow, and put an end to treachery. Crane steadied himself. The matter was not finished. The harder part was to come. He had to conceal the body and destroy the evidence of death.

Gower's fingers gradually relaxed. Outside a car pulled out of a neighbouring garage and children jabbered before jumping into it and being driven off with much slamming of car doors. Pigeons were calling in trees. Inside, nothing disturbed the silence but Gower's breath and the soft sounds of his clothes as he straightened.

Quickly he felt along the mantelpiece to where he had left a light bulb in readiness. He lifted the chair, climbed on it to reach the socket. With total equanimity he looked down on the face of Mel Conlon.

Conroy's facial expression in death was one of surprise. He had been given no time for indignation or fury. The easiest emotion is surprise, and he had ended on that note. Richard Crane looked down on him in triumph.

Gower rolled back a couple of yards of linoleum near the window, far enough to uncover a wooden trap giving access to the air space beneath the wooden floor. He opened the trap. Then he took Mel's keys from his pocket, the money from his body belt, and he wrapped Mel's head in a plastic bag. After that, he was ready to drag the body towards the hole.

Crane's planning was impeccable, although he could have wished for a greater depth of space. There were a couple of difficult moments, when Conroy seemed to resist, before the body was manoeuvred out of sight. Crane replaced the trap and the floor covering.

Gower completed tidying up by returning the chair to its usual place, washing the iron bar at the kitchen sink and wiping over the linoleum in places where there were suspicious marks. The wiping was a mistake because the floor had been so dirty to begin with that the cleaner patches he created were obvious.

For a second he could not think what to do, but then the answer came. With the iron bar he attacked the mantelpiece. Loosening it and smashing into the plaster around it he freed dust and rubble that he trampled liberally over the suspect patches. His final act before leaving the house was to break the panels of the door to the room.

It was a long, long time since he had been on a motorcycle. In the years when he and Rob Watson had spent every spare penny on keeping the *Jumble* afloat, he had used one as it was cheaper to run than a car. But it had not been a symbol of viciousness as Mel Conlon's was.

Wearing Mel's gloves and Mel's helmet, and a black leather jacket belonging to one of the squatters and borrowed from the attic room, he trundled the great machine down the alley beside the house.

Crane wrapped himself in Conroy's things, convinced that anybody who glimpsed him with the machine would accept him as Conroy. If ever the time came for questions, people would say they had seen Conroy leave the house alive and wheel the motorcycle to the garden himself.

Gower dumped the machine behind the shed. He laid the helmet beside it, with the gloves inside the helmet. And he went away, re-entering the house by the back door and tossing the leather jacket where he had found it. Then he made tea, two plastic beakers of it, one of which he drank and the other he tipped down the sink, leaving about an inch in the bottom.

He carried the two beakers to the ground-floor room and set them down, one near the fireplace and the other near the chair. As an afterthought he sprinkled dust and a little rubble into them.

434

'It was all right,' he told George when he met him in the square. 'I made him a cup of tea and I told him he wasn't getting paid. I don't think we'll see him again.'

George was incredulous. 'He took it? Just like that?'

Gower assumed false modesty. 'Well, I had to be pretty tough about it, but he got the message. Actually he got a bit rough, broke a few things up.'

He stopped, sensing George examining him for injury and wondering what violent scene Richard's calm words belied. George wiped his mouth on the back of a hand. 'Well,' he said doubtfully, wanting to share the belief that Mel would not trouble them again but knowing how improbable it was. 'Well, you're just lucky he didn't kill you.'

Gower smiled an arrogant smile. 'I can look after myself.'

Actually, it had never entered his head that Mel Conlon might have killed him instead.

When people traipsed back to the house that evening they found Gower supervising the dismantling of the white marble fireplace. Rod, while puzzling how his iron bar had been discovered in the cistern, put all his teenage muscle into getting the marble surround down. Joe and another young man slaved at it too. Gower drank a celebratory can of lager offered by Cowboy who had spent a profitable day singing Dolly Parton numbers outside Sainsbury's.

There was an air of levity at the news that the rent collector had been sent packing. This feeling did not run deep. Those who were one minute saying 'Well done, Richard,' were subsequently found muttering: 'He'll be back with some heavies. He's only gone to tool up.'

Somebody flaunted the knowledge that Mel's bosses had no need of tools. They could stun a man and hang him and leave him to dangle like a suicide, and there had been suicide verdicts recorded at inquests on people in the squats who had been dispatched this way.

Gower affected not to hear their misgivings and accepted the congratulations. At any event, as George said, they had won a respite.

Next day, when the fireplace was completely dismantled, Gower detailed Rod and Joe to stack the pieces in the back of the Ford estate car belonging to one of George's friends and to sell it to a specialist dealer in the locality. Their spiky haircuts nodded obediently. His triumph over Conlon had become theirs because he was their friend. If Joe could not run the house himself any more, he could enjoy loyalty to Richard Crane whose exploits had won him control.

Gower told Rod: 'Tell them you work for a firm of builders and it comes from a house that's being modernized.' He gave them the name of a builder, a name he had spotted on skips parked near houses undergoing renovation.

They returned with a fair price in tattered £10 notes and Gower shared the money with them. After that he sent them off with the metal fire grate and surround, to another dealer with a similar story. This time they did not come back.

Kenny, the owner of the Ford, was livid to learn it had been started under the bonnet and used without his permission. Gower was tempted to soothe his conscience by giving the man some of the proceeds of the sale of the fireplace, but in the end he did not as it could be interpreted as a sign of weakness.

Kenny was ranting and demanding to know where his car was, and why Gower had put it into the hands of two thieving magpies like Rod and Joe. No one could curb him and there was a danger he would go too far. A man like Richard who had broken up the fight in the attic and had put the rent collector to flight was not a man to be crossed.

But Kenny could think of nothing but his precious vehicle being used for joy-riding or possibly sold on the streets. He was shouting, fists clenched, chancing his luck.

When he put out a hand Gower had him, twisting the arm and thrusting him away. The man staggered against a chair, regained his feet and dived at Gower, head down, unstoppable. Gower did not attempt to stop him. He sidestepped and let the fool thud against the wall. An echoing thud came from elsewhere in the house.

'Conlon!' screamed Cowboy. The others merely thought the word.

Glass smashed, wood cracked, feet crashed along the passage from the back door and up the stairs. In the big room Kenny recovered his temper and took cover the other side of the chair. George was ghastly white. Men shrank and faded. Only John Gower stood his ground. The door of the big room was open and he was facing it. He was the first to see the men with the guns.

The notion that the men with guns had been sent by Mel and his bosses was a long time dying. Bereft of news, the squatters could provide no other explanation.

The newcomers were accepted with stoic resignation, as all the other arrivals had been in their turn. The gunmen themselves said nothing to clarify the position. They rapped orders, singling out the meek of eye for this dubious distinction.

'Send them away,' one of the gunmen ordered the duty guard at the window when Rod and Joe came back with the Ford intact.

The guard opened the window and called down to them. Rod and Joe went round the back but found the back door had been made secure in their absence. They went away.

The few squatters who had been on the premises when the men broke in were forced to stay, no one else was allowed in. And because the men kept out of sight and used other people to arrange what they wanted, the secret of their presence was maintained.

'Tell them to bring fish and chips,' was one order.

The man's companion changed the order. 'No, get a take-away Chinese.'

On the pavement those locked out conferred about the strange instructions and eventually complied. Gower kept in the background. He was experiencing what Rod and Joe had been through when George arrived, and what George had suffered when Gower himself had asserted authority. He kept quiet and wrote the Richard Crane diary and hoped to avoid confrontation.

No one queried his decision to sleep in the attic instead of the downstairs front room that he had used until then. Everyone was behaving differently under changed circumstances. George tiptoed up to the attic one afternoon while he was writing. George checked the stairs to make sure he had not been followed. There was always one gunman guarding the first-floor landing.

'Richard?'

Gower dragged himself back to a kind of reality. 'What?'

'Who do you think they are?'

Gower shrugged. Should he claim they were sent by Mel and his bosses in the rent-collecting racket, or should he stick to the assertion that there would be no more trouble from that quarter?

George said: 'I'll tell you one thing, they've never heard of Mel Conlon. I mentioned his name and they asked who he was. It was genuine.'

Gower tapped his notebook with the pen. He was writing so fluently it would soon be full, and Rod and Joe were unavailable to acquire a new one. He shared the thought he had harboured for a long time. 'They aren't interested in us. They haven't come because of us, they're using this place to hide.'

Nodding, George agreed. 'Hiding from the police.' He rolled his eyes, adding: 'I thought I'd seen everything in the squats, but I've never had one used as a bolthole for men on the run before.'

Squats were plainly not what they used to be. Maliciously, Gower said: 'What are you going to do about it? Shop them or continue to show solidarity?'

George scowled. 'We're trapped in here. There's always one awake with a gun in his hand. What *can* we do?'

'We can get a message out. The next time the window's opened we can throw a piece of paper down. But I don't know that we should risk it. If the police come round we'll find ourselves used as hostages in a siege.'

438

George was nodding frantically. 'Yes, we would. And if we're right and those two are on the run, then it probably means they aren't afraid to shoot.'

'Or,' said Gower, 'we could drop down a message asking for room service to be discontinued. If the food and drink and cigarette supply is cut off, then perhaps they'll lose interest in this house and move on. It would mean we'd go hungry too, of course, but it might be worth it.'

George preferred the sound of that. He wrote a note, on a sheet from Gower's book. It did not say precisely why he made the request but it begged his friends on the outside to stop coming round and running errands. He made it clear that whatever they were told by the man at the window was to be ignored, only the contents of the note were to be taken seriously.

The note was smuggled to the squatter on window duty and when he saw two of George's group come up to the house, as they had been asked to the previous day, he opened the window to call out an order for pizza and he let the note flutter down. The gunman near him did not notice it fall.

The pizza did not come. George's glittery eyes would meet no one's, he appeared shifty. The gunmen grew twitchy, sensing that something was afoot. Everyone was ordered into the big room. During the early evening Joe came and stood outside the house, puzzled, twiddling his earring, just looking up without calling or ringing the bell. The guard stared out, without reporting Joe's arrival to the gunmen. Then Joe left.

He went down the alley to the garden. Under cover, as best he could, he ran to the back of the house, sprang on to a windowsill, threw an arm around a drainpipe, leapt again and used the pipe to scale the wall as high as the first-floor kitchen. The room was empty. Joe got on to the sill to open the sash.

And then a man with a gun in his hand walked into the kitchen. Joe automatically ducked, scampered down the drainpipe and dashed for the cover of shrubs by one of the hedges. The window did not open, nor the back door, but he did not wait to see what might happen instead. He scuttled, terrified, alongside the hedge, aiming for the protection of the hedge and the apple tree on his way to the gate. Joe entered the slot between the hedge and the shed, and he fell over Mel Conlon's motorcycle.

Running as far as the street corner, he spilled out to Rod that he had seen Conlon in the house with a gun and Conlon's motorcycle in the garden. 'He's a psychopath,' he said. 'He's holding them all in there at gunpoint, George and all those, and Richard.'

'Perhaps Richard's gone,' said Rod, scratching his ragged coxcomb.

'No, of course not. He hasn't got any money.'

Rod pointed out, not without sourness, that Richard had taken the bulk of the money from the marble mantelpiece. But Joe would have nothing to do with such quibbling. 'We've got to get them out, we've got to do something or that Conlon will shoot them all.'

'Yeah. A carnage, like that video we saw.'

'We've got to call the police,' said Joe. 'Anonymously. We won't say it's us, we'll just tell them to get round here.'

'Yeah,' said Rod.

21

While Joe was disguising his voice and telephoning the police, Rain Morgan was ringing Ratcliffe's bell in the house where Alf Wilson had died. The old man was taken aback to see her again. He greeted her in the brisk military way that had inspired his neighbour to nickname him the Colonel.

Rain eased her way into his flat with appropriate smiles and solicitous questions. He was fine, he replied.

And the noisy drummer who had taken Wilson's flat?

He had left, said Ratcliffe. The demon drummer had been properly scared by whatever nonsense Rain had told him.

They laughed, recalling her pose as Ratcliffe's niece. Then she got down to business. 'I'd like you to tell me about the men you let into the building the night before Alf Wilson was found dead.'

Ratcliffe's knees trembled beneath the heavy tweed. She was convinced she had hit the target. Ratcliffe had lied. Once before she had tackled him and he had revealed an extra portion of the truth, but this time she was not to be fobbed off. She meant to hear it all.

They had rung his bell, he said, and told him they could not make Wilson hear. There had been two men, well-dressed, educated types aged nearer forty than thirty but athletic. Medium height, light brown hair, with long lean faces and very dark eyes.

'Both of the men looked like that?' Rain queried.

'Yes, very similar, but one a shade taller than the other. Brothers I would say, such a strong likeness.' Ratcliffe was in his chair by the fireplace now, bony fingers interlaced on a knee.

Rain said: 'Did they threaten you?'

'They told me to keep my mouth shut, that was all. And

after we found him dead, I thought what difference could it make if I did? He'd been scared, and he'd hanged himself.'

'Did you notice anything else about them, apart from their voices and physical appearances?'

'They wore suits, expensive ones. And their car was a long white foreign one. A sticker in the rear window had the name of a garage in Leeds.'

Rain tried not to appear excited but Ratcliffe was filling in important pieces. Then she grew doubtful. How did he know? He would not have gone out late at night to inspect a vehicle driven by two men who had intimidated him.

He explained. 'You're forgetting, they were there on previous occasions. I didn't come face to face with them then, but I spotted the car on my way home and then saw them leave the building and drive off in it. The night Wilson died, I noticed their car outside. It was perfectly clear in the streetlight.'

Another Yorkshire connection, she thought, walking home to Kington Square. *The woman Drummond was with in the nightclub said the Shelbourn brothers went up north at weekends. To Ilkley?*

She already had a reason to ring Alf Wilson's cousin. Pat Jarvis sounded pleased to hear from her, wanted to chat. Rain kept it to a polite minimum. She did not have much time to spare and she needed to use it wisely. Coming to the purpose of her call, she reported that her copy of Wilson's play had been stolen when her flat was ransacked.

'Ooh, no! Ooh, you poor thing. Ooh, that's terrible.'

Rain stemmed the sympathy. 'Could you get another copy made for me?'

'Of course. You'll not want to drive up again will you? We could risk the post instead.'

Rain said she preferred to collect it. She put her question. 'Are the people at Bibury Farm called Shelbourn?'

Pat Jarvis said definitely not. They were Bentons.

Rain checked the regional telephone directories in the *Daily Post* library but found no Shelbourns in the Ilkley area. And yet the coincidences were piling too thickly to be ignored. Pat

442

Jarvis had once said there was something odd about the way the folk at Bibury Farm ran their business; Bibury had been a word among Alf Wilson's telephone notes; another word she and Pat Jarvis had guessed might be Sherborne could equally be Shelbourn; Rain knew the Shelbourn brothers went 'up north' at weekends; Ilkley was not far from Leeds, and the men who had frightened Wilson had driven a car with a Leeds garage sticker.

Yorkshire was a long way for her to go on a wild-goose chase. There was somewhere in London where she might accumulate more evidence. Rain drove to the charity office over the run-down café south of the river.

The young man with the lank hair had expected never to see her again. 'I'd written you off as another journalist who wasn't going to bother.'

'I'm sure you did.' She pulled up a chair and sat across the desk from him. 'Please, I'd like you to tell me the rest.'

He fidgeted but he did not repeat the surprise.

Rain said: 'How much do you know about the Shelbourn brothers?'

'Twins,' he said. 'They've been in all the housing rackets – fake accommodation agencies, spurious hostels that grab the residents' social security payments, bed-and-breakfast hotels, charging rent for squats . . .'

She was nodding, indicating this was no more than she knew or guessed. She said: 'Where can I find them?'

He whistled softly through his teeth. 'Dangerous.'

Thin-lipped she said: 'So dangerous they must be left alone and allowed to get away with it? Is that how you and your charity protect the homeless?'

He sneered. He lit a cigarette before replying. 'We don't hire contract killers to stamp out vermin, we try to get publicity about the problems and influence public attitudes until the system gets changed.'

'Very effective,' she said sarcastically. 'Now, where are the Shelbourns?'

'I don't know.'

She challenged him. 'It's your business to know. Where are they?'

He denied he could help.

She said. 'Tell me whether there's a Yorkshire connection.'

His interest intensified but he sucked on his cigarette instead of answering.

She badgered him. 'An Ilkley connection, perhaps?'

He moved away from the desk, blew smoke, said defiantly: 'What is this? If you know, why are you asking?'

'I want confirmation. You can give it.'

He took another drag before saying: 'Yes, Ilkley Moor. I don't have an address. All I know is they go up that way most weekends.'

But squeezing that much out of him was not enough. 'And where can I start looking for them in London?'

'I thought I'd given you contacts for that.' He could be sarcastic too.

'And that's all you did. You sent me trailing around for information that was here all along. Why did you do that?'

He flicked ash, with a contemptuous gesture. 'Because I wanted you to see for yourself. I wanted *you* to go into the squats and see the way people have to live in this so-called civilized society. I wanted *you* to walk into a bed-and-breakfast hotel and understand the living hell families have to suffer because there aren't enough homes to go round. And I wanted *you* to go out at night and meet the down-and-outs, the way Alf Wilson did.'

She raised her voice to his level. 'Yes, I'm glad we've got to Alf Wilson. You didn't give him any more than you gave me. Contacts, that's all. And they led him down a trail to death.'

He advanced on her, furious, banging his fist down on the desk in front of her. 'I wanted him to see what the system was doing to people, not to sit here in this office hearing it at second hand.'

An echo down the years, her first editor: 'Never trust a promise, always see for yourself.' Fine as far as it went, but who wrote the story if you got killed?

She shouted back. 'You should have warned him. You should have warned me. He's dead and I've been threatened because I tried to find out what happened to him. Now will you answer my questions?'

The glared at each other, their faces close. She could smell his sweat and the tobacco smoke on him, see the dandruff in the dirty hair. She held her ground. Suddenly he drooped, sat down again but dragging his chair further from her. He liked her no more than she liked him.

She said: 'Give me the address of a squat where the Shelbourn brothers are currently preying on people.'

He recited an address. Her pen poised above her notebook.

'No,' she said. 'That was an eviction weeks ago. The councillor you sent me to said that, but she didn't know of an up-to-date one because her borough was cleaning up the problem.'

He repeated her phrase with disgust. She pointed out she was quoting the councillor, his friend. Resigned, he stubbed out his cigarette, lifted the telephone receiver, spoke a couple of sentences and gave her a different address. She blinked at it.

'Are you sure?'

'What's wrong now?' He was back to sneering. 'Did you think squats only happened in tatty areas?'

She did not tell him the address was a street where her friends lived, where she had briefly lived herself. She said: 'Is there anything I ought to know before I walk in there? I don't want to get killed if it's at all avoidable.'

'Watch out for the rent collector, Mel Conlon. He's a lunatic. Carries more knives than the café downstairs. Only sharper.'

He loved watching her try not to shudder. Rain got up to leave. She reached the door when he said: 'Have fun.'

She retorted that at least she was trying to do something, whereas all he was interested in was political point-making instead of action. He said it wasn't true, that he rang the newspapers, that he did a lot of things but nobody took any notice, that when Alf Wilson died he had . . .

He had *what*?

He wanted her out of the room, out of his life. She stood in the doorway, refusing to budge. 'What?' she demanded. 'What did you do when Alf Wilson died?'

And when he prevaricated it came to her. Through his obfuscation and denials she pictured him as he had been, with the telephone in his hand making the anonymous call that had sparked the rumour that Wilson's death had been murder and not accident, the rumour that had set her on the trail that had convinced her of Wilson's murder and nearly brought about her own.

She got it out of him. The Shelbourns hit people, made them unconscious and hanged them. It had happened in the squats, in the hostels, in all their rackets. They got away with it. It looked like suicide. Troublemakers could be got rid of without trouble.

He was torn between showing off that he had all this knowledge that she did not, and hating her for forcing him to reveal it. On the whole he hated her.

She left. His words followed her down the stairs. 'The Shelbourns are part of the system. Create a dependency and someone will always exploit it, catch the Shelbourns and somebody else will fill the gap they leave, because extortion won't end until society changes.'

At the foot of the stairs she shouted back: 'Words. All you can do is talk. Come to the squat, you might get the chance to tackle the rent collector and the Shelbourns. I'll hold your hand if you're scared.'

To reach the street she had to go through a corner of the café. Two old men and the woman behind the counter watched her in wonder. She put on a very polite smile and said good afternoon to them.

A choice faced her. Go direct to the squat, or leave that until after the weekend and get up to Yorkshire? She went home, undecided, and unsure why she was delaying the decision.

446

There was a light on her answering machine. Paul Wickham had left her a message. He was sorry he had been too busy to call before, he was not going to be free over the weekend, and on Monday he would be at Roger Fleet's funeral, but he would ring later next week. Her decision was made. She opted for a weekend in Yorkshire.

Early next day she packed a bag with overnight things, a camera, a few lenses and rolls of film, walking shoes and a green showerproof jacket with a hood. She caught the train at King's Cross and hired a car in Leeds. Her own car had been seen in the area once and she did not want to be recognized.

The patchy sky suited her ideally. A few showers, a light wind and sunny spells were exactly what she would have chosen. Taking the Guisely road out of Leeds, she made straight for Ilkley.

Sheep that dotted the moors had lost the heavy weight of winter wool they had worn when she had previously been up here, but there was a freshness and a clarity of colour that defied the summer. The natural beauty of it brought a smile to her face. All that was missing was music. Delius, or Elgar with his evocations of the English countryside, would have rounded off her pleasure to perfection. The hired car, alas, came without music.

Rain drove past the turning to Bibury Farm and some way on turned off the road down another grey-walled track that began parallel and then curved away around a rise. She stopped to consider the map before going on about half a mile and finding a place to park.

Clad in the hooded jacket, the map in her hand and her camera concealed beneath the jacket, she set out to walk over the rise towards Bibury Farm. Curlews distracted her, sheep ignored her. Eventually she sat on the far side of the rise and looked down on the farm and beyond to its track.

She saw nobody and no white car, merely horseboxes, farm vehicles and half a dozen fine horses in the stable block. Then a stocky old man walked from the house to the stables. Over the next quarter of an hour Rain observed him working in the yard. She photographed the farm, with the man saddling up a horse.

A young woman came out of the house, mounted and rode away over a field on the other side of the farm track. Rain photographed her too. But what she hoped for was a long white car and twin brothers. They did not come.

She walked on towards the farm, relying on her map and her clothing to disguise her as a casual weekend walker. But the lie of the land meant that the nearer she approached the less she could see of the yard, and so she arced back towards the lane where she had left her car.

Rain returned to Ilkley and looked up the telephone number of the Bentons of Bibury Farm. When a man answered she simply asked: 'Is Tony there?'

'Who wants him?'

Rain hung up. *A pity about the name, an Archibald would have made it more conclusive.*

But the call had added a scrap of information where she had been increasingly seeing doubts. Encouraged, she went to Addingham and Pat Jarvis.

'I'd like you to come on a country drive,' said Rain, and watched Pat Jarvis's pleasure cloud as the woman discovered she intended to take her to Bibury Farm.

Pat Jarvis said: 'They're not nice folk up there, they won't like us being around them.'

'It's a public road, not their own personal track. Come on, we'll take a picnic.'

The woman laughed in wonder. 'A picnic? From what you've already said I got the idea you wanted us to stake the place out like a couple of plain-clothes cops. And I must say that sounded more exciting than a picnic.'

'Can you think of a better cover for hanging around in the countryside than posing as a couple of gossipy women having a picnic tea?'

Pat had to say no. She took to the venture with delightful enthusiasm. 'Ooh, it's like those thrillers I get from the library,' she said, as she packed a thermos of tea into a shopping bag. 'And we can wear dark glasses, can't we? It's that sunny this afternoon we'll look suspicious if we don't.'

Rain laughed with her, promising her it was going to be far more like the boring door-stepping that journalists indulged in than like any thriller Pat had ever read. She hoped it was true. And she refused to ask herself whether she was being wilfully unfair to Pat Jarvis in not telling her of the potential danger, as unfair, perhaps, as the charity worker had been when he had not warned Rain about the risks of antagonizing the Shelbourns.

Specifically, Pat had not been told of Rain's conviction that Alf Wilson's death had resulted from his interest in the brothers. Rain doggedly closed her mind to the hazards, and encouraged the older woman in her lightheartedness.

As they drove from Ilkley up to the moor, Pat Jarvis contributed a good idea. 'Why don't we call on my friend who lives over there and ask her if she's heard of any Shelbourns living around here? I mean to say, we know the people at Bibury Farm are Bentons and we might be planning to spend our time at the wrong picnic spot.'

The detour would take them no more than minutes. Rain agreed. The woman Pat was looking for was in her front garden and the conversation took place over the gate.

'No,' said the woman. 'Nobody of that name lives up this way. What line of work do they do, these men you mentioned? There aren't any farmers of that name, of that you can be sure.'

Pat Jarvis saw that it was hopeless and began her thanks and goodbyes, but Rain popped in a different question. 'It's a fairly unusual name, have you ever heard of it?'

'Well, yes, but not for years. There was a divorcee of that name who worked in a pub in Skipton. She wasn't a local lass, she came from the south.'

Pat Jarvis butted in. 'My, your memory, Alice! Nothing gets by you, does it?'

Her friend laughed modestly. 'The only reason I remember is that there was a road crash and she was a witness. My family knew the man who died, you see, and so we took an interest.'

Rain asked what had become of the divorcee.

Alice said: 'Went up in the world, she did. Married that Benton who snatched Bibury Farm from under our noses. Marjorie Benton, she is now.'

'Well!' cried Pat Jarvis, admiring, triumphant, confused.

Her friend let her down over the final question, though. She could not remember ever hearing that the divorcee had children.

The picnic was eventually successful. Long after the tea had grown cold in the plastic cups and wind was buffeting the shopping bag on the grass beside the car, a long white shape oozed down the track. As arranged, Pat jumped up with the map in her hand and stopped the car to ask whether it was possible to drive beyond the farm and reach another lane.

There were two men in the car, men with similar faces and very dark eyes. Rain, from inside her car, snatched a couple of photographs of them. Then she slunk down in her seat, ostensibly packing up picnic things and making sure she was not studied and recognized.

After curtly telling Pat Jarvis she would have to go back the way she had come, the men moved off. The encounter had taken perhaps a minute and a half. For Rain it had been long enough.

'You were terrific,' she told Pat.

'Yes, but did you shoot them?' Pat helped stuff the remains of the picnic into the shopping bag.

'The one near the window certainly, the other one won't be very clear. But as they look alike I doubt that matters.'

Rain started up the engine. Pat said: 'I wonder which one is Roy and which is Tony?'

'I know you're enjoying this, but I don't think we should go after them to ask.'

More seriously, she impressed on Pat the need for secrecy, now and in the future. She knew it would be tough for her to keep the adventure to herself because she had few lively moments in her life.

'Even your friend, Alice, shouldn't be told. Let her suppose it was an ordinary picnic.'

Pat was alerted by Rain's sombre determination. Subdued, Pat remembered everything she had been told about the matter and spotted the gaps where she had been told nothing. She said: 'Did they find out that Alf was inquiring into their business for his research?'

'I'm sure of it.'

Pat absorbed this in silence.

Neither spoke again for a mile or two. Then Pat Jarvis said: 'I always said our Alf wasn't the type to kill himself.'

Even at this time, Rain had not told her everything. The newest piece of information she hugged to herself. She did not want to worry her by saying that the voice that had answered Pat's questions was the same voice that had once left Rain a threatening message.

The photographic department at the *Daily Post* developed the film for her and blew up the shots of the farm.

'Not bad, for an amateur,' said one of the photographers. 'But you can always ask me to come with you on these snatch jobs, you know.' He was alluding to the time they had posed as a courting couple in a parked car so that the prey would take no notice of them.

Rain left some prints for safety in the office and took a set to Chelsea. 'All I need is Ratcliffe's identification of the men in the photographs, then I really will know that it isn't all conjecture.'

But she did not get it. She met the doctor in the entrance hall in Hunt Road. Mrs Dobson's roly-poly shape blocked the doorway to Ratcliffe's flat.

'Heart attack,' said Mrs Dobson. 'Not a great shock at his age, but as my late husband used to say, a death always gives you pause for thought.'

If she had known Rain's thoughts she would have paused

for longer. *If only he hadn't fiddled with the facts and delayed me getting at the truth!* Rain turned helplessly away.

Mrs Dobson called after her, lumbering down the front steps. 'Looks like you had a letter for him.'

Rain shook her head. 'It doesn't matter.' And she put the envelope containing the photographs in her bag and coerced herself into a conversation with Mrs Dobson who had discovered Ratcliffe ill and summoned the doctor. They had been sometimes scathing of each other, often mocking, but Mrs Dobson was going to miss the Colonel.

Returning to the charity office, Rain spread the photographs on the desk in front of her adversary. 'Are these men the Shelbourn brothers?'

Now that Ratcliffe had died, this difficult man was her best chance. He picked up one of the shots of a long-faced man looking out of an open car window. The length of time he spent over it persuaded Rain he did not know.

She said: 'If you don't know, can you tell me who would?'

'Did I say I didn't know?'

She choked back a groan of exasperation. 'You didn't say anything.'

'Right. Look, I think it's them but I'm not prepared to be definite. They don't drop in here for a chat, you know. I've seen them once, but I didn't get a clear sight of their faces. They were running from a house and jumping into a car. Two men in suits, that's about what I saw.'

Rain gathered the photographs up. He was not the end of the line. There was a chance someone at the squat would be able to identify them, and it was certain that Drummond, who worked for them, would.

The very idea of approaching Drummond made her queasy. The last time she had asked him about the Shelbourns, it had resulted in her home being destroyed.

She put if off, going next to Kingsway where she looked up Shelbourn in the Registrar General's files until she discovered a Marjorie Shelbourn who had been married to a Nicholas Shelbourn and had given birth to twin sons, Nicholas Roy and

Anthony James. After that, she felt obliged to give some of her time to the gossip column. Holly had taken over her Sunday duty but it was unreasonable to burden her unnecessarily. Not that Holly grumbled, she greeted Rain with one of her biggest smiles.

'Rosie has given in her notice at Wapping,' said Holly. 'She couldn't stand being chased around the office by the lecherous fool she works for.'

Rain beamed too. 'When is she coming back?'

'As soon as you like.'

'How about an hour's time?' Then, more moderately: 'I'll ring her.' But the matter had to wait because the temporary Sylvia appeared with the latest crop of post. Holly dropped on to Rain's desk her most recent fancy from the literature with which the estate agents were strafing her.

'Hackney,' said Holly. 'But so close to Islington we could easily lie.'

'Snob.' Rain scanned the details of the flat. It was dearer than the earlier choices but it was better.

'This one has a big plus,' said Holly. 'And that is that Dan likes it too.'

'Then what are you waiting for?'

'We're not. We're going to see it this afternoon and if it's as good inside as these details and our nosing around the outside suggest, we'll make an immediate offer.'

Rain wished her luck and sent her to Hackney, then rang Rosie and welcomed her back without so much as an I-told-you-so. She was sure both ventures would work out satisfactorily. There was a sense of unfinished business being concluded, a little of the restlessness going out of life.

Drummond could not be looked for until very late at the riverside nightclub, therefore Rain decided to visit the squat first. An evening visit would be best, she thought, because the squatters were more likely to be 'at home'. And because of the location, she invited herself to drop in on Marion Dudley after her interview at the squat.

Over the telephone Marion gasped. 'You can't go in there!

453

Those people are absolutely frightful. They've been breaking into houses all round here. I can't tell you how how terrible it's been. And the police don't do anything. They went to the house last week and they just stood on the doorstep and spoke to them, and then they went away. My neighbour saw it all, the one who got burgled while you were here in April. Do you remember him? Anyway, come over as soon as you've finished there and tell us all about it. I'll feed you. I'm trying out a wonderful recipe I persuaded the chef at our local restaurant in France to give me, so you're in luck.'

Rain left Marion Dudley in a state of high excitement, over the squatters and the *canard au sang*.

The Sylvia had a call waiting for Rain on the other line. The girl whispered: 'This one sounds queer.'

It was Mrs Dobson. 'There was a letter for you in the Colonel's flat. I thought you'd like to have it, and I took the liberty of taking it away. You could pick it up from me when you're passing.'

Rain thanked her, wondering how much else Mrs Dobson had taken the liberty of scavenging from the dead man's flat.

The letter was addressed and sealed but had not been stamped. Rain thanked Mrs Dobson again but chose not to open it in her presence. She hurried through wet streets to Kington Square without examining it. Home, she kicked off damp shoes, clicked on the coffee-maker and flopped on her torn couch, eager to know what Ratcliffe had to tell her. Something he had remembered about Alf Wilson? Something about the men with the white car?

It was the kind of letter that demands to be read and reread until the reader has extracted every nuance, every implication, every inference. Tense, on the edge of her seat, Rain ran through it over and over. It was a startling letter. It began with a belated warning and an apology, but the rest amounted to a confession.

Suddenly she realized how rapidly time was passing. She raced to put the letter in her bag, to shower and change, to swill down a cup of coffee and leave for the squat and thence the Dudleys' house.

He knew he was going to die. He needed to tell someone what was on his mind, and he told me. I hope Mrs Dobson never saw inside that envelope. What did he want me to do with the knowledge?

Her mind was a kaleidoscope of shifting responses, each mutating to the next, no logical progression discernible. In this state she arrived at her destination, parked at the nearest kerbside space and walked back to the squatted house. She recognized it from her walks with the dog, Fred, recalled his escape into its derelict garden.

Her ring at the doorbell was answered only by a face at the first-floor window. The ground-floor window was boarded, as was the glass panel in the front door. She rang again and stood back, looking up to where there had been a face.

The Ratcliffe letter compelled her attention but she could no longer give it. She concentrated on composing a few pleasant phrases of introduction, a way of talking herself into the house if the inhabitants were less than happy to accept her.

The words played through her mind, the smile was poised to flash across her face as the door was unlocked. A clattering of chain heralded the moment. She went up the steps, close enough to discourage it being slammed in her face, but not meaning to risk her foot in the gap if the words and the smile failed.

What happened next was the last thing she had ever expected. The door opened wide. She smiled at a man in the passage, her words tumbled forth. But she did not reach the end of her first sentence. The man lunged forward and dragged her inside, slamming and locking the door behind her with an alarming finality.

22

John Gower was in the big room upstairs when Rain Morgan came in. They all were. They spent most of their time in there, talking or not talking depending on how edgy their captors were.

The gunmen had been at the house a week. One day Gower had believed they were on the brink of freedom but Kenny, the man who owned the Ford estate, had been ordered at gunpoint to tell the police everything was all right, and he had convinced them.

Rain, bewildered, took in the row of ashen tense faces and the second armed man at the window. She addressed the man who had grabbed her. 'What's this about?'

He ordered her with a movement of his gun to sit down. 'And keep quiet.'

There were no chairs in the room. The captives were sitting on the floor, backs to the wall facing the window. They made a space for her. She continued to stand.

'I came here to talk to squatters. I'm a journalist.'

Chancy, she thought, *if these are the Shelbourn brothers' henchmen, but I'll probably be recognized anyway.*

The same man said: 'We know who you are. Now sit down.' He jerked the gun and she sat.

'All right,' she said. 'Now tell me who you are.'

Her effrontery surprised both the armed and the unarmed, but the *frisson* was soon over. She was told to keep her questions to herself. Unwilling to accept the situation, she continued to argue and demand information until she was shouted at and frightened into submission.

She's like a flower, thought Gower, *fragrant and delicate, and she's going to be crushed as we've all been crushed.*

He included the gunmen in that, imagining the crucial steps

in their lives that had led them along a path of criminality. Nobody set out in life with the aim of being a criminal, they had ends and adopted fatal means.

For the first few days he had written the Richard Crane diary but now the second notebook was full and he could write no more, although the story continued to tell itself inside his head. He also entertained himself by inventing life stories for the men around him. George, for instance, who had his own standards to live by and qualities of leadership. What had set him adrift? Gower supposed ill-favoured plans, for education and family life, and ultimately a refusal to face any more rebuffs from a society whose rules barred him.

Then there was Kenny. Gower and Kenny had submerged their differences since the gunmen had burst in on them. What did it matter to either of them any longer that Kenny's car had been used without his consent to ferry hunks of marble? The car had been returned and it remained outside the house, a minor comfort to Kenny who had stopped bemoaning its theft by Rod and Joe.

Gower was especially intrigued by the behaviour of Rod and Joe. Locked out themselves, startled at the first-floor rear window by a gunman, they had nevertheless hung about the place. They were trying to help. Specifically, they were trying to help him: *Richard* had been scrawled across the wrapping of a can of sardines that thudded through the letter box one evening once it was dark. Never dreaming it was his plan to cut off food supplies and starve the gunmen out, Rod and Joe were sending in food parcels.

Rain Morgan was speaking to the man next to her, George. The hostages' acquiescence both calmed and annoyed her. There were five of them, six now she had come, and only two gunmen. How was it that they had not overpowered and disarmed their tormentors? What made them docile?

Tactfully, she tried to find out. George knew what she was getting at. 'Look over there.' He stuck out a stubby finger. High on a wall a plaster cornice was shattered. Its dust lay like icing sugar on the carpet.

George said: 'That was a shot. The one named Jerry did that. Jittery Jerry we call him. He thought we were going to jump him and he pressed the trigger. The bullet went wild. Next time it might not.'

'But . . .'

He looked sidelong. 'But what? What does it matter if one or two of us get killed as long as the rest go free? No, we're sticking together in this. No dramatics, no heroics.'

She chewed her inner lip, unable to argue further. Conversation lapsed. The gunmen went out of the room, one staying on the landing and the other running downstairs.

Rain opened her mouth. George advised her to keep her voice low. There was always one of them listening, he said.

Whispering, she asked them who the gunmen were and why they were there. In reply they told her how the men had arrived and the little they had gathered from overhearing exchanges between them. They also told her about the squat, how the house had been squatted first by a couple of teenagers who had been obliged to let George's commune join them, and how the racketeers had seized control of the house and put more squatters in, and how there had been a frightened, shifting, population until everything changed alarmingly when two gunmen had stormed in.

George did most of the talking. Four men next to him, including the one in a cowboy hat, nodding silent agreement from time to time.

Another man voiced the fear that if the gunmen left they might steal his car which was standing outside. Next to him was a whey-face youth who sat with his eyes shut and rarely spoke. At the end of the row, and facing Rain, was a man whose gaze had made her uncomfortable ever since she had become aware of him. He was watching her acutely from beneath a denim hat worn over tangled, once-dyed hair. It was a gaunt face, unhealthily grey and lined. Yet there was a challenging intelligence in the dark eyes. George told her his name was Richard Crane.

In the street outside there were sounds of a vehicle. The

man got up and went stealthily to the window, shook his head and came back. 'A car at a house on the other side of the road but the trees cut off the view.'

George said testily: 'Richard, we agreed to do nothing to precipitate more shooting. Now for all our sakes keep away from that window.'

The man shrugged. He sat rubbing his left arm, hugging it to him.

George wiped sweat from his face with a shirtsleeved forearm. 'Sorry, Richard. It's getting to me. I thought we'd have been out by now.'

Kenny said: 'I've told you. We could crash through the window, jump into my car and make a dash for it. Like now, when they're both out of the room.'

'No,' said George and Gower together.

George added: 'Jittery Jerry would be in here at the first sound of breaking glass and he'd be firing at everyone. He missed last time, he won't go on missing.'

They explained to Rain that Jerry had missed because his companion had flung himself on him, forcing his arm up and the shot astray. George pointed out that it had not been Kenny in the sights, it had been Cowboy, and if it *had* been Kenny then Kenny would now be taking a different view.

Out on the landing the gunmen conferred, no useful snippets reaching their captives. Inside the room Rain, who still did not know why she had been pulled into the house, said that she expected to be missed fairly soon.

'My car's parked in the street. My friend knows I was coming here. She's sure to search for me.' And she pictured Marion Dudley utterly engrossed in the *canard au sang*, a few hundred yards away. Would Marion worry about her, come looking for her? Rain could not rely on it. She was a journalist, her friends were used to her unreliable social life, to the sudden dash to cover a story, the empty place at the dinner table and the following day's apologetic phone call.

But Marion's possible appearance was Rain's only positive contribution. 'We ought to decide what to do when she comes. Unless she gets captured too, she's our best chance of sending for help.'

'The window's locked,' said George, 'and Jerry has the key. We can't drop a note out, and if – '

The gunmen came into the room. Jittery Jerry suited his name. He was reedy and twitchy, rarely still, eyes flickering, movements abrupt. His companion was marginally more solid and by comparison slower although his nervous tension exhibited itself in other ways. He licked his lips a lot, rubbed sweaty palms against his thighs. Jittery Jerry called him Del.

Rain Morgan thrust away knowledge she would rather not have. She set about the interviews she had come for, quizzing her fellow hostages about life in the squats, getting her answers mainly from George. Yes, he knew about the Shelbourns. Who, in the squats, did not? Yes, he knew about Drummond, and Drummond had been one of the men who had broken in, changed the locks and signalled the arrival of the Shelbourns' rent collector. Yes, he knew Mel Conlon.

Kenny put in a word, jerking a thumb at Gower and saying: 'Richard's a bloody hero. He saw him off.'

Rain had not cast Richard Crane as hero material. She raised an eyebrow. He responded with his sardonic smile, saying: 'Conroy won't cause any more trouble.'

Kenny slapped his hand to his thigh and corrected him. 'Conlon, not Conroy. Gawd, you're always getting it wrong!'

The hero began to say something about the rent racket, but a woman's voice in the street snatched everyone's attention.

'Fred?' she called. 'Fred, come here.'

Marion, thought Rain. *Already, and we haven't made a plan.*

Jerry darted towards the window but Del reassured him. 'It's only a dog. The stupid thing's come to the front door and it's standing there wagging its tail.'

Rain heard Marion's voice, closer, and then Fred's scuffling protest as his collar was held and he was pulled away. Rain had sat with her head bent, concentrating on the sounds outside, hoping to give away to her captors nothing of her excitement at Marion's proximity. Then she sighed deeply, looking up as she did so. Her eyes met Richard Crane's. He was still studying her, registering her reactions, guessing at her emotions. She felt a tingle of unwelcome interest in him.

George, she could tell, was schooling himself to be unobtrusive but Richard Crane was contained. He was not like the rest. He was apart. Intelligent. Compelling. He was not to be read as she, with a journalist's ease, was able to read the others. There was an undefined element in Richard Crane. She hoped to discover what it was.

The evening drew in, the room darkened. Only street-lighting lit it, Del and Jerry having removed the light bulb to protect their privacy. With self-pitying looks, Rain shared her dismay at Marion Dudley's unquestioning retreat, at her disinclination to return.

Absurdly, she found her resentment centring on Marion's enjoyment of the *canard au sang*, just up the road, while Rain herself fasted. She clamped her eyes shut but the pictures would not recede. Marion Dudley in her local restaurant in Normandy cadging the recipe from a red-cheeked and flabby chef. Marion in her superbly fitted kitchen, with the duck on her marble slab and a half cup of good red wine reducing in a saucepan. Marion wiping over the duck press she had bought on an earlier visit to France, anticipating a supply of Rouen ducklings, crossbred domestic and wild creatures with a distinctive gamey flavour, smothered and not bled. Marion lifting from the oven, after a scant eighteen minutes, the partly cooked bird and carving the breast into fine slivers that she arranges prettily on the dish containing the reduced wine. Marion cutting up the rest of the carcass, splashing it with more red wine and pressing it, then enriching the juices with two tablespoons of brandy and pouring this sauce over the sliced and seasoned meat. Marion dotting the meat with butter, then heating the sauce, gently, not boiling it. Marion, flushed, from kitchen heat and activity, carrying into the dining room her triumph, her *canard au sang*, pale meat in a sauce blackened with its own blood.

Rain swung back to the present as something crashed into

the downstairs hall. Jittery Jerry went to fetch it. He swore, came more slowly upstairs. He kicked back the door of the big room, his usual fashion of entering. 'These things again,' he said, and held out a packet of custard creams.

Rain was bemused. Other people tutted their exasperation. Richard Crane hid a smile.

Del nervously moistened his lips with a pink flash of tongue. 'Go and take another look. Might be more stuff outside.'

He tossed a key that Jerry plucked out of the air with the hand that was not glued to a gun. Then Jerry went down again. They heard the front door open and close. He came back with a couple of cans of mulligatawny soup and a sliced loaf.

Cowboy was dispatched to the kitchen to heat up the soup and given instructions to add water to stretch it. Richard Crane had acquired the custard creams. He ripped open the packet and lobbed one to Rain who caught it neatly.

From canard au sang *to custard creams, just like that,* she thought, and bit into the vanilla-flavoured pastry and the hard, improbable cream.

'Where,' she asked, 'did these come from?' She was addressing him this time, not George. Whatever else Richard Crane was, he was the guardian of the custard creams.

He told her about Rod and Joe. He could not, because Del was in the room, tell her that their help amounted to sabotage of his plan to rid the house of the gunmen. He was ironic, making the tale amusing. She actually caught herself laughing, especially at the episode concerning the packet of teabags that Rod jammed in the letter box one night. Joe had hacked at it with his knife until the teabags (those he had not slashed apart) toppled into the porch and the empty box fell into the passage. The teabags had then been fed through the letter box singly and Joe had disappeared into the night leaving a mess of torn paper and tipped out tea in the porch.

'However,' he ended, 'he returned next morning with a bottle of milk. From somebody's doorstep, I dare say. I have to admit their milk delivery has been reliable, better than some milkmen I've known.'

Del and Jerry took turns to go and drink some soup in the kitchen, then the others went in pairs. Rain and Richard Crane, who had been eating the custard creams which everybody else loathed, went last.

They had been ordered to keep the kitchen door open so that whichever of the gunmen was near the entrance to the big room could hear them, but he shut it. His ironic manner changed. He stood very close to her and kept his voice a shade above a whisper.

'Something's going to happen, Rain,' he said. 'I heard them whispering about bargaining if they're found here. Apparently we weren't important enough for their purposes, then they recognized you and couldn't believe their luck. If the police trace them to this place, then you are what they intend to use to buy their way out.'

She was looking at him in horror. She stammered when she spoke. 'I . . . I haven't really been frightened until now.'

'No, well we've tried to reduce the tension as far as we can. If you'd been around when Jittery Jerry shot the cornice off you'd have been scared to hell.'

'Do the others know why they grabbed me?'

Impatient, he shook his head. 'I haven't told them. George would want a committee meeting to discuss it at a democratic level, Kenny would do something rash like jumping through a window and Cowboy would make up a song about it. Oh, don't smile, he's made up two already. I won't sing them for you, your turn to hear them will come soon enough.'

'And you? What will you do?'

'I thought I'd severed the food supply to starve them out, but Rod and Joe . . .'

'Oh dear.'

'If this escalates and gets dangerous then we must separate them. I'll go for Jerry. He's the wild one and he'll have to be stopped. We'll have to take a chance on Del. I can't see any of the others tackling him, not successfully anyway.'

Rain's words stuck. Her head was full of violent images. The knowledge she had shunned could not be unlearned. His eyes were searching hers for the truth, measuring her anguish before she spoke. 'Richard, I know who these men are.'

'Go on.'

'They're Gerald Marks and Derek Lilycombe. They shot a policeman at King's Cross and went into hiding. There's a huge search for them. They're small fry with the Goad gang, and they were already wanted for killing a security guard in a raid on a warehouse. They . . .'

But he turned away to the window. He had heard enough.

She insisted he be told the rest. 'The policeman who died, well, he tackled them. They've killed twice. We've got to face that. I don't think they'd jib at shooting any of us.'

'Do you know which one did the shooting?'

She said not, said Del was not to be relied on any more than his jumpy pal. While she stood weakened by the realization of the danger she, above all of them, was in, he was washing out plastic beakers, filling them with watery soup, holding one out to her. Automatically she took it, barely conscious of the warm plastic in her hand, the faint curl of steam rising in front of her face.

'Drink it,' he said. 'There's no knowing when we'll get anything else.'

She tried to sip, but her teeth clenched in resistance. Food was the last thing she wanted to think about. She wanted to be sick. He put the sliced loaf on the surface beside her. Folding one of the thin unsatisfactory slices in his hand, he ate it between mouthfuls of soup. He was coping, being very cool and sensible. She made a better attempt at sipping the soup.

He said: 'Pretend it's something else, something you actually fancy eating.'

A wry smile lightened her face. '*Canard au sang*? That's what my friend was offering me for supper tonight.'

'Then you'll have to think of something else.' He gave his beaker a disapproving inspection. 'This could not be confused with a bloody duck.'

464

Rain helped herself to the bread. He was right, she had to eat while she could. Soon he had finished, was rinsing out the beaker beneath the cold tap and filling it with water to drink. He said: 'When it gets difficult . . .'

She had been thinking about that too. She interrupted. 'Yes, there's something I've got to say about that. When it gets difficult, I don't want anybody to risk his life for me.'

'No dragon slaying?'

'Preferably not.'

There was a pause during which he did not promise not to protect her from dragons and during which she persuaded herself not to stress the point. She gave way, sufficient to say: 'If they do put me in special danger, then I'll face it alone. It would make it worse for me if I thought you were going to be shot because of me.'

He looked at her, without a word. He held out his hand to her. Stupidly she looked back, not understanding. Then she collected her wits and passed him her empty beaker which he washed out for her and refilled with water.

The scene, intense and confused, and made more so by the events that were to follow it, lodged in her memory. Years later the faint smell of curry would trigger the recollection of the moment she faced the possibility of her death and his, and asked him not to save her. And always it was encapsulated in that instant where he stood against the dying light and held out his hand to her, and she failed to understand.

Rain Morgan told John Gower, whom she knew only as Richard Crane, why she had gone to the squat. That is, she told him the fundamental reason: she was pursuing the trail taken by the playwright Alfred Gervase Wilson during his research.

They were in the big room again, talking well into the night, softly because George and Cowboy were sleeping. So was Del. Kenny and the whey-faced lad were talking in another corner. Jittery Jerry was near the window, gun in hand. His shadow fell diagonally across the room, the echo of another shadow that had signalled death.

It was partly this echo that spurred Rain to pour out what she knew about Wilson. Partly also that she wanted to draw from him his experience of life in the squats and she therefore had to explain her own interest.

The mention of Alf Wilson roused him from a torpor of mild interest. He was an admirer of Wilson's work. Rain had met few of these, most with whom she had discussed Wilson had either lamented the fate of the man, or converted his worth into pounds and pence, or congratulated themselves on helping re-establish his status in his profession. No one else had ever appreciated the writing.

'Take *Dead and Alive*,' he said. 'They put it on television again shortly after he died. I hadn't seen it before. What I'd heard was that it was an influential play that had forced a shift in public opinion and a change in a law.'

'Yet it wasn't dated,' said Rain, anticipating.

'That's exactly my point. What I saw was relevant to society today. The thing that caused the fuss seems minor, but other aspects that were overlooked at the time now assume greater importance.'

She agreed, admitting she had closed her eyes to shut out the old-fashioned clothes and décor, and, listening purely to the dialogue, she had found the play to be as fresh as anything written in the current year.

He singled out one character as particularly appropriate in the modern context. 'You remember, the woman who is described as "insulating herself with beauty".' And he went on to quote other examples of Wilson's dialogue.

Rain felt her smile solidify. She no longer heard him. *Insulating herself with beauty*. The phrase had not impressed her when she had watched the play, but Richard Crane had plucked it out and waved it under her nose.

She accused herself. Mozart at the end of the day. Her home with its garden and *objets*, ruined now but soon to be restored with a more ambitious garden scheme and more beautiful

466

possessions. Schubert from the window of a discreet hotel. *Babette's Feast*. Opera. Art galleries. Expensive clothes. Richard Crane talked on and Rain Morgan accused herself of using beautiful things to blot out the ugliness around her.

If I get out of here alive . . . she thought. And stopped thinking it because vows under duress were no vows at all.

Sleeping uncomfortably, she leaned into the angle between the chimney breast and the wall, above her head the damaged cornice. Whenever her eyes opened she made out in the half-light the mounds of sleeping figures and the erect shape of the gunman at the window.

Despite the circumstances she slept surprisingly well, waking early and rereading Ratcliffe's letter to her. He had known he might die and he had wanted to tell her what he had done.

Quaintly and sometimes pompously to begin with, he had set it all down. All, but not entirely enough. After warning her against confronting the brothers who drove the white car, and apologizing for misleading and prevaricating, he went on:

> I let them into the house as I described to you and within a short time I heard a disturbance upstairs. When they were leaving, they knocked on my door and told me that for my own peace of mind I had better keep my mouth shut and forget they had been there. They threatened to have me evicted if I said anything. I had no intimation what they had done but I remained in my flat with the door locked, and I could hear someone moving around upstairs. After a while Alf Wilson came and called through my door, and I let him in. He was extremely agitated. He said: 'Please never let those men into the building again.' Naturally, I wanted to know what it was all about but he refused to tell me. He kept saying it would all come out soon and it would be in the media and then everything would be all right.

Rain turned the sheet over. The handwriting was thin and spiky, not always easy to read. The letter continued:

Wilson explained he had a friend who was a journalist and he intended to ask her to be at his flat next morning. He wanted me to attend too. Apparently, the men had threatened to return the next day. Then Wilson left me, saying he was going out to deliver a note to his friend who lived near by. I never saw him alive again. Sometime during the night I was woken by footsteps running on the stairs. Then, at around six in the morning, I got up and went downstairs to see whether the milk had been delivered as I had run out. The street door was unbolted, which is most irregular. Remembering the events of the previous evening, I went up to Wilson's flat. The door was unlocked. He was hanging, exactly as you saw him three hours later.

Somewhere in the street a driver was having difficulty starting a car. Rain moved to Ratcliffe's second sheet. She read:

I knew someone was to come at nine and I was afraid of the consequences for me if the two men assumed Wilson had confided in me. I preferred not to stand out in any way, such as being named as the person who reported the death to the police. Then I saw the solution: if everyone in the house were to be summoned at nine, I would be protected. I regret to say I typed those notes and pushed them beneath the doors of Mrs Dobson and our neighbours in the other flats. One other thing: two days earlier Wilson had complained that his windows were jammed and he lacked fresh air. I loaned him the extending pole to open them. The hook is supposed to slide into the metal ring in the top sash and help draw it down. I did not hear whether he succeeded – it would not have worked, as I warned him, if the frame had been painted up. When I entered his room and found him dead I noticed my pole lying near the table. I took it away and stood it behind the curtains in my room, where I usually keep it. It was obvious to me that this was the means of getting the rope into place over the chandelier. Again, I was afraid that the loan of the pole could suggest to the two men that I had rather greater contact with Wilson than was actually the case, and would encourage them to believe he had confided in me.

And then there was a diminuendo of regrets and apologies, including the sad revelation that the army career was an exaggeration and that he had been afraid of being exposed if he had become involved in a police inquiry into the activities of the men and the manner of Wilson's death.

Safety in numbers, she thought. And looked up and caught Richard Crane's gaze. She passed him the letter. Ratcliffe was dead, so was Wilson, what harm could their secrets do now?

George came over too and was allowed to see it. Rain explained briefly. George said: 'Mel Conlon knows about this sort of thing. He said so once, not at this squat but at another one friends of mine were in. He said his bosses had ways of dealing with people who didn't play by their rules, he said they could incapacitate them with a blow and then string them up so it looked like suicide. And Mel said he didn't go in for fancy tricks like that himself, he liked lots of blood. He was fondling his knife all the time he said it. Evil.'

The three of them went through to the kitchen where there were teabags and milk. George made the tea, handing beakers to the other two and then going into the big room to ask: 'Would you like a cup of tea, Del?' And he returned and poured the sweaty-palmed gunman a cup of tea.

Rain watched in disbelief. George gave her a very straight look. 'Policy,' he said. He carried the gunman's tea to him, carefully.

Before George came back to drink his own, Rain tossed in a conversational titbit, picking up the thread of an earlier talk with Richard Crane. 'Funnily enough, Alf Wilson wanted to adapt one of John Gower's novels for television. It was because he couldn't get permission to do so that he began to research and write his own play about homelessness.'

He said: '*A Candle Lit*.'

'Yes.' And then they meandered through a discussion about John Gower's novels, he being knowledgeable but less complimentary than he had been while quoting Wilson's work to her the previous evening. Under any other conditions she would have enjoyed the argument. As it was, Del and Jerry were having a fractious meeting on the landing outside the kitchen door. Something was afoot.

George had come back and he and Richard Crane wisely kept up a steady flow of conversation rather than confess to overhearing. 'What,' Richard Crane asked Rain at one point, 'would you say John Gower is worth these days?'

She said one hell of a lot, although tabloid figures were fanciful and varied. And she might have been tempted to slide deep into gossip if Cowboy had not begun wailing a dreadful song he called 'The Ballad of Del and Jerry'.

George huffed and set off to hush Cowboy.

Richard Crane said: 'They hate this song, because it ends up with them being killed. There was a fantastic row about it the first time Cowboy sang it. Jerry said he wasn't to use their names because they were copyright. And Del said if he was going to sing about them he had to make them happy songs and not shoot them.'

Rain stifled hysterical mirth. 'They don't seem to have deterred him.'

'No, he cited precedent. Bonny and Clyde, Butch Cassidy and the Sundance Kid . . . you know, all those pairs who got gunned down in the final reel.'

Through the wall Cowboy was on to the second verse and George was remonstrating with him. Rain asked: 'Hasn't he got another song he could sing instead?'

As if he had heard her, Cowboy cut short the first song and his twangy guitar brought them one about 'The Siege of Barnsbury' in which all ended happily with the SAS swinging through the window and saving everybody, except those who got killed by accident. Rain buried her face in her hands and tried to make sense of it, of *any* of it.

'Is it better or worse,' she demanded with tearful, laughing eyes, 'to have your life in the hands of fools? Or is it just funnier?'

'Try insulting,' he suggested bitterly. 'Don't you think you deserve better than to be snuffed out because of something that idiot Cowboy sings, or because George is too damned courteous to put the boot in, or because your life has been taken over by a couple of incompetent, trigger-happy crooks?'

She sniffed, wiped her eyes, battled to keep a straight face. 'We all deserve better. They do too. Cowboy probably deserves to make up better songs.'

'For all our sakes.'

She needed to release the tension in laughter, defuse the anxiety building within her. But she had to do without the release. She said: 'It isn't really funny, of course it isn't. I suppose it's a way of dealing, or not dealing, with the situation.'

She did not mention hysteria. She did not have to. He said: 'Humour, one of the saving graces?'

She nodded, blew her nose, controlled herself. When it came to the point, she would not have room to amuse herself with paradox and absurdity. She would be facing death.

The police came mid-morning, a young man and a young woman in a squad car. The young woman straightened her hat over her upswept fair hair as she walked up the path to the house. The young man was bare-headed.

They had been sent for by Marion Dudley whose morning walk with her dog had shown her Rain's car at the kerbside further down the street. Marion had called on a neighbour. Together the two women had rung the doorbell of the squatted house and looked up perturbed at the unanswering figure at the first-floor window.

The policewoman and her colleague also looked up at the first-floor window. They called up and they hammered the door in case the bell was not working. Then they stood back from the house to make sure their uniforms and identity were unmistakable. 'Police. Open the door.'

The figure near the window did not move. It was Jittery Jerry standing there, stock-still and with his gun held down against his side. The police could not see who it was because he stood to one side of the window, partly concealed.

Inside the room all vestige of relaxation vanished. The worst was going to happen. Del had taken up position in the doorway to the room, blocking escape. He had forced the hostages back against the wall facing the window. Cowboy wanted his guitar and took a couple of steps to fetch it. Del hissed at him, lashed out with the gun and struck him on the shoulder with it, and Cowboy shrank whining against the wall. Nobody else dared move after that.

John Gower measured the number of paces from where he stood to the fireplace. Four? He observed the tremors that began to wrack the body by the window, the quivering arm that ended in a gun. He knew that Rain Morgan, beside him, was noticing it too. He heard only breathing. His. Hers. Cowboy's coming painfully. Del's, light and rapid. He saw Kenny's fists clenched against his thighs, saw George's stony face, saw the nervously tapping boot of the pale-faced youth who had grown paler. After a week of intermittent dread and hope it had begun.

The knowledge forced a decision on him. How much should he tell her and how soon? They had talked, so long, talked about the beautiful things – literature, art, music – and not about themselves because, of course, he knew about her and because, of course, she was tactfully sparing him a recital of failure. He had liked their talks, her company. He could not bear to think that once this was all over they would not meet again.

Gower was wary of exaggerating the attraction he felt for her, as a human being with similar interests, as a woman. He blamed it on the contrast between Rain and the kind of people he had surrounded himself with since he had come to London, people whose pain was too sharp too be dulled by contemplation of beauty.

And also she filled a gap that had opened up within him.

The Richard Crane narrative had ended. He did not know how the story went on. The fiction that had run through his mind, entertaining and sustaining him, had petered out. Crane had killed Conroy, lost all desire for Julia, and had gained control of an underworld gang. And there he was stuck.

Crane had moved a world away from his riverside penthouse and his champagne-swilling evenings on the balcony, and Gower could not get him back there. The step was too big, the experience too wounding.

Rain Morgan had said of John Gower's novels: 'There's an accuracy about his characters, an intensity, that makes their experiences affect the reader. They progress and change during the stories, and I think the reader does too.'

The burden of truth had lain heavily, but he had maintained the interest of an apparent reader and the conversation had flowed without him revealing what was in his heart. In his heart, he wanted her to be the first to read the Richard Crane story. He was bursting to tell her how superior it was to the earlier novels, how wide and deep the experiences it would share with the reader, how much it had absorbed him, and how much he had sacrificed for it. He said none of it, and held it to himself, another secret among many secrets.

Jittery Jerry was quaking from head to toe, hand flexing on the gun. The police were pushing at the door. Del was scanning the hostages with a threatening face, shifting his stance to dry sweaty palms on his thighs. Rain had wrapped her arms around herself, against the cold, or for comfort.

John Gower again measured the space between his position and the fireplace. Cowboy's guitar, scratched and scored, leaned against the wall, between Gower and the fireplace.

'Christ!' shouted Jerry, an explosion of sound after the long, aching silence. 'They're coming in.'

Del said: 'Relax, they can't.' He did not sound relaxed himself.

Jerry said: 'They're not going to go away, I know they're not.'

From downstairs came the thud of the policeman's fist against the front door.

Del said: 'We'll have to tell them to clear off.'

Kenny who, on the previous occasion the police called, had been forced to deliver a similar message with a gun barrel in his back, tried to make himself small and unobtrusive. Del picked on Cowboy anyway. His hand sank on to Cowboy's injured shoulder and he propelled him across the room to the window. Cowboy was made to call out, saying everything was all right and the police were to go away.

As he was not heard in the street, his voice being choked and uncontrollable, Jerry made Cowboy open the window and try again. Cowboy's head was shoved into the gap and he repeated the dubious information.

The policeman answered him, Cowboy replied and then Cowboy did an alarming thing. He thrashed out with his legs and dived headlong through the window. The shock on the faces of the police officers as they broke his fall and heard his unintelligible gabbling, deepened considerably when they looked up and saw the gun pointing at them. They sidestepped, bundling Cowboy out of the line of fire and then the policeman scrambled over the wall into neighbouring property and took a circuitous route to the car where he radioed for help.

The fresh air that flooded the upstairs room, even the sounds of traffic and the police radio, were comforting. Kenny reminded his fellow hostages with a look that he had always said it was a great idea to dive out of the window.

Later, thought Gower wearily, *somebody will have to explain to Kenny that if it had not been for Cowboy leaping out, we might not now be in for a shooting match.*

The window stayed open. Jerry stayed by the window. He shouted occasional abuse at the police. Reinforcements arrived and a new voice began to address Jerry, advising him to throw the gun out and come into the street. Jerry answered with abuse.

Soon Jerry closed the window and stepped back out of view.

With the slamming of the sash, the real world was excluded once more. George wiped sweat from his face with his shirtsleeve. Gower rhythmically rubbed his sore arm. Del repeatedly moistened his lips with his tongue. The pale lad's boot continued to tap and Kenny huddled, seeming to grow smaller and smaller.

'When this is over.' Nearly all their murmured conversations began like that, stated or inferred. When it was over Rain Morgan would like George's help in proving Alf Wilson had been incapacitated and hanged by the Shelbourn brothers in the manner Mel Conlon had once described. When it was over George planned to find an empty council house to squat, because the eviction process took longer. When it was over Kenny was going to see a man he knew in Dalston who could get him a set of retread tyres for his Ford estate, cheap. When it was over the pasty youth was going to see whether his parents in Newcastle would take him back.

'When this is over,' said John Gower to Rain Morgan, 'I have a lot to tell you.' He pictured himself arriving at her office, well dressed, well groomed, giving her the exclusive story of his disappearance and resurrection. He imagined David Gerrard's fury and Linda's gall as she found herself still married and not rich with all his riches.

Rain, misunderstanding, said: 'About the squats? Yes, I need all the help I can get.'

He fancied them together, he and Rain. It would take an age to tell her everything. He would pay the story out over restaurant meals, visits to Butlers and Stream Cottage, to Cornwall too. And she would . . .

A terrible thought interrupted him. *What* had she said to George just now?

Chill sweat beaded his forehead beneath shaggy, concealing hair. *Rain's the last person I can tell my story.* And as fear knotted his insides: *There's nobody I can tell. Ever.*

Horror at the thing that lay beneath the floorboards of the ground-floor room brought vomit to the back of his throat. He clapped a hand over his mouth, smothered the retching.

Mel Conlon, his pulped head wrapped in a plastic bag, his body stuffed into a cavity, his identity tattooed on his arm . . . Before long Mel would be found, was sure to be. They would know, George and Cowboy and Kenny, that Mel had been killed by Richard Crane. Rain Morgan would know it too.

The vomit rose again. He swallowed it back. His throat burned, his vision dimmed.

Killing Conroy – no! Conlon – was justifiable for Richard Crane, unavoidable. And as long as the people who knew me as Crane never discovered my true identity, the killing would be blamed on a man who could never be caught because he didn't exist. But now Rain Morgan knows me as Crane.

Beside him Rain was concerned. Outwardly calm, she called over to Del. 'It's terribly hot in here. Can we get some water?'

'OK. And make some tea while you're at it.'

He stepped back to let her go through the door and then he stood on the landing with the gun, guarding her in the kitchen as well as the exit from the big room. She put the kettle to boil and then carried a beaker of cold water to Gower. The hands that took it from her were shaking. She smelled the sourness of fear.

For a moment she stayed, making sure he had the beaker steady, putting an encouraging hand on his arm. He avoided her eyes. They had talked, and smiled and even laughed together, shared much and lightened the dangers that beset them, and now he could not meet her eyes. She was puzzled.

Gower heard her back in the kitchen making tea. A woman in a kitchen making tea. It ought to have been innocuous, pleasant. It was neither of those things. The more time was measured out, the nearer drew the climax when Jerry and Del would come to the end of their adventure and the captives, unless disaster intervened, would pick up their own lives, dust them off and go on their way.

But he, like the fictitious Richard Crane they all believed him to be, was stuck. He found no comedy in the paradox that by hiding beneath an alias, to avoid being accused of murdering the boy in Hampshire, he was now guilty of killing Conlon and could not escape responsibility by reverting to his own name.

The beaker clattered against his teeth. George gave him an assesssing look, of surprise or maybe disappointment, which subtly changed his features.

Rain brought in the tea. She took a beaker to Jerry, addressing him in an unconcerned way as she did so to be sure he did not leap with fright at her approach and do something fatal. Then she gave tea to Del and to the others, whispering as she went along the row. 'There are police in the back garden and across the road.'

'Gawd, my car's out there,' groaned Kenny. 'I'll kill them if they shoot up my car, the murdering bastards.'

Rain was not sure whether it was the gunmen or the police Kenny had in mind. She carried her own tea back to her place, near Gower.

John Gower was coming to terms with the enormity that until this moment he had never faced the appalling fact of Mel Conlon's murder. He had obliterated the fact, refused it a place in his consciousness, in his *un*consciousness too because the killing had not troubled him at nights. Mel's final, surprised look had never returned to haunt him. Until now.

Shadows coursed the room as the sun coursed the sky. The day was being spent in outbreaks of fear, when police addressed Jerry and Jerry cursed them, and lapses into tea drinking and desultory talk. Fear heightened when Del and Jerry spoke to each other about their plans, across the room because neither could risk leaving a door or a window unguarded.

Jerry argued: 'We ought to make those demands, like you said.'

'I dunno,' said Del.

'We've got to do it, keep on top of this thing,' said Jerry, who seemed in control of nothing, least of all his own agitation.

'If you like,' said Del.

Jerry ordered Rain to the window. 'You're to tell them we want a car . . .'

Del said: 'A fast one, mind.'

Jerry said: 'A Ferrari, say. And we want a clear run to Heathrow.'

'And tickets to Marbella,' said Del.

Jerry said: 'And that's it.' He looked at Del for confirmation.

Del wiped his lips with his tongue, then said that would do for now, they could say the rest later.

Rain was made to recite the childish, foolish, pointless demands until Jerry was satisfied she had them off pat. Then he pushed her up to the window, opened it, jabbed a gun against her head and told her to announce their demands.

As her words fell into the street, she saw the blur of blue uniforms, the figures crouching behind the parked cars, the distant white flutter of what the police called incident tape that cordoned off the street. She could make out the upper window in Marion Dudley's house. And she saw yellowish London-brick walls, slate roofs, white paintwork around Georgian windows, leaves and flowers. Birds were singing all the while she spoke.

At the end of her speech a disembodied voice told her that the request had been heard. Then she was the medium for the to and fro of negotiations: the police resisting, giving a little, resisting again and Jerry standing firm, caving in, standing firm again. She prayed the police would get in at the back before much longer.

I could jump, she thought. *Like Cowboy did. Like Kenny would have. Why not? Go on, topple forward. Let go. That's all it takes.*

She did not do it. She stood there, the cold steel cruel against her scalp, and she could not free herself.

Then she failed to follow what Jerry was saying, was unable to repeat exactly, extemporized, and he cracked the gun barrel against her skull and swore at her. She hated him and Del and the humiliation, especially the humiliation of being used by them.

Out there would be her journalist colleagues, at a safe

distance, not daring to get an inch closer, and thankful to the police who would not let them attempt bravado. Some would be there because it was a siege with a famous person in it. Television cameras with long lenses would be trained on her, providing the leafy street allowed them a clear view. Overhead a helicopter circled.

Jerry got fed up with the noise of the helicopter and demanded its withdrawal. Moments later it veered away. Jerry was elated by this success. He made Rain repeat the other demands, the fast car (it having been decided to drop the brand name as a concession) and the flight to Spain (Marbella having been similarly dropped because the airport was at Malaga).

The response to his demand for the helicopter to go away lured him into believing the other demands were being met. Via Rain, he got into tortuous discussion about the cubic capacity of the engine of the car that was allegedly being arranged.

'When it comes,' said Rain, repeating faithfully, 'you'll have to get right back to the end of the road. Oh, and leave the keys in the car, of course. And we'll come down and go. And if anybody tries to stop us, we'll shoot.'

Gower thought: *Kids' stuff. How long before it strikes them that this is a kids' dream, they aren't going anywhere?*

He had quashed all thought of Conlon lying in wait for him. *I can decide when this is over how much to tell Rain and what to do about Conlon. It's hopeless trying to think clearly with this going on. And she's not somebody who's going to vanish, like a girl you meet on a train. She works in Fleet Street. I can ring her office and find her any time.*

Except that they might neither of them get out of that room alive.

From the rear of the house came the scrabbling sounds Gower recognized as evidence of men scaling a drainpipe. Del knew it too. He was out of the room and into the kitchen, screaming to Jerry that the garden was swarming and the police were going to break in the back way.

Jerry bawled at him to shoot. Del's reply was missed because Jerry leaned past Rain and yelled into the street. He had the gun to her head and she was pinned against the window frame by its pressure.

Gower moved fast. Four paces? He made it three. He reached the fireplace. He snatched from the chimney what he wanted and then he kicked the guitar skidding over the carpet to George. George hesitated. Kenny picked it up.

Del came running into the room. Gower was back in his place as though he had never moved. Kenny lounged against the wall, the guitar obscured by his body.

Jerry held Rain in front of him, his fingers twisted through her curls. He waved his gun and he shouted. 'Get away from the back of the house or I'll shoot. Get away, all of you. I'm going to shoot the first thing I see moving down there.'

The police attempted to reason with him but the time for that had gone. He felt cheated because the car had not come and while they had talked to him about it they had been creeping up behind him. He said so.

'The first thing that moves,' he threatened. 'I'll shoot it.'

And that was when Fred came flopping through the hedge dividing the front garden from a neighbour's. Jerry shot him.

Rain quaked as the gun fired close beside her. She saw the big black dog stagger, try to run on, collapse sideways with a scream. And lie appallingly still.

Numbed, she stared at Fred, unable to close her eyes and blot the scene out. Then Jerry was shouting, deafeningly near to her, shouting that he had proved he was serious and where was the car?

Del raced into the kitchen, smashed glass, fired a shot into the garden, ran back to maintain guard on the hostages. Jerry, through Rain, had told the police all about the hostages, how they would be shot if the demands were not met.

'We're going to start shooting them,' warned Jerry. He turned into the room and nodded at Del.

Del raised his gun, looking maliciously along the row of hostages. Beyond belief, beyond hope, they stared back.

Like this, thought Gower. *It's to end like this.*

Then Del smirked. He lifted his arm and shot another chunk from the cornice. But the sighs of relief were curtailed.

'Christ!' exploded Jerry. 'Are you going to do it or is it all talk?'

'Jerry, listen . . .' Del brushed a sticky hand over a trouser leg. Habit. Fear.

Jerry swung round, his gun pointed at Del. 'We're in this together. Remember that.'

'OK, OK. Only don't point that my way.' Del edged back, nearer the doorway and the refuge of the landing.

A voice from outside was urgently demanding Jerry throw the gun down on the path. Jerry shouted back that they had killed one hostage and if that car was not there in ten minutes there would be another body.

This was a very long ten minutes. Rain spent it with her back to the window, leaning against the frame, Jerry's gun alternately clamped against the side of her head or waving wildly in the corner of her right eye. Gower stayed where he had been most of the time. He looked better now. His colour had returned and his firmness.

No dragon slaying, she remembered. *It would be worse for me if I knew someone was going to risk his life too. Well, would it be? And if so, how much?*

Gower was watching her, in the appraising manner she had initially found disconcerting. *When this is over, he's going to tell me all about squats. But that's not all I want to know. There are secrets. I can see in his eyes there are secrets. How can I get him to tell me those?*

The ten minutes were up. Del blasted a skirting board. Rain made a morbid calculation. Five hostages, since Cowboy had escaped. Two shots fired to represent two deaths. Two to go at ten-minute intervals, then she would be the last 'survivor' and Jerry might feel it necessary to shoot her at the window. What did that give her? Half an hour to live?

Gower was counting too. Six shots, unless Del was reloading. One into the cornice, one into the skirting board, and one through the kitchen window. Three to go, before he had to break the gun and reload? Maybe. Maybe not.

And Jerry? One shot into the cornice the other day, and one into the dog. That left him four shots, less however many had been fired when the policeman was killed at King's Cross. Gower had made up his mind that it was Jerry who was the killer.

Morbid calculations. A miserable way to die. He sighed, turned it into throat clearing. *What's Rain thinking? She said no dragon slaying. Meant it too, then. Wonder what she thinks of dragon slayers now?*

With his eyes he signalled to her to look at Kenny, at Kenny's legs. In a few seconds she picked up the signal, saw the guitar. It was all he had to offer her, a tiny hope of resistance.

Rain grasped the importance of the guitar, ready to hand as a weapon if the opportunity to use it ever arose. But she could not indicate her understanding with a nod because Del was looking her way. She willed Gower to understand her.

Another ten minutes. A bullet smacked into the marble of the fireplace and ricocheted treacherously before embedding itself in the wall above Gower's head.

As the following ten minutes began, the tension eased slightly, to rebuild as the minutes were counted off on Del's watch. Jerry twisted Rain round, held her to shield him as he shouted down to the invisible policemen, giving them a tally of the number of hostages he claimed were dead and cursing them for their failure to provide the getaway car.

Rain saw the sunlight fading on leaves, the sheen leaving slate roofs. She prayed the end would come before nightfall. Then prayed it would not.

Down the street the incident tape fluttered like wedding ribbon. Safely the other side of it would be the *Daily Post*'s crime reporter, with all the other reporters. As he knew her, were they pestering him for quotes about her? And what was he saying?

She knew a lot of the people out there, invisible, in the

street. But she knew Paul Wickham would not be there because he could not be involved in a siege where she was a hostage.

He'll be furious with me, she thought. *He wanted to catch the Goad gang, all or any of them. When I joked about helping him find them he said he'd rather do it by himself.* It took her a minute to realize how ridiculous she was being.

Jerry fired two shots to where patches of uniforms protruded from behind parked cars. Kenny's car took one bullet, straight through the driver's window. She did not see where the other one went. She was counting. Gower was counting.

Then Jerry twisted the screw tighter. 'We're going to chuck a body out.'

Rain shut her eyes. *Jump*, she thought. *Go on, now. No. I'll be dead before I hit the ground.* Behind her head she heard a metallic click, an inexplicable and therefore threatening noise.

Gower sprang forward, the iron bar held high. In a blur of movement he saw Kenny go into action, knew the guitar was splintering on Del's head as he hunched over the gun to reload. Gower's body thrilled to the exertion, the satisfaction with which he brought the iron bar down on Jerry's skull.

He heard the crack of bone, saw the gunman crumple, heard Jerry's gun fire into the wall beside the window as he went down, glimpsed Rain falling back out of the way and scrambling after Jerry's gun. Behind him, across the room Gower heard the commotion as Del was beaten and kicked and subdued.

It happened so fast, sensation crowded sensation, culminating in achievement and release. And mystery.

Gower never knew about the bullet through the window. He barely felt its touch on his forehead, it seemed nothing. *Nothing.*

23

Rain Morgan met David Gerrard at Linda Gower's wedding. It was a glamorous occasion and the media circus had pitched its tent there for the day. Gerrard was buoyant, a big, bouncy man looking thoroughly pleased with himself and all the world.

'Rain!' he summoned her with a sweep of his cigar.

Obediently she went to him. 'Hello, David.'

They were in a grand reception room overlooking the River Thames. Everything Linda Gower did these days was grand. An obsequious waiter refilled their glasses. Gerrard raised his.

He said to Rain: 'You may join me in a celebratory sip to applaud the news that I have this very day been exonerated of murder. One knew that it was only a matter of time, of course. But how I wish those country coppers had gone about their business and arrested that diabolical old gardener months ago. One does not enjoy having one's reputation besmirched, one's friends whispering behind their hands.'

'Oh, quite. To the restored reputation of everybody's favourite literary agent. Will that do?'

He bowed graciously and they drank the toast. 'Details?' he inquired.

She shook her head. 'Not yet. Only that the old man who cut the grass at Butlers has been charged with killing the boy and has made a confession. I'm not sure in which order.'

'Now your turn,' he said, raising his glass again. 'One cannot let the moment pass without offering you a minor accolade for exposing the Shelbourn brothers as the killers of Alf Wilson and the scourge of the homeless. To Rain Morgan who made the houses of London safe to squat in.'

'Not too fast. Nobody's been charged yet. They're still discussing their future with the police.'

Gerrard swilled back another mouthful of champagne. Rain was telling him that the money from the rent extortion in the squats and from the bed-and-breakfast hotels had been laundered through the farm in Yorkshire, that it had paid for racehorses. But Gerrard was less than enthralled with the intricacies.

'My dear, this is too sordid,' he said. 'But that reminds me, while speaking of the sordid, I have yet to hear your first-hand account of the siege.'

She laughed it off. In the weeks since it ended she had spent too much time describing and picking over the events to want to do it any more.

'No, David. The hour has passed.'

Gerrard nodded sympathetically. Then: 'I have heard that your friend Wickham was displeased about your little adventure.'

Wryly she said she had been fairly displeased herself.

'Prevarication,' he accused. 'Now come on, is it true?'

She ticked him off. 'David, stop it at once. You sound like a gossip columnist on the prowl and this is not one of my days for encouraging rivals.'

He smirked. 'Very well. Then I shall take that as a "no comment", and we all know what that means in your world.'

Rain shrugged a don't care. And said: 'If you want to know what Wickham thinks, why don't you ask him? He's over there.'

'Ah, hired to guard the wedding presents, I suppose. I didn't know you could buy officers of detective-chief-superintendent rank for such duties, although it's always nothing but the best for Linda Gower, of course.' And when Rain declined to rise against his gentle malice, he went on: 'He's said to be the best, isn't he? Although he appears to have made a hash of corralling the Goad gang. What optimism, to be quartering the capital for Goad when gangland has pensioned the fellow off to one of those Costas the package tours head for!'

'I'm sure Paul would be interested to hear your views, David.'

But he resisted her offer to introduce them although it would have amused her to do so. Gerrard preferred to revert to the siege. 'And what stupendous folly for the police to shoot between the eyes their best potential witness to the "Terror in the Squats". However, the dead man's diary seems to have been of inestimable value to them.'

'You're fishing,' said Rain. 'And I can't tell you anything.'

'You've read the diary, I don't doubt.'

She guessed at the reason for his interest. 'It's not publishable in my opinion. The names are all wrong, no, *some* of them are wrong, so it becomes a guessing game to match up real-life villains with people in the diary.'

'But I understand it was all in there, about the man he claimed to have killed and buried beneath the floorboards.'

Hating his gleam of prurient interest, she thrust back the memory of her own horror when, during a sleepless night at the Dudleys' house once the siege was over, she had read Richard Crane's diary and come upon an account of the murder. She refused to share with Gerrard her feelings of disloyalty when she told the police they would find a corpse in the front room. The man who had saved her life, who was emblazoned as a hero across the newspapers one morning, was the next day named as a murderer.

The police had taken the two notebooks from her, scarcely bothering to complain that she had removed them from the squat. Gerrard was asking her a question about that.

She told him: 'Richard Crane was a man with secrets. I was nosy, I hoped his diaries would reveal them.'

'You . . . er . . . didn't get hold of any other documents belonging to him, did you?'

'Such as?'

'Oh, I don't know.' He pursed his lips, awaiting her answer.

'No. I had nothing else. Besides the notebooks, his bag contained only a cheque book, a library ticket and bank cards.'

Gerrard finished his drink, flicked cigar ash which landed on heavy linen beside an ashtray. 'I saw you on television at his cremation, the chief and almost the only mourner.'

Rain desperately wanted to get off the subject. *If Gerrard had any feeling*, she thought, *he'd drop it*. She said: 'I had to go. I felt responsible for his death in a way. And I wanted to meet any of his friends or family who might have turned up.'

The police had been there for the same reasons. She had met them and she had met an untidy youth called Joe, that was all. Joe had told her his friend Rod had meant to be there but had that morning been arrested for stealing from a shop.

She said to Gerrard, with an air of finality: 'There were no answers. Richard Crane will remain one of the unsolved mysteries of my life.'

Gerrard appeared happy with that. They talked then about the *Daily Post*, where Rosie had returned to work as Rain's secretary and where Holly was deeply engaged in purchase of a flat on the borders of Islington. It was always referred to that way, rather than on the borders of Hackney. Then they talked about Rain's holiday, beginning next day, in France.

'Marion Dudley owes me a *canard au sang* and is taking me to Normandy for a month to enjoy it.'

'That's an awfully long time of Marion Dudley.' He and Marion had taken against each other years before, a little misunderstanding over who had first claim on the best of their favourite fishmonger's catch.

'Marion won't be there all the time, and Paul will come out for a while.'

Gerrard was sifting out a teasing reply when there was a stir in the room and a couple went out on to the balcony. Linda Gower and her new husband, with a photographer in tow.

'Rain, as you're going to be away I must tell you now,' said Gerrard. 'This isn't idle chatter, you know. I have a story for your column.'

She adopted an exaggeratedly attentive pose, wondering what fraudulent nonsense she was about to hear.

He said: 'Linda Gower has a contract to write a novel.' He named a famous publisher and a sizeable advance on royalties.

Rain's jaw dropped. She snapped it shut, trying, too late,

not to give him the pleasure of seeing her amazement. 'But, David – '

'But what?'

'But that's more than John Gower ever received.'

'Mmm. I know.' He wore an aren't-I-clever smile.

'Can she write?'

'So naïve, Rain. Linda's the widow of a famous man, she's a television personality. She doesn't require talent, too.'

Their eyes swivelled to the balcony. Linda Gower and her bridegroom posed there, smiling at each other, sunlight shimmering on champagne. The photographer waited until a boat sailed up river on the tide. The perfect shot.